I MARRIED AMRETH

Prime Mating Agency

REGINE ABEL

CONTENTS

He's the dark angel of her dreams.

When Ciara attends the Intergalactic Medicine Symposium, the last thing she expects is to run into Kayog, an infallible empathic matchmaker, who declares he knows who her soulmate is. Her excitement at the prospect of meeting Amreth, a magnificent and powerful Obosian Hell Lord, is crushed when a pirate attack results in her near-death and abduction.

After years of loneliness as a Warden on the prison planet Molvi, Amreth is elated when Kayog informs him he found his soulmate. Devastated to hear she's been abducted, and even though he's never met her, he doesn't hesitate to go rescue his Ciara. Kayog is never wrong. But once he tracks down the kidnappers and connects with his mate, Amreth realizes that nothing is ever as it seems.

As tragic events unfold, will Amreth and Ciara's efforts help save an entire species from extinction, or will they also fall to the evil external forces threatening them?

DEDICATION

To the medical professionals who put themselves in harm's way daily to save the lives of countless strangers, reduce suffering, and bring hope where there once was none.

To the scientists and specialists who tirelessly work in the shadows to defeat the invisible enemies that attack our bodies and minds, thwart the epidemics that decimate too many communities, and develop new medicine and technologies to help prevent tragedies.

You are the unsung heroes of entire generations. Some may deny or challenge the miracles you perform but know that a silent majority sees you and thanks you.

CHAPTER 1
CIARA

I brought another fancy hors-d'oeuvre to my lips as I gazed upon the diverse crowd around me. I couldn't decide if amusement or disgust dominated within me as I watched them sucking up to each other. Although their behavior was expected, it still boggled my mind that after having achieved such high levels of expertise in their respective fields, they still had to debase themselves in this fashion.

Then again, I couldn't blame them. Getting an invitation to the Intergalactic Medicine Symposium pretty much qualified as a lifetime achievement in and of itself. The biggest names in the medical and pharmaceutical fields throughout our sector of the galaxy always attended. This constituted the ultimate opportunity for lobbying, jockeying for a prestigious job, securing much needed funding for a new project or research, as well as sweet talking potential donors into becoming your patron.

Personally, I had no time for this shameful but necessary administrative aspect of the medical field. I was just happy to have earned a ticket so that I could meet my hero. As an epidemiologist with the Interstellar Doctors Organization—a galactic entity similar to Earth's Doctors Without Borders—I always dreamt of being part of the type of life-changing discovery Dr. Elias Jacobs achieved a decade ago.

During a routine research mission, his team was attacked by a wild beast from whom he derived the revolutionary Simian Serum 12—commonly referred to as SS12. That wondrous chemical transmitter not only stopped but also reversed degenerative diseases for multiple sentient species. Things such as dementia, Parkinson's, and Alzheimer's were now a thing of the past. And that included their equivalent among most non-human species.

I just hoped for a chance to get even a five-minute one-on-one with Dr. Jacobs. But that would require me to be a bit more aggressive. Most of my colleagues, current and former, were boldly approaching all the people they wanted to interact with. While I wasn't the skittish or easily intimidated type, I didn't particularly care for having to elbow my way through the throngs for a bit of attention. Still, it would be dumb of me to let this once in a lifetime opportunity go to waste just because I didn't feel like coming out of my comfort zone.

Heaving a sigh, I popped another of those overly fancy—but insanely delicious—amuse bouche, chugged down the remaining two sips of my sparkling wine, dropped the empty glass at the corner of the table, and headed towards the other end of the room where the masses were surrounding Jacobs.

It was slow progress, with so many people of diverse species forming clusters of varying sizes. I politely exchanged smiles, nods, and even a few words with acquaintances along the way. But it wasn't until halfway through that my steps faltered. The golden and maroon feathers of a tall bird-like male caught my attention. I did a double take upon realizing it was the famous Kayog Voln.

He ran the highly reputable Prime Mating Agency. They specialized in finding life partners for primitive aliens. Unlike most other matrimonial agencies, they had a 100% success rate for all the actual matches they performed. The challenge was actually getting matched. Over the years, they got flooded with countless requests. But it wasn't like they—although I should probably say *he*—could simply wave a wand to pull out the name of your soulmate. Kayog needed to have met both partners to be able to recognize them as the perfect pair. From my understanding, as an Edal—a rare trait for the people of his species— he could hear the songs of two souls and recognize them as being in harmony.

What the hell is he doing in a medical symposium?!

The question no sooner popped into my mind than the answer revealed itself. One of the many people surrounding him shifted to the side, thus revealing the stunning silhouette of his mate, Linsea Voln. Where he was fully maroon with golden down feathers on his chest and face, with a fluffy, long, white tail, she would compare to a snow owl, with her pristine white feathers and a smattering of dark spots on her chest.

Linsea worked as an ambassador for the United Planets Organization. As such, among the many high-profile cases she got involved in, the Temern female often facilitated collaborations between species when it involved access to rare medical resources, among other things.

I couldn't help but to stop dead in my tracks to admire the couple. They were holding hands like two young lovers. Every time he would glance at her with his silver eyes, the tenderness —if not adoration—that shone within melted me from the inside out… not to mention stirred a hint of envy. From what I seemed to recall, they met in college and had been married for a little over thirty years.

What wouldn't I give for someone to look at me the way he did her after such a long time together?

Despite the stiffness of his beak, he was warmly smiling at Demetra Stamos. I didn't need to be within range to know she was telling him about her romantic woes. The poor woman had been married and divorced more times than I could count. Unfortunately, she was one of those who tended to be in love with the idea of love more than with their actual partner. For her, being single for even a day meant that somehow, she failed as a woman. It saddened me to the extent that Demetra was otherwise a beautiful, extremely smart, and delightful person. She just kept settling for the wrong guy. A compliment and a seductive smile sufficed for her to be swept off her feet.

Hopefully, Kayog can give her the happily ever after she desperately seeks.

Just as I was going to turn away and resume my arduous journey towards Dr. Jacobs, Kayog suddenly frowned. His smile faded, and he jerked his head to peer at something towards the back of the room to his right. His frown deepened as he stared intently in that same direction. Curious as to what prompted this odd reaction, I followed his gaze.

It took me a moment to realize what had caught his attention with so many bodies moving about. A woman I didn't know was leaning against the wall for support, her brow creased. She took in a couple of deep breaths then straightened, casting discreet glances around her as if to make sure she hadn't brought any attention to herself. I narrowed my eyes at her, looking for any signs that she might require an intervention. Although she outwardly looked fine now, one look at Kayog indicated that his concern had increased.

As if in response to that thought, the Temern excused himself to his mate and Demetra and made a beeline for the woman. Without thinking, I followed. The swarm of people made my progress challenging. But I no longer focused on Kayog. Beads of sweat were appearing on the woman's forehead as she once more winced. Understanding she had something likely too serious to just wait out, the woman headed towards the exit.

Having attended many of these large events where a variety of alien foods were served, I'd grown used to at least a handful of people getting sick and feeling embarrassed about it after eating something they shouldn't have. But where else would you get such an opportunity to sample as diverse a selection of off-world cuisine?

The woman exited the room a good minute before either Kayog or I managed to reach the door of the massive reception hall used for the event. Just as he was about to step outside, the Temern suddenly jerked his head to the left to look at me over his shoulder. For some stupid reason, my stomach dropped, as if I'd been caught red handed committing a crime or stalking. He locked eyes with me, tension visible in his.

"Are you a doctor?" he asked as a greeting.

"Yes," I replied.

"Good. Follow me. This woman is unwell."

Without waiting for my response, he turned around and rushed outside the room. He wasn't running, but his long strides had me half jogging to keep up. His massive wings partially blocked my view as we exited into the large promenade of the humongous vessel the event was taking place in. From here, we could look at the four stories above us as well as glimpse at the three more below. Each level had its own balcony which grew narrower the higher up you went, giving almost the illusion of the promenade being an amphitheater. Various sets of elevators at each end, and in the middle of each side provided a quick way to the other floors. However, majestic staircases also provided a more casual access.

I finally spotted the woman a short way ahead. She appeared wobbly on her feet. I couldn't tell whether she had intended to go to one of the hygiene rooms, back to her quarters, or to the Infirmary. Whatever her plan, she clearly wasn't going to make it.

With everyone busy inside, none of the handful of people loitering on the promenade appeared to notice her distress. A soft gasp escaped me when, with two powerful flaps of his wings, Kayog suddenly lunged forward. Barely a couple of seconds later, the woman collapsed. Swooping in, the Temern caught her right before she would hit the ground. I ran towards them, my movements impeded by the formfitting evening gown I was wearing as well as my high heels.

That didn't stop me from typing a few instructions on my bracer to activate my medical scanner. The Temern turned around to face me just as I was reaching them. He didn't say a word, content to hold her like a bride while I ran my scanner over her. The woman was moaning in pain, more beads of sweat dampening her forehead.

"Looks like she's having an anaphylactic reaction," I said, glimpsing at the scan results populating the holographic screen that projected off my bracer. "We need to get her to the med bay at once."

I glanced at the elevators located about fifty meters away even as I spoke those words. "I will fly up. It will be much faster than waiting for the lift," Kayog said.

"Good idea. I'll meet you up there," I replied with a nod.

With one powerful flap, the Temern soared and quickly flew up to the top balcony, four floors higher. As I raced to the elevators, I couldn't help but admire his strength and the grace of his movements. From my understanding, Kayog was in his early sixties. And yet he looked no older than someone in his early to mid-forties. This was in no small part due to his incredible fitness level.

That male was buff, although with the slender body of a swimmer rather than the bulky one of a bodybuilder. It shouldn't surprise me as he had been a jock in his teens.

As expected, the lift took far too long to arrive and get me to my destination. You would think such a luxury cruise ship would have much faster elevators. However, it had been a deliberate design to make them slower so that people could enjoy the view of the promenade and the relaxing orchestral music within. Patrons on these vessels were expected to be laid back, not rushing like one would in a shopping mall. But this also made for a frustrating experience when in a rush.

Thankfully, the staff elevators had no such speed restrictions.

Although it had only been a couple of minutes, I finally reached the top floor after what felt like an eternity. I ran to the Infirmary to find Kayog standing alone in the waiting area by the reception.

"She's inside with Dr. Alicent," Kayog replied to my unspoken question.

"Oh, excellent!" I said with relief. "Alicent is an excellent doctor. That poor woman is in good hands. Thank you for being so swift. It must be amazing to be able to sense things the way you do. As a doctor, it would be the greatest gift."

He chuckled and gave me an indulgent smile. "It is indeed quite practical. People so often convince themselves that they're fine when they in fact are not. But while I have that gift, you're not lacking either. You were quite sensitive to the situation as well."

I waved a dismissive hand. "I'm merely observant. And even then, without you drawing my attention to her, I probably wouldn't have noticed."

"Fair enough," he conceded. "However, many others noticed my reaction, but only you and my mate wanted to help. It says a lot about your character. You're caring, which is a wonderful trait to have in your profession. But it doesn't surprise me. Your soul is quite beautiful."

My cheeks heated as his words deeply moved me. Although masters in the art of diplomacy, Temerns weren't known to be flatterers. He wouldn't say something so kind unless he truly meant it, which made it even more special.

I was struggling to find an appropriate response without making a fool out of myself when the door to the examination rooms opened.

"Ciara! What a pleasant surprise!" Alicent said, her blue eyes sparkling as smile lines wrinkled their corners. "Am I to under-stand you are the doctor who swiftly assessed a potential allergic reaction?"

I nodded.

"Well, you were right on the money. The alien seafood in the hors-d'oeuvre did not agree with her," the older lady said with an overly exaggerated air of discouragement.

I snorted. "A classic. Do you need any help?"

Alicent shook her head, her curly black locks streaked with gray bouncing around her wizened face.

"I'm good. You go have fun. And thanks for bringing her so swiftly. She would have had a very unpleasant time getting here on her own," Alicent said, smiling in turn at the Temern and me.

"Our pleasure," Kayog replied.

We waved goodbye and headed out of the infirmary with a nod to the nurse who also acted as the receptionist.

"The Intergalactic Medicine Symposium seems like quite the change of scenery for you," I said teasingly as we walked towards the elevators.

He raised a feathery eyebrow as he gave me a sideways glance with a hint of amusement. "What would make you say that?"

"Aren't you the famous Kayog Voln, the Matchmaking God of the galaxy?"

He threw his head back and burst out laughing. It was full, throaty, and powerful in a way that was incredibly contagious. I found myself chuckling as well.

"Matchmaking God… That has a very nice ring to it. My beloved Linsea will not approve of you stroking my considerable ego on that matter," he said teasingly. "But you have an unfair advantage over me."

"Oh? And what is that?" I asked as he pressed the button for the elevator to bring us back down to the main floor where the symposium was taking place.

"You know who I am, but I only overheard your name when the doctor greeted you," he said with a dramatic air of being wounded.

I couldn't help but chuckle again while shaking my head at him. I had heard of his playful and mischievous personality, but I never expected he would be this delightful in person.

"Apologies," I replied in the same overly dramatic fashion while pressing a palm to my chest. "Forgive my epic rudeness, Master Voln. My name is Ciara Stark, medical doctor with an epidemiology specialization, and a proud member of the Interstellar Doctors Organization for the past fourteen years."

"Fantastic! I'm impressed. Well, Dr. Stark, would it be too bold of me to address you by your first name?"

I grinned. "Not at all, Kayog. These events may be a bit stuffy, but I'm far more laidback."

"Thank the Maker!" he replied with an exaggerated relief that made me smile further. "My Linsea constantly rolls her eyes at me for my lack of decorum in these types of settings."

I gave him a sympathetic look, even though I knew he was grossly misrepresenting how badly he misbehaved. Although brief, the period during which I observed him with his mate showed he perfectly handled himself in these stuck-up environments.

"I can only imagine. What I have a harder time picturing is how a matchmaker and an ambassador ended up getting married. I never thought such a pairing would work, and yet you two look absolutely perfect together," I mused aloud.

His face melted with that same tenderness he displayed the few times I caught him glancing at his wife.

"We're indeed perfect for each other. She's my soulmate. And this pairing is quite useful. Every time I accompany my beloved to these types of events, I get to meet countless people, which further helps me find the right match. And that usually occurs in the most unexpected places."

I nodded as the lift came to a stop. "That makes sense," I said while stepping out of the cabin.

"But what of you, Ciara?" he asked as we walked back towards the gathering hall at a leisurely stroll. "I do not see a ring on your finger. But feel free to tell me to mind my own business."

I shrugged. "It's okay. My life is nothing like the type of stories you've probably heard a billion times before. There's no ring because I threw it in his face before kicking him to the curb once I found out he was stealing my research."

"Oh no!" Kayog exclaimed with a genuine air of sympathy.

For some silly reason, that touched me. I gave him a resigned smile.

"Sadly yes. Collin also worked with the Interstellar Doctors Organization. Like me, he specialized in epidemiology. We worked on a couple of projects together and started dating. I like to pride myself in being a smart woman, but I was so freaking blind. He never loved me. The entire time, he was using me to prepare the type of article that would open many doors for *him*."

"Ambition can be a cancer in many relationships," Kayog replied with an apologetic expression.

"Right, except it was completely dumb in our case since I've never been the ambitious type. All the idiot had to do was to ask for my help, and I would have given it freely. I didn't need the glory. He would have been entirely welcome to it," I said, the old anger resurfacing.

"I'm sorry. You certainly deserved better. Was that recent?" he asked, in a gentle, almost paternal fashion.

I smiled reassuringly and shook my head. "No. It all went down a few years ago."

He hesitated and appeared to carefully choose his words as he came to a stop near the railing at the edge of the promenade looking down onto the lower floors. I stopped as well and eyed him with curiosity.

"Do you still have feelings for him?"

I snorted and looked at him as if he had lost his mind. "Good God, no! I'm definitely not pining for that asshole. The feelings I still have for him are a strong urge to punch him in the throat. But no, I'm beyond over him. I was devastated when it happened, but I'm glad it did. I dodged a major bullet. Next time, I'm steering clear of anyone who is also in the medical field and who has big ambitions."

He cocked his head in that odd way birds often did as he eyed me with great intensity. "No medical field... Hmm. And what else would you like or not like in a potential mate?"

I chuckled, suddenly realizing that he was doing his thing of assessing every person he met as a potential candidate for him to matchmake. Although I'd been single for a while, I wasn't actively on the market to find a mate. That said, now that I had the Matchmaking God's full attention, I suddenly found myself caught up in the game and wondering if he actually could find my soulmate.

"Well, since you're asking, I would want someone who is Collin's opposite when it comes to values. He would need to be honest, with solid morals, generous, selfless, and in this relation-ship for me, not what he can get out of me."

The Temern nodded, his beak stretching in as wide a smile as its stiffness allowed. "Someone trustworthy and highly princi-pled like an Obosian?"

"Oh, God!" I said, fanning myself in an overly dramatic fash-ion. "You should know better than to tease a woman with the prospect of marriage to one of those fine specimens," I added, casting a not-so-subtle look at one of the two Obosian guards patrolling the promenade. "Too bad they won't give us the time of day."

It was his turn to chuckle. "I do get an insane number of requests from human females to be paired with one of these impressive males. So does that mean you would love to be matched with an Obosian?"

"Of course! What a silly question to ask," I said, giving him a playfully chastising look.

"Excellent! Because your soulmate happens to be one!" Kayog exclaimed enthusiastically.

My brain froze, and I gaped at him, wondering if he was pulling my leg.

"Are you serious?!"

He nodded. "While you were helping me with that poor woman, I realized that your soul felt familiar. I wanted to talk to you to confirm my suspicions. And there is no doubt in my mind that you are Lord Amreth Vahna's soulmate. He is a Warden on Molvi, and a most wonderful male."

"Are you for real?!" I insisted, my mind reeling at such a prospect.

"Yes, Ciara. This is real. I can be quite the mischievous brat when I set my mind to it. But when it comes to pairing soulmates, I never play, and I'm never wrong. You and Lord Amreth were made for each other. Of this, I am certain."

"Oh, my God!" I whispered, pressing my palms to my cheeks.

An Obosian… My soulmate was one of those hot as fuck Hell Lords!

Kayog grinned. "Am I sensing that you approve?"

"Well duh?!" I replied, as if he had said something dumb.

He burst out laughing. "I'm glad to hear it. Sadly, now isn't the time to discuss. My beloved is waiting. But in the morning, before we depart, you and I should talk further."

I nodded enthusiastically. "Absolutely!"

"Good. Why don't you come with me? I'll introduce you to my Linsea."

"I would love to," I said as we headed back towards the large doors of the gathering hall.

I couldn't help but stretch my neck to get another glimpse at one of the Obosian guards, my fertile imagination going wild wondering what mine looked like. I was especially curious about the piercings their people were so fond of. I immediately clamped down on those naughty thoughts for fear the Temern's empathic abilities would rat me out.

"By the way, you should be aware that the Prime Mating Agency will not handle your pairing," he explained carefully. "As neither of you belong to a primitive species, we cannot get involved in an official capacity. However, I will make the introductions between you as a friend."

"Thank you," I said with genuine gratitude as we made our way to his beautiful mate.

"There you are!" Linsea said with a slightly disapproving tone—although I didn't miss the underlying playfulness. "I was starting to feel abandoned."

"Never, my love. Ever!" Kayog said, drawing her into his embrace before gently rubbing his beak against hers.

The love that radiated between them felt like a living entity. This time, the wave of envy that wanted to surge within me was quickly squashed by an overwhelming sense of anticipation. Would I, too, have something this powerful with my Amreth?

"My Linsea, I bring a new friend. Please meet Ciara Stark," Kayog said, after releasing his mate. "Ciara, please meet the love of my life, Linsea Voln."

"It is a pleasure to meet you, Ciara," Linsea said in a friendly voice that felt like being wrapped in a warm blanket.

"The pleasure is all mine, in more ways than one," I said with a similar tone.

"Should that reassure me that my mate wasn't up to any mischief?" she asked teasingly.

Kayog scoffed as if she had said something offensive. "I'm *always* up to mischief... *and* to matchmaking..."

"To matchmaking?" Linsea echoed, her eyes widening.

He nodded with a smug expression while I gave her a timid smile, suddenly feeling self-conscious for no good reason.

"Absolutely. I forgot to add that Ciara also happens to be Lord Amreth's soulmate."

"No!" Linsea exclaimed, pressing both her palms to her chest with an air of incredulous happiness. "That is the most wondrous news! Amreth is such an amazing and selfless male. Not to mention very easy on the eyes!"

"Hey!" Kayog exclaimed with false outrage.

Linsea and I both burst out laughing. She playfully elbowed him while giving him a dismissive look. "Oh, hush, husband. Anyone with eyes can see how handsome he is. Even you have said as much."

"Right, but I'm a male, and a pathetically insecure one at that," he said in a pouty tone.

She snorted. "Your ego is too immense for you to even begin to understand what being insecure could be like. And yet, I love you regardless."

"Because I'm lovable, huggable, and insanely adorable," he said smugly, wrapping a wing around her to draw her closer to him.

His mate facepalmed while I laughed. They were both ridiculously adorable. I opened my mouth to say as much when a loud explosion rocked the ship.

Fearful screams filled the room as the alarm went off and blinking yellow lights started flashing around the edges of the high ceiling.

"The ship is under attack," said the soothing voice of the ship's artificial intelligence through the com. "Emergency lockdown activated. All civilians, please shelter in place."

CHAPTER 2
CIARA

Two of the five Obosian guards inside the room rushed to Elias Jacobs. Two more headed outside, while the last one opened a hidden compartment in the wall, revealing an impressive arsenal of weapons—mostly shields, swords, and staves. Although I understood their reluctance to have accessible range weapons, it distressed me that they only had a handful of blasters, all of them appearing to be basic stun guns.

To my dismay, the first set of two guards escorted Dr. Jacobs out of the room through a secret passage. Judging by the look on his face, this wasn't a surprise to him.

"Jacobs expected this," Kayog said in a frosty voice, as if he had read the thoughts crossing my mind.

The hard glint in his eyes took me aback. Gone was the jovial and mischievous older male he often portrayed himself as.

"Stay with my Linsea," he commanded.

I gave him a stiff nod, while trying to quell the panic wanting to take root deep within. He caressed his wife's cheek then walked briskly towards the hidden compartment with the weapons. Linsea squeezed my shoulder in a reassuring fashion although she kept her eyes glued to her husband, her back tense.

I glanced back towards the direction Jacobs fled. The ornate paneling of the walls that had parted to let him through were now closed again. Had I not seen it open for him to escape, I never would have suspected its existence. He had planned for this probability.

What the heck is going on?

Kayog grabbed an impressive battle staff before making his way back to us. Moments before he could reach our side, another series of explosions rocked the ship. This time, people gave in to panic. The yellow lights turning orange did nothing to calm things down. A couple of people rushing for the doors sufficed to start a stampede.

The single Obosian remaining in the hall flew towards the entrance, his silver-blue eyes glowing. It took me a moment to realize what he was doing when he started circling over the masses. The frantic push that threatened to crush the people in front against the sealed doors ebbed. He was using his calming aura called *bakaan* on the guests. But there were too many. With the ongoing explosions, it would only be a matter of time before their fear overwhelmed his ability to appease them.

Kayog slipping a protective arm around my shoulders startled me. Linsea held onto his other arm, in which he kept the staff firmly gripped in his hand. With a determined expression, he carefully led us closer to the doors, but out of the main crush.

The sound of the alarm took on a shriller pitch moments before the voice of the A.I. resonated again.

"The ship has been breached. All passengers, please stay calm and head in an orderly fashion to the nearest escape vessels. I repeat, the ship has been breached. All passengers, please stay calm and head in an orderly fashion to the nearest escape vessels."

Her words opened the floodgates that even the Obosian's appeasing powers could not stem. For one dreadful moment, I feared that the people closest to the doors would be crushed against them. Thankfully, the automatic locks opened, and the massive doors parted, allowing people to rush out. It didn't prevent some of the ones in front from being knocked onto the ground.

Before they could get trampled, using both his calming aura and the stunning abilities of his Lumiak, the Obosian forced the fleeing crowd away from the fallen right before he swooped in to pick them up and get them back on their feet so they could escape. Under different circumstances, I would have marveled at witnessing first hand an Obosian using his powers in a non-lethal fashion.

Among other things, they could invoke their Lumiak, which was essentially lightning. Its luminous tendrils writhed around his hands and shot out from his fingertips. At a low level, they would simply give you a small jolt. At mid-level, they acted like a Taser. But at maximum intensity, they could literally reduce their target into ashes.

A startled yelp escaped me when Kayog's arm slipped down around my waist, and he effortlessly picked me up. I barely had time to cling onto his shoulders before he flapped his wings and flew over the panicked crowd pouring out onto the promenade. Over his shoulder, I watched Linsea pick up a frail older woman in a similar fashion and take flight with her, following in our wake. We emerged into the promenade where complete mayhem greeted us.

A sea of people invaded the space. They were recklessly pushing and shoving each other. The majority were attempting to reach the elevators while others were rushing up and down the stairs. Sadly, people traveling in opposite directions made circulation harder. The only reasonably controlled areas were the upper floors as most guests were with us on the main floor.

Although escape vessels were available on every level, everyone was attempting to reach the larger ones, creating bottlenecks that further fanned the flames of panic. With the elevators being slow, people were elbowing each other to try and get inside every time the lifts returned. The A.I. probably should have locked their access.

Half a dozen Obosians were flying in the massive gap between the promenade, blasting their appeasing aura and intervening where people appeared on the verge of getting crushed against the railing or tumbling over.

I took in this apocalyptic scene in the seconds it took Kayog to fly me to the highest floor where the smallest crowd had gathered to access one of the escape vessels. He set me down on my feet, his face tense, as his mate landed moments later with the elderly woman.

"Get on the vessel and leave immediately," Kayog ordered.

"What about you?" I asked, worry audible in my voice as I glanced in turn at him and his wife.

"We must help get the most vulnerable out of this madness. We will follow shortly. Go," he said in a tone that brooked no argument.

Throat constricted, I gave him a stiff nod. "Thank you!"

He smiled, turned around, and took flight with his mate. A part of me felt guilty about escaping instead of also staying to help. But from experience, I knew very well how people filled with good intentions often ended up creating a lot more problems for the first responders by getting in the way instead of following instructions to evacuate when asked. I wouldn't be one of those people.

The elderly lady Linsea had brought was already standing with the crowd making its way through the vaulted doors to the fourth floor's northeast escape vessel. I joined them, grateful that people here were still mostly civilized, in no small part thanks to the line steadily moving forward.

With about five meters to go before I could enter the hallway leading to the escape vessel, another violent explosion rocked the ship. I fleetingly found the absence of bellowing smoke in the promenade or of any sign of apparent fires rather strange.

My jaw dropped when the Obosians suddenly stopped their crowd control efforts and all converged towards the northwest corner of the promenade on the main level, three below the one I was standing on. Where they previously cast weak Lumiak on the panicked passengers to snap them out of their problematic behaviors, this time they were blasting something that seemed lethal at targets I couldn't see from my location.

It could only mean the pirates had boarded us.

How was that even possible when this vessel possessed the most advanced defense technology in this sector of the galaxy?

But it was what followed that took my breath away. Within seconds of the Obosians going on the offensive, they suddenly stopped casting their lightning, half of them blinking while the others flat out held their heads with both hands as if in reaction to a massive headache or shaking their heads to clear their minds. Their flight patterns became erratic, forcing most of them to make an emergency landing on the closest level of the promenade.

The invaders had to be using some kind of psionic attack on them.

To my shock, Kayog suddenly swooped in, his right palm raised in the direction the Obosians had been casting their lightning as his silver eyes glowed. Within seconds, the Obosians closest to him appeared to recover from whatever had been affecting them, and they charged forward again to fight back the invaders. Too many questions fired off in my mind. Was he using some kind of kinetic ability or did he have some sort of psychic disrupting skill?

I knew Kayog possessed special powers that were extremely rare to his people, but this defied anything I'd ever heard about a Temern's abilities.

Another passenger bumping into me with a bit too much

force reminded me to get a move on. Forcing my eyes away from the spectacle unfolding, I took a few more steps forward only to hear a shrill scream to my right, moments before I was to enter the hallway to the vessel.

My blood turned to ice upon seeing a Darwandir female dangling from the railing. Someone must have accidentally bumped into her in their haste to come to the exit, knocking her over the rail. To my dismay half a dozen people ran past her, ignoring her cries for help as she struggled for purchase.

Cursing under my breath, I pushed past the people behind me, many glaring or yelling at me for blocking their way out. Ignoring them, I forced my way out until I could run to the female. I reached for her overly long and skinny arms. As soon as I closed my hands around her wrists and started pulling, something appeared to snap inside the older female. She screeched like a banshee, the sound painful to my ears as she frantically tried to climb on top of me.

In a moment of pure dread, I realized she'd become too terrified, her survival instincts overshadowing any rational thought in her desperate efforts to save herself. I cried out as she sank her claws into me.

"STOP!" I shouted. "I'm trying to help you. You're hurting me!"

But she was too far gone. She kept screeching, clawing at me as blood began trickling down my arms. I tried pulling away from the railing, hoping as I fell backward it would draw her with me in the process. Once she was safe, she would stop lacerating me. But my movement only freaked her out more. She tried to jump, pushing herself upward with her feet at the bottom edge of the railing, and digging her claws into my shoulders.

As she hadn't given herself a strong enough swing, she fell back down, jerking me forward in the process with such force, I found myself folded in two over the railing. I shouted in pain and fear as I blindly reached for the railing to hang onto it and keep myself from falling to my death—and hers. But more terrified than ever, the Darwandir female went berserk in her desperate attempts to use me as a ladder to safety.

My head spun as pressure on my chest made it difficult for my lungs to expand and allow me to breathe. My screams as she continued to lacerate me to shreds didn't help. I could feel my hands tingling and going numb as her claws dug in my flesh on each side of my spine. A choked sound escaped me when she rested her knee on the back of my head as she continued to climb over me.

I vaguely remembered thinking I would likely die any minute now from a broken neck or spine. Then something—probably someone running past us—violently struck my left hip. It destabilized the crazed female, sending her falling backward. She screeched in terror, further digging into the back of my thighs to propel herself forward but only achieved to throw us both over the edge.

My scream mingled with hers as we plummeted to our deaths.

In the brief seconds it lasted, a million thoughts and regrets flashed through my mind. I should have just gotten on that escape vessel. Or at least, I should have observed the safety measures when rescuing a panicked person. I should have asked for help. I should have…

I should have had a chance to meet Amreth.

Just as that thought popped into my head, and despite the haze of agony from my countless cuts and lacerations, I realized my descent had slowed, as if a force field was dampening it. I came to a full stop mid-air, then started gliding sideways, to the safety of one of the lower floors of the promenade. I couldn't say which one as I struggled to remain conscious.

"Hush," a female said, her voice soft although affected by the strangest vibration.

For a split second, I thought she was talking to me. I didn't believe I was making any sound, aside from maybe moaning in pain. But the dreadful noise assaulting my ears that suddenly stopped made me realize it had been the Darwandir female still screeching.

Through blurred vision, I stared at a male from a species I'd never seen before. He had soft brown fur and ape-like features, although he appeared to stand upright like a human. Next to him, a female—also of a species I'd never seen before but different from his—observed me with an unreadable expression. Her pale, whitish-gray skin was adorned with dark veiny streaks.

Despite the excruciating pain threatening to overwhelm me, it was fear that tore a whimper out of me when the male leaned forward to run a strange device over my face. I suddenly realized it was some sort of scanner.

"She's one of them," he said to the female.

"But not Elias. The coward fled," she replied in a clipped tone.

"We expected as much," the male said dismissively although anger lingered in his voice. "No matter. This female will do."

"I… I'll do what?" I stuttered, another wave of fear sweeping through me.

He bared his fangs at me and hissed angrily. Simultaneously, a powerful energy blast emanated from him. It didn't hit me physically, and yet it felt as if my brain had been bitchslapped. A veil of darkness descended before my eyes, and oblivion claimed me.

CHAPTER 3
AMRETH

I reveled in the intense sense of power blasting out my Lumiak always procured me. My fingers tingled as pure electricity flowed out of my hands as I refilled the crystals of my Light Quadrant. The crystals provided energy to the inmates serving their sentences in the less savage area of the four Quadrants of my Sector. Those Quadrants were ranked from Light to Dark, the former hosting the least dangerous criminals, the Gray Quadrant Q2 and Q3 holding increasingly foul individuals, and the latter containing the worst of them all, mainly unredeemable.

The survival chances of the inmates exponentially decreased based on the Quadrant in which they were incarcerated, as did their quality of life. In accordance with the law, as the Warden of my Sector, I had to provide my prisoners with the minimum requirements for their survival. That meant a certain amount of food, energy to power their basic electrical needs, a place to shelter in, and the means to improve their lot.

Food and energetic resources were provided in a flat amount every month. However, should they so choose, prisoners could work at harvesting and transforming some of the natural resources located in their Quadrant. It was entirely on a voluntary basis. But I would buy at market rate whatever they produced. In turn, they could use those credits either to upgrade their living conditions, acquire additional crystals for greater power reserves to be spent over that month, or to put in a savings account that would give them a comfortable leg up once they were released.

As was often the case in most Sectors managed by other Wardens, my Light Quadrant fared a lot better on that front. The inmates made a coordinated effort to be productive rather than spend all their time protecting themselves from the other prisoners—or plotting against them—which tended to be the norm in Quadrants Q2 to Q4.

And yet, for the first time in nine years, the extra crystals the inmates had acquired in my Light Quadrant wouldn't be filled, nor would there be any leftovers owed to them. Thanks to Gaelec, they enjoyed that extra comfort for a while. During his twelve-year sentence, he performed impressive maintenance and optimization work. He wisely devoted most of his time here learning new skills that allowed him to improve all their lives in the process.

The first signs of decline appeared after the seventh month mark. The fools kept whining about how their living conditions had deteriorated. But that was all on them. They had known all along that Gaelec's time among us was quickly drawing to an end. Someone else should have stepped up and learned what they could from him so that they could pursue his work after his departure. But they had been too lazy.

Their loss.

Still, it warmed my heart to know that, nine months after his liberation, Gaelec was not only thriving, but he had been paired with his soulmate who was now expecting their first child. Despite the countless rehabilitation programs I put at the disposal of my inmates, far too few people took advantage of them, and especially those from his species. I could only hope that his success story would be an inspiration for other Nazhrals like him.

In a silly way, thinking of Gaelec made me feel like a proud father. Well, okay, more like a proud big brother. After all, I wasn't *that* old.

But I am growing older and feeling lonely.

The face of Malaya flashing before my mind's eye immediately filled me with shame. Too many times over the past few years, the fleeting thought that she could have been my mate would resurface. It shamed me all the more that she was my best friend's soulmate. Granted, I was not *in love* with Malaya, but I did love her. While genuine happiness filled my heart for my friend Kronos, I couldn't quell the envy seeing them always awakened deep within.

I ached for that same type of wonderful connection they shared. Their love felt like a living entity that you just wanted to grab and hold forever.

That means your stupid self needs to socialize more to find your one and only.

Sadly, that was easier said than done. There weren't all that many females overly keen on settling on a prison planet. The worst part was that Kayog could not even assist me in this endeavor. Us Obosians were far too advanced to fall under the umbrella of the Prime Mating Agency. And the odds of another wrongfully accused mate conveniently landing on Molvi needing the protection of a Hell Lord—like had been the case with Malaya—were slim to none.

Just as I was starting to fill Q2's crystals, my com went off. My jaw dropped upon seeing the name of the sender. Kayog was requesting a call with me in forty-five minutes.

"What in Tharmok's name is this about?" I whispered to myself.

My mind immediately went wild with speculation. Was it news of Gaelec? Had the Temern found a match for yet another inmate? Could the highly improbable wrongfully accused mate I'd been thinking about just moments prior actually have turned up?

I forced myself to focus on my tasks rather than losing myself in pointless conjectures. I swiftly filled the crystals of my other Quadrants. While I was a strong proponent of upholding the laws and dishing out fair but stern punishment to those who broke them, I wasn't heartless. Looking at how little the prisoners from Q4 had produced over the last month discouraged me. Their earnings would barely top off their basic energy reserves. As they utterly failed to ration their usage, they would run out early and suffer this month… again.

But that was on them. My task completed, I took flight from the small island upon which the crystals rested. A small body of water surrounded it, filled with the kinds of fiendish creatures that would wreck anyone foolish enough to attempt to cross it in order to tamper with the Sector's power grid.

I flew over the forest that divided my sector into the four Quadrants. No guards were necessary to keep the prisoners from escaping as the even more dreadful creatures that inhabited the forest made certain anyone foolish enough to venture too deep would meet a horrible demise. I absentmindedly tracked the Faernych populating my forest. Those giant, five-headed, draconic creatures constituted the main guardians there. Their acid and lethal venom could kill in minutes. Their insane flight speed also made them nearly impossible to outrun.

Finding everything in order, I flew up the mountain bordering my Sector, and at the top of which my dwelling had been carved directly within it. Even before I landed on one of the countless terraces looking over the breathtaking view of the landscape, I telepathically broadcast my emotions to my Nundars. Having sensed my arrival, they would start preparing dinner right away. But I wanted to wait until after my call with Kayog was completed.

Like every Obosian, I hosted a clan of Nundars, who we usually called our familiars. The highly intelligent species lived as recluses and fed off the energy we emitted. In exchange, they took care of all house chores, including cleaning, cooking, and even repairs or construction. The best part was that they also possessed impressive magic of their own, allowing them to defend our homes in our absence against potential invaders, as well as tremendous healing powers. Those talents had allowed Kronos's own Nundars to save Malaya when rogue Faernychs attacked their home.

As I entered my office while removing my breastplate, a thought suddenly struck me. Malaya was expecting their first child. Could this be the reason Kayog was reaching out to me? He had shown an almost paternal affection towards her. Were he and Linsea planning some sort of baby present for them and wanting my input?

A few minutes later, my com went off again with the incoming call. I settled in front of my computer to accept it, projecting it onto the screen. My warm smile upon seeing his face immediately stiffened. Although I couldn't read auras through technology, his face lacked the usual joyful enthusiasm that I always associated with the Temern.

"Greetings, Kayog," I said carefully. "It is a pleasure to see you, as always."

"As it is to see you," Kayog replied, in an oddly tired voice.

"What's wrong?" I asked, this time my worry audible in my voice.

He heaved a sigh and rubbed the side of his beak with an uneasy expression that threw all my senses into high alert. I had never seen him like this.

"The past two days have been quite stressful and disturbing," Kayog said, as if choosing his words.

"How so?" I insisted, surprised by his somewhat evasive response.

From my experience with him, Kayog usually preferred the straightforward approach. What could possibly have him behaving in such an odd fashion?

"You may not be aware, but my mate and I were on board the Gladius," he replied with a dejected expression.

My eyes widened in shock. "For the symposium?!" I exclaimed.

He nodded grimly. "Yes."

"Tharmok take me! Are you okay? Is Linsea all right?!"

He nodded again and gave me a sad but reassuring smile. "Yes. We're both fine. Thank you for your concern."

I sighed with relief. "I'm glad to hear it. From what I saw in the news, many people were injured, but fortunately no deaths were reported."

"That's correct. Some people did suffer some serious injuries that they will thankfully fully recover from. But they all stemmed from the stampede of panicked people and not from the attack itself. What the authorities have not made public was that twelve people were taken during the attack."

"What?! Who? And why?" I exclaimed, stunned that they would keep such a thing secret after more than forty-eight hours.

"Every single person kidnapped worked for the Interstellar Doctors Organization," he answered calmly.

"Dr. Jacobs?!" I asked, my mind reeling at the revelation.

The Temern shook his head. "Jacobs was whisked away as soon as the attack began. He made it out safely."

I narrowed my eyes, feeling instantly suspicious. "That's odd. Why would they feel the need to take *him* to safety? A lot of high-ranking officials attended the symposium. Were they also escorted out early?"

Kayog once more shook his head. The hard glint in his eyes —something I had never witnessed before—had the seed of suspicion further taking root.

"The missing doctors all had different specialties. However, yesterday, nine of those doctors were returned," he continued.

"Returned?!" I echoed, utterly baffled. "In exchange for what?"

"In exchange for nothing. They were placed inside escape pods that were launched onto the moon Delta 5. A beacon was activated an hour after their landing, informing us of their location so that we could rescue them."

"The abductors wanted enough time to leave," I said with instant understanding, as Kayog nodded. "It is very good news, although a strange one. You would expect abductors to either ask for a ransom or to kill prisoners deemed useless. That said, why are you telling me this?"

"Because of the three people still missing, one of them is of great importance to you," the Temern replied, the oddest expression of guilt, sadness, and commiseration on his face throwing me for a loop.

"To me?" I repeated, confused. "In what way? Who is it?"

"Her name is Ciara Stark. She's a forty-one-year-old human. Like the others, she works for the Interstellar Doctors Organization with a specialty in epidemiology. She's been with them for over fourteen years now," Kayog explained before displaying an image of her.

My heart skipped a beat upon seeing the stunning female. For half a second, I almost thought she was an Obosian. She had dark brown skin and pure white hair. An organically V-shaped white spot on her forehead almost looked like a silver circlet. However, I suspected it was the result of piebaldism, which would explain the unusual color of her hair for someone of her ethnicity. Obviously, she lacked the horns, pointy ears, and bat wings of my people, but that took nothing away from just how breathtaking she was.

"She's stunning," I blurted out.

"I'm not surprised you would say that," he replied with that same sympathetic expression, making me frown.

"What does that mean? And why the sad face?" I asked, my stomach knotting with tension as another even more potent suspicion reared its head.

"You know why, Amreth," he said in a dejected fashion.

I stared at him as his words sank in, the realization I refused to acknowledge forcing itself on me.

"No way. You can't be implying what I think you are," I said, unconsciously shaking my head.

"Yes, Amreth. I am indeed implying what you think. Ciara *is* your soulmate."

"That's impossible!" I exclaimed.

"It's undeniable. I met her the night of the attack on the Gladius. I instantly recognized her soul as belonging with you. In fact, she and I had a long talk where I told her about you. We were supposed to pursue that conversation in the morning so that I could put the two of you in contact. But the raid occurred."

"That was two fucking days ago!" I snapped, suddenly angry, my chest constricting at the thought that I might have lost my soulmate before I ever even got a chance to meet her. "Why are you only telling me now?"

Although visibly upset by my reaction, he forced a stoic expression on his face and responded with a controlled and reasonable voice.

"Because there were over twenty-six hundred passengers and crewmates on board. It took time to get all those people to safety and account for them all. I didn't want to message you with some terrible news before knowing for certain what had become of her."

"Where was she when the attack occurred?" I demanded, my mind still reeling.

"Ciara was with my mate and me."

"And you left her behind?!" I shouted, shock, anger, and disbelief filling my voice.

This time, the Temern clenched his jaw, his silver eyes darkening with outrage, although their rim appeared to slightly glow as if from constraining some sort of psionic powers. Did he possess any?

"Absolutely not!" he snapped. "As soon as they opened the gathering hall's doors, I flew her to the safest exit so that she could board one of the escape vessels. She should have been safely gone while I went to fight and assist other people in distress. But while I was fighting, she went to rescue someone who was hanging on for dear life to one of the railings of the balcony. And unfortunately, both of them fell down."

"SHE DIED!" I shouted, jumping to my feet, horror clawing at my heart.

"No!" Kayog exclaimed, raising his palms in an appeasing gesture. "She did not die from the fall. The attackers caught her and the Darwandir female she had been attempting to rescue. They released the Darwandir but kept Ciara."

I ran a shaky, nervous hand through my long, silver-white hair while dropping back down onto my chair. Relief and worry twisted my insides.

"But why? What do they want from her?"

"I don't know, Amreth," Kayog said with discouragement. "The security videos showed her being carried away like the other nine who have been recovered."

"So there's a chance they might return her as well?" I asked with a sliver of hope, instantly crushed by his defeated expression.

"Everything is possible, my friend, but it is highly doubtful. If they intended to release her, why not do it at the same time as the other nine?"

Obviously, that thought had entered my mind. I simply wanted to cling to any possibility that she could be safely returned to me. I examined the Temern with confusion while trying to sort out my conflicting emotions regarding this entire situation.

"Why bring this to me instead of to the Enforcers? Are they not setting up a rescue mission?" I asked.

His shoulders slouched, and he uneasily shifted his massive maroon wings. "Because there currently are no plans for the Enforcers to take on this mission. They do not handle cases where there are 'only' three civilians involved. Such a matter is left to the local Peacekeepers."

"You and I both know they will be useless in that matter!" I said angrily. "Whatever happened to the UPO's harsh new rules against piracy? Those kidnappers went after a top-of-the-line vessel on board which countless high-ranking officials had been present. And they walk away?"

"They're not walking away from this entire incident," Kayog amended in a soothing voice. "But their focus is on identifying the pirates as well as understanding the type of technology that was used to disable the vessel without actually damaging it. They also want to know why they left after Elias did."

"So what you're saying is that the missing people are not important enough to be worth the time of the Enforcers," I hissed.

I was being unfair to the Temern by directing my anger at him. Nothing he said surprised me. Those were not only the standard procedures, but they also made sense. It would be illogical to send the elite law enforcement team to investigate every small case of missing people. Their skills would be more useful specifically tackling the issues they were currently going after. It didn't make it any easier knowing that the people entrusted with rescuing my soulmate possessed far less resources and talent.

Thankfully, Kayog seemed to read my remorse for snapping at him on whatever expression my face displayed. He gave me yet another apologetic smile laced with understanding.

"What about Maeve?" I asked, suddenly struck by a thought. "She and Helio really came through for Malaya and Kronos. Technically, they aren't Enforcers anymore."

The approving smile that stretched his beak indicated he always meant for us to get to this point. I almost asked him why he hadn't stated as much right from the start, but I suspected he was toeing a fine line as to what he could say or the suggestions he could do.

Although he was technically merely a matchmaking agent, Kayog Voln possessed an extremely high security clearance. In theory, it was due to his marriage to one of the top-ranking ambassadors of the United Planets Organization. But like Maeve and Helio—who were officially bounty hunters but unofficially secret agents for the Enforcers—I was increasingly suspecting that the Temern also performed covert missions for the UPO.

"Technically, you are correct," he replied in a non-committal fashion. "The main reason Maeve resigned her position within the Enforcer was so that she could take on the type of cases that would be deemed too small by them. That said, while I do not doubt she would be eager to assist you, both her and her mate are already working on an important mission. But that shouldn't stop you from reaching out. Whatever they can do, they will."

He didn't have to go into further details for me to understand his underlying meaning.

"I will make sure to contact them at once," I grumbled. "I need to see all the files available on the attack, and especially the recording. Do we even know who the attackers were?"

The strangest expression fleeted over his features. He hesitated for a second before appearing to settle on the answer he wanted to give me.

"I do not have the files. After all, I am just a matrimonial agent. You, on the other hand, are a Hell Lord. Surely, you have access to far more things than I do?"

I snorted and smiled. "Correct," I conceded.

As a high-ranking Warden, I indeed had access to a lot of things. But in this specific instance, I would have to stretch the limit of my clearance and get creative in pushing those boundaries further in order to get the answers I sought.

"Find her, Amreth. Ciara was truly eager to meet you. She has a beautiful soul."

"I *will* find her and bring her home. Thank you, Kayog."

He smiled then ended the communication. I immediately contacted Maeve. Thanks to the fantastic work she did helping prove Malaya's innocence, I also collaborated with her, sharing my own testimony and information about the unlawful sentencing the corrupt judge had done.

The speed with which Maeve responded hinted that she had been waiting for my call.

"Hello, Amreth," Maeve said in a gentle voice. "It is unfortunate that we should speak again under such circumstances."

"Greetings, Maeve. It is good to see you seem to be faring well. The circumstances are indeed unfortunate, but I dare hope you can be of some assistance."

She pursed her lips in a way that indicated she was carefully choosing her words before answering. "As you may be aware, my mate and I are currently working on a very sensitive mission that we cannot stray from. However, I will assist in what little capacity I can."

"I'll take anything I can get. Right now, I have nothing, not even the species of the attackers."

She nodded, a slight frown creasing her brow. "This is a very unusual situation. Our biggest asset is the fact that all the members of the Interstellar Doctors Organization who go on field missions are required to receive an organic tracker implant. It helps with rescue efforts if anything happens to them while on some godforsaken planet."

I instantly perked up, my heart soaring with hope. But a single look at her face dampened my blossoming excitement. Of course, it wouldn't be that easy.

"The good news is that we were able to follow her to the

edge of the Northern Quadrant before we lost the signal," she said apologetically.

"Lost the signal?" I echoed. "Did they detect the tracker and block it?"

She shook her head. "We do not have any communication satellites or relays in that area. It is the Dead Zone before entering the Eastern Quadrant."

My eyes widened with shock and disbelief. "Are you saying that the pirates are Sectarians?!" I exclaimed.

Her frown deepened, and she shrugged in a way that expressed uncertainty. "In truth, we don't know. Some facts seem to be pointing in that direction, but we don't have enough concrete evidence to confirm it. And that's why the Enforcers are so adamant about figuring out their identity."

"Exactly!" I said as if it was self-evident. "What better way to identify them other than finding her?"

"Because wherever they dropped her isn't where they ultimately headed afterwards," Maeve explained. "You see, the ship that we managed to capture on the surveillance cameras of the Gladius doesn't belong to any species from our Quadrant, at least none that we know of. The cameras on board also kept glitching, preventing us from performing any type of facial or species recognition. Even the bio scanners faltered."

"So they deliberately sabotaged our technology," I replied.

She nodded. "But they didn't damage anything. They only disrupted them for the duration of the raid, which confirms they wanted to hide their identity."

"But what of the guards? I understand they fought the pirates. Surely they saw them and could give some kind of description," I challenged.

"All the guards were Obosians. Every single one of them reported that they sustained some sort of psychic attack that completely messed with their heads and even their ability to fly," Maeve replied. "The enemies that they could see wore some sort of holographic disguise that made them look blurry and disjointed. It was impossible to say what they were except that they seemed humanoid. If not for Kayog, they wouldn't have been able to fight back at all."

"Kayog? What did he do?" I asked, taken aback.

"He is an Edal. It grants him a broad range of unique powers that other members of his species do not have. His ability to recognize soulmates is merely the one he makes public. There's more to the Temern than meets the eye," she added in a mysterious tone. "He can disrupt psychic attacks, which allowed the guards to resume pushing back the enemies. But their technology was far too powerful, and I suspect it involved more than that. We honestly have no idea what we were dealing with."

"Are we talking about a potential invasion?" I asked, my mind reeling from these revelations.

Relief flooded through me when Maeve shook her head with conviction. "This was targeted. They wanted something, although we believed it was someone."

"Ciara?" I asked with confusion.

She shook her head again. "We believe they were after Elias Jacobs."

"Why?" I asked, the suspicions that had taken root while talking to Kayog resurfacing.

"We're not sure. He claims he doesn't know either, but he lies. His early escape seems a little too convenient. He suspected an attack was imminent and planned accordingly. Rest assured that we are investigating."

"But why take Ciara and the other two doctors? What could they possibly have that the kidnappers might want?" I insisted.

"That is the main question. Ciara is an epidemiologist. Mehreen is an immunologist, and Ernst is a molecular biologist," she said pensively. "The three of them together is an ideal team to investigate an epidemic."

"You think they're sick? Or are they trying to develop some

sort of biological warfare?" I asked, my sense of unease cranking up another notch.

"We're leaning towards the first hypothesis," Maeve replied. "Their attack was surgical. All the injuries that the passengers sustained came from their own panic, none from the actions of the kidnappers. Like with the Darwandir female that fell with your mate, the attackers protected all the people who fell or would have sustained grievous injuries. Whatever they want, we don't think they're evil. But their technology makes them an undeniable threat that we need to assess."

"Be that as it may, they still kidnapped three people after attacking a vessel that caused injuries, despite their best effort to limit them. If they only needed help, they could have asked. Why this? Why come from the Eastern Quadrant for this? Where have they taken them?"

"Truth be told, we're beginning to suspect the kidnappers might have been hired hands for a third party," Maeve said carefully. "Like I mentioned earlier, we lost Ciara's signal at the edge of the Dead Zone. But after the ship dropped the nine people they released, it left our Quadrant from a different direction. That vessel is back in the Eastern Quadrant, but Ciara's implant never left the Dead Zone."

"What's over there?" I asked, baffled.

"Just a handful of extremely primitive planets under the strictest Prime Directive guidelines. The only species over there with whom strictly controlled interactions are allowed are the Sangoths. They possessed a certain level of technology, and we interact with them to a comparable extent as we do with the Ordosians."

"You think they have her?"

"It's a long shot and pure speculation," she admitted with an apologetic look. "The Sangoths do not have the capacity for interstellar travel. We have to go to them. But they have ways of contacting us through very slow relays."

"Even assuming some Sectarian came to our Quadrant to help them out, why wouldn't they simply request our doctors if we already have a relationship with them?" I challenged.

"I don't know, Amreth. But maybe it is because the trust was breached. The serum that made Elias famous was derived from a random event that occurred on Kestria, the Sangoth homeworld."

"Why in Tharmok's name didn't you mention that earlier?!" I exclaimed. "That's the obvious connection!"

"Maybe, but maybe not. We have to handle this whole thing extremely carefully. If Jacobs wronged them somehow, tipping our hand too early might jeopardize the welfare of the prisoners. There is also the matter of the extremely strict restrictions to go onto that planet. Even the peacekeepers will not be allowed to land without strong enough probable cause."

"You have the three doctors' implants!" I said in an evident tone.

"Yes, but the Peacekeepers do not have powerful enough technology to track them without entering Kestria's atmosphere, which they can't do without cause."

"Then give them the damn technology!"

"We can't. It is too powerful and could be abused in the wrong hands. That's why the Enforcers strictly control who has access to it."

"So we're supposed to sit back and do nothing?" I exclaimed, anger seeping into my voice.

"No, Amreth. I'm merely explaining that the Enforcers are tied up elsewhere. And the Peacekeepers do not have the necessary tools to enter Kestria without cause. But if a civilian ship going through that region happened to have an unexpected malfunction, nobody could fault them for making an emergency landing."

I gaped at her. She smiled shamelessly.

"The Peacekeepers—and the Enforcers for that matter—only need the slightest evidence of probable cause. An image or video of one of the three missing people would suffice to justify them entering Kestria's atmosphere."

I shifted uneasily in my seat.

"This would be a deliberate violation of the laws," I said.

The 'Are you fucking kidding me?' look Maeve gave me had my cheeks burning with embarrassment.

"Seriously, Amreth… I realize your species is raised indoctrinated about the importance of upholding the law. But with all due respect, you need to remove that self-righteous stick out of your ass and focus on what matters. What is more important to you? Rescuing your soulmate, or righteously upholding some law?"

"That is an unfair question! However good one's intentions may be for breaking the law, they were created for a reason. Don't you humans have a saying about the road to Hell being paved with good intentions? What if me going there with a conveniently timed accident ends up creating even more diplomatic problems?"

She shrugged. "Then don't go, and hope for the best."

I bared my fangs at her, her unimpressed look stinging even more. Obviously, I would never just sit back and do nothing while my other half was potentially in danger somewhere and being held against her will. But breaking the law…?

"You mentioned occasional interactions with the Sangoths. I seem to recall that they offered contracts for seasonal trade workers. If I joined one of those teams, I would legally enter their airspace," I offered.

Maeve slowly nodded. "You heard correctly. Unfortunately, there won't be any such trade missions for another five months. Are you willing to wait that long?"

I didn't have to answer. My face did all the talking. She once again gave me a sympathetic smile although her dark brown eyes sparked with mischief.

"Look, I know how difficult this must be for you to even

contemplate. Sometimes, bending the rules is necessary. What do you think I'm doing right now even sharing all of this with you? More often than not, the Enforcers—and their greater network that I am a part of—have no choice but to toe the line, and sometimes even trample it. What do you think would have happened to Malaya and Kronos had we not bent those rules? How many more innocent lives would Judge Wuras and his father have destroyed?"

I gave her a stiff nod.

"I'm telling you all of this because we implicitly trust you. You are a highly regarded Warden and an elite Warrior. Both Kayog and Linsea vouched for your outstanding moral compass and diplomatic skills. You are the best candidate the Enforcers could have wanted to investigate the situation in that area without making waves."

My jaw dropped from sudden understanding. The Enforcers were not washing their hands of the fate of those three missing people. They were recruiting me as their silent agent to protect their plausible deniability.

"I understand what you are saying," I said at last.

She smiled with approval. "I will transfer all the tracking info you require to your com. Go in stealthily. To the extent possible, avoid contact with the locals unless absolutely necessary. Get the proof we need and then leave. Do not try to play the hero. Communications will be slow as any message you send will need to travel to the nearest relay before it gets picked up. But keep us apprised as much as you can about any development. We will assist you in any way possible."

"Thank you, I will."

"Good luck, Amreth. And bring your girl home. You deserve every happiness."

As soon as we ended the communication, I began preparation for my immediate departure.

CHAPTER 4
CIARA

I woke up with a start. The bright lights of the room made me blink a few times before my vision adjusted. A glance at my surroundings revealed it to be the fanciest medical bay I had ever set foot in. In all my years, I had visited the infirmaries and laboratories of countless ships and species. None of them rivaled this one.

I fleetingly wondered if this belonged to the Xurgens. After all, they were the most advanced species in our sector of the galaxy. But for having drooled over their technology more times than I could count, I could say with great confidence that this didn't feature in their line of products.

I tried to sit up from my lying position only to realize some sort of energy field kept me immobile. My initial confusion quickly gave way to a sliver of panic as memories of the recent events came rushing back. The pain from being torn to shreds by the terrified Darwandir female flashed through my mind. However, a quick self-assessment revealed no true discomfort aside from a little stiffness and soreness. Considering the grievous wounds she inflicted on me, I should be in complete agony without heavy sedation. As my mind was clear, this meant that whoever attacked the ship and stopped my deadly fall apparently also healed me.

I wanted to believe this to be a good sign that maybe their intentions weren't as evil as my fertile imagination suggested. My heart leapt when I turned my head to the side. Through a glass wall, I stared in shock at a strange female with the simian-looking male I vaguely remembered from the ship. They were talking with Brett Dunham, another of my acquaintances with the Interstellar Doctors Organization.

What do they want with us?

Whatever questions she asked him, his answers prompted a rather unimpressed reaction from her. Her male companion stood there stoically, occasionally speaking. I would have given anything to be able to hear their exchange. If nothing else, I took some small measure of comfort in that Brett didn't seem scared, just confused.

A glance at the opposite side of my room revealed a second glass wall separating me from another staff member of the IDO. Discovering an unconscious Mehreen Aziz freaked me out. Sure, many physicians and medical professionals had been aboard the Gladius. But countless politicians, investors, corporate magnates, social and ethics advocates, and people from various other fields had also been present. Why did it feel like only members of the Interstellar Doctors Organization had been targeted?

They mentioned something about Elias Jacobs…

That he was one of the most prominent figures of our organization seemed to confirm that they were indeed after our members.

My stomach knotted when I glanced back at Brett and our abductors. He appeared to be arguing with the female, who suddenly waved her hand with an air of aggravation. A gasp escaped me when Brett's head fell back onto his pillow, and he appeared to lose consciousness.

Does she have psionic powers?

Even as that thought crossed my mind, I remembered how the simian seemed to knock me out on the ship. But he hadn't moved or even seemed to react when the female made that gesture.

The mattress—which had been tilted upward to have Brett in a semi-sitting position—lowered back to a horizontal state. As it did so, the two aliens started walking towards the glass wall separating my room from Brett's.

The entire glass pane slid open with a soft swish. Heart pounding, I watched them silently come my way, their gazes assessing me. Despite the absence of apparent aggression from either of them, fear twisted my insides.

As they approached, and now without the debilitating pain that had blurred my vision back on the ship, I got a better look at the pair. There was no question I had never seen either species before. The strangest black patterns adorned the female's grayish-white skin. For the briefest instant, it brought to mind the sickness that previously affected the Xelixians, a species located in the Western Quadrant. But beyond the fact that their illness had been cured over a decade ago, her markings were a lot more organized, not the random chaos of the disease that had spread black, veiny tendrils all over the Xelixians' bodies. This felt more like the patterns of a tiger but restricted to specific areas of her body.

She had long, pitch-black hair and very pale eyes with an otherwise very human appearance. Her companion also possessed the body of a human except covered in the same brown fur of an ape. His face had undeniably simian traits, especially the nose and eyes. But his mouth could have belonged to one of us. The thicker fur around his head acted like a fluffy and lustrous mane. He, too, was observing me with yellowish brown eyes brimming with intelligence. Thankfully, they were devoid of the anger he displayed on the ship before knocking me out.

Even as they completed their approach, the upper half of my

mattress started tilting up, putting me in the same semi-sitting position that Brett had been. I didn't see either of them activate the switch or issue any type of command that would have set my bed in motion.

"Greetings, Ciara Stark. I am Svira, and this is Kald Aku Ebaki," the female said with a polished voice as she waved at her companion. "We have a few questions for you."

For some dumb reason, my brain latched onto her undefinable accent. I couldn't say why South African popped into mind. Although she spoke in Universal—which was a major relief—my translator kicked in when she spoke the word *Kald*. I initially assumed it to be part of his name, but the word Chieftain kept wanting to worm its way in. I could only presume my implant was attempting to translate what it perceived as a foreign language.

I meant to return her greeting, but my mouth had different ideas.

"Where am I? Why did you take me? What are you? And what did you do to Brett?" I blurted out back-to-back.

Svira snorted while Aku merely raised an eyebrow.

"Slow down, human," Svira replied with a hint of amusement. "In case you had not paid attention, I said that *we* had questions for *you*. But fair enough. I will indulge you this once so that we can proceed with the important matters. Brett is fine. He's only sleeping as he is of no use to us."

"Who is *us*?" I asked, my eyes flicking between the two of them.

"I'm a visitor to this Quadrant and a friend of the Kreelars, Aku's species. They need help righting the wrongs done to them by humans," she replied, her voice taking on a slightly harder edge.

"What? How did we wrong them? I've never even seen or heard of their species before!" I exclaimed, although I didn't miss how she conveniently avoided naming her own species.

"And you never would have in your lifetime without Elias Jacobs' trespass."

My blood turned to ice. Her words reminded me how odd it seemed for Jacobs to get so swiftly escorted off the ship the moment the attack began. What did he do? When and where did he interfere with the lives of people from the Eastern Quadrant?

The UPO and the Galactic Alliance controlled different areas of the known galaxy. We remained in the Northern Quadrant. The Galactic Alliance controlled the Western and Eastern Quadrants. The Southern Quadrant was still a heavily disputed no man's land. Residents of each Quadrant observed strict rules forbidding them from crossing into each other's territories.

Earth was one of the very few planets that was a member of both the UPO and the Galactic Alliance. This privilege stemmed from the fact that our solar system was located in the Dead Zone between the Western and Northern Quadrants. Once we achieved warp travel, both the UPO and the galactic alliance attempted to lure us to their side. We were greedy enough to demand to be part of both and totally got away with it.

While it greatly benefited our home world, it didn't subtract us from the strict rules observed by everyone else. Any human who left Earth couldn't ping pong back and forth between the Sectarian territories of the Galactic Alliance, and the Allied territories of the UPO. The people from the Eastern and Western quadrants hated to be referred to as the Sectarians. But it was an appropriate description as the planets over there were extremely divided and firmly indoctrinated in following their own rules, their own way. Furthermore, where planets of the Western Quadrant still heavily followed organized religions, mainly the worship of the Goddess, the Eastern Quadrant had abandoned all forms of faith and had rather interesting rules about indentured servitude and the ability to subject oneself to pretty much anything through a binding contract.

Therefore, Svira's presence here violated enough rules to

potentially trigger a major diplomatic incident between the Allies and the Sectarians. They had attacked a vessel hosting countless high-ranking officials from various planets of our Quadrant. What wrong could humans have caused that was so dire for Svira to take such a risk?

"What did Jacobs do?!" I asked, my mind reeling.

"What do you know of SS12?" Svira asked instead of answering my question.

I felt myself pale. Had he done something immoral to obtain the serum that propelled him to the very top of medical excellence in this generation?

"It is a revolutionary cure that Dr. Jacobs discovered a decade ago during his study of the Sangoths," I replied carefully. "As I understand it, one of his team members was attacked by a rabid beast and got sick. They were able to track down the beast and derived the miraculous treatment from it."

"A beast, was it?" Aku interjected for the first time, anger seeping into his voice. "Is that the description he gave?"

It was deep and a little breathy. Under different circumstances, I would have found him attractive. But a deep anger simmered under the surface. Whatever Jacobs did, it had to be terrible.

I licked my lips nervously and nodded. "Obviously, everyone in the medical community had countless questions about the source of the cure. But Jacobs—along with his entire team—stated that it was some kind of a wild beast that they couldn't identify. It decayed too quickly from whatever disease was eating it from within. It had also mutated far too much to allow them to identify the original species it belonged to."

"And you believe that?!" Svira asked with obvious disbelief.

I hesitated and then shrugged. "It was indeed a rather disturbing accounting," I conceded. "Quite a few people expressed feeling troubled by it that they didn't even have sketches or any preserved samples that could have allowed more advanced computers than the field ones to try and recreate the original creature from the DNA. But you cannot challenge an entire team of highly regarded scientists without solid proof or at least a strong cause."

"And no one thought of coming back?" Aku challenged.

"Many of us wanted to. But the Sangoths' home world is under strict Prime Directive guidelines. That *beast* did not naturally dwell in the areas inhabited by the Sangoths. Trying to track down a creature whose actual appearance they weren't even certain of would have greatly risked disturbing the ecosystem. It didn't feel justified under the circumstances. Anyway, the entire Quadrant was too hyped about further digging into SS12."

"Well they lied to all of you," Aku ground between his teeth. "That wild beast was my older sister. She was training her son at tree hopping when she stumbled upon two humans. They were coupling by the river where they had been eating. We had never seen humans before. But my nephew, who was only five years old at the time, focused on the food left on display. He ran from his mother to go eat some of it."

"Oh, no!" I breathed out.

If that couple had been on a romantic escapade, there was no way they would have brought the sterile rations that were authorized when eating in protected environments. God only knew what kind of negative reaction the local population could have to it. As if he had heard the thoughts crossing my mind, Aku confirmed my fears.

"The human male noticed my nephew grabbing the food. He chased after him. Naturally, my sister intervened to protect her son. The human shot her," Aku snarled.

"Oh, my God!" I whispered, horrified. I would have pressed my hand to my face, but the energy field kept me restrained.

"She still managed to fight him. She bit and clawed him. The human female shot my sister as well. That succeeded in knocking her out. And they both fled, abandoning my sister and my nephew distressed about the state of his mother."

"She died?" I asked, my voice constricted.

"No. They shot her with tranquilizers," he replied.

I flinched upon hearing his words. You never injected new species with any types of drugs before performing extensive tests to see how they would react. In this specific instance, beyond the fact that they never should have been there, they should have used a stun gun to incapacitate their target. How the fuck did they compound so many mistakes in one go?

"What you need to realize is that the river where this took place is located more than a day's run from the closest Sangoth village," Aku added angrily.

"This means at least an hour flight in a personal shuttle," Svira specified. "Those humans didn't stumble there by accident. It was a deliberate choice, knowing they were violating the Prime Directive just so they could enjoy a pretty setting to fornicate."

"I'm sorry this happened. The way they handled it was beyond poor. They certainly panicked, which made them act irrationally," I said in an apologetic tone.

"And that makes it acceptable?" Aku hissed.

"Of course not," I said in a soothing tone. "They never should have been there in the first place. But what happened? If I'm here, I'm assuming that she had some sort of negative reaction?"

"At first, she seemed to fully recover once the sedatives wore off. But then she started getting sick about a week later. As she was a wet nurse, she was breastfeeding many of our infants, including my nephew."

"Oh, heavens!" I whispered, my chest constricting.

"The younglings got sick, as did the ones who no longer breastfed but played with them. And then it passed on to their siblings, their parents, and to the entire village. Our young breastfeed until the age of six or seven. Most of our females only have two, or maximum three, babies in their lifetime. In the two months that followed the incident, four out of five of our infants died. Barely a third of our females remain. Some are starting to show early signs again. We are becoming extinct!"

Despite the horror his words awakened in me, my scientific mind kicked into gear, thanks to years of dealing with these types of situations.

"Only the females, not the males?" I asked.

"Both genders are affected, and have similar death rates, except it becomes even more fatal for the females, if they become infected after puberty," Aku explained.

Could it be impacted by estrogen levels?

If their hormonal development followed a pattern similar to humans, males and females would have similar testosterone levels in their infancy, but females would see a significant increase in estrogen once they hit puberty.

"What do your doctors say about it?" I ask carefully.

"Our healers do not possess advanced enough technology to be able to fully understand what is happening," Aku said begrudgingly.

"Kreelars fall under the strictest guidelines of the Prime Directive for a reason. They've only recently developed basic electricity. They don't even have connectivity," Svira explained.

"But *you* do!" I challenged before giving a meaningful glance at the high-tech med bay around us.

She shook her head, her face closing off. "We have reached the limit of how much we can interfere in this matter."

"What the heck is that supposed to mean?" I asked, baffled.

"The Oracles saw the paths. If we meddle any further, things will end extremely badly for the Kreelars, and for many others. Our contribution in saving their people is coming to a close."

"Oracles?" I echoed with confusion before my eyes widened

with shock and sudden understanding. "Wait! Are you saying that you're Korletheans?!"

I recoiled, and my heart skipped a beat when she bared her teeth, an air of pure hatred descending over her features.

"We are *not* Korletheans! We *hate* those sons of krilliks! They have done to us what you have done to the Kreelars. But they did so with malice!"

"Hold up right there!" I exclaimed with outrage. "*I* did nothing to the Kreelars. *Humanity* did nothing to them. From what you are telling me, it appears that Elias' team did. What I can promise is to do everything in my power to help undo some of the damage and prevent this tragedy going on any further. But… but you don't look Xelixian either."

From what little I remembered of the Sectarian history, the Korletheans had harmed a heck of a lot of species with reckless experiments. The only one that I could think of in those Quadrants that had a grayish skin with dark markings were the Xelixians. But they had oversized irises without pupils, chevron shaped bone ridges on their foreheads, and unusual ridged ears, none of which matched Svira's appearance.

She snorted and shook her head. "We're not Xelixians either."

"Then what…?"

She waved a dismissive hand, interrupting me. "Never mind that. The only thing you should focus on is undoing the damage to the Kreelars. You have an epidemiology background which will be of great use for the challenge ahead."

"Absolutely. I can and want to help. But shouldn't Elias—"

"He will be dealt with," Svira interrupted again. "There's a reason he fled the minute our vessel attacked yours. He knew what was coming."

Although I didn't voice it, I had suspected as much. Nevertheless, I narrowed my eyes at her, still struggling to understand why they were handling things this way.

"All right, but why attack the Gladius? If what you're saying is true—and I have no reason to doubt it—why not simply expose him? The UPO and the galactic community would hold him accountable and do everything in their power to do right by the Kreelars. This attack could trigger a major political conflict between your Quadrant and ours."

She nodded. "Believe me, Ciara, that had been the original plan. Sadly, all those paths lead to tragedy. But you..."

To my surprise, her voice trailed off, and her eyes went out of focus. I cast a confused look at Aku, who simply observed quietly. Moments later, Svira blinked and returned her full attention to me. A triumphant smile stretched her lips.

"You can be the key," she said at last. "So long as you work with your mate, you will find the solution."

I recoiled again, this time truly confused. "My mate?! I don't have one!"

She gave me a mysterious smile. "Not yet, but soon."

Oh, my God! Is she talking about Amreth?!

Her smile broadened as if she had read the thought that fleeted through my mind.

"What are you?" I whispered more to myself than truly to her. "You are not a Xelixian or a Korlethean, and you display the type of powers that the Veredians possess. And yet you're clearly not one. So what are you?"

"We are the Korletheans' worst nightmare," she said with a hint of cruelty in her pale eyes. She then turned to Aku with something akin to a triumphant smile. "She's the one."

An air of relief washed over him.

"I'm the one what?" I asked, instantly worried again.

She ignored my question, and the outer rim of her eyes began to glow as she stared at me with great intensity. "Ciara, obey my command. Once I leave this room, you will fall asleep and forget you ever saw me as well as any discussions and allusions ever made during this discussion regarding my people, the Korletheans, the Veredians, and the Xelixians."

"But why? Wait!" I exclaimed when both of them simply turned around and started walking towards the glass wall separating my room from the one Mehreen was lying in.

Before exiting, she stopped one last time and looked at me over her shoulder. At first, I thought she was going to answer my question, but her eyes went slightly out of focus again.

"There should never be red rocks in the river. Remember this well."

"What?!"

She didn't respond and looked back towards Mehreen's room. The upper half of my bed began lowering again as I once more called out to Svira. But as soon as she stepped through the open glass door, I felt my consciousness get swallowed into a dark void, and I knew no more.

CHAPTER 5
CIARA

Unlike the previous time, I didn't wake up with a sudden jolt of panic. Instead, I comfortably emerged from what felt like the best, most restful sleep I've had in ages. That didn't prevent a brutal wave of confusion from crashing over me once I took in my new surroundings. Despite the fog that now wrapped my memory of recent events, I knew beyond any doubt that I had fallen asleep in a completely different environment. I vaguely remembered a ship, but not which one it had been.

I was now lying on an insanely comfortable bed inside what looked like a decent sized mud house. Wooden shutters covered a set of large windows. I removed the plush comforter covering me and carefully got out of bed. That movement brought back the fact that I had been immobilized previously. It was odd that I would remember that detail but not the actual place I had been held in. I made my way to the window to open the shutters. Daylight immediately flooded the room. At a glance, it appeared to be mid-morning.

Exposed wooden beams and clay walls gave the space a warm feeling. The furniture, which included a queen-sized bed, a dresser and two nightstands, was all carved in the same pale wood. Although beige, it had a slightly greenish tinge to it, like dry bamboo.

Unfortunately, the window looked out onto what I presumed to be a private garden, preventing me from getting a better idea of what was happening outside. Although still slightly worried, I didn't feel afraid. The strangest sense of determination filled me.

It suddenly struck me that I was wearing some kind of light but demure nightgown. The fabric felt unfamiliar to me, as did its design. In the corner of the sparsely, but tastefully decorated room, a chair sat near the window with a set of clothes properly folded on top. At the foot of the chair, a pair of comfortable shoes just the perfect size for me also awaited. My cheeks heated upon realizing they added fresh undies to the pile.

I wanted to believe one of the Kreelar females provided these for me. It felt awkward that Aku might have handled it.

And yet, even as that thought flashed through my mind, with a certainty I couldn't explain, I believed someone else, not of their species, got these for me. For a moment, I considered donning those garments right away then decided to explore the rest of the dwelling before taking any action.

I exited the bedroom to be greeted by a rather nice living area. A large couch and a chair, both made of wood with some very comfy looking beige cushions sat straight ahead from the bedroom door. To the left, a table with six chairs faced another large window on one side, and a small counter with a sink and cupboards on the other. Although this clearly served as the dining area, I couldn't see anything that even remotely resembled a stove or cooling unit. But then, I didn't recall seeing any type of night lamps or anything that hinted that they possessed electricity.

And yet, a part of me believed that someone had mentioned that the Kreelars were sufficiently advanced to harness electrical power. It suddenly struck me that, if they didn't, helping them without the comfort of the advanced technology that had always been at my disposal would prove extremely challenging.

Still, I strolled over to the table upon which they left a few covered plates. I lifted the lid off the first one to find dry breads, jam, what I assumed to be cheese, cured meats, fruits, and some kind of clear juice. To my shock, right next to the plate that contained the fruits, I spotted my bracer.

My heart leapt as I greedily reached for it. Although I expected it, I couldn't help a sliver of disappointment at the absence of any connectivity. But that didn't make it unusable. As a member of the Interstellar Doctors Organization, I had been vaccinated against pretty much everything and anything under the sun. I also received a variety of intelligent nanobots that could detect most toxins and do quite a number on them should I find myself stranded somewhere without access to medicine.

Nonetheless, I scanned the food for any potential risk. It wasn't wise to think that, because I had protection, I should recklessly expose myself to unnecessary bacteria. Even if my system could fight almost anything, there was nothing to be gained by putting myself through the discomfort—and maybe even the agony—of a random illness.

The green light on the interface of my bracer signaled the all clear. I took a bite of the cured meat. It tasted like a mild version of chorizo. The yellowish white slices indeed turned out to be some kind of cheese, which strongly tasted like Swiss cheese— my favorite. It paired perfectly with a bit of jam on the bread that could have been some multigrain cracker. Although slightly hungry, I didn't settle down to eat and decided to complete the tour first.

The door near the dining area was locked. I presumed it was the main entrance. Saying it didn't bother me to be locked in would be a lie. But under the circumstances, I could see Aku not wanting a random human to traipse around his village. For all I knew, his people hated my kind for what had befallen them.

I backtracked to the door on the other side of the living area. It turned out to be a second bedroom. The bed was a little smaller than the one I had slept in. The dresser was also smaller, leaving plenty of room for a large work desk which would be perfect for me to use as my office. The door on the back wall of the living area opened onto the backyard. It was small and cozy with tall fences for privacy. It only took me a second to realize the reason for it. They didn't have a traditional bathroom, but an outdoor shower next to an outhouse.

To my delight, the outhouse wasn't as rudimentary as I expected. As a field doctor, I had experienced my fair share of latrines and chemical bathrooms along the way. This one actually appeared to be linked to some sort of sewer system, which suited me just fine. It was clean, with the strangest toilet paper, almost like napkins, and a small sink likely hooked to a well system. I quickly relieved my bladder and then took a shower. A recessed shelf contained a set of towels. I grabbed one, dried myself off, and wrapped it around my body before returning inside the house. I put on the clothes that were left for me. It disturbed me what a perfect fit they turned out to be. They were comfortable, the type of durable outfit that we often wore on these kinds of missions.

I returned to the dining area and ate while assessing my current situation. The gaping holes in my memory seriously pissed me off. I should be worried about it, but a part of me felt like that loss had been expected. It was as if I had been warned beforehand, even though it didn't really make sense.

The main question was who else had been brought here? I clearly remembered Brett Dunham and knew beyond any doubt that he would not be here. I also recalled seeing Mehreen. Having her here would be wonderful. I just wished I could contact someone off this planet to let them know that I was fine. My parents would be freaking out as they undoubtedly had been warned of my abduction by now.

Unsure what to do, I neatly packed the leftovers on a single plate which I covered and took the empty ones to the sink. Just as I was about to start washing them, a knock on the door startled the living daylights out of me.

"Come in," I called out, my palm pressed to my chest.

The lock clicked, and then the door opened. I clasped my hands in front of me, feeling suddenly nervous when Aku's broad frame filled the doorway. His eyes quickly glided over me before flicking towards the table.

"Good, you are ready," he said in an approving tone. "Do not fret with the dishes. Someone will take care of cleaning up. Come."

He gestured for me to follow and immediately exited the house without waiting for my response. I hastened after him, fascinated by the slow movement of his long, fluffy tail. It surprised me that he should have one. More advanced primates like humans and apes didn't have tails, unlike monkeys. And this Kreelar clearly possessed an intelligence and sentience level on par with a human.

I stepped out of the house and into a rather charming inner courtyard. Within, eight other dwellings similar to mine lined the edges of the circular area. To my utter delight, a deployable field lab with solar panels sat next to the last dwelling across from my own home. Packed dirt served as pavement, although a series of flowers and small bushes adorned the front-end edges of each small residence. To our right, a tall gate restricted our access to the rest of the village. A single guard stood watch in front of it.

Like Aku, he was wearing some poofy long pants, an adorned belt, and a decorative loincloth on top. His bare chest hid nothing of his well-defined abs. Leather bracers around his wrist boasted the same dark green shade as his leader's. The main difference between them was the intricately carved circlet on Aku's forehead, which I assumed served to mark him as the Chieftain, or *Kald*, if I had properly interpreted my translator.

As we approached the lab, I recognized it as being the official property of the Interstellar Doctors Organization. Did they steal it?

"How did you get your hands on this lab?" I found myself blurting out.

"We got creative," Aku replied in a noncommittal fashion.

"How creative?" I insisted.

A single glance from him sufficed to make it clear I was to drop the topic. Although it didn't really matter under the circumstances, I hated working in the dark and having so many unanswered questions. It also worried me to the extent that having top notch and reliable equipment was essential in my line of work. Faulty gear meant results that couldn't be trusted. Which in turn translated as cures that could in fact be even more harmful than the disease we were trying to combat to begin with.

But all such wandering thoughts flew right out of my head when the door parted to reveal the presence of two familiar faces.

"Mehreen! Ernst!" I exclaimed, my face lighting up as both scientists rose from the workstations they had each been sitting at.

"There she is!" Mehreen said.

While we were on friendly terms, I wouldn't call either of them close friends. And yet I immediately rushed to her and gave her a big hug, which she happily returned. At forty-eight, the petite woman of Lebanese descent barely looked a day over thirty. She had perfect, luminous skin, long, dark-brown hair, pale-brown eyes, and obscenely long natural lashes that had me drooling with envy. She had earned the respect of the scientific community with her impressive work in immunology.

After releasing Mehreen, I turned to Ernst Wagner. Tall and lanky, he towered over me by a good head. The warmth of his embrace slightly took me aback. I knew him even less than

Mehreen. From my limited interactions with him, while I wouldn't call him cold and distant, he'd never seemed the demonstrative type. As if realizing it, he dropped his arm, and straightened before running his fingers through his short, light-brown hair. The glimmer of embarrassment in his blue eyes would be adorable if not so odd from the usually very stoic fifty-four-year-old man.

As a cell and molecular biologist, he was an expert at researching the physiological health ramifications of plant chemical interactions on living tissues in animal species with a specialization in xenobiology.

"I'm pleased to see that you already know each other," Aku said, reclaiming our attention. "It will make things easier for everyone. Please," he added, gesturing at the meeting table in the center of the front room.

The space had four workstations on the left and right side. A large door at the back gave access to the actual lab split into three sections. One was only accessible after going through a decontamination space. Another section had two isolation suites for patients, and the last offered a variety of cages and cells where we could keep animals.

We took our seats around the table, Mehreen and I on the left, Ernst across from us, and Aku settling at the head.

"The three of you were chosen because you have the skills and right moral compass to fix the tragedy that Elias caused," he said in a calm voice before turning to me. "As Mehreen and Ernst will be able to tell you, these devices contain all the information that you require."

He was pointing at the computers on each workstation. Without connectivity, we would still be limited in some of the tasks we could perform and information we could access. However, these labs had been specifically designed to operate in remote areas, often for primitive species that also didn't own this type of technology. Therefore, the local drives possessed an extensive database with almost anything we could need for cross-reference and analysis.

"If you have any questions, my people and I will be happy to answer them. You can examine Yekka, the latest member of our tribe to present symptoms," he continued. "We have settled her in the first house right next to the lab."

"We found a file about her in the system," Ernst said with a slight frown. "Did you enter that data there?"

Aku shook his head. "Our friends did."

"Are your friends the ones who taught you Universal as well?" I asked.

He gave me a strange look before nodding. "Yes, they did. But enough about them," he added when I opened my mouth to further pry about them. "They are not the reason for your presence here."

"You said you would answer our questions," Ernst challenged.

"I said I would answer questions regarding the illness plaguing us, nothing else," he retorted, his tone hardening.

Mehreen gave Ernst a look that implied that he should drop it. I also wanted to press the issue, but I realized that they had been in this lab for a while now. God only knew what had transpired in the meantime. Making waves until I had a better understanding of what was going on didn't seem wise.

She turned to Aku. "Based on the issues your people are facing, if we had more help—"

"No one else comes," he interrupted sharply. "The three of you is already too much, not to mention her mate. Off-worlders are a scourge to this world. We only brought you here because we had no other choice. Rest assured that we want you gone as much as you want to leave."

"Her mate?" Ernst repeated, confused.

Aku waved a dismissive hand, clearly uninterested in deepening the matter. A part of me wished he would have answered while another really didn't want to discuss the improbable state of my personal life with the others.

"You are free to move around this courtyard," he continued. "We initially built it to keep the sick isolated from the rest of the tribe. Do not try to escape. We do not wish you harm, but we expect you to do everything in your power to fix what your people wrought. If you need to exit the courtyard, ask one of the guards. Note that the forest beyond is not safe. Should you venture there unaccompanied, you will not survive. Understand that this is not a game or empty threats. Any questions?"

I had a million of them. Judging by my companions' expressions, they also had plenty they wanted to drill him about. However, a silent communication passed between us as we exchanged glances. We needed to discuss a few things among ourselves before giving him a full inquisition.

"Good!" he said, getting on his feet when we all nodded in response. "Meals will be served in the green house at 1:00 and then at 6:00. If you require sustenance earlier, simply warn the guard. His name is Enre. There will always be things to munch on in that same dwelling. May your day be productive."

With that, he got up and walked out of the deployable building.

"What the fuck was that?!" I whispered as I watched the door close behind him.

"That was our grumpy host, Kald Aku Ebaki," Mehreen said with a long-suffering sigh. "But it was about time you stopped napping and joined the fun."

"How long was I out? And how long have you guys been here?" I asked.

"We all arrived here two days ago," Ernst replied. "Mehreen and I started going through the files yesterday. This entire thing is an epic clusterfuck."

"Yesterday?! Why was I not awakened?" I exclaimed.

"You sustained some grievous injuries on the Gladius,"

Mehreen explained. "Your nanobots have been working overtime getting you back to 100%."

"But I was fine when I first woke up before arriving here," I argued.

She shook her head. "You were only partially mended and enjoying the effects of some pretty incredible painkillers. You would have hated being up and about yesterday."

"I see. But what of you two? Are you okay?"

They both nodded.

"We've been treated very well," Ernst said. "No one has threatened or tried to harm us. Our dwellings are clean and comfortable, and they provide us with plenty of food."

"That's good to hear. But are you suffering from any type of memory loss?" I asked.

Once again, they both nodded.

"They wiped our memories," Mehreen said firmly. "There was someone with Aku on that ship, but I can't remember who they were, what they looked like, or even what type of vessel we traveled in."

"Same," I replied with a sliver of frustration.

"But why?" Ernst asked.

"For the same reason that they won't tell us where they got this lab. Whoever is helping them would get in deep trouble," I said pensively. "As much as I wish he would open up about them, Aku is right that this is not relevant to our current purpose. But those accusations against Elias are wild."

"Wild but true," Ernst said with an air of disgust.

"What?!" I asked, stunned by the depth of contempt I could read on his features.

"I've worked with Jacobs. That man is as foul as he is ruthless. Based on my experience with Elias, everything that Aku said sounds probable. That's why I left his team. That wretch is a leech. He passes off his interns' work as his own. What most people fail to realize is that SS12 saved his career. He was about to lose his funding. And with so many people refusing to work with him, he was getting desperate."

"What are you saying? You think this entire tragedy was caused deliberately? Are you accusing him of foul play?"

My stomach dropped when he hesitated. It struck me hard to see someone I held in such high esteem turn out to be nothing like the idealized image I built up in my head.

"No," he said at last. "I doubt he would have provoked something like this on purpose. For all his faults, Jacobs is an opportunist, not an evil mastermind. He has just grown increasingly lazy with protocols, and that has trickled down to the members of his team. When we leave this planet after resolving this crisis, you realize that we're going to walk into a major shitshow, right?"

"*When* we leave, or *if* we leave?" Mehreen countered.

I frowned as I studied her face. "Why do you say that? You think they will harm us once they've gotten what they wanted?"

She shook her head. "I have sensed no malice from these people. So I don't think they will try to hurt us, but I believe they will want to keep us."

"Whatever for? You heard him clearly expressed that he cannot wait for us to be gone," I argued.

"He did," she conceded. "But they've also seen how the disease came back one year after Jacobs initially cured it. Their people are on the verge of extinction. In their shoes, I wouldn't be too swift about allowing the only people able to fix it to leave, especially since they have no direct way of communicating with us if anything else happens."

I waved a dismissive hand. "The Prime Directive has already been violated where they are concerned. Following this incident, we are compelled to do regular checkups with them."

"The three of us know that. But *they* don't. And even if we tell them that we will come back to make sure everything is still fine, they have no reason to trust us."

"I hear what you're saying, but I'm convinced they will want us gone so that they can forget we ever existed. Time will tell. For now, we need to get back to work. I would appreciate it if you both could update me as to what you have discovered so far."

And with this, we began our race against the clock.

CHAPTER 6
AMRETH

After eighteen hours traveling to the edge of our sector of the galaxy, and four days after Ciara's abduction, I finally began my descent into Kestria's atmosphere. Despite the unofficial mandate given to me by the Enforcers, the deep-rooted Obosian side of me that demanded I abide by the laws still twitched about violating the Prime Directive. In truth, I expected to borderline feel physically ill at that prospect. But the need to rescue my mate—a woman I had never even met—superseded everything else.

My heart soared when only minutes after I pierced through the atmosphere, my tracker went off, indicating it was finally picking up the signal from Ciara's implant. Two additional signals confirmed that Mehreen and Ernst were also with her. That was a major relief. Had they been split up, it might have significantly complicated any rescue effort.

To my surprise, the signal didn't emanate anywhere near the Sangoth villages, but on the other side of the mountain range where they dwelled. It was in the valley, at a nearly two-hour flight from there. Although confused by this, it also brought me some measure of relief. The Sangoths dwelled in the frozen peaks of the mountains. Without proper winter equipment, humans would struggle in those frozen temperatures.

The whole journey here, I dug up everything I could about my Ciara. All that I read further fueled the pride I felt knowing that she was mine. Beyond her stellar record and flawless background check, she had been a prodigy in school, obtaining her first doctorate at the age of twenty-three. She received countless prizes and awards over the years, many of which opened the type of doors people would beg to have access to.

Despite the numerous fancy appointment offers she received, Ciara declined them all to pursue selfless missions on primitive planets in dire need. She also focused on research that could have a tremendous impact on the medical world, but that wouldn't give her the type of glamour and exposure that many of her colleagues sought, like Elias Jacobs.

But will she want to settle on Molvi?

That question plagued me relentlessly. Obviously, as the Warden of my Sector, I couldn't leave. Sectors actually belonged to a bloodline. My family had managed ours for many generations. It was a tremendous honor to be the Warrior chosen to take over that responsibility. For all its challenges, I loved what I did. Even now, I felt guilty for being absent and unloading my duties onto my best friend Kronos, and my cousin Silas.

It shamed me all the more that Kronos already had his hands full taking care of his own Sector on top of preparing for the arrival of his first child. I could only hope that we would be able to swiftly resolve the issues here. At least, I took comfort in the fact that I had kept my Sector in good order, and unless something totally unexpected derailed things, handling my prisoners in my absence shouldn't be too heavy a burden.

As I flew over the dense forest framed by a wide river, I absent-mindedly scanned for the local wildlife. While most of them seemed fairly small, a few larger ones traveling at high speed indicated some areas might not be safe to wander. Those creatures definitely looked like vicious predators.

My confusion steadily grew as I closed in on the location of the implants. They clearly emanated from a sprawling village up ahead. Although of pleasant appearance and sturdy construction, it was undeniably primitive. Beyond the fact that they clearly had not achieved space travel, I doubted they even possessed electricity.

On my journey here, I heavily speculated as to what could be going on. My main theory had been that an advanced species secretly established a base here, and that they abducted these scientists to complete the project they illegally began with Jacobs.

But this definitely was not it.

I flew over the village in stealth mode to get a first view of the lay of the land. The incredibly large number of males to the much lower ratio of females disturbed me. The drastically low number of younglings raised even more flags. On my way here, I had not detected any of them traipsing in the surrounding wilderness, which might have explained such an imbalance had they been out on a field trip or on the hunt.

That everyone remained at the village—at least in appearance—also seemed odd. About thirty males and a handful of females labored outside the main gates of the village, plowing the fields that spread on both sides of the main road to the entrance. I shifted my vision to glance at their souls. To my relief, they had the overall peaceful shades of common, decent folks. None of them displayed the orange or reddish hue of evil or ill intentions.

But what does evil look like for them?

Over the years, I encountered some rare species who would never qualify to join the United Planets Organization. Their moral values clashed too radically with ours. Things we would deem unconscionable and atrocious were considered normal and as part of the survival of the fittest. They didn't commit those acts out of cruelty. Our shock and outrage genuinely confused them. How did you prosecute people who saw the world through completely different lenses from your own?

I zoomed in on the males outside to get a better look at them. Their simian appearance threw me for a loop. The bioscan confirmed that there were no records of such a species in our database.

"What in Tharmok's name is going on?" I whispered to myself.

The scan indicated a single high-tech building, which turned out to be a missing deployable laboratory of the Interstellar Doctors Organization. How in the world had such a primitive species gotten their hands on it? Why did they have those three scientists working inside it? The thought that Sectarian invaders were using this village as a staging area wouldn't go away. And yet, I didn't detect any cerebral implant or control collars that might indicate that this simian species had been enslaved to the service of powerful off-worlders.

After a brief hesitation, I circled back to the inner courtyard where the lab was located. I proceeded to another scan to confirm the absence of any kind of technology that could detect the signal I was preparing to send to the three doctors' implants. The organic device was designed in a way that it would fool most scanners into believing it was merely a mole on the person's skin.

Once signaled, the host would feel a small pulsation indicating we were attempting to contact them. Based on protocols, if the target was able to move around, they were expected to go out in the open to allow facial recognition. If they couldn't come outside, they had to provide one of four potential responses.

The first indicated that they could not come outside, which generally meant that they were physically restrained, be it by being locked in a space or shackled. The second expressed that they would need a bit of time before they could come out. In that case, they would attempt to give a time range for the wait. The third signal informed us that they were injured and therefore either unable to come out or in need of immediate assistance. The last signal indicated danger requiring us to leave at once before we got caught or attacked.

The target could respond with a mixture of all of the above. The challenge was that it required them to apply pressure on the subdermal implant in a specific pattern. If they were shackled or injured, it made that task nearly impossible.

My heart leapt when the doors of the lab opened less than a minute later. I held my breath and zoomed the camera as three humans exited the building. Tharmok's teeth! My mate was even more gorgeous in person!

She had the face of a goddess, with high cheekbones, a delicate nose, plump and sensuous lips, with stunning eyes whose color I couldn't quite define. Her file labeled them as gray, but they were too dark to truly be described as such, but too pale to be black. Her brown skin looked good enough to lick, it contrasted in the most wondrous fashion with the silky strands of her silver-white hair. Under the light of the early afternoon sun, they shone like a sea of diamonds. Despite being very generic, her field uniform hugged the perfect curves of her body in just the right way. It took every ounce of my willpower not to land my vessel right away and run to her.

Seeing Ciara raising her right hand and caressing her right cheek before sliding her palm down the side of her neck snapped me out of my dazed fascination. It was the sign indicating that they were unharmed and not in any danger. I sent a signal back acknowledging their response, as they continued to pretend to be casually chatting while stretching their legs.

They lingered a few seconds longer before going back inside. One final scan confirmed that there was no one else inside the laboratory with them. I only detected two female simians in the dwelling next to them. The superficial readings seemed to indicate that they were asleep. A single guard was casually standing watch by the gates closing off the inner courtyard where the doctors were detained.

After one final fly over to assess the best way to break them out, I flew a relatively short distance away—approximately a ten-minute winged flight for me—to a tall rock formation with a sturdy overhang upon which I landed my vessel still in stealth mode. I couldn't risk leaving it in the forest or any other open area where the locals or an animal might run into it.

Anyway, I wouldn't break out the prisoners just yet.

First, I wanted to enter the village, possibly set up a few diversions to help their escape, and ideally speak to one of them to get a better sense of what was happening. Before leaving the ship, I sent a message to Maeve with the coordinates of the village as well as the data and photos gathered so far from my scans. As there were no relays nearby, the message would travel for a while before it eventually got picked up.

And yet, a part of me suspected someone might conveniently be lurking in the vicinity of Kestria, ready to intervene should things truly become dire. Although I had limited interactions with the Enforcers on a daily basis, I had seen enough reports involving some of the foulest convicts incarcerated in my Sector to know what creative methods were used to capture them. The Enforcers rarely left things to chance. They simply excelled at finding workarounds to maintain plausible deniability. The same way they enabled me to come here, I didn't doubt they had someone else ready to pick up any trail that could lead them to the identity of the Sectarians threatening the sovereignty of our borders.

Even without proof of that speculation, it still provided me with some measure of comfort. If things went belly up for me, at least someone would know for certain where my mate was so that they could take her to safety.

I opened the hatch of my vessel, activated my personal stealth shield, then took flight. Once again, I marveled at the beauty of the landscape. It reminded me of home, with the lush forests, colorful flora, clear skies, and fresh air softly laced with the sweet aroma of fragrant flowers. The sun caressed my wings with its warm rays, the weather perfect for an extended stay outdoors without the type of crushing humidity that could ruin places such as these.

As much as I wanted to fly directly into the courtyard, I couldn't risk the sound of my flapping wings giving me away. Although my stealth shield also had a strong sound dampening feature, it didn't fully mute it. I didn't know enough about this species to dismiss the possibility of them having highly sensitive hearing. The position of the guard by the gate would make it nearly impossible to land without getting noticed.

Anyway, the goal of today's infiltration was mainly to see how I could walk them out safely or make plans to fly them out individually at the most appropriate time. I landed in the forest located in front of the village, the tree line beginning about one hundred meters in front of the last row of their farm field.

I started walking carefully towards the village. At least twenty-three males and four females were working the fields on each side of the wide path that led to the gates. I welcomed the noise they were making, which further drowned the very discreet sound of my own steps. Even without it, they wouldn't have been able to hear me from this distance and with the dampening effect of my shield. But you couldn't have too many things on your side. They were harvesting what appeared to be some sort of corncobs, although the shape slightly differed, as did the color. Others seemed to be pulling out weeds and working the soil.

However, it was the color of their aura that retained my attention. During my flight, it had a bluish white hue that had been quite safe. Considering the distance and the blocking effect of the vessel itself, it wasn't uncommon for our readings to be impacted or skewed. Now, in person, they all had a pale, yellow tinge that made me uneasy. As it remained far from anything that could remotely translate as danger, I continued my advance, my eyes flicking this way and that as I observed them, looking for any sign of potential trouble.

That they all focused on their work, aside from the occasional chatting, lessened some of my tension. Halfway through the path, I noticed the first shift in the color of their auras. The yellow tinge noticeably intensified. It had not turned orange or red—which would have been terrible in the latter case. It still made me consider aborting the mission. I hated not having a baseline for the color palette of these people's emotional range.

They still paid me no mind. A couple of the males and a female picked up the heavy crates filled with vegetables to bring them to a chariot by the entrance of the village, before returning to their spots. The effortless way with which they carried them testified to their tremendous strength. It also told me that their females—at least this one—were as strong as the males. Then again, although more slender and with narrower shoulders, the females were at a height with their counterparts, the muscles in their arms well-defined like those of a fitness model.

Just as I was closing in on the last five meters to the village's entrance, where the gates lay wide open, the color of their aura shifted again, this time with a hint of orange. My stomach dropped, and I stopped dead in my tracks. There was no way this was a coincidence. While the original yellow only told me that I should be on my guard, the increased intensity hinted that they might have been plotting something. But this was the color my convicts usually displayed when they were waiting for just the right moment to spring a trap on their unsuspecting target.

I didn't know if these colors had a different meaning for these people, but my every instinct was yelling for me to get out of here. Silencing my urge to move forward and make contact with my mate, I slowly started to back away, my eyes fluttering in every direction for any sign they were onto me.

And did it ever come.

I had only taken three steps backwards when every single simian jerked their heads in my direction. My blood turned to ice when they all made direct eye contact with me. I instinctively glanced at my shield to make sure it was still active. And it was. Somehow, they could see right through it. As one, they dropped their gardening tools and ran towards me.

I flapped my wings and darted towards the forest. To my dismay, they ran at impossible speeds, closing in on me. Their perfect coordination accompanied by an eerie silence—other than the thumping sound of their feet—made it even more frightening. My heart skipped a beat when a male with a circlet jumped at least four meters high, his fingertips brushing my left heel. Only a couple more centimeters, and he would have grabbed my ankle to yank me back down.

I flew even harder as an odd tingling sensation manifested itself at the back of my eyes. My initial plan of losing them in the forest was quickly thwarted as they all leapt at insane heights, latching onto the first lower branches of the surrounding trees, swinging with incredible strength over a few meters onto the next tree. Many were climbing at the same time. A couple of them released a high-pitched shout, reminiscent of those emitted by monkeys. They didn't sound random, but appeared to act as some sort of tactical direction to help them better coordinate their attack.

With the growing discomfort in the back of my eyes, it took me too long to realize that they were attempting to get enough height to be able to jump on me and tackle me to the ground.

I immediately soared, hoping to put enough vertical distance so that the upper branches would be too weak to support their weights, giving me a chance to escape. But no sooner did I begin my ascension than a loud noise exploded inside my head. My vision blurred, and I suddenly found myself struggling to control my movements. It sounded like an unnatural white noise, confusing my synapses and scrambling my motor system.

I started falling and barely managed to recover enough to go into a glide so that I wouldn't plummet to the ground. The noise lessened, partially restoring my control over my wings and senses. But as soon as I tried to outrun them again, the noise came back with a vengeance, making me falter some more.

Having no choice but to land or risk grievous injury, I flew towards the ground but brutally crashed, my blurry vision making me miscalculate the distance. My teeth rattled in my head, but I rolled with the momentum and jumped back onto my feet. The unrelenting noise made my eyes water and my muscles tremble. I tried to focus on the silhouettes closing in on me as I invoked my Lumiak. My fingertips tingled with the electrical energy half a second before it fizzled. My knees buckled, and I fell down. A wave of dizziness crashed over me. Kneeling, my palms resting on the forest floor for support, I struggled to remain conscious.

In one last desperate effort, I blasted my *bakaan*. If nothing else, it might keep them from killing me. I couldn't tell if it succeeded, but after multiple thumping sounds of the Simians jumping down from the trees and landing all around me, the noise in my head dimmed as they all stood still.

"A calming aura?" a male voice said with a hint of amusement. "That must be a useful talent to have with turbulent infants. But there is no need to appease us. We are not your enemies, Obosian. You may calm yourself and drop your shield. We expected you."

How in Tharmok's name did they know what I was when I had never heard of their species? How could they possibly expect me? How did they speak Universal so fluently? And especially, how the fuck could they see me?

In a way, that last question was stupid. Clearly, they

possessed some form of psionic powers. I, as an Obosian, had the power to see souls, even through camouflage. They apparently shared similar abilities.

My mind still reeling, I deactivated my shield. I looked up at the tall and muscular male that seemed to be their leader, if only judging by the circlet on his forehead that none of the others possessed.

"You expected me?" I asked, hating to find myself in such a vulnerable position.

He nodded. "Do not give us reasons to hurt you, and all will be well."

"Who are you?" I asked, as the pressure on my brain continued to fade. To my relief, their auras were steadily shifting to blue, the standard color for the absence of threat.

"My name is Aku. I am the Kald of Bryst, the village you were trying to sneakily enter. And these are my tribemates. Our people are called Kreelars. But do stand. You should be steady enough now."

He didn't have to say it twice.

I rose to my feet and dusted the dirt off me before readjusting my breastplate. No words could describe the extent of the mortification I felt right this instant. As an elite Obosian Warrior, deemed the best of my bloodline—which had earned me the management of our Sector on Molvi—I never should have been so easily defeated. Granted, I was seriously outnumbered. But they were primitive, land bound off-worlders without weapons. I had psionic powers of my own. I also possessed a blaster and a sword, neither of which I used.

Considering the current outcome—at least for the time being —I was glad I had not. Attacking or killing these people was the last thing we needed if the prisoners were to stand a chance of coming back home unscathed.

I just poorly handled the whole thing. The warning signs had been loud and clear. But in my arrogance and overconfidence in my ability to escape thanks to my wings had been my downfall.

If Father finds out, I'll never hear the end of it.

While I doubted that he could read minds, the Kreelar named Aku gave me a teasing smile that seemed to hint he suspected what self-deprecating thoughts swirled in my head.

"We will relieve you of your weapons for the time being," Aku said, extending a hand towards me. "You will get them back later, once we feel confident we have an understanding. Fear not, they will not be tampered with."

I silenced my instinctive urge to argue. The unyielding glimmer in his eyes belied the polite sweetness of his voice. The aura of authority emanating from him screamed loudly what a formidable foe he could become if needed. A peek at his aura thankfully confirmed once more that he held no ill intentions towards me. Not that it would have made a difference. If I tried to resist, they would have no problem beating me into submission and still take away my weapons, as demonstrated by the ease with which they captured me.

Pinching my lips, I complied, which only had the Kreelar's smirk expanding a notch. He handed them over to another male, comparable in size and musculature, but with a grayish-beige fur. At least, the care with which that second male handled them appeased me. It didn't scream of fear of the unknown, but more of respect towards items of value.

"Walk with me, Obosian," Aku said, gesturing towards the village.

"My name is Amreth," I said grumpily.

"Then Amreth it is," he replied in a conciliatory tone, as we began walking.

"But you haven't answered my initial question. How come you expected me?" I asked.

He gave me a sideways glance and raised an eyebrow that clearly indicated I was being a bit too cocky. Obviously, I wasn't in a position of power. However, my people had the tendency of being blunt and straight to the point about everything. It occasionally came across as being rude, entitled, or arrogant, which actually was not intended.

To my surprise, he indulged me.

"Our friends warned us that you would come to rescue your mate. Except, she doesn't need to be rescued. She requires your help," Aku said in a factual manner.

"Help with what?" I asked, confused.

"With completing her task. Once that is done, all of you can return home," he replied in the same neutral tone.

"And what task would that be?" I insisted, starting to feel annoyed by the slow drip-drip of information.

"Righting the extreme harm humans inflicted upon us," he replied, his eyes and voice hardening.

"Humans?!" I exclaimed, stunned. "When? How? Your planet is under very strict restrictions from the Prime Directive."

"And humans violated it by traveling in forbidden areas well beyond Sangoth territories," Aku snarled. "Because of their carelessness, the humans infected us with a deadly disease that now has my people on the verge of extinction."

"Tharmok's blood!" I breathed out, shock giving way to understanding. "So that's why you took the prisoners. You want them to find a cure!"

He nodded, his expression grim as we cleared the tree line and stepped onto the wide path leading to the village. With a stiff gesture of his head, Aku signaled to his tribemates that they could go back to their duties tending the fields. All of them complied, but for two males who remained with us as we continued down the wide path towards the village.

"But if you found a way to travel off-world to abduct these scientists, why not simply go public with how humans wronged you?" I asked, baffled. "The UPO and all the allied planets would have put every resource at your disposal to fix things and make the culprits answer for their crime."

Aku shook his head with a conviction that took me aback. "We explored all such scenarios. Every single one of them ends up in a much worse fate for us. Some powerful people in your world stand to lose a lot if this is exposed the way it ought to be. Exterminating a primitive species that no one has ever heard of to keep their secret can be tempting for those with the means to accomplish that."

My back stiffened, my protective instincts firing on all cylinders, while my bone-deep need for justice demanded I hunt down the culprits and subject them to the righteous retribution they deserved.

"How do you know that a worst fate will befall you if you bring them to justice? They cannot be allowed to get away with something so atrocious, if it's true. Beyond the fact that they must answer for their crimes, if they are allowed to get away with it, what prevents them from causing similar or maybe even greater harm to someone else?" I challenged vehemently.

He gave me the type of indulgent smile one would give an overly excited child. "Have no fear, Amreth. Those responsible will pay for it."

"We need justice, not vigilantism," I countered with a frown, my voice stern.

He snorted, and his amusement cranked up a notch. "There will be no vigilante activity involved. *You*, Amreth, will see to their punishment."

I recoiled, stunned not only by his words, but also by the certainty with which he spoke them.

"Me?" I echoed.

"Yes, *Warden*," he said, his emphasis on my title making me even more curious.

"Who in Tharmok's name are your friends?"

"Just good friends," Aku replied in a tone that made it clear he would not expand further.

"How do they give you this foresight?" I insisted.

"They just do," he said with a shrug, his expression broadcasting loudly that I should drop the topic.

Annoyed, I sorted through the billion questions I wanted to ask him, especially when it came down to the identity of the powerful people he had alluded to. But he didn't give me a chance to do so.

"This is our village, Bryst," Aku said as we finally walked through the open main gates.

Although primitive by galactic standards, the village was actually quite beautiful. A large square greeted us, covered in colorful pavement forming an abstract motif. I didn't doubt it usually served for mass gatherings, and possibly an open market. All around it, various one-story buildings made of wood and clay created little clusters akin to street blocs. They had erected a handful of much bigger buildings with stone and bricks. All of them boasted light colors of beige, brown, and khaki, with proper glass windows. The streets were all made of packed dirt delineated by a decorative stone or pavement border. Plenty of plants, trees, and colorful flowers gave the place an inviting feel to it.

I detected no clear signs of electrical power or of any type of transportation technology like vehicles. Very few people loitered in the streets, mostly females and a handful of children who eyed me with undisguised curiosity. To my relief, none of their auras expressed hostility. Whoever their friends were—undoubtedly Sectarians—they convinced these people that I would be some kind of ally. While that served my purpose and prevented my initial blunder from having an unfortunate outcome, it made me all the more eager to find out their identity, and how they got involved in the first place.

We immediately made a right towards the other gate which

controlled access to the inner courtyard where my mate and her colleagues were held. My pulse picked up at the prospect of meeting my Ciara in person. She seemed well when she stepped outside the lab earlier. Judging by my interactions with Aku so far, I had no reason to worry she had come under any type of mistreatment.

But how will she feel about my presence?

Had Aku told her that their friends had foreseen my arrival? Was she looking forward to it? According to Kayog, she had been eager to meet me. However, she certainly had not expected it to be under such circumstances.

To my surprise, instead of leading me to the lab, Aku took me to a dwelling on the opposite side of the inner courtyard, directly facing it. I glanced at the deployable building over my shoulder only to see one of the two males accompanying us make a beeline for it. The one who remained with us held my weapons.

The Kreelar leader opened the door to the dwelling and waved me in.

"You will share this dwelling with your mate," he said as soon as we entered the humble, but comfortable living area.

"What?!" I exclaimed, staring at him in shock.

"Peace, Amreth," Aku said with that obnoxious taunting tone I was starting to grow familiar with. "I am aware you two have never met. There are two bedrooms. She will have her privacy. But if sharing a dwelling is truly problematic for either of you, we will make arrangements to move you elsewhere."

"I see," I said, tension bleeding out of my shoulders.

Obviously, I much preferred sharing a home with Ciara, if only to be able to protect her in whatever capacity I could. But I wanted her to feel comfortable with me, and not like my presence was being imposed upon her simply because a Temern had declared us soulmates.

"We will not shackle you, or spy on you," Aku said, his face taking on a serious expression with a hint of warning. "I will trust your honor to do right by my people before you depart, and that you will not attempt to escape before this situation is resolved."

"Trust? You don't know me. That seems like a reckless leap of faith," I challenged, my wretched Obosian mouth speaking my mind when I should rejoice about this.

"I can shackle you if you insist," he replied, his tone only partially teasing. "But no, Warden, when it comes to this specific matter, no decision I take is reckless. But a leap of faith? Yes, I will concede to that. I have total and complete faith in my friends. They say you can be trusted, and that you will remain until this matter is solved, just like they foresaw that you would come here. So yes, I will trust in your honor."

I tilted my head to the side, unable to resist the need to poke at his logic, but also to get a better sense of who I was dealing with.

"I do not know your friends or how their foresight works. But what if I do not want to help your people? What if I choose to challenge their assertion that I will aid you? After all, however good your intentions, you committed a crime to achieve your purpose."

To my surprise, he shrugged, seemingly unfazed by my words. "It will sadden me and delay the resolution to this tragedy. In turn, it will likely cause more unnecessary deaths. But I cannot coerce you into helping solve a situation you did not create. So should you refuse to assist, you will simply have to remain here until it is safe for us to release all of you."

I stared at him in shock. A glimpse at his aura revealed no deception. He would truly not twist my arm or use my mate as a cudgel to force me to obey their demands. To my shame, he struck me as being a much better person than I wanted to believe myself to be.

I opened my mouth to respond, but a bright light at the edge of my vision drew my attention.

"Your mate approaches," Aku said in a soft voice.

My mouth instantly went dry as the most beautiful light I had ever seen—although dampened by the closed door between us—held me in a thrall. The glow of her escort's aura annoyed me to no end as it mingled with hers due to his proximity.

Moments later, the door opened, and my brain ceased to function.

Tharmok smite me, she's pure perfection!

"We shall leave you with your mate," Aku said.

The slightly mocking edge in his voice barely registered in my mind. I was too enthralled by my woman. She gasped, and her eyes widened as she stared at me, before casting a confused look at Aku.

"My mate?!" she exclaimed, seconds before she seemed struck by a thought. She jerked her head back towards me to examine me with shock and disbelief. "A... Amreth?" Ciara asked in a hesitant voice.

"Yes, Ciara. It is I," I said, stunned that I even managed to form any words.

Aku's soft chuckle snapped me out of my dazed trance. I glanced at the Kreelar only to catch him looking in turn at my mate and me with a satisfied grin. In a flash of sudden under-standing, I realized he had somehow known this exact scene would take place. Something in the way it played out pleased him.

Without another word, he gave each of us a farewell nod then walked out of the house with his tribemate.

CHAPTER 7
CIARA

Too many thoughts simultaneously fired off in my brain to allow it to function properly. Amreth's breathtaking beauty made it even harder for my mind to act rationally. From the moment Kayog told me of my soulmate, my fertile imagination began creating all kinds of scenarios as to what our first meeting would be like. Then my whole world came crashing down during that attack.

"What are you doing here?" I blurted out, instantly flinching that those would have been the first words that came out of my mouth after he confirmed his identity.

By the way he blinked and the uncertainty that flashed over his stunning features, that had not been the reaction he had expected or possibly hoped for.

"I came to rescue you," he said carefully.

"To rescue *me*?" I repeated, my confusion audible in my voice. "How did you get here? How did you find us? Aren't you a Warden?"

I pressed my palms to my cheeks and shook my head in embarrassment for that sudden surge of verbal diarrhea. I didn't mean to bombard him with so many questions, but this entire situation seemed surreal.

"Yes, Ciara. I am a Warden on Molvi, and I came as soon as I heard what fate befell you," he replied with a guarded expression.

"But… Did Kayog tell you about…?" I gestured between the two of us when my voice trailed off.

He nodded. "As soon as it was confirmed that you were missing, Kayog contacted me about you."

"And you came for me?" I whispered, my voice filled with disbelief.

"Of course," he replied as if it was self-evident. "What kind of male wouldn't come to the rescue of his soulmate?"

I stared at him, speechless. A part of me wanted to melt from the inside out that he hadn't hesitated to come for me when we had never met, let alone spoken to each other. Another was just too blown away to fully understand my conflicting emotions. Aku mentioned that my mate would come, but I kept dismissing it as being way too far-fetched. And yet, here he was, looking good enough to eat.

"Wow," I said at last, with a mix of wonder and bewilderment. "Who else is here with you? The Enforcers?"

My brow further creased with confusion when he shook his head with an apologetic expression.

"I'm afraid I am alone. The situation is a little tricky," Amreth replied, carefully choosing his words.

"Let me guess," I said with an unimpressed tone. "Three Interstellar Doctors aren't important enough to send in the big guns."

He nodded again. "The Enforcers couldn't justify taking on this mission for three civilians as it should be a matter handled by the Peacekeepers. It also doesn't help that this planet is located inside the Dead Zone. There is no simple way of tracking you here."

"But you did," I challenged, my frown deepening.

"I had to… hmmm… skirt around certain rules to come here," he said reluctantly.

Under different circumstances, the mortified look on his gorgeous face would have been adorable. This male truly was stunning.

He had to be at least 6'5, with broad shoulders and bulging biceps left exposed by the sleeveless, ornate leather breastplate he wore. His skin was on the darker spectrum for an Obosian. Like dark elves, they tended to have very somber skin, usually in the midnight blue tinge or very dark grey. His had a lot more grayish-brown in it in what I would call charcoal. His black sclera made his silver white eyes starkly stand out, drawing me in an almost irresistible fashion. He had a noble nose, and the most sensuous, plump lips made to kiss.

Like all his people, a series of dark scales adorned his forehead, shifting into the main set of black horns on top of his head, with a smaller recurved set behind his ears. They, too, contrasted sharply with his long, silver-white hair, the same color as mine. Where that hue was standard for Obosians, for me, it was due to the fact that I had the rare human piebald trait. Even folded, his black, leather bat wings looked massive, not to mention lethal with the sharp talons at the tips and lining the bottom edges.

Naturally, I couldn't help my eyes lingering on his many visible facial piercings. It was a cultural thing for Obosians and a great source of pride. Their people couldn't simply slap a piercing on themselves. They needed to earn that privilege through a multitude of potential accomplishments for which they were given a varying amount of a rare metal called algarium. From it, they could forge the piercing in a shape they liked for the spot on their body that tempted them the most.

Amreth had a small ring on the side of each of his nostrils, a little spike in his labret—the spot right below the bottom lip, but above the chin, two rings in his left eyebrow, and a few more along the sides of his ears. I couldn't see any piercings on his arms, but I didn't doubt for a minute that a few more hid beneath his breastplate.

I immediately shut down the thought rearing its head as to whether he also had some in his naughty bits. By all accounts, both male and female Obosians made sure to have some in their private areas for extra sensations. Considering they possessed erotic powers that often had them labelled as Incubi and Succubi, it wasn't all that surprising.

"Wow," I said at last, genuinely touched. "I know how important abiding by the rules is for your people. So it really means a lot to me that you would bend them a bit to come save me."

"Always, Ciara," he said with a gentle smile that softened his face in the most wondrous way.

"So what did you do? You just walked up to the village?" I asked with sincere curiosity.

The sudden embarrassed look on his face and the way he shifted uneasily on his feet took me aback on top of sending my curiosity into overdrive.

He rubbed a spot behind his lower right horn, just above his nape while searching for an appropriate response.

"Not exactly. I was attempting to scope out the area for the best way to get the three of you out when I got captured," he said sheepishly.

I blinked.

"They used psionic powers against me that I had no way of counteracting. It all but paralyzed me," he added quickly, sounding a little defensive.

"Right," I replied pensively. "I remember the Obosian guards on the Gladius almost crash landing on the promenade when they were affected by similar attacks. In fact, Kayog did something that helped them resist it. I'm surprised he didn't mention it to you."

Amreth rolled his shoulders and stretched his neck, visibly trying to loosen some of the tension building there while his embarrassment appeared to crank up another notch.

"Kayog did mention their psionic abilities," he conceded.

"And you came unprepared for it?" I blurted out, my voice laced with disbelief, then immediately inwardly flinched again.

Fuck me! Could I sound more judgmental and ungrateful? My wretched mouth had a tendency of just speaking its mind, which could sometimes involuntarily come across as mean or hurtful.

"I didn't just go in recklessly," he said, sounding even more defensive. "I had my stealth shield activated. Considering my scans didn't reveal any form of technology, other than the deployable lab you were working in, I had no reason to think they possessed powers that could see through it. After all, my people enjoy some of the most advanced technologies out there. I only planned on going in and out quickly and maybe planting a couple of diversions to help your escape."

"I can see that," I said in a conciliatory tone, feeling like a total bitch towards the poor male. "In your stead, I would have assumed the same. No one would suspect them of having the type of psionic powers they displayed. In truth, they didn't use to. This is not a normal trait for the Kreelars. Whatever happened to them a decade ago caused this mutation."

"What?!" Amreth exclaimed, stunned.

I nodded, my brow creased in a frown. "But please, have a seat. I'm being quite the poor hostess," I added with a nervous laugh.

He smiled. "It's okay. This entire situation is kind of surreal. None of us can be expected to act in our usual way."

After an awkward moment of hesitation, I guided him to the dining area rather than the living room. One side of the table had a wide bench while the others had chairs. I figured the absence of a backrest would be more comfortable to accommodate his wings. He seemed to share that thought as he made a beeline for the bench. Still, he remained standing until I settled down first across the table from him. It was odd that he should observe some of those old school human courtesies.

As soon as I sat, I suddenly remembered I hadn't offered him anything to drink or eat.

"No, Ciara. I'm fine," he said with an amused expression when I once more blurted out if he needed any refreshment. "Do not fret so much. I will let you know if I require anything."

"Okay," I said, feeling insanely clumsy. This was not the first impression I wanted to give to my soulmate.

"So you were about to tell me about the Kreelars' mutation. But first, I would know how you are faring," he asks, his silver-white eyes studying me intently. "Based on the recordings from the Gladius, you were seriously injured."

By the way his gaze went slightly out of focus, I suspected he was peering at my soul or aura to get some additional information about my current emotional state.

"I'm fine, all three of us are doing good. Thanks for asking," I replied with a smile. "The Kreelar and their friends fully patched me up. I don't know what kind of technology their friends have, but it could give the Xurgens a run for their money. And since our arrival here, they have treated us like esteemed guests. They need us... badly."

"I'm grateful they were able to mend you. None of this makes much sense. What have you found out since your arrival?" he asked. "Aku claims that humans harmed them."

I nodded grimly. "What happened is truly messed up and the reason why there are strict Prime Directive guidelines. It's all the more infuriating that this entire tragedy was caused by the very people who should know better."

"What do you mean?"

"This whole mess started a little over ten years ago. You

probably heard about the incident that led the UPO to make contact with the Sangoth for the first time, right?"

He nodded. "Smugglers were stealing some of the rare metals in their mountains. Competition over those rare resources led to some criminal factions battling over that wealth. If I recall properly, the losing faction ratted out the winner."

"That's correct. The Timmons Cartel didn't take well to losing. They figured if they couldn't harness that wealth, then no one else would. Without them tipping off the UPO, we never would have known of the Sangoths' existence. Except a lot of damage had already been done to their population. The UPO initiated some diplomatic talks, and the Sangoths consented to allowing some of our scientists to perform non-intrusive studies of their people."

"And that's where Elias Jacobs comes in," he said with sudden understanding.

I nodded. "His team was there for a one-year study. The Sangoths have extremely strong bones, nearly unbreakable. It stems from the mineral residues in the water that streams through their mountain. Jacobs was hoping to figure out a way to adapt it to other species and help solve things such as brittle bone disease and osteoporosis. But that research went nowhere. The Sangoths possess unique genetic traits that allow them to assimilate those minerals like no other species could."

"But it allowed him to discover that SS12 serum. Or was that a fabrication?" he asked.

"The Sangoths have nothing to do with that serum," I said angrily. "During that time, two of the doctors on his team decided to have a romantic getaway in the valley by the river. It was well outside of the authorized area. They were having sex by the water after having a picnic. A Kreelar mother and her child stumbled on them."

"Blast! I'm guessing that didn't go well?" Amreth asked with a frown.

"That's quite the understatement. They had never seen humans before, but that wouldn't have been the problem. The five-year-old child went after the food and started eating it. The man noticed and went to stop the child."

Amreth flinched, no doubt guessing what followed.

"Thinking that he was trying to hurt her child, the mother attacked him and bit him. The couple managed to escape by shooting her with tranquilizers."

Amreth cursed under his breath. "I'm not even a doctor and I know better than to inject primitive species with chemicals with no idea how they might react."

"Exactly. She was knocked out for a few hours. The sedation eventually wore off and she was able to take her child back to the village. At first, all was well. But it was the following week that she started showing signs of illness. The problem was that she was a wet nurse for her people."

"Tharmok's blood! She infected others?" Amreth asked grimly.

I nodded. "The sad part is that she stopped nursing as soon as the first symptoms appeared. But the damage was already done. A few days after she got sick, so did many of the children she had been feeding. The Kreelars breastfeed their young until they reach the ages of six to seven."

"And Jacobs' team did nothing? Did they even investigate the potential fallout of what they caused?" he asked, outraged.

"Actually, they did," I conceded. "They quickly realized something was off and intervened. Sadly, it was too late for eight of the children who died. They managed to save the mother, Sora, but she wished she hadn't survived."

"What?! Why?" Amreth exclaimed.

"Sora blames herself for what occurred then, what has happened since, and what is currently taking place," I said, frustrated.

"But that's not her fault! She was merely defending her child.

She had no way of knowing the stranger would have passed on some illness to her," he argued.

"I fully agree with you, but things turned into something much bigger than what anyone anticipated. We've only been at this for three days, but everything we've discovered so far only enrages me further."

"What do you mean?" he asked, tilting his head to the side.

"We performed some tests on Sora. And guess what? Elias's great discovery, SS12, actually came from her. He derived the serum from the antibodies she developed from surviving the disease that the human doctor passed on to her."

"So it wasn't the sedative that she negatively reacted to?" Amreth asked, surprised.

I shook my head. "No. It came from the bite, which caused her to swallow some of his blood. But the problem is that whatever she suffered from isn't the same illness as what is killing the others. Had it been the case, we could have derived a quick cure for all of them. But something else happened."

"You think Elias did something to their people?" Amreth asked, his expression darkening as suspicion filled his voice. "Could he have made them sick on purpose to further validate his serum?"

I hesitated. "Actually, no. I don't think he made her sick on purpose. After all, from our analysis and their retelling of the events, it was purely unfortunate circumstances that she bit him and became infected with that disease. The problem is that as soon as he cured her, he left and never looked back. This is a grievous breach of the Prime Directive. The terrible fallout imperatively should have been reported. The Kreelars should have remained under discreet observation for at least five years to make sure that nothing resurfaced."

"Why didn't he? It wasn't like he was at fault for those two foolish doctors breaking protocol. *They* would have faced the consequences. At worst, it would have been a slight blemish on his reputation, but it wouldn't have been a devastating blow," Amreth argued.

"And that's the part that truly bothers me. The consequences now for being exposed are going to destroy his career. Why risk it? The incredible discovery of SS12 would have made the shame of this situation fade away in a heartbeat. This was ideal timing for him, however tragic as it had been for the victims. There's something else we're missing."

"Aku mentioned that they had to be secretive about this because extremely powerful people would have made things even more tragic had they gone public with this instead of abducting you," Amreth said pensively.

"He hinted at that as well," I said with a frown. "Once we have saved these people, we need to get to the bottom of this."

"Agreed," Amreth said with a determination that almost made me smile.

He truly was the embodiment of the extreme law-abiding Obosian.

"It's just frustrating that no one really prodded at some of his inconsistencies. First off, he labeled his discovery SS12, which stands for Simian Serum. Although the Sangoths have some very distant links to apes, we mostly compare them to Yetis. Whereas the Kreelar clearly have simian traits. When asked to describe the species he derived the serum from, Elias gave some random explanation that the illness the creature suffered from acted like a virulent flesh-eating bacteria that not only consumed the flesh at an accelerated rate but also made it decompose much too quickly for them to have any viable tissue that would enable them to identify its species."

"That's ridiculous!" Amreth said, incredulous.

I snorted. "Tell me about it. But people were too busy raving about the serum and its applications to really dwell over its origins. And down here, all was well for nearly a year after their departure. And then, that illness came back. But it was different.

No one bit anyone, and it wasn't restricted to a specific subgroup like it had been with Sora and the young she breastfed. Random members of the tribe of all ages and genders started getting sick."

"Some kind of virus?" he asked.

I shook my head. "No. Whatever it is, it isn't airborne, isn't a blood borne pathogen, and isn't physically transmissible via touch. It's causing severe headaches and swelling in the brain. It's almost like encephalitis with the headaches, fever, fatigue, joint pain, and eventually confusion and hallucinations. Both genders get it, but females who contract it after puberty rarely survive. The biggest problem is that it began happening in every other tribe, not just the people here in Bryst."

"That doesn't make sense. When Sora first got sick, did she infect a child from another tribe?"

"No. The illness exclusively struck here. So something else happened that is now spreading to other Kreelars, but not the Sangoths. But then, those two species don't interact with each other. Over the past nine years since the sickness returned—or rather this version of it manifested itself—the Kreelar females have been decimated. They now account for less than a third of their population. If we don't find a cure quickly, they will become extinct. So as you can guess, we can't leave. We *have* to fix this."

He nodded slowly, a deep frown creasing his brow. "Aku said you can solve it, but even faster with my aid."

I perked up. "He did. They have some kind of seer who said you would come and that you would help. That first part was clearly accurate."

"It was. Which means I must help. Whatever you need, it is yours."

Although his words pleased me, for a reason I couldn't explain, I felt the need to challenge his motivation.

"Would you still offer your aid if I wasn't involved?" I asked.

He slightly recoiled and looked a bit offended.

"Yes, Ciara. I would still offer. I may have come here specifically for you, and as your soulmate it is indeed my duty to assist you in every way possible. But I also have a duty of conscience to do right by those in need. Obosians may come across as cold and rigid at times, but we are not heartless. We're just… stuck up when it comes to upholding the law and following rules."

"Then you might find having me as a mate quite problematic. I'm the rebellious type," I challenged.

Although he narrowed his eyes at me, his lips stretched into a subtle smile laced with a hint of provocation.

"Are you now?" he asked in a dubious tone. "It sounds a bit contradictory for an epidemiologist."

I shrugged. "Those rules, I follow. But others…" I waved a dismissive hand as my voice trailed off.

"Well then, you'll just have to be disciplined."

I snorted and gave him an incredulous look, unsure how to interpret his expression, which was the perfect mix of serious with a hint of mischief.

"Good luck with that!" I said with a dare.

"On that front, I do not need luck, Ciara," he said, his voice dipping an octave in a way that sounded both threatening and full of promises.

My stomach did a backflip, and I suddenly found myself again admiring his insanely attractive appearance. I didn't know how I felt about him. Physically, he was a billion out of ten. Personality wise, it would take me some time to adjust to him. I just took comfort in this glimpse of his playful side.

Part of me wished that I didn't know he was my soulmate as our relationship would then be given a chance to grow organically. Instead, I felt compelled to just be swept off my feet because I knew we were meant to be. That would have been fine if not for my stupid excessively analytical mind that always needed to look for the potential flaws that could have bad repercussions later down the road. I needed to relax and just let things happen. After all, he had traveled halfway through the galaxy to rescue me on a leap of faith.

And Kayog was never wrong.

"But on a more serious note, what can I do to help? I am many things, but definitely not a scientist," he said with an apologetic look.

I smiled. "Actually, your arrival could not have been more perfect. These people do not yet have advanced transportation or communication systems. They do have the equivalent of CBs for radio communication. But as you can guess, that's far too restrictive for our needs. We must visit the other villages to try and get a better sense of what could be the cause of the illness spreading to other tribes."

"Of course, I'll be glad to fly you. Somehow, I doubt Aku would be too keen on letting me take you inside my shuttle," he added pensively.

"Agreed. At least, not right now. The people here in Bryst have been nice to us, but the other villages have never met a human in person before. Since their only knowledge of us is of how our actions may be the cause of what is destroying their people, I doubt they would welcome a shuttle until we've had a chance to establish some sort of rapport. I was going to ride on one of their mounts, but it would take hours to reach our destination. So you flying me would be great, assuming I'm not too heavy?"

I flinched as soon as I stated that last sentence. Obosians were reputed for their strength. I had a healthy weight which would put very little strain on him. I didn't want him to think I only said that in order to fish for compliments.

The strangest emotion fleeted through his silver-white eyes. "Are you calling me weak, woman?" he asked with false outrage.

I snorted and instantly relaxed. "Not flat out, but I do have to account for the fact that being tall and broad-shouldered doesn't necessarily mean being strong. There would be no shame in being on the feeble side," I said teasingly.

"You will soon discover that your soulmate is many things but not weak."

He opened his mouth to say something else, hesitated, and then decided not to proceed. That had me burning with curiosity. With a certainty I couldn't explain, he almost said something flirtatious. It sucked to want to court each other but having to tiptoe around because of the serious circumstances under which we met, on top of how unusual our situation was.

And yet, I secretly rejoiced that we got thrown into a relationship like this. There was no greater test for the strength of a couple than to face adversity together. So far, I truly liked his responses to this whole thing.

"Don't mind if I put all of that to the test," I replied with a taunt before sobering. "But you might also be of great help on a different front. I understand that Wardens are great hunters. From what Aku has told me, they've found increasing cases of wild beasts becoming rabid over the past nine years."

"About the same time that second wave of illness started!" he exclaimed. "Had this type of rabies occurred before then?"

I shook my head, impressed by his analytical skills. "No. And we suspect that they are linked. Or rather Ernst emitted a few hypotheses as to what the cause could be. But we still need more data to be certain."

"Hypothesis like what?" Amreth insisted.

"Our preliminary tests indicate no anomaly in their people. But we suspect that it might be the case of a misfolded prion," I said pensively.

He raised an eyebrow, his face taking on a confused expression that immediately had my cheeks burning. As I rarely discussed my work with non-scientific people—as it usually puts laymen to sleep—I tended to forget to explain some of the notions that were common to me.

"Oh, sorry. Prions are like proteins inside organic things like people, animals, plants, etcetera. But if something contains a misfolded prion—meaning that it's deformed—and you consume it, it is possible that it will cause catastrophic illness."

"Consume it? So you think they're eating something that's poisoning them?" Amreth asked, looking taken aback.

I nodded. "Like I said, we're still speculating, but it seems like the most probable theory."

"If it is in the food, why is it only a small number of people becoming sick? Why not everyone? From what little I've seen, they seem to grow food for everyone. I would assume they also hunt as a tribe for the entire village. Or did I misinterpret things?"

"You are correct. However, some people are already immune because they got sick before and developed antibodies against it," I explained. "For others, maybe they ended up eating from the safe batch. But again, it is too early to say. We could be completely off."

"Have you tested their food stores?" he asked.

I smiled, feeling stupidly proud of the keen interest that he was displaying as well as the ease with which he was following and asking insightful questions. I didn't need a nerd, but I definitely wanted someone witty who could quickly think on their feet.

"That's exactly what we've been doing. Unfortunately, no luck so far. But that's not surprising. If we are correct by assuming that it is a misfolded prion causing the disease, then symptoms can take days or weeks to appear. So if a contaminated batch caused this, it would be long gone by now. Therefore, narrowing down the cause will be tricky. But you could really help us scan the local wildlife for the potential source in the upcoming days."

"I will be happy to do that. You will be hard pressed finding an Obosian who doesn't enjoy flying, especially in such a stunning and pure environment as this one," he replied with a smile.

"Thank you. It means a lot. Pinning down the source is the toughest part of the investigative work. Please bear with me if I become nerdy. Once I start talking about this stuff, I tend to ramble on. So don't be shy to tell me to shush," I said sheepishly.

The soft and almost tender way in which he smiled did funny things to me. "Never apologize for being passionate about something, especially not your work. And yours is extremely important. You change other people's lives for the better. I am honored to be able to help you in this endeavor."

My toes might have curled a little upon hearing his response. Just as I was opening my mouth to speak, the sound of bells went off. Amreth stiffened, immediately alerted.

"It's okay!" I said, raising my palm in an appeasing gesture. "It's just the bell indicating that the hunters have returned with meat. I should go test it for any signs of contamination."

"Lead the way, my mate."

CHAPTER 8
AMRETH

I followed Ciara outside the house while trying to sort out my conflicting emotions. From the moment Kayog revealed her existence to me, I pictured a million different scenarios as to what our first meeting would be like. As much as I prided myself on being the rational and stoic type, I hadn't been able to resist fantasizing about countless heroic scenes of me rescuing her, dashing through the skies with her in my arms while being pursued by fiendish enemies. She would cling to me, confident in my ability to keep her safe despite the extreme peril we faced.

Being captured on my first excursion, in no small part because I hadn't properly prepared, couldn't have fallen shorter from those grandiose expectations. My gut still burned with embarrassment at having her calling me out on it.

Although she was undeniably physically drawn to me, Ciara had not seemed particularly impressed by me as an individual. It stung. But what had I expected? I didn't believe in love at first sight, even though she took my breath away the moment Kayog shared her image with me. Still, I had hoped for more of an instant chemistry that would have confirmed what the Temern claimed about us being meant for each other. In truth, without that assertion, I probably wouldn't have pursued her further, in light of her lukewarm response to me.

Nevertheless, I took heart in the one or two instances where she seemed to let her guard down and show a less distant and reserved side of her personality. That was rich coming from an Obosian. We were reputed to be quite stiff. And that certainly had always applied to me.

But I had truly wanted a hug from her.

For a reason I couldn't explain, I felt it deep in my bones that physical contact between us would be required to initiate the bond. And I didn't mean sexual. Even something as simple as holding hands would help break the invisible barrier separating us.

A part of me wondered if I was overthinking things. But another strongly felt that if we didn't manage to fill the gap between us early on, it would simply widen with each of us increasingly struggling to find a way to establish that connection. In a way, knowing that we were meant to be created this strange expectation that things should flow a certain way. Under different circumstances, had our first meeting been on a romantic date carefully planned by us, I believed it would have been a lot smoother than this awkwardness.

That didn't stop me from being even more impressed with my Ciara. Beyond her physical beauty and the enchanting marvel that was her soul, my woman was smart, strong, and no pushover. I loved that she bluntly expressed her thoughts on a few occasions, even if it put me in a bad light. It was very Obosian of her. I had no use for a meek and skittish female who couldn't speak her mind or call me out on my failures. The absence of cruelty as she did so, and the sliver of guilt that emanated from her for having possibly hurt my feelings reassured me as to her being a kind person.

But it was her determination to do right by those who had been wronged, and to use the skills she honed over the years to better other people's lives that truly warmed me from the inside out. People often wrongfully assumed that we Obosians had a sadistic side that made us enjoy the prisoners' suffering. They couldn't be more mistaken. It actually broke my heart every time one of my convicts failed to redeem himself or met a dire end because of their poor choices.

They didn't see the amount of effort and work we did to get inmates to use their time in prison to improve themselves so that they could have a brighter future by making better choices thanks to the new skills and wealth they acquired.

Although I couldn't deny having far less sympathy towards the criminals in our Dark Quadrants, some of them actually went out of their way to redeem themselves. Considering the atrocity of the crimes that had landed them there to begin with, seeing one of them complete their sentence and turn their lives around was probably one of the greatest accomplishments for us.

My mate hurrying up to the two humans I recognized as Mehreen Aziz and Ernst Wagner put an end to my wandering thoughts. Her two colleagues had already gathered around the wheeled cart pulled by a beast I didn't recognize. A large animal lay dead on it. Ernst was looking at the interface of an analysis device, having likely drawn some blood from the beast. Mehreen was running a handheld scanner over every inch of its body.

My mate caught up with them and exchanged a few words with Ernst, who showed her the interface. She tapped a few instructions on it then pulled out what looked like a long needle from the top of the device. She held it up while Ernst replaced the needle with a fresh one and fiddled with the device while Ciara pricked the creature again.

Not wanting to get in the way of their work, I stood back and observed the villagers. Quite a few of them had entered the inner courtyard, although they remained by the gates as if worried about trespassing. They were observing the scientists with unde- niable wariness, but devoid of any aggression. It struck me then that the concern was likely more about the safety of their food than about the doctors themselves.

Once again, it sent my mind down a spiral of speculation as to who in Tharmok's name were the friends who had so thoroughly convinced them that we could be trusted to do right by them. I needed to write to Maeve to set her on the trail of whatever powerful entity Elias might be in cahoots with.

Or could it be beholden to?

I made a mental note of the things I would want her to look into. As one of the Enforcers' top hackers, there weren't too many secrets that escaped Maeve once she set her mind on discovering it. So long as it had some sort of digital print, she would find it.

The thought that I couldn't just take off right now and go to my ship didn't sit well with me. I hated being a prisoner in that courtyard. How ironic for a Warden. My inmates wouldn't let me hear the end of it if they knew of my current predicament. Technically, I could leave. They were clearly giving us enough freedom of movement so that I could grab Ciara and fly to my vessel before they could get into close enough range to disable me with their psionic powers.

But I would never do it.

Beyond the fact that I felt a strong moral duty to help them, I was honor-bound to stick around. With a certainty I couldn't explain, I knew that Aku was not the type to easily grant his trust. And he had granted me his. It didn't matter that some Seer's prediction cemented that conviction. A part of me believed that our interactions convinced him that I was a male of my word. Had he felt I couldn't be trusted, Seer or not, I didn't doubt he would have shackled me.

Anyway, trying to bail now would be the surest way to torpedo any hope of a smooth relationship with my woman.

I refocused on the scientists just as they finished their tests. Based on their body language, they hadn't found anything suspicious or that could aid their research. Ciara gestured to the Kreelar hunters, indicating that they could take the meat away. She then faced me while her companions turned towards the lab only to stop dead in their tracks as they finally noticed me.

"An Obosian!" Ernst whispered with shock, quickly replaced by excitement.

He swiftly approached me, followed by the two women. I remained still as he closed the distance between us.

"My Lord, we're so glad to see you. Where are the others?" he asked, peering over my shoulder.

"I came here alone. There's no one else, only me," I replied in a calm voice. "And you can simply call me Amreth."

In theory, he should indeed address me as Lord Amreth as I was of noble descent. Many of my peers were sticklers for hierarchy. I didn't particularly care. And under the circumstances, those stiff protocols didn't seem appropriate. The approving glimmer in my mate's eyes did something delightful to me. I hadn't done it to impress her, but I welcomed anything that could help smitten her towards me.

He blinked with confusion. "Alone? Whatever for?"

With a will of their own, my eyes flicked towards Ciara. I caught myself right before I would have told him that I came to rescue my mate. While true, it didn't feel appropriate for me to expose the nature of our bond without her consent. Although she had acknowledged knowing of our connection, she was yet to express any eagerness to see it through.

"He came for me," Ciara responded in my stead, stunning all of us.

"For you?" Ernst and Mehreen echoed simultaneously.

The most adorable timid expression flashed over my woman's face even as she tried to look nonchalant.

"Guys, please meet Amreth Vahna, a Warden on Molvi, who also happens to be my soulmate. Kayog matched us right before the Gladius was attacked."

The way her companions' mouths dropped, and their eyes nearly popped out of their heads would have been hilarious if I had not been too busy preening to have thus been publicly claimed. Ciara didn't strike me as the type who loved to boast. To me, that she openly revealed this to the others broadcast that she was committed enough about us working out that she had no qualms sharing it.

"Kayog? The Temern matchmaker?!" Mehreen exclaimed.

Ciara nodded.

"Holy cow! I didn't know you sought out his services," she added.

My mate snorted and shook her head. "I didn't. We met on the ship and started talking after assisting a woman who was feeling a little under the weather. And next thing you know, boom, he told me he knew my soulmate."

"But… But when did you two get to talk before we got abducted?!" Ernst challenged.

"We didn't," Amreth replied in a factual manner. "Once it was confirmed that Ciara was among the missing, Kayog contacted me."

"And so you decided to come rescue her?!" Mehreen asked, an air of pure awe descending over her features.

"Of course. What kind of male would I be if I did not?"

My mate burst out laughing, while Ernst rolled his eyes with false despair when Mehreen pressed both her palms to her chest and stared at me with an air of wonder.

"Be still my heart! That's so freaking romantic. Please tell me you have a single brother!"

It was my turn to burst out laughing. "I do," I replied with a nod.

"I demand a formal introduction," Mehreen said before shamelessly batting her eyelashes.

"Woman, rein yourself in, and stop flirting with my man," Ciara said with false severity.

That, too, did funny things to me. It was silly how much pleasure I derived from her possessive display of me, however playful as this current situation was.

"Spoil sport," Mehreen replied with an exaggerated pout. "Anyway, the name is Mehreen, and he is Ernst."

"He already knows and has read all our files on his way here. Now let's go eat. We can catch him up on the parts I haven't gotten around to."

We all fell into step following her lead. It was starting to become apparent to me that the two scientists deferred to my woman's authority. She led us into one of the houses adjacent to the lab. To my surprise, the interior had been set up as a meeting room next to a dining area. The table was already laden with a generous amount of food. To my dismay as we took our seats, I noticed the substantial percentage of fruits and vegetables with only a small portion of meat and some dry breads.

Ciara chuckled upon seeing my expression, her own face taking on an air of commiseration laced with a hint of mockery.

"Someone isn't vegan?" she asked teasingly.

"Definitely not," I replied in a grumpy tone. "Our Nundars make the most delicious gastronomic dishes one could dream of."

"Nundars? What are they?" she asked with curiosity.

"We call them our familiars. They are a spiritual species of hermits who require living with an Obosian to thrive. They are highly intelligent and possess extremely powerful psionic powers. They feed off emotions but are also extremely sensitive to them. Negative emotions greatly distress them, which explains their need for isolation," I explained.

"Why do they thrive around your species specifically?" Ciara asked.

"Like my people, they mainly feed off emotions. Obosians naturally constantly emit a certain energetic aura that we can deliberately expend more of as needed. Therefore, around the time we reach maturity, we will be surrounded by young Nundars in the hope some of them will like our energy. Those who do will choose us as their patron and move in with us in the section of our dwelling reserved to them."

I deemed it wiser to skip the part where that selection occurred during the wild weeks when young Obosians reached their maturity around the age of eighteen. Prior to that, we were basically asexual. But once that moment occurred, we practically became rabid and were thrown into an orgy with other teens our age while we worked out our unbridled libido with everything and anything that moved. Young Nundars would supervise, making sure we kept hydrated, fed, and rested during that time when our minds were completely addled. Seeing us at our most uncontrolled and primal state helped them better assess if they could see themselves serving us for the rest of their lives.

"Isn't it a bit invasive? It sounds like you could end up with a lot?" Ciara asked carefully.

I snorted and gave her a reassuring smile. "They truly are not. Like I said, they enjoy living in isolation. You will be lucky to see them even once a month. Normally, you're only aware of their existence because they take care of all the chores around the house, including cooking, cleaning, and doing the laundry. But as they can sense our presence and state of mind, they know exactly how to make themselves scarce and only show up if they feel that we want to speak or interact with them."

"Wow, invisible and efficient helpers, who cook great food and take care of all the house chores? Sign me up!" Mehreen said, her voice dripping with envy, although her tone remained playful. "About that introduction to your brother…"

We all snorted, and my mate shook her head with false severity at her colleague as if she was a hopeless case.

"So it's true then that Obosians are like Incubi," Ernst said pensively.

"To the extent that we feed off the emotions of our partners, yes, we are. We don't need it, but it sates us far more than regular food. However, we do not drain the life force from our mates when we do so. They're not negatively affected in any way," I said teasingly.

"Well then, you're all set," Mehreen said with exaggerated enthusiasm. "No need to torture yourself with all that bird food," she added, waving at the mostly vegetarian meal on the table before casting a meaningful glance at Ciara.

"Hey! I'm not food!" Ciara exclaimed with false outrage.

"Technically, yes you are," I said with a shit-eating grin. "Or rather your emotions are."

I silenced the part that her pleasure would be the most succulent feast I would ever indulge in when the time came.

"But fear not, Ciara. I shall never feed without your express consent," I said in a reassuring tone.

Apparently determined to cause as much mischief as possible —although without any malicious intent—Mehreen further playfully needled my mate in a clear attempt to make her blush.

"Seeing as you two are soulmates—not to mention that you are every shade of hot—I'm sure Ciara will be more than happy to grant you that consent," Mehreen said with a dismissive wave of her hand. "By the way, are we to assume that you'll be sharing Ciara's house?"

Ernst bit the insides of his cheeks to keep from laughing while my mate gasped in disbelief, still stuck on that first comment. Mehreen was growing on me. It was strange as my people tended to be on the stiffer side. I also unfairly assumed that scientists would be boring and stuffy. A part of me suspected that her humor was also a coping mechanism for the stressful situation they'd been thrust into.

"Uhm… according to Aku, we are indeed meant to share her dwelling. I challenged him, saying that it was highly inappropriate. He informed me that there was a guest room, so it should be a non-issue. But if it was truly problematic for either of us, then he would provide different accommodations for me," I explained, factually.

"Wow!" Ciara whispered, looking at me with a hurt expression that took me aback. "Do you find it that dreadful to share a house with me?"

I recoiled and gaped at her. "What?! No, not at all. I just found it extremely presumptuous of him to assume you would be fine with it."

Her shoulders relaxed. "Did he tell you why he wanted us to share a house?"

"He said we were soulmates," I replied calmly.

"Which is accurate," Mehreen said with an obvious tone.

"Yes, but how does he know?" I challenged before glancing at my mate. "I doubt either you or Kayog told him."

"Their friend did," Ciara said with certainty before scrunching her face in frustration. "I hate that our memories have been wiped. I just know that their friend claimed that we all play an important role that will lead to the success of our efforts."

"It sounds like the vision of a Seer or Oracle," I said pensively. "Could those friends be Korletheans?"

To my shock, all three humans responded in unison with a definite no. That surprised them, and they exchanged amused looks at their instinctive reaction.

"I don't know why I can say this with complete certainty, but the Kreelars' friends absolutely hate the Korletheans," Ciara said carefully, to which her colleagues nodded.

"Yeah, I feel something very icky when their name comes up. It has to come from those mysterious friends," Ernst said with a frown. "I wonder if their friends could be Sarenians."

Ciara nodded. "It's plausible considering they possess mind controlling powers. With a single command, they could have wiped our memories. They also hate the Korletheans. But what would they be doing here in the Dead Zone? They mostly stick to their own region at the opposite end of the Eastern Quadrant."

"Does it matter?" Ernst countered.

"Absolutely!" I exclaimed sternly. "Unlike humans, who are also part of the Galactic Alliance of the Eastern and Western Quadrants, the rest of us here in the Northern Quadrant know very little about the Sectarians. They helped perform an attack against one of our most powerful Ally vessels. Was this an isolated event or are they up to something more nefarious?"

"Fair question," Ciara said in an appeasing tone. "But the Kreelars truly need our help. Without their friends' intervention, they might have become fully extinct in the next few years. Also, so far, I've perceived absolutely no evil or deception from Aku and his tribemates. They only want to save their people."

I nodded begrudgingly. "I also do not perceive any treachery from them. But why are their friends so secretive?"

"You know why," Ciara said in a reproving tone. "They broke the law to help the Kreelars. Even though they have done this for good reasons, you would breathe down their necks if you could get your hands on them."

"With valid reasons!" I exclaimed.

She gave me a hard stare, her face closing off in the most unpleasant fashion. I didn't like stirring that type of response from her.

"If I have to break the law to save a dying species, I will do so without hesitation," she said in a harsh tone.

"There were other ways they didn't explore," I argued.

"Were there?" she challenged. "They believe we are the one hope with the best outcome for all. So far, their foresight has been right, including you coming here."

"A crime is a crime," I said stubbornly. "People got hurt because of their attack."

"And they made every reasonable effort to mitigate injuries, including saving my life and fully healing me," Ciara said in the same stern voice. "You violated the Prime Directive to come and rescue me. Should you be sentenced to Molvi?"

I waved a dismissive hand. "Some exceptions are made when helping relatives and also based on the intentions of the person who committed the trespass."

"Exactly!" Ciara exclaimed as if that should be obvious to me. "You don't know what their intentions were."

"Fair," I conceded. "But what were they doing here on Kestria in the first place?"

I shrugged. "What were we, humans, doing here as well? What were Elias and his team doing here? This is the Dead Zone. The UPO has no more jurisdiction over the Sectarians who come to this planet than the Sectarians do over us. Whoever their friends are, they might have had legitimate reasons to be here. And clearly, they have a strong bond that strikes me as having spanned many years. So technically, if there are any intruders, it appears to me that *we* are."

I pursed my lips as I reflected on her words before nodding slowly.

"You make valid points. But why are you so protective of them?" I asked with genuine curiosity.

She appeared taken aback by that question. To my delight, rather than instantly denying or going on the defensive, Ciara took a moment to assess her thoughts and feelings about it before responding. That pleased me a great deal.

"When I became a doctor, I pledged to do no harm and to aid those in need. The Kreelars are in desperate need. Without their friends, they were guaranteed to die. You spoke of an attack, but not of a slaughter. Aku swore that they harmed no one, not even the guards, who they had also psychically disrupted. You confirmed as much. Yes, people got injured in the panic. But that was not the Kreelars' fault, or rather not directly. The way they saved me proved they were trying to mitigate any damage done to innocents."

Once again, I found myself begrudgingly forced to nod in concession. That seemed to please and embolden her.

"I think the Kreelars are good people, and their friends saw it, too. They could be treating us like shit for what they've endured, even if Elias and his team are the ones responsible for it," she continued.

"They have been extremely kind to us," Ernst concurred while Mehreen nodded in support.

"Ciara says you might have found a trail. You think you can help?" I asked.

Ernst nodded, his face lighting up with hope. "We found the responsible prions—the infectious agents that are causing this variation of prion diseases," he added quickly in an apologetic tone, although that explanation would remain less-than-clear for most people.

I smiled in a reassuring fashion. "Ciara already did a great job of explaining to me what prions are."

"Oh, excellent!" he exclaimed. "So we found the prions in the brain cells of the four current patients here. Two of them only started showing symptoms yesterday. We knew for sure that it was a prion disease because of the initial spongy plaque formation in their brain tissue seen in scans. As Ciara likely told you, prions must be ingested. We've scanned every food in the village as well as their water sources. Everything is clean. We must find what they are eating that's causing it, and that's a total Hail Mary."

I didn't know the formal meaning of that expression, but in the context, I suspected it meant that it would be an extremely difficult task to achieve.

"The important thing is that since this is happening in other villages, we know that the problem isn't restricted to one herd or one farm. There is something out there infecting these people," Ernst said.

"Can you cure it?" I asked.

All three of them shook their heads.

"There are no known cures for prion diseases. Normally, we

can only make the human patients as comfortable as possible while the illness progresses until their passing," Ciara said with a troubled expression. "But it is behaving differently with the Kreelars."

"How so?" I asked with genuine curiosity.

"The symptoms appear faster where with most other species it can take many weeks to months to manifest. But more importantly, some of the Kreelars survive whereas humans die within two years. Sora was the first case, and she's still alive. She's Aku's sister and the wet nurse who attacked the doctors by the river. Not only does she have antibodies, but her brain tissue also mutated to grant her psionic powers."

"Do the others, like Aku, have the same antibodies?" I asked, fascinated.

Ciara hesitated, seeming unsure how to respond.

"The antibodies are fairly similar but not the same," Mehreen said. "We believe the prions shared the same origin but that the source of contamination was different, and the variant Sora consumed through that doctor's blood was a mutated version of the one that has been infecting the others."

"We're still trying to figure out why females are more likely to die," Ciara said.

"I would have assumed it was a hormonal factor," I said carefully.

"That's what we suspect as well, but what specifically? How is it interacting with the prions to precipitate the catastrophic failures that killed them?" she said pensively.

"At least, we can now detect who is infected, even if they are not yet showing symptoms," Ernst said. "We must test everyone and provide them with test kits to ensure infected mothers and wet nurses aren't passing anything to their children."

"I'm assuming they have many villages spread over a vast territory. Do they have quick communication systems?" I asked, trying to assess how many villages we could reach in the shortest time possible.

"Yes and no," Ciara replied. "They have the equivalent of old CBs, which basically only require an antenna and a receiver to catch the radio frequencies. They can talk over them, but there is no vidcom. So we can't show them virtually what to do. It at least allows Aku to give them a heads up of what's going on and that we will start visiting them as of tomorrow with test kits and medicine."

"Medicine?" I echoed with a frown. "I thought you said there was no cure?"

"We've prepared something derived from Sora's antibodies with synthetic immunoglobulins that will help prevent normal prions from turning abnormal. This should significantly slow the progress of the disease and give the patient's body a chance to fight back and mutate instead of dying. So far, it has been working well for our first two patients."

A sudden thought struck me. "Is there any chance that they are in fact consuming whatever this is on purpose? Is there a possibility that the Kreelars *want* to undergo this mutation? After all, it has given them the type of offensive psionic powers that many hunters would love to have."

To my surprise, they all simultaneously shook their heads.

"Definitely not," Ciara said with certainty. "They were happy the way they were. But they will take the mutation over death. They just fear what other changes may occur in the future and would love confirmation that this mutation is the final result of their exposure to the prions."

"Fair enough. So what's the plan?" I asked.

"We travel to nearby villages with a couple of Kreelar escorts in the morning," Ernst said. "With your wings, you could take Ciara to one of the more distant ones."

I nodded. "We were discussing it before the hunters returned with their catch. My shuttle would be a lot more efficient though.

Hopefully, things will go well tomorrow enough that their people will feel more comfortable with our advanced technology. It would allow you and Mehreen to travel farther while I fly my mate."

I flinched inwardly when I caught myself using that term of endearment. It was the second time I had done it. I cast a nervous glance at Ciara but was relieved to find her smiling with approval. I doubted it was because I had claimed her. But I welcomed the fact that it didn't seem to trouble or displease her.

"Sounds like a plan!" Ciara said.

We finished our 'bird' food meal in an amiable atmosphere. Afterwards, Ernst and Mehreen went back to making more medicine while Ciara taught me how to administer the test so that I could help her in the morning.

In a way I couldn't explain, it felt good.

CHAPTER 9
CIARA

Finally as ready as we could be for the morning, we exchanged our good nights, and I headed back to my house accompanied by my mate. I still struggled with the idea that he was mine. It wasn't that I had an issue with it, but more that I didn't really know how to go about it. For the first time, I realized just how awkward I actually was on the romantic side.

Amreth made a couple of attempts at flirting since his arrival, but he was also being cautious. It was a difficult balance to strike to avoid coming across as too bold, too soon. His earlier comment about disciplining me had skirted that fine line. The thing was that I couldn't swear he intended for it to hint at kinky spanking. His people were all about disciplining misbehavior. Therefore, his words could have been totally innocent.

But then, I'd always been the oblivious type when it came to that. My traitor of an ex-fiancé flat out had to tell me that he was interested and was running out of subtle ways of expressing it before I realized he had indeed been flirting with me.

And now, my romantically challenged self was going home with the total stranger that was supposedly the other half of me.

Had he been of any other species—except maybe a Temern

like Kayog—I couldn't swear that I would have been fine with him spending the night under the same roof as me this early on. Separate bedrooms didn't mean anything if the person was a psycho or the type not to respect boundaries. But Amreth inspired trust with an intensity that defied logic.

To my surprise, halfway across the courtyard towards my house, Amreth gestured for me to wait a minute and headed towards the gate, waving at Enre, the Kreelar guard sitting on top of the small tower at the edge of the gate. Enre leapt down the three meters, effortlessly landing with the grace of a cat. He approached us with a calm demeanor laced with curiosity.

"Sorry to disturb you, but I must run an errand to my ship," Amreth said.

I gaped at him before quickly schooling my features. Enre narrowed his dark brown eyes at him with a hint of suspicion.

"Why?"

"If I am to stay here, I need clean clothes and a few of my personal items," Amreth replied matter-of-factly.

The Kreelar studied his features in silence with an unreadable expression. His eyes slightly glowed. It always freaked me out when they did that. To my utter annoyance, when I questioned Aku about their powers, he told me that such knowledge was irrelevant to the pursuit of my task here. When I challenged that notion, saying that a better understanding of their powers could lead me to make certain associations that could help identify and resolve the problem faster, he flat out shot me down. Apparently, those wretched friends of his confirmed that giving me that knowledge would not help their cause.

Considering the occasions under which they used that ability, I strongly suspected that it allowed them to read the emotions or intentions of their target. I didn't believe they could read minds. More than once, they'd been genuinely taken aback by something we said or revealed. If they could read minds, they would have known ahead of time what we were preparing to say or do.

"That is a decision for Aku to make," Enre said at last.

"Of course," Amreth replied graciously.

Although now wasn't the time to shower him with compliments, I gave him a grateful smile that he was showing so much consideration and being so cooperative. Technically, as he wasn't officially a prisoner, he could have snuck out and then attempted to return discreetly once he'd been done with whatever was calling him back to his ship.

I would have hated that. I couldn't tell whether he could have pulled it off, but after my ex-fiancé's betrayal, I had some trust issues. Any act from him that would even remotely hint at him being loose with his word would significantly undermine whatever relationship we could have.

To my shock, less than ten seconds later, Aku walked through the gate into the courtyard. By the way Amreth narrowed his eyes, I knew the same question was crossing his mind as to whether Enre used some form of telepathy to call him. That could explain the glowing eyes.

"Enre says you want to leave?" Aku asked in a non-confrontational manner, confirming my suspicions.

"Not *leave*," Amreth corrected. "I just need to get fresh clothes and personal things. When I came down, I did not expect to remain here."

Aku pursed his lips while giving him an assessing look.

"Listen, I'll be flying to a nearby village with Ciara in the morning. If my intention is to escape, it will happen regardless at that time. Your 'friend' says I can be trusted, and I have committed to see this through. So if you are going to trust me, it needs to start now. I didn't come here to play games."

"Our people are wary of strangers. You coming and going so soon will only make them even more uncomfortable," Aku argued.

"Amreth is an Obosian," I interjected softly. "His word is his bond. If he says he will return, then you can count on it. Your friend has been right about everything so far. Why doubt them now?"

To my surprise, he gave me a strange look before casting an even stranger one on Amreth. I would have given lots of credits to get a hint as to what thoughts were crossing his mind.

"It is not *my* trust you need to earn. You both already have it. My people are dying. They need someone to blame. You just happen to be the closest thing that they can turn on. Please be swift and be discreet."

I gaped at him, robbed of words. Of all the things he could have replied, I had not expected this.

"I will," Amreth said, snapping out of the same stupor I felt first.

He glanced towards the northeast where a series of low mountain ranges could be seen on the horizon then turned back to face me.

"Do you need me to bring you back anything from my ship?" he asked.

I shook my head. "We have everything we need. The deployable lab is perfect. But whatever you're fetching over there, *do not* bring back any food!"

I burst out laughing at the way he scrunched his face. I doubted he had actually considered doing it, but this reminder that he wasn't enjoying the mostly vegetarian food they had here cracked me up. He looked like a little boy pouting over having to eat his broccoli.

"Understood. I'll be back soon," he replied.

Then, with a powerful flap of his wings, he took flight. I couldn't help but admire his grace and strength. Amreth was magnificent. Obviously, his physical appearance didn't hurt my eyes. But what I had seen so far of his personality was seriously growing on me. It was exceedingly early in our relationship, so we had ways to go in getting to know each other. However, I loved his intelligence and his ability to quickly understand things and focus on topics that usually had people's eyes glazing over in seconds.

My main concern was how rigid he sometimes seemed to be when it came to observing the law. I understood that it was nearly indoctrinated in his people from birth. But nothing was ever completely black or white. At least, he was open to arguments, listened with an open mind, and seemed willing to make concessions.

A strong sense of being observed had me jerking my head suddenly towards Aku. Finding him and Enre staring at me with a slightly amused expression had my cheeks burning with embarrassment.

"He pleases you," Aku said in a factual manner.

I shifted on my feet, feeling a little awkward and shrugged dismissively. "I hope so. We're soulmates after all."

"You don't know him yet," Aku challenged.

"You're right, but that doesn't mean there can't be natural chemistry. Your friend said that we were meant for each other, as did my own," I said nonchalantly. "Sometimes, you don't need to know someone for a very long time to get a good sense of who they are and of their true nature. I don't know you, and despite you kidnapping us, I trust that you're a good person. Your actions and devotion to your people broadcast it loudly. I feel the same towards Amreth."

A strange expression fleeted over both his face and Enre's.

Aku nodded slowly. "Your words are kind. But as stated earlier, the feeling is mutual. That said, it is fascinating to witness this attraction between such different species," he added pensively, which prompted Enre to nod in agreement.

I smiled. "It is very common off-world. People from many planets of our alliance marry each other. Soulmates are not deter-mined by species. I mean, your own soulmate could be human."

Aku recoiled. "Ewww! Absolutely not!" he exclaimed with the same horrified expression that Enre displayed.

"Ouch!" I said, pressing a palm to my chest as if I had been mortally wounded with an overly dramatic expression on my face.

"Apologies," Aku said, his ears darkening with embarrassment even as I burst out laughing. "I meant no disrespect. You and your companions are charming enough, but no, me ending up with a human is highly unlikely. In truth, an off-worlder mate would not be welcome here after all of this. It will take my people quite some time to heal and to see strangers as anything other than bringers of doom."

"Right," I said, sobering.

"But I'm glad for you," Aku said in a gentler tone. "He truly seems honorable. For what it's worth, he was not easy to capture, even though he believes so, and it wounds his pride. Ten of us had to use our powers on Amreth to bring him down. And even then, he still fought back. It has been a while since we've had to chase anyone or anything for that long. They usually don't make it to the tree line."

"Oh wow! You should tell him that. He indeed felt quite mortified for getting captured," I said, a silly wave of pride surging through me.

"Not happening! We wouldn't want that getting to his head now, would we?" he said in a taunting tone.

I snorted and shook my head at him. "Then maybe I'll just do it myself. I kind of owe him that much. He came all the way here to rescue me without us ever even meeting," I added wistfully before giving him a serious look. "I understand that you cannot tell us anything about your friends. But are they a threat to us?"

Although I had no reason to trust that he wouldn't lie to protect them, the swiftness and conviction with which he shook his head at least convinced me that he genuinely believed they weren't. Not that it proved anything.

"They are not. Their affairs are in the Eastern and Western Quadrants. Dark things are brewing over there. I can only pray they will come out on the winning side once all is said and done," Aku said in a mysterious tone laced with a hint of worry for his friends. "But now we shall leave you. Your companions and I will ride out early. Enre will leave tonight to Jaln Village ahead of your arrival. Rest well."

"Will do," I said with a smile.

After one final stiff nod in response, Aku turned around and walked out with Enre shadowing him. I watched them until they vanished from view then headed for my house. To my surprise, I caught myself rushing in to take a shower and pick the outfit I would wear from the respectable selection that had been provided for me. There were a few nightgowns, sexy enough while remaining prim and respectable—the type of nightwear I could wear in front of him without it coming across as me trying to get frisky. Still, I suspected whoever picked those clothes for me knew I would be with Amreth.

Judging by the outfits worn by the Kreelars, they had not created these clothes. Their people—both males and females— mostly wore trousers that reminded me of those puffy harem pants with colorful belts or loincloth on top. Neither gender wore tops, aside from the occasional sash, weapon strap, but more often a series of colorful beads and necklaces around their necks, which tumbled down to the middle of their chests.

Their females didn't have prominent breasts like we did, just an extra set of nipples. I couldn't tell if their garments meant to hide their nudity or were simply a fashion statement. But I appreciated not having to stare at their naughty bits. The one male patient we examined gave us more than an eyeful. If the Kreelars were all made the same, they might have simian features, but they were hung like horses.

After settling on a coral, sleeveless negligee that flattered my dark complexion, I brushed my hair and teeth, making extra sure I didn't have anything funky stuck between them. I was that person wildly grinning at others while oblivious to the fact that I had a piece of spinach wedged between my front teeth.

A swift glance at my watch indicated that twenty-one minutes passed since Amreth flew off to his ship. Considering he said it was nearly a ten-minute flight in each direction, it would probably take him another twenty before he returned. Feeling restless, I went back to my laptop to try and get a bit more work done, but my mind just kept wandering off.

He'd been here less than a day, and yet my entire life felt as if it had been turned upside down. I wished we weren't here, that this whole thing was already resolved so that we could just focus on getting to know each other and exploring our relationship.

Among other things, I needed to figure out how I wanted to handle things between us over the upcoming days. Should I just let things follow their normal course and go with the flow? Should I suggest that we put anything between us on hold while we sorted out this mess and then start fresh with our minds at ease once we were done? What did he even expect?

"Oh, my God! Cut it out!" I whispered angrily to myself.

I had the tendency of overthinking and over analyzing things. Sometimes, things didn't need to fit neatly inside a little container with a proper label. Chaos held its own beauty.

I nearly jumped out of my skin when I heard a knock on the front door. Heart pounding, I jumped to my feet and bolted out of the guest room where I'd been working—or rather daydreaming —and rushed to the door. It wasn't locked. My heart fluttered when I found Amreth standing behind it, his hands carrying two large bags.

"Come in," I said, feeling a little awkward as I stepped out of the way.

He smiled with a hint of amusement, no doubt perceiving how flustered his mere presence suddenly made me feel.

"Technically, as you're going to live here now, you don't have to knock in the future," I said with a nervous giggle.

"Thank you. It just felt presumptuous not to do so at least this time," he replied.

"And I appreciate you being so considerate," I said, tucking a strand of my silver-white hair behind my ear. "But please, this way. Your bags look heavy," I added, gesturing towards the guest room.

He followed me into the room only for my stupid brain to finally realize that I had been using it as an office. The whole time I'd been waiting for him, it didn't register once that I should move my stuff out. Granted, it was only a laptop and a 3D holographic display, but I still should have thought of it.

"Oh, sorry!" I exclaimed, rushing to remove them. "I had been using this room as my office."

"You can leave them here," Amreth interjected while setting one of the bags on the bed. "I will only need this room to sleep. You can still work here the rest of the time."

"I don't want to bother you or invade your privacy," I said sheepishly.

He shrugged and looked at me as if I had said something silly. "Your presence can never bother me. But mine could definitely bother *you*," he added teasingly.

"I doubt it. I've really enjoyed your company so far, and you're far more pleasant to look at than all that medical data," I retorted tauntingly.

He snorted. "Not to boast, but I couldn't agree more with you on that last point. I get cross-eyed just looking at those reports you and your colleagues have been poring over. I'll ogle myself any day over that," he said with an exaggerated shudder.

I chuckled, seriously liking that playful side of him. I doubted he realized it, but where people would occasionally say I had quite the resting bitchface, he had the typical Obosian resting haughty face. Anyone who didn't know him would likely assume that he was stuck up and holier than thou.

"But you also are very easy on the eye, Ciara. I love the color of this nightgown on you. It makes your skin glow."

My stomach fluttered with the most pleasant feeling. It wasn't just the words, but the soft way he spoke them and the admiration in his eyes devoid of lurid undertones. This could have gone in so many different directions. I just liked that he didn't seem to just look at me as a sex toy.

I glanced down at myself with a timid smile, my right hand absent-mindedly flattening nonexistent creases on the short skirt of my nightgown.

"Thank you. Whoever picked the clothes for me had a really nice taste. I don't naturally tend to go for colorful clothes, but the selection they provided has made me rethink that stance. Once I leave here, my wardrobe will get a notable update. I just wish they had a bath here and not just a shower. I have a thing for bubble baths while reading a good book."

"I have a jacuzzi tub on my ship that I personally never use. If the urge becomes too great for you, I'll have to sweet talk Aku into allowing you a well-deserved escape for an hour or so."

I smiled. "You're sweet, and I'll definitely keep that offer in mind. In fact, I will set it as a reward for when we pinpoint the source of the illness plaguing them."

"Deal! Now I have an extra incentive to see that it happens sooner than later. But with that said, I could use a shower myself," Amreth said, glancing around the room. "I did not notice the hygiene room when Aku first brought me here."

"This place is fairly primitive," I said in an apologetic tone, as if somehow this was my house that I feared wasn't up to par. "They have an outdoor shower, and an outhouse."

The crestfallen look on his face had me bursting out laughing. I didn't mean to make fun of him, but as a noble Lord, he likely wasn't used to roughing it out. Added to that, his wings were quite massive. Although the shower wasn't tiny, it would likely be a little cramped for him in there.

"I should have listened to myself," he mumbled under his breath.

"About what?" I asked, curious.

"About taking a shower on my ship before returning. But I had been gone long enough and didn't want Aku to think I had reneged on my word. Oh well, it will be a good reminder of what it was like during my Warrior training. They made sure we forgot the meaning of creature comfort during those four brutal years," he said with resignation.

My heart melted. "Thank you. You really are very considerate. Aku has taken a huge leap of faith trusting us. I didn't expect him to say what he did before you left. It's silly, but that made me even more determined to prove he was right in putting his trust in us."

"I feel the same, especially since he was sincere when he spoke those words. He has an unusually pleasant soul."

"I'm not surprised. But I admit that I'm really jealous of your ability to see souls. That would have spared me from getting taken advantage of by a few jerks in the past," I said with a hefty dose of self-derision.

Amreth gave me a mysterious smile as he began removing his breastplate. "Don't be jealous, Ciara. You will be able to as well in the not-so-distant future... I hope."

I blinked with confusion. "What do you mean?"

"The day you and I formally bond, I will pass on some of my abilities to you. Specifically, you will gain night vision and the ability to see souls. It will not be as powerful as mine, but you will be able to know who wishes you ill and who is honest. You will also heal faster from injuries and be more resistant to illness in general."

I gaped at him as he chuckled smugly, the sound deep and throaty in the sexiest of ways.

"Damn, sign me up," I whispered.

He laughed, placed his breastplate on the bed and turned

back to face me. It took every ounce of my willpower not to let my greedy gaze roam all over the perfection of his body. That didn't stop me from noticing the piercing in his left nipple and the one in his navel. Their presence further reinforced my conviction that I would eventually discover a few more farther south on him.

"Would you mind showing me that primitive shower?" he asked, the mischievous glimmer in his eyes hinting that I was doing a terrible job of keeping myself from ogling him.

Then again, my gut told me that the wretch partially stripped on purpose to make my mouth water.

"This way," I said, escaping with a wee bit too much eagerness to hide my embarrassment.

I led him to the private backyard where the shower was located. Once again, I couldn't help another less-than-charitable laugh at his crestfallen expression when he saw what he had to work with.

"Enjoy!" I said teasingly in a sing-song voice.

He muttered something under his breath while I made my way back inside. I'd never been the sex starved maniac type of woman, but the burning urge to go get a peek of my man washing was almost overwhelming.

My soulmate was fiiiiiiine!

Just thinking about the perfection of his body had me drooling, especially that impertinent piercing in his nipple. I'd never really been into any type of body modification, whether implants, piercings, or even tattoos. Sure, I could admire them on someone who had really nice ones done, but it had never been something that I felt drawn to.

On Amreth, it was sheer perfection.

Obviously, I was super biased where he was concerned, but I was genuinely turned on by everything about him. To my shame, my wicked mind started taking a deep dive into every type of naughty fantasy involving him. I wanted to kick Mehreen for making all those innuendos earlier and especially for bringing up the topic of his incubus powers. At the same time, I wished she had made him delve even farther into it to give me a more complete picture of what awaited me the day Amreth and I got down to business.

When will that actually happen?

To my dismay, a wave of disappointment washed over me knowing that this wasn't an official Prime Mating Agency union. Although Kayog paired us, we didn't receive any of the benefits of the PMA nor were we subjected to its rules and commitments. With both of us belonging to advanced species, we were left to our own devices as far as our coupling was concerned. That meant we had no obligation to consummate our union tonight. Hell, we weren't even married to begin with.

This behavior was all the more confusing to me that I wasn't the type to have sex on the first date. Granted, Amreth wasn't just some random dude I was getting to know to see if things could develop into something more meaningful. The question was how much of my attraction and impatience to deepen the relationship with him was due to the natural chemistry between us or the bias created by the knowledge that we were meant to be?

My mind wandered back to his incubus powers. I had read a thing or two about them in the past. However, considering the possibility of a relationship with an Obosian had been slim to none back then, I hadn't looked into it much. How I regretted it today.

A glance at my watch had me frowning. Already twenty minutes had elapsed since he hopped into the shower. As he didn't strike me as the type to linger or a daydream while washing, this felt overly long.

I waited a bit longer, but when it started pushing into thirty-five minutes, I finally decided to go check up on him in case something had happened or if he needed assistance with anything. I had analyzed their soap and water, and neither represented the slightest threat to humans or Obosians.

Feeling a little nervous about intruding in case he actually was just the type that spent forever in the shower, I pressed my ear against the door to hear if the water was still running. It didn't seem to be, but a muffled woosh seeped through the door. Intrigued, I knocked to announce myself before cracking the door open.

"Amreth? Are you okay?" I called out through the narrow opening.

"I'm fine, you can come out," he replied.

Pushing the door a little wider, I poked my head out to get a glimpse of what was happening. My jaw dropped, and I fully opened the door to step outside while staring at a rather annoyed-looking Amreth. He was leaning forward, his palms pressed against the outer wall of the shower, a towel wrapped around his waist to hide his naughty bits, and his massive wings slowly flapping behind him.

"What are you doing?" I asked, baffled.

"Drying my wings," he said in a grumpy tone. "I had forgotten how obnoxious it is not to have the proper shower heads specifically set to wash our wings or the dryer to take away all the water between the creases. You have no idea how itchy it gets to try to sleep with damp wings. Flying around would have made it a lot faster. But I doubt our hosts would be overly thrilled to see me circling their village at night like a predator ready to pounce."

I snorted before slapping my hand over my mouth to keep myself from laughing. "You're right, I have no idea what it's like. I'm guessing washing them was also quite the headache. I struggle washing my back without a back brush. I can't imagine trying to clean those huge wings."

"I gave up halfway through," he said dejectedly. "Extreme contortions only get you so far with these things."

"Poor baby," I said teasingly. "You know, you could have asked for help."

"I didn't want to bother you," he mumbled.

"It doesn't bother me, you silly male," I said in a chastising tone while heading towards the recessed shelves near the shower that held the towels.

To my surprise, he suddenly looked almost shy when I approached him with the large towel. That took me aback. I wasn't seeing much more of him now than when he had removed his breastplate. The only difference was that he was barefoot and with a towel around his waist instead of the tight leather pants he previously wore.

But I'm about to touch him... more like caress him with the towel...

The moment that wretched thought entered my mind, my stomach instantly fluttered, and my fingers began to twitch with anticipation.

"Any spot in particular I should focus on?" I asked, proud that my voice was a lot steadier than I expected it would be.

"The base of my wings, where they connect to my back, and the creases along the spines, please," Amreth said.

"All right. Don't hesitate to tell me if I'm doing it wrong," I said as I parked myself behind him.

Amreth spread his wings wide. Aside from the fact that they were magnificent, I truly got to admire their impressive span. The muscles of his back rippled and bulged under the effort that position required. Despite that, it seemed effortless for him.

I began to rub the towel on his back, to the left of his spine and along the base of his wing. A shiver coursed through him. It was subtle, but strong enough for me to notice. My stomach did a backflip at the thought that enjoyment of my touch prompted that reaction. I didn't bring it up and neither did he.

"Your wings are truly gorgeous," I said wistfully as I admired their obsidian, leathery texture. "But they must be terribly heavy."

He glanced at me over his shoulder, an amused smile stretching his lips. "Technically, you are correct. But to me, they feel no different than any other limbs on my body. I've had a lifetime to get used to them."

"Still, it must have been challenging at first," I insisted.

He shrugged. "We're born with them. We stumble around at first as we adjust to their weight. But it's not much different than human babies trying to find their balance as they learn to stand up. We just have an extra set of limbs to take into account."

I ran the towel over the leathery surface, taking a bit more time than necessary to thoroughly dry every bit of moisture in the corners where the spines connected. I was seriously itching to just rub my palm all over it. But it felt a little too bold.

"What about the first time you had to fly? Wasn't that terrifying?"

"Not for me," he said firmly. "Some Obosians get very nervous about it. We even have a very small fraction of our people who hate being winged. It goes beyond not wanting to fly or being afraid of it. They just hate having wings, which I truly struggle to comprehend. I love my wings. I couldn't imagine a world where I would be forever land bound."

"Oh wow! I never imagined that could be an issue," I said with genuine surprise as I shifted to his other wing. "What happens to those people? Can therapy help?"

"For some, therapy will help them overcome it. Those cases are usually because the person faced some grievous trauma related to flying. But the very low percentage of people who are truly against having wings normally express that aversion fairly early on as younglings. A majority of them end up having their wings removed."

"WHAT?! Are you serious?!" I exclaimed.

He nodded grimly. "As the procedure is not reversible, they

have to wait until they reach adulthood. If they still want to go through with it at that point, they are required to spend an entire year living wingless in a holodeck simulation. Only then, should they still want to do it, will they receive the surgery. Thankfully, although 8% of our population want to be rid of their wings, only 2% actually get them clipped. The others keep them but simply never fly."

"Damn. Even if I may have vertigo simply standing on a chair, I still highly doubt I would have my wings removed. But I could see myself living as a land bound person," I said sheepishly.

Amreth gasped and turned around to stare at me in shock. "You're afraid of flying?"

"I'm afraid of heights," I said with a guilty expression.

"You realize I will be carrying you in my arms as we fly tomorrow to that village, right?" he said, looking a bit perplexed.

I nodded. "Yeah. I'll just keep my face buried in your chest, and my eyes tightly closed."

"But you'll be missing the view!" he exclaimed, sounding scandalized. "This planet is gorgeous! It would be a crime for you to miss out on its beauty."

"Believe me, Amreth, it's better that I miss the scenery than have me puking all over you or peeing myself out of fear," I said teasingly while working on the front of his wings, not that those ones truly needed it as he had clearly been able to reach that part on his own.

"There will be no puking or peeing," he said with an assurance that bordered on arrogance.

"Is that so?" I challenged.

He nodded. "I will appease you so that the height won't be as frightening for you."

"Appease me?" I echoed. "Now you have me curious. How will you do that?"

"With my *bakaan*, of course," he said.

He no sooner spoke those words than a tingling sensation washed over me, quickly followed but the most fantastic sense of peace and well-being.

"Whoa! Okay, that's freaking awesome!" I said, my voice slightly slurred like when you just finished receiving the best body massage ever that left you feeling almost groggy but not quite. "I wish I had that power when dealing with distressed or panicked patients. I'm guessing that's not one of the powers you'll pass on to me?"

He shook his head and gave me an apologetic look. "It's not. But I'll be happy to use it on your patients on your behalf."

"You're too kind," I replied teasingly. "I knew Obosians could do that, but I never experienced it directly. On the ship, during the attack, one of the guards used it on the panicked crowd to stop the stampede, but I was outside the radius of his *bakaan*. That said, aside from this and your Lumiak, aren't all your other powers sexual in nature?"

He hesitated. "Technically my aura actually is. I used it at its lowest level on you just now. But the greater the intensity and the more erogenous its effect. In fact, at its maximum intensity, I can make you climax without even touching you."

I gaped at him. "Your *bakaan* on its own could give me an orgasm?" I asked, wanting to make sure I truly understood him.

His silver-white eyes darkened while his smug smile took on a sensuous edge that instantly ignited a little spark in the pit of my stomach.

"Mmhmm, it can. But I also have pheromones that can drive you completely mad with lust. And as for my Lumiak, it's not just an offensive power. At low intensity and used on very strategic erogenous points, I can drive you insane with instant and powerful pleasure even greater than someone precisely targeting your G-spot."

Damn the man… or rather male. The way his voice dipped lower with each of his words, not to mention the words themselves, had me throbbing and aching in no time. How the fuck could he just tease me with so many promises of a good time knowing he wouldn't act on them? The naughty side of me wanted to ask him to give me a sample… for science of course. By the taunting way he was staring at me, the wretch knew exactly what thoughts were coursing through my mind.

"Well, it sounds like I have many interesting things to look forward to as you and I grow closer. Just be aware that you set a pretty high bar for yourself. I have all kinds of expectations now."

He snorted and puffed out his chest with a confidence bordering on arrogance. "Giving you more pleasure than you could ever imagine possible is not a challenge for me. I am an Obosian. We are the embodiment of sexuality and sensuality."

Saying my toes curled something fierce would be the understatement of the century.

"Someone is boasting," I said teasingly to hide how much his words were affecting me.

"No, my Ciara. I *never* boast, least of all about this. You'll find out soon enough."

I scrunched my face at him. I didn't need to read minds or see souls to know he wasn't kidding. For the second time this evening, I caught myself wishing we were under the PMA guidelines so that I could put all of this to the test.

Instead, I heaved a sigh and bunched the damp towel that I had been drying him with.

"Well, I guess we're all done, unless you feel I missed a spot," I said nonchalantly, although dismayed by the sliver of hope that sparked deep within when I said that last part.

"Thank you, Ciara. But don't be so sad. You can touch me anytime, and not just to dry me," he said teasingly.

I gasped and gave him a stunned look.

"We are soulmates," he replied in an obvious fashion in

response to my expression. "All of me, everything that I am is yours."

And there went my ovaries exploding. A billion replies burned my tongue. Instead, I surprised myself by blurting out a completely different question.

"How much did it freak you out finding out you were paired with a human? With me?"

I instantly flinched inwardly. Although that question had plagued me from the moment Kayog told me Amreth was my one and only, I wondered how he would feel about it. From my understanding, his people weren't particularly impressed by my species as a whole. Humans had too great a propensity to break the rules or stretch them to their limits. Our morality could be very fluid especially when it benefited us, even to the detriment of others.

"It did not freak me out in the least. To the contrary, I was elated," he said with a conviction that had a swarm of butterflies taking flight in the pit of my stomach.

"Really?" I asked, wondering where that irrational need to be reassured came from.

He nodded. "I've been longing for a life partner for a while. In fact, the very day Kayog called to tell me about you, I was bemoaning the fact that I couldn't retain the services of his agency because my home world was too advanced. No news could have made me happier, especially knowing that whoever you were, together, we would achieve perfect harmony and share the type of love my best friend Kronos has found with his Malaya."

I tucked a strand of hair behind my ear and smiled at him. "I had not been looking at all. So Kayog dropping this on me totally took me by surprise."

"Not a bad one, I hope?" Amreth asked, tilting his head to the side.

The underlying vulnerability and uncertainty in his voice—

subtle though it was—threw me for a loop. How could such a fine specimen even remotely doubt that any hot-blooded woman would ache to throw herself at him?

"Are you kidding? Do you not know how human women constantly drool about your species? We know how picky you are. So finding out that my soulmate was an Obosian was a huge honor. And so far, you're exceeding everything I hoped for. And I'm not talking about your hot appearance—which you are. You also seem to have a good heart, compassion, integrity, and the ability to not only keep up with my nerdy gibberish, but to also be interested in the scientific stuff I spew. You made me feel seen and heard instead of annoying like laymen often do."

"You're many things but not annoying, Ciara. The first time Kayog showed me a hologram of you, I was blown away by your beauty. I remember thinking that you could be one of ours with your dark skin and silver-white hair," he said wistfully.

I snorted, my mouth running away with me to hide my embarrassment. "Most people find me weird because of my piebaldism. It's what causes my hair to be white and that discolored patch of skin on my forehead," I said with a nervous laugh.

"You're not weird. Only a fool would think so. Beyond the fact that your hair matches the colors of my people, I find your discolored patch to be stunning. It is like your own organic circlet. I wish you could see yourself through my eyes. Your aura is mesmerizing and lights you up from within. It makes your crown glow."

My throat tightened with emotion. Sure, his words touched me, but it was the look in his eyes and the sincerity in his voice that wrecked me.

"You speak of my compassion and integrity, but do you not see your own? Many people in your circumstances would have turned their backs on the Kreelars for abducting them. Aku trusts you because your kindness and determination to help his people radiate out of you with the strength of a thousand suns. I don't know to what extent I'm smart, but you have a talent for explaining complex concepts in a way that is both understandable and fascinating."

"Jeez! If you're trying to make me like you, you're doing a great job of it," I mumbled, my cheeks heating with pleasure.

"Success! By the time we're done helping these people, I intend to have you head over heels in love with me," he said in a voice full of promise. "But come, let's get back inside."

I nodded and hung the towel to dry on the rack by the inner wall of the shower. To my surprise, Amreth extended a hand towards me. On instinct, I took it. His grateful smile did funny things to me. He gently caressed the back of my hand with his thumb before leading me back inside the house. My mate stopped in the middle of the living area, which also happened to be directly between the two bedrooms, and he turned to face me.

"I guess we should turn in for the night as we must rise early in the morning," he said in a gentle voice. "Despite the dire circumstances that have brought us here, I'm happy that we are together at last. Would it be too bold of me to ask for a kiss goodnight? Feel totally comfortable saying no."

My stomach did another somersault, and it took every ounce of my willpower not to over enthusiastically agree.

"It is not too bold," I said with far more poise than I felt. "And yes, you may."

The softness of his smile, and the way his silver-white eyes darkened as he carefully drew me into his embrace had my girly bits standing to attention. I pressed my palms to his bare chest, a delicious shiver coursing down my spine as his strong arms closed around me. I wanted to rub my hands all over him, having been cheated by the towel between us when I dried his wings earlier. His skin was soft and warm. My fingers itched to travel farther up to his shoulders and the side of his arms that were covered in dark scales.

Forcing my hands to remain still, I lifted my face towards

his. He leaned forward, slanted his head to the side, and then pressed his lips to mine. Although I knew beyond the shadow of a doubt that he hadn't used his aphrodisiac pheromones or *bakaan*, the bolt of desire that exploded in the pit of my stomach at that mere contact left me reeling. It made even less sense that the kiss was devoid of any lust. It was gentle, tender, and highly respectful.

Too soon, he broke the kiss. I almost whimpered, not yet ready to part from him. To my utter delight, just when I thought he was going to push me away, Amreth tightened his embrace around me and buried his face in my hair while I buried my face in his neck. This time, with a will of their own, my hands glided upwards, caressing the dark, chevron-shaped scales that covered the curve of his shoulders, and then sank into the silkiness of his long, silver-white hair on his nape. Another shiver coursed through me when his wings wrapped around us.

I always wondered what it would be like to be hugged like this. It went beyond feeling sheltered and protected. I felt at home.

I couldn't say how long we remained like this, quietly in each other's embrace. But when he opened his wings and loosened his hold around me, a brutal sense of being bereft crushed me. I could have stayed like this with him forever. The tenderness in his eyes as he locked gazes with me melted me from the inside out. I didn't know him well just yet, but I knew with unshakable certainty that this was just a first glimpse of the deep love that would eventually burn bright between us.

He cupped my right cheek with his hand, leaned forward again to brush his lips against mine one last time.

"Sweet dreams, my mate," he said in a deep whisper.

His thumb caressed my lips, then he dropped his hand from my cheek.

"Good night, Amreth," I whispered back.

He turned around and walked to his room. I stared at his

receding back, two of my fingers absentmindedly finding their way to my lips as if to rekindle the sensation of his kiss. It wasn't until the door closed behind him that I finally snapped out of my trance.

I went to my own room, still torn by my disappointment that we didn't fall under the PMA rules and relief that we would get to set things between us at our own pace. But the dominant thought as I climbed into bed and settled my head on my pillow was that I was developing a major crush on the male I would get to spend the rest of my life with.

I closed my eyes and smiled.

CHAPTER 10
AMRETH

That first night sharing this house turned out to be a lot more restful than I expected. A genuine connection occurred last evening. Instead of tossing and turning while longing to hold her again, the memory of how perfectly she felt in my arms kept me company until morning.

A part of me was embarrassed to be so keenly aware of her arousal as her aura loudly broadcast it. Obviously, it pleased me a great deal that she should be attracted to me. But I wanted an emotional and spiritual connection with Ciara before we took things farther. Because sex with one of us was guaranteed to be phenomenal, I needed to feel like we had more than just lust as a foundation.

But that hug…

I'd never been one to have an addictive personality, until now. There was no question my mate would become my new drug. And I welcomed it.

We woke up almost at the same time. After quickly getting dressed, we met in the living area where I shamelessly stole a kiss from her, followed by a much-too-brief hug without wings. I

139

might have tried to make it linger a bit, but the bright lights of approaching souls forced me to put an end to it.

As an Obosian, I could see souls in a very wide radius even through walls and other obstacles that blocked people's normal sight. Even stealth shields could not fool me.

It turned out to be Aku inviting us to join the others for a quick breakfast before we each parted in our own direction. After the meal, the spectacle that greeted us outside blew us away. A handful of mounts awaited our companions and their escorts.

"These are Saguls," Aku explained. "They allow us to travel much greater distances a lot faster than if we run or swing on trees. The previous humans who came here said they resembled horses and behaved the same."

My mate nodded. "They certainly are the same size as a horse with a similar head. But the curves and shape of their bodies remind me more of a greyhound with the stripes of a zebra, the mane of a lion, and the horn of a unicorn, although three horns in their case."

Aku and a couple of other Kreelars whose name I didn't know stared at her with some of the confusion I shared. I knew of horses, lions, and unicorns, but greyhounds and zebras meant nothing to me. I suspected our hosts never heard of any of those other creatures either.

"They are beautiful!" Mehreen exclaimed with almost childish excitement. "Am I to understand we each get to ride one?"

Aku nodded. "Yes. I hope it will not be a problem?"

Ernst and Mehreen simultaneously shook their heads. "Horseback riding is compulsory training to be an Interstellar Doctor assigned to some of the primitive planets. It is often not possible or allowed by the locals for us to use shuttles. So we need to be able to adapt to whatever local transportation is available."

A wave of shame surged through me at the instant jealousy I felt when Ciara eyed her companions with envy while the Kreelars taught them how to ride the Saguls. I'd been counting the hours, minutes, and seconds until I finally got to hold her in my arms as we raced through the skies to our destination. There was no way I would let some pretty alien creature steal my moment of proximity with my mate.

Thankfully, our destination was much too far for us to ride that mount. In fact, our escort—Enre—left ahead last night so that he could make it by the morning. To my shock, right before the two other doctors and their escorts were about to set off, a female entered the inner courtyard carrying a small package. She handed it over to her leader who then came to me.

"Here, in case you need them. I doubt it, but I would hate for you to find yourself in a precarious situation with little means to defend yourself or your mate. I trust you will show wisdom as to *when* or *if* they should be used at all."

My jaw dropped upon seeing he had returned my blaster and my sword.

"Your trust honors me," I said in all sincerity as I took the weapons from him.

"As your integrity honors us. Safe travels to both of you. May your trip prove fruitful," Aku replied.

With one last nod, he turned around and hopped onto his own mount with incredible grace and dexterity that screamed of a lethal predator contained behind his controlled exterior. The extent of the importance of the work we were doing here and of the relationship we were currently developing with his people finally struck me.

Between their natural physical abilities and their newfound powers, the Kreelars would be extremely lethal foes on the battlefield. The fact that they hadn't achieved interstellar travel on their own meant nothing when clearly more advanced species interacted with them on multiple occasions in the past. Should one of those visitors—or worse still their friends—convince them to turn on us, things could get ugly quickly. Humans already gave them a reason to resent us. And their raid on the Gladius proved they could wreak havoc beyond their planetary borders if they wished.

I secured my weapons around my waist as we watched their mounts take off. Once they cleared the gate to the inner courtyard, I turned to look at my woman to find her staring at me with an air of pride that warmed me to the core. I hadn't done anything special for our host to show me this level of trust, but it pleased me that she should delight so much in it. Her pride confirmed she'd claimed me and saw us as an extension of each other.

"Let's go," I said in a soft voice.

Ciara nodded and passed the strap of her bag around her neck so that it would dangle sideways across her chest. Thankfully, Enre took with him most of the equipment and medicines that my mate required last night, strapping them on his mount.

A flame sparked in the pit of my stomach when she approached me and slipped her right arm around my shoulders when I picked her up like a bride. She settled her bag on top of her stomach before glancing back at me. Ciara's expression was unreadable, but a part of me believed she was also enjoying that proximity. It wasn't lust swirling deep within, but a tender possessiveness mixed with an odd sense of well-being to have her so close, in my arms, where she belonged.

"Here we go," I said gently before flapping my wings and taking flight.

As I ascended, Ciara gradually tensed, her hand around my shoulder gripping it more tightly while she pressed herself against me. She closed her eyes and buried her face in the crook of my neck. Tharmok take me! She felt so wonderful against me. But shame immediately crushed that warm feeling. As much as I loved that increased closeness with my mate, my protective instincts overrode my selfish needs.

"Calm, my Ciara," I said in a reassuring tone while emitting some of my *bakaan* to appease her.

A shiver coursed through her, and her hand tightened a bit more around my shoulder for a split second before she looked at me with an air of wonder.

"See? It's not so bad," I said gently.

She scrunched her face, then peeked warily below before closing her eyes and burying her face in my neck again. I chuckled and tightened my embrace around her before kissing the top of her head. I loved the soft and bouncy texture of her hair. It was like rubbing my face on a cloud.

For all that, my mate stole a few more glances at our surroundings as we flew, and her fear gradually subsided as the beauty of the landscape increasingly retained her attention.

"Flying is one of those things that I would be devastated to lose," I said wistfully as I spread my wings wide to glide over an air current. "It's the feeling of total freedom, of being in complete harmony with the world. Sometimes, I will just do wild acrobatics in the air for fun. My brother and I used to chase each other, issuing ridiculously dangerous dares to see who would veer off first as we barreled towards a rock wall, or down a cliff."

"Why do I have a feeling it didn't always end well?" Ciara asked with a disapproving tone.

"Because it didn't," I confirmed with a chuckle. "It's a good thing we have an accelerated regeneration on top of access to some of the best medicine available. I might have broken more than my fair share of bones because of reckless behavior. Reining in the wild antics of younglings once they get a true taste of speed can be challenging."

"So how do you learn how to fly?" she asked, peering at my

wings over my shoulders as I resumed flapping them. "Do they kick you out of a shuttle or drop you off a cliff?"

I snorted and shook my head. "Parents usually are the ones trying to stop the little ones from trying to fly too soon. Some reluctant children need a bit of coaxing to get going. But for most of us, the need to imitate our parents and elders is just too strong, not to mention the instinctive urge to just flap our wings. The only thing that keeps us from flight early on is the weakness of our muscles."

"Meaning you try to take off but can't flap hard enough?"

I nodded. "We'll rise a couple of centimeters and fall right back down. Needless to say that our surroundings get rather roughed up in the process. You'll find that dwellings with younglings tend to be very minimalist in their décor."

She chuckled. "Does that mean we will have to pad every surface in the house the day we have kids?" Ciara asked teasingly.

A powerful longing exploded in my chest at that thought. I definitely wanted children. Since we'd just met, that obviously had not been a discussion between us, but it pleased me beyond words that she appeared to be not only open to the idea, but even thinking it was a foregone conclusion that we would.

"It may not be a bad idea for certain things. If they are half as rambunctious as my brother and I used to be, it would be a wise course of action," I confessed, unrepentant.

"I have a hard time picturing you—or any Obosians for that matter—as troublemakers," she said with an amused expression. "You all always seem so proper and disciplined."

I laughed. "It's the quiet ones you should be the most wary of. Do not be fooled by that stuffy expression my people project. We're just like everyone else with our sense of humor, mischievous behavior, and vast emotional responses, including diva tantrums as humans like to describe them. We just tend to do it behind closed doors."

"Okay, now I totally want to see you having a full drama queen melt down," Ciara said, her eyes sparkling with mischief.

"Deliberately break the law, and you might get your wish," I said teasingly.

To my surprise, she didn't respond with a dismissive huff as I expected. She sobered and studied my features with surprising intensity.

"No, Amreth. I don't think that would do it. In truth, I believe only deep and devastating pain would ever cause you to lose control. But I have no doubt you will berate me until my ears fall off."

"That, I most certainly will. Why do I have a feeling that you are plotting to deliberately push my buttons?" I asked, eyeing her suspiciously.

The smug and shameless grin she gave me was all the answer I needed. Unable to resist, I leaned forward and kissed her forehead. She smiled and lifted her face to press a kiss on my cheek. My heart melted further, and I gave her a gentle squeeze before looking back down at our destination.

I gestured forward with my chin. "This is it, Jaln Village. We should land in the next five minutes."

Ciara nodded, although I didn't miss the tension that returned, stiffening her back.

"It will go well, and we won't be alone," I said reassuringly. "Enre is already there, waiting for us."

She smiled, its stiffness indicating that she was still apprehensive about the greeting that awaited us. I used a bit more of my *bakaan* to soothe her. However, I needed to be careful with how much of my calming aura I emitted as it could either make her groggy or greatly aroused. Under the circumstances, neither would be ideal.

As I began my descent, I assessed the village. Its size was comparable to Bryst, maybe even slightly bigger. It also appeared to be older, with a clear evolution from some of the older buildings to the newer ones. As in Aku's village, a series of houses had been separated from the rest of the village by an inner courtyard. I was beginning to suspect all the tribes had been forced to erect that separation to isolate their members who became ill once the disease began to spread.

Heading towards the open area that served as the village square, I altered my vision to assess the overall state of mind of the villagers. I would have hoped for far more blue halos, but the overall shade of yellow was pale enough to express wariness and not hostility. At least, as far as the majority of the people were concerned. A non-negligible number of them thankfully radiated an aura that usually reflected relief and even anticipation. Only one Kreelar had all my senses on high alert. They were angry. Unfortunately, I couldn't say whether that anger was aimed at us or at something completely unrelated.

To my own relief, I spotted Enre in the middle of the square waving at us in greeting and making sure we had seen him. Before our departure from Bryst, Aku confirmed through their radio system that all was well and that we were expected.

It bothered me to no end that Ciara still felt nervous—if not a little scared—as I landed in front of Enre. He was standing next to a Kreelar female with a potent aura of authority. She appeared to be older than Aku, and closer to my own age of forty-six. Like most of their females, she was tall, fairly muscular—but not in a masculine fashion—with light grayish beige fur and stunning blue eyes. Like Aku, a circlet adorned her forehead marking her as the leader of the tribe.

"There you are," Enre said with a big smile. "I'm glad you were able to quickly find your way."

Although he spoke those words in a jovial tone, I didn't miss the underlying relief in his voice. It struck me then that, as much as his people respected Aku's authority, they didn't necessarily share his views on everything. They had trusted his judgment in allowing me to fly my mate here on my own, but they had not equally shared his faith in me. It didn't hurt my feelings but increased my respect for Aku as a leader. Considering all that was at stake for them, it said a lot as to the level of loyalty his people bore him.

"The directions were perfect," I said gently as I put my mate down on her feet.

She adjusted the strap of her bag across her chest, ran her fingers through her hair to comb it after the wind seriously ruffled it and smiled politely at Enre and our hostess. Despite her lingering nervousness, the poise and calm demeanor she displayed filled my heart with pride. If not for my ability to read a limited range of emotions through one's aura, I would have been fooled by her apparent stoicism.

"Good, good! Amreth, Ciara, let me introduce you to Kald Vala, leader of Jaln Village. Vala, these are the off-worlders we told you about, Amreth and Ciara, who are working diligently to help save our people," Enre said, gesturing in turn at my mate and me.

"It is a pleasure to meet you, Amreth and Ciara," Vala said in a gentle voice. "The people of Jaln welcome you and thank you for whatever assistance you may provide with our plight. We—"

"*Samra telankay!*" an angry male voice suddenly shouted, interrupting her.

Unsurprisingly, my translation implant didn't recognize the language. However, I didn't need it to guess as to the nature of his words. He repeated them in a litany while charging towards us.

As one, the other villagers, who had gathered at a short distance around the square to witness our arrival, moved towards the male to restrain him. He was the angry aura I perceived during my descent. On instinct, I pushed Ciara behind me and spread my wings to hide her from view. They grabbed his arms and tried to hold him back while he struggled to free himself, shouting the same words in a loop. The depth of pain and sorrow in his voice and on his face told me all I needed to know.

The illness had taken a loved one.

Enre and Vala took a protective stance in front of us. That erased any lingering concerns I might have had as to their intentions or the safety of my mate in this village.

"Muti, calm yourself!" Vala commanded.

I placed my palm on each of Enre's and Vala's shoulders and gently pushed them aside so they would no longer obstruct my view of the shouting male. They cast a worried look at me, but I kept my eyes locked on Muti. I made no threatening gesture and instead cast a focused blast of my *bakaan* on him. As it had an area of effect, the people in his direct vicinity also felt some of my calming aura, tension bleeding out of them but also loosening their grip on him as they were trying to restrain him.

With him receiving the greater concentration of my power, his efforts to free himself weakened, his eyes slightly glazed over, and his angry shouts devolved into unintelligible words before turning into choked, teary sounds. My heart broke for him when he fell to his knees, his body rocked by violent sobs. Many of the people around him crouched by his side. They intertwined their tails with his, caressed his head and back, and whispered soothing words in their language.

Ciara pushed on my left wing, clearly wanting to see what was happening. With most of the threat now under control, I folded my wing and drew her to my side. Vala walked towards Muti, knelt directly in front of him, and pulled him into her embrace. She whispered to him in their language in an almost maternal fashion. I continued to send appeasing waves his way, and his sobs gradually faded. Vala pulled back, cupped his face with both hands, and wiped his tears with her thumbs.

She spoke a few more words to him. He nodded, his features

tortured by sorrow, despair, and something akin to guilt. Vala kissed his forehead then helped him up at the same time she rose to her feet. She gestured with her head at a couple of villagers. They promptly approached, each holding onto one of Muti's arms, and gently escorted him.

His tribe leader continued to stare at him walking away with a sad expression filled with pity before she turned towards us. As if following her cue, the rest of the villagers also shifted their attention back to us. A quick survey of their emotions reassured me that this incident had not turned them more hostile. But a definite hint of despair now infiltrated their emotions.

"Because of the disease your people brought to us, Muti is about to lose his mate. She's in a critical state, and his two infants are fighting for their lives," a female to our right said bitterly.

Despite the harshness of her tone, her anger wasn't aimed specifically at us, but at off-worlders in general and at the situation that was destroying their people. A single stern glance from Vala quieted her.

"No words can express the sorrow we feel for the tragedy that befell your people," Ciara said to the female in a soft voice filled with sympathy. "The few of us here are not your enemies. You have every right to be angry. None of this ever should have happened. We personally didn't cause this, but we will do everything in our power to make sure to stop it. It will not bring back those who have already been lost. We can only devote ourselves to prevent it from ever happening again."

"Can you?" Vala interjected with a sliver of defiance in her voice. "The sickness came back after the first humans said it was cured. Throughout the past decade, it kept coming back. It *always* comes back. And this time, it is hitting my tribe harder than it ever has before. Twenty-three of my people started showing signs just three days ago."

"The same day you arrived!" that same female said, the underlying accusation audible in her voice this time.

A few heads nodded while some other people in attendance muttered their agreements in their language. Another swift peek at their auras reassured me that they still were not turning hostile, although their anger was blossoming. There was nothing even remotely alarming yet, but I mentally prepared to act quickly to take my mate to safety should things turn sour.

Having learned my lesson from the first time they'd captured me, I made sure to bring back a psychic disruptor so they couldn't mess with my mind again. I didn't actually believe they would turn on us. But when it came to my woman's safety, I didn't take risks.

"Our arrival on that day is a pure coincidence and not linked in any way," Ciara said in a tone that brooked no argument. "The type of illness that is afflicting you only transmits through something you eat. It also takes a certain number of days before the first symptoms appear. So whatever caused this new wave, the sick tribe members ate it long before we arrived on Kestria."

"But what food?" Vala asked. "And why only them, not the rest of us?"

"That's what I am hoping you can help us determine," Ciara said. "I have many questions about it that will hopefully put us on the track to finding the source. But Enre has also brought test kits for us to detect if any of your food stores are currently contaminated as well as find out if anyone else among you has been infected but isn't showing signs yet."

"The tests were kept in a cool environment, as per your instructions," Enre said swiftly. "Should I go fetch them?"

"In a minute," Ciara said. "First, we need to set things up in a way that we can do this in an orderly fashion and ensure we keep track of everyone that has been tested. There's also a small questionnaire that we need them to fill."

"Yes," Enre said. "Ernst explained the procedure to me. We will set up the tables and chairs and have the forms ready."

"Thank you," Ciara said with a grateful smile before turning back to Vala. "Naturally, I would need to examine the patients. But I also would like to know if there's anything specific or unusual that happened to all of them over the past week or so."

She frowned as she pondered on the matter. "There isn't really anything we can think of. At first, we thought it might be due to their pilgrimage to Svast Temple. We all go there once a year for prayers and purification. The rituals last for a week before they head back."

"It sounds like they all ate something over there that made them ill," I said pensively.

Vala shook her head. "We initially assumed that something at the temple made them sick. It would have been a tragedy considering it is the holiest of places. Why would the gods punish us when we went to honor them? On average, seven or eight different tribes participate together. This time, there were nine tribes. As soon as the first person fell sick, we contacted the other villages whose members were present, but only one had people falling ill."

"Only one?" Ciara echoed pensively. "How long is the trip from here to the temple?"

"It is a two-day journey on foot through the forest in each direction," Vala replied, in a factual manner. "We could complete it faster, but the pilgrims stop along the way to cast blessing prayers over the land, to eat, and rest. They will camp for the night at the midway point."

"How long ago did they return from the temple?" Ciara asked, her voice intense.

Excitement would not have been an appropriate term to describe her emotions, but she clearly seemed to feel like she was onto something.

"They returned eight days ago, but only started showing symptoms five days later," Vala replied.

"This is critical information," Ciara said, while absent-mindedly glancing at Enre who was setting up the tables a short distance away with the help of other villagers. "It gives us a much narrower window as to when the infection occurred. The other village with infected people, how close is it located from here?"

"Not close at all," Vala said with discouragement. "That is another reason why we eliminated the possibility that the journey to the temple might be the cause. There is a wide river between Baki Village and us that they must cross using a boat. And once on the other side, they have a long way to travel on foot. They left on completely different routes."

"But they hunted for food along the way, right?" Ciara argued.

Vala nodded. "We hunt and forage along the way."

Sudden understanding struck me.

"So something they gathered in the forest or hunted along their respective paths was infected," I said pensively. "Any chance the animals could still be infected, or would they all be dead by now?"

"It really depends on whether the prion hurting the Kreelars is normal for the animal, fruit, or vegetable they consumed. If it is normal for them, then they will still be thriving in that area. But if it's not, then we would need to find one that is still alive."

"It would take us a bit more than half a day—approximately twelve hours—to run to the temple on foot, and maybe seven to eight riding a Sagul," Vala replied.

"Which means it would take me barely two to three hours each way," I said.

"It should take me about six hours to test everyone as well as the food. So that would work perfectly," Ciara said with an enthusiastic spark in her beautiful eyes.

But even as I spoke those words, a wave of unease swept through me. I didn't really want to leave my mate here by herself. Granted, Enre would protect her, and I didn't doubt the same from Vala. The aura of the people around us had gradually lost some of its wary edge, more and more having streaks of blue indicating they were relaxing around us. But it still unnerved me. At the same time, I could do this much faster than they could.

Oblivious to my inner turmoil, Ciara began typing a few instructions on her bracer, seconds before my own beeped from an incoming message.

"I've sent data regarding the prions we're looking for," Ciara said. "I would need you to do an aerial scan of the flora and fauna between here and there. There's a good chance that your bracer will not be able to detect the prions without actually testing a sample. But it will be able to pick up on any anomalies between plants and animals of the same species."

"So it will flag any animal or group of plants that are abnormal compared to others of the same type," I said to confirm I properly got her meaning while uploading the new data to my scanner.

"Exactly," Ciara said, beaming at me with that same glimmer of pride in her eyes that did the sweetest thing to me.

I had never thought of myself as dumb, but simply as someone of standard intelligence. And yet, over the past day, my mate had increasingly made me feel almost like a genius. I was discovering a new passion in trying to solve these little mysteries.

I smiled before casting a wary glance around the crowd. To my surprise, Ciara immediately sensed my discomfort.

"I will be fine in your absence," she said in a reassuring tone. "Enre and Kald Vala will make sure I'm safe."

"No harm will come to your mate," Vala confirmed with a firmness that did wonders to alleviate some of my concerns. "There can be no greater dishonor than for a host to allow their guests to be mistreated in their home. On my honor, and with my life, I pledge to keep your mate safe for so long as she is within our walls and until she is returned to Bryst."

"Thank you, Vala," I said with sincere gratitude.

I turned to Ciara and gently caressed her cheek. To my delight, she pressed her palm to the back of my hand and leaned into my touch. Unable to resist, I leaned forward and kissed her. She returned it with a tenderness that messed with my head. Fighting the urge to draw her into my embrace and deepen the kiss, I straightened and reluctantly let my hand drop.

"I'll return soon."

"Be safe out there," she replied with an encouraging smile.

I nodded, cast one last meaningful glance at Vala, then took flight.

The first hour proved totally uneventful. My scanner collected data on the flora and fauna below without picking up anything unusual. Thanks to previous sanctioned visits to Kestria by Elias Jacobs' teams to work with the Sangoth, the UPO already had a pretty extensive database regarding this planet's plants and creatures. With everything checking out so far, I allowed myself to revel in the untainted beauty of this new world.

As much as I hated how those foolish doctors tragically derailed the lives of these tribes by their careless actions, I could understand the temptation that led to this. This place truly was a paradise with countless perfect settings for romantic getaways. I spotted so many along the way where I would love to take Ciara for a proper courtship. To my shame, I caught myself wondering if it would be acceptable to have such an escapade before our departure. As we wouldn't be bringing anything alien into their ecosystem, surely it would be fine?

But all such wandering thoughts flew right out of my head when my scanner beeped. A look at the interface indicated a number of moving orange spots of varying sizes, which belonged to animals. I looked up and altered my vision to peer at the aura of those creatures. A mix of shock and excitement surged through me upon seeing the grayish burgundy color of their auras. This corresponded to a state of mindless rage. Those creatures were rabid.

Who or what infected them?

I circled around the area, marking the coordinates on the map of my scanner while attempting to see how far the infected creatures had roamed. I also noticed that not every animal registered as rabid. In fact, only a handful did. Although I only quickly surveyed the results, it struck me as odd that not all the animals of the same species displayed the symptoms. I couldn't tell if it was because they were still in the early stages of the disease, if they hadn't been infected yet, or if they were somehow immune.

But that would be for more competent people than me to assess.

To my surprise, as I traveled farther to the west of the path I had been following, a dense patch of red appeared at the edge of my scan radius. It was located on the other side of the river, which initially made me hesitate. Intrigued, and not wanting to leave any stone unturned, I crossed the large body of water. Once over the western shore, I tapped an inquiry into the scanner. My jaw dropped when a small holographic display popped up from my bracer with additional info indicating an intrusive plant.

"How is this plant intrusive?" I asked my device.

"This plant does not belong to Kestria's ecosystem," the artificial intelligence replied. "It is a 94% match with two different species of berries from Earth: strawberries and raspberries."

I muttered a curse under my breath even as a thrill coursed through me. Granted, the berries were rather far from the location where the infected creatures roamed. But if it also took a while before the symptoms manifested themselves, the animals would have wandered off in the days after they consumed it.

Across the river?

That didn't add up. I continued flying farther west until the scanner stopped picking up more of the berries. But it did detect a few sick animals, although in far smaller numbers than the ones I had found on the east shore. I backtracked and continued nearly a kilometer to the east to see if I could find more berries but failed to do so.

For a moment, I considered picking up a few samples then decided against it. I wasn't a scientist and didn't know what potential consequences my actions could have against the Kreelars. It didn't matter that Ciara said that the infection only occurred through consumption. These people were suffering enough without me gambling further with their lives by taking risks. At least, I knew specifically where they could be harvested under proper safety and containment procedures. Instead, I flew down to some of the largest patches and took close-up pictures.

With time ticking away, I came back to the main path the pilgrims had taken and pursued the journey to the Svast Temple. A haunting melody reached me long before the forest opened in front of me to reveal its splendor. I didn't need to know that it was indeed a holy place. It radiated divine energy. I suspected some of it could be explained by physics, but a part of me believed that people could imbue an area with either positive or negative energy when enough of it was expanded repeatedly over a long period of time.

The temple itself had been carved directly into a mountain face framed by a waterfall. The tall pillars and massive doors were intricately adorned with carved symbols in a foreign language my translator didn't know. There didn't seem to be a direct access to the front entrance by land. One had to walk through the water to reach the stairs. I presumed it was a form of cleansing ritual before being allowed in.

And exactly what appeared to be happening right now. At least a hundred pilgrims of all ages had gathered in the water.

The youngest stood closest to the stairs, which was the shallowest part. The older people took position in the deeper part, with water reaching up to the middle of their waists. They formed a continuous chain with everyone on the same row holding hands. The people standing at the end of each row would link to the row in front or behind by holding the tail of the person ahead of them.

They were chanting while not exactly performing a dance, but they were stepping from side to side, front and back, and occasionally tilting their heads at various angles in a synchronous fashion. In front of them, standing at the top of the four stairs to the entrance, three Kreelars also sang while performing wider gestures with their arms and hands. They were wearing sleeveless robes with faceless masks that made it impossible to know their gender for sure.

I wanted to fly in closer to get a better look and further enjoy the fascinating proceedings but turned around instead. Although Vala didn't tell me to steer clear of the temple, it felt sacrilegious to spy on their devotions and intrude in their shrine. Anyway, I was only here to determine whether more infected plants or animals could be found in the area. The fact that I didn't seemed to confirm why only a small number of the previous pilgrims had been infected instead of all.

Although I hurried on my journey back, I still ended up reaching Jaln Village after an absence of nearly eight hours. Despite feeling tired and famished, the emotion that dominated within me as I began my descent towards the square was relief to find Ciara rushing towards its center with a broad smile.

Relief also radiated from the other villagers, and especially from Enre and Vala. I could only imagine how much the trust the people had in them would have been undermined had I not returned.

Ciara throwing herself into my arms as soon as I landed did

the most wondrous thing to me. I could get used to this type of warm welcome every day for the rest of my life. It touched me all the more that it wasn't fear and the need for protection that prompted it, but genuine joy at simply having me back.

"Welcome back, Amreth. We feared you might have gotten lost," Vala said in a teasing tone, though I didn't miss the underlying lingering worry that she had genuinely felt.

"I did not, but I did wander off much farther than initially intended to investigate some anomalies," I replied before turning to my mate. "I believe you're going to like this."

With a couple of taps on the interface of my bracer, I called up the pictures I took and displayed them on the holographic screen that deployed over it. Ciara gasped, her eyes popping with excitement. I swiftly recounted what I encountered, between the rabid animals and the patches of berries.

"You were wise not to bring samples," Ciara said absentmindedly while browsing through the scan reports before glancing at Vala. "Are you familiar with those fruits? Are these a part of your diet?"

She shook her head and looked at them with a confused expression shared by Enre.

"I have never seen those berries before. They certainly aren't anywhere near the areas that we hunt or forage in."

"It's not really surprising," I said pensively. "Without the scanner, I likely wouldn't have noticed their existence. They were not visible from above, and even after I landed, I had to lift a few leaves to expose them."

Ciara pursed her lips and slowly nodded as she reflected on my words. "That's pretty common for wild strawberries. This explains a few things. Ideally, we would have a field lab directly in that area. Maybe we could set something up using your shuttle?"

I quieted my instinctive desire to say yes and glanced questioningly at Vala. My heart sank when she stared at us with a closed off expression.

"I will discuss the matter with the other Kalds," she said in a non-committal fashion. "Anyway, the hour is drawing too late for you to return to Bryst. You must be tired and hungry. Come, rest and eat. You will all sleep here tonight. In the morning, we will have a decision."

CHAPTER 11
AMRETH

As much as I understood their reluctance, I hated feeling shackled. By now, I felt as if we had proven ourselves enough to be given even more freedom to move around and do what was needed to solve this crisis. Seeing no point in making waves, I went along with it.

They led us to a small house. Surprisingly, it wasn't in the inner courtyard but in the village proper. All the ones in the courtyard were already full with the infected pilgrims. Two males were walking out as we approached. Only once inside did I realize that they had brought food for me. To my utter embarrassment, my stomach loudly expressed its approval, making everyone chuckle.

"Enjoy your meal. We will see you in the morning," Vala said.

We thanked her and watched her leave. As soon as the door closed behind her, I removed from my belt the weapons that I thankfully didn't have to use today and glanced at the right wall where the door to the guest bedroom had been located in Bryst. Finding none, I jerked my head around to look at the opposite wall. Only then did I notice that this dwelling didn't have a guest room.

"Tharmok's blood. It seems there's only one bedroom. I can go ask if they have a bigger dwelling," I said, scratching my nape. "Or I could sleep on the couch."

"Absolutely not!" Ciara said, looking at me as if I'd gotten hit once too many on the head. "Have you looked at the size of you compared to that couch? Are you itching to sleep with your knees pressed to your forehead?"

I snorted and shook my head, almost feeling like a child being scolded by his mother.

"We're grown adults, not rabid animals. I'm sure we can share a bed and behave like civilized people. But if it makes you uncomfortable, I will let you have the bed, and I'll sleep on the couch."

"Absolutely not!" I said, echoing her previous words but with total outrage. "I will not sleep comfortably in a bed while my mate is cramped up on a couch."

"Exactly!" she said with an exaggerated air of relief that I was finally seeing the light. "See how outrageous that felt to you? Why would you assume I would be fine doing that to you?"

I scrunched my face at her, failing to find an appropriate answer.

"We both need proper rest. So this matter is settled. Now let's feed you," Ciara said in a tone that brooked no argument as she waved for me to take a seat at the table.

As a noble Lord and Warden of my own Sector, I couldn't remember the last time anyone ordered me around. The only person that had me jumping to attention with a single word was my father. Then again, Kronos's sire had a way of making your insides liquify with a mere look. And yet, behind his stern and intimidating exterior, Lord Aramon was the sweetest of males with the dryest sense of humor. You never knew if he was chastising or teasing you until you caught his very discreet smug smirk.

I smiled, amused by her take charge attitude, and settled at the table. She didn't sit but immediately started digging in the three serving trays they had brought us, piling on all the meat she could find onto a plate, which she then settled in front of me.

"I told them you weren't into bird food," Ciara said teasingly.

I burst out laughing, my chest warming with affection as she grabbed only a couple of vegetables with a piece of roasted white meat before settling across the table from me.

"That's all you're eating?" I asked, frowning at the tiny amount on her plate.

She shrugged. "I already ate. I'm just joining you because it sucks to eat on your own while your companion is staring at you. Now dig in. You're not starving on my watch."

I nodded again, grateful for yet another thoughtful gesture from her, and complied. To say I was famished couldn't begin to describe the hollowness in my stomach. Flying required a lot of energy. As grateful as I was for the food—which was actually quite delicious—I hungered for a much different type of sustenance. My mouth watered at the thought of how her emotions would taste. She couldn't begin to imagine how much more filling and satisfying feeding from her would be.

Attentive as ever, Ciara didn't strike a conversation right away, allowing me to get a few bites in to appease the most brutal pangs. I all but inhaled the first few chunks of meat. Although she tried to hide it, I didn't miss the amusement in her eyes as she discreetly peered at me.

"I was worried about you," I said at last after swallowing another mouthful. "Everything went well in my absence?"

She nodded. "Thanks for the concern, but there was no need. Everyone was very kind to me. Anyway, Enre and Vala totally went into Mama bear protective mode over me.

Keeping me safe was truly a matter of pride and honor for them."

"I'm glad to hear there were no incidents," I said while cutting a piece of meat.

"Actually, there was some partially good news and a minor incident," Ciara amended. "The semi-good news is that I was able to put Muti's wife in a semi-stasis. It keeps the disease from progressing. I've injected her with some nanobots that are targeting the prions killing her and eradicating them. It's a very slow process. But it seems to be working."

"Will it cure her?" I asked, perking up.

She shook her head. "No. It's just going to bring her down to a less critical state where her body will hopefully be able to fight back the prions while it adjusts to the changes of its evolution. Their two children have taken really well to the medicine, so I'm keeping my fingers crossed."

"That's wonderful news. I cannot imagine a greater gift for that poor male. His pain was so vivid, I could almost touch it. What you and your team are doing is phenomenal," I said with deep admiration and respect.

She smiled shyly. "Thank you. But don't forget that you're now a part of that team, too. And with your discovery today, we could get even closer to success."

"Like you said, fingers crossed," I replied gently. "But you mentioned an incident?"

Ciara nodded. "After we finished testing everyone—and thankfully found no other cases—we began to administer the vaccine to all the people who had not been infected before. Two of them were adamant about not being injected."

I pursed my lips and nodded pensively. "That's not surprising. Frankly, I expected far more resistance from a greater number of people. But you cannot force someone to receive that type of treatment."

"I know. All I can do is explain the benefits, but in the end, it remains their choice. Hopefully, seeing the others are fine and do not suffer negative effects from it may end up changing their minds. Either way, I pray that we can actually find a treatment or eradicate the source."

"You think the berries are the source?" I asked.

"With its foreign origin, it's extremely likely. There should be no strawberries on Kestria. From the events that Sora and Aku recounted to us, the doctors had been eating by the river. After Sora bit the man, they stunned her and then ran away. They never came back to pick up the food that they left behind. Neither did the Kreelars."

"So the local fauna feasted on it," I said with sudden understanding.

"Exactly. Berries are a nightmare for this because each one has a very high concentration of seeds. Those seeds will pass through the digestive system and will often come out intact in the stool," Ciara explained. "Of all the fruits they could have come up with, it had to be the one that is very easy to spread and grow. Strawberries only need wet soil, some fertilizers, and plenty of sun."

"All conditions that were met," I replied pensively.

"Yes. Whether the animals that ate them got sick and regurgitated the seeds, or simply passed them through their stools, they disseminated them. I don't know what quantity of berries there were or how many different animals ate them, but the location you showed me is very far from the area where this initial incident occurred."

"So it's spreading. But how did it appear on the other side of the river?"

"In the morning, we will need to do a thorough breakdown of their wildlife's food chain. The small rodents and mammals that ate the berries would only travel so far with them. We have to assume that some birds also ate those fruits, and they travel much greater distances. And then you have the larger predators who feed on both the birds and the small mammals. If any of those animals tend to roam or migrate, they would move along with them."

"It's been nearly ten years though," I said with a frown. "Wouldn't it have spread a lot farther and wider?"

My mate shook her head. "Not necessarily. These types of things tend to be exponential. It starts small, with one little patch here and then another one there. But the more patches you have the more creatures feed from it, and the more they spread it. Not every seed released in the wild will take root. The probabilities simply increase with the number of occurrences."

"Can we wipe out all those berry patches?" I asked while shamelessly refilling my plate, this time with a mix of sides and vegetables.

She frowned and put down her fork on the side of her empty plate. "It is extremely difficult, and often impossible to fully eradicate an invasive plant. Once it starts spreading, there's always some seed somewhere that will have escaped detection, or that is sitting in some creature's digestive system just waiting to be released when and where you least expect it. So as much as you manage to cull their number, they almost always come back. It becomes a permanent chore to control their propagation."

"So there are no solutions," I said, crestfallen.

"There are mitigation measures that we can use. But it will take quite a bit of time of thorough testing to make sure we will not harm the local flora or fauna in the process. We need to study all the animals in the area, both those who were infected and those who appear immune. We have solved similar problems in the past with nanobots designed specifically to prevent a certain type of protein from attaching to specific cells, keeping them from reproducing and thereby killing the organism."

"That sounds like the perfect solution!" I said in a self-evident manner.

"It is if that cell is unique enough not to be found in other life forms in the area. We do not want to accidentally exterminate other plants or animals in the process," she explained.

"Right, I didn't think of that. That's why *you* are the scientist," I said teasingly.

She smiled. "We each have our skills and purpose. You were fantastic today. From the way you made me feel safe during the flight here despite my fear of heights, to how you help appease that poor male, when others would have just responded to his aggression with violence. And how you handled the mission we entrusted you with. You went above and beyond thoroughly investigating wider than the original path agreed upon."

"It was just common sense," I said, my voice sounding a little grumpy when it was in fact prompted by shyness at her praises.

"Believe me, common sense is far too often a rare commodity. Do not underestimate yourself. And for the record, I don't think you noticed, but you earned a great deal of respect by not approaching the temple. I saw the look in their eyes when you said you turned around. No words can describe how freaking proud of you I am."

My chest warmed, and I caught myself extending a hand towards her over the table. To my delight, she placed hers in mine without hesitation.

"The feeling is mutual, Ciara. I guess I didn't notice what you saw because I was too busy noticing how they were reacting towards *you*. When we arrived this morning, their auras radiated distrust and despair. When I returned tonight, I saw relief but especially hope. What you and your colleagues are doing is saving an entire species. There could be no greater honor for me than to be a part of this."

"And you certainly are proving to be an important part, in more ways than one," she said with a smile.

I gave her hand a gentle squeeze and caressed its back with my thumb before releasing her.

"Well, I sweated all day. I should go shower," I said, rising to my feet and picking up the empty dishes on the table.

Ciara grabbed the other ones and followed me to the sink so that we could wash them. There was something oddly intimate to us performing such a menial task together.

"Do you want me to wash your wings?" my mate offered, as I finished drying the last plate.

My stomach did a backflip, and I hid how strongly her words affected me by plastering a taunting expression on my face.

"I would need to be naked while you do that."

She shrugged, raised an eyebrow, and held my gaze unwaveringly. "Yes, and? I'm a medical doctor. There isn't much I haven't already seen. So unless it makes you uncomfortable, or if Obosian nudity is somehow lethal for humans, then I have no problem with it," she deadpanned.

"Lethal nudity? That's a first. But no, seeing me undressed will not cause you any harm."

"Then, it is settled, big boy. To the shower we go!"

"Big boy?!" I exclaimed with a mix of amusement and disbelief.

"I said what I said," she replied in a singsong voice while strutting her way ahead towards the door to the back.

Following in her wake, I removed my breastplate and put it down on the counter before exiting the house. She kicked off her shoes and turned on the water. To my shock, Ciara stripped out of her own clothes, placing them neatly in a pile next to the recessed shelves that contained the clean towels. When she turned around to face me in her glorious nudity, she found me staring at her, mouth agape, and my hands frozen on the waist of my pants with the magnetic clasps half opened.

"What are you doing? Take it off!" she said, gesturing with her right hand in a way that meant for me to get a move on. "And don't gape at me like that. I'm not getting my clothes drenched while washing your wings, and I need to shower, too."

That snapped me out of my daze, and I promptly complied. Despite her direct and no-nonsense tone and demeanor, I didn't miss the sliver of self-consciousness in her eyes. A billion words pressed themselves on my tongue. I wanted to tell her how gorgeous she was, just as much as I wanted to ask if that meant I got to wash her back for her, too.

A part of me felt that pointing out that her stripping changed the dynamic between us would only make it awkward. But another part believed that not acknowledging it would make it even weirder, like when something was so bad you would rather convince yourself it wasn't happening instead of dealing with it.

"Apologies. Your beauty addled my brain," I said at last. "But you make a fair point. Practical and efficient. I approve!"

Although she snorted and made a face at me, I didn't miss the subtle way her shoulders relaxed. I wanted to believe I'd handled it adequately.

"Those are but some of my countless qualities," she said, flicking her hair over her shoulder in a theatrical way that had me laughing. "But thanks for noticing."

I removed my boots and then stepped out of my pants as a wave of nervousness washed over me. It seemed silly for me to worry about what she might think of my appearance. I was extremely fit, and doubted she would find my body lacking. However, did she know what an Obosian penis looked like? Would it turn her on or distress her?

I straightened, and stood facing her, my chin lifted with a hint of defiance. Ciara didn't look fazed or distraught by the spectacle before her. With incredible boldness, she let her gaze slowly roam over me with a possessiveness that had my blood rushing to my groin. Although undeniably appreciative, there was nothing lurid or objectifying in the way she admired me.

"You truly are a stunning male," Ciara said almost wistfully.

"I'm glad you think so," I added, feeling inexplicably timid.

She quickly plated her hair into a single braid which she

wrapped around in a bun, cleverly weaving the end through her hair so that it would stay up. The gesture had her perky breasts slightly push forward, drawing my eyes to the dark areolas and taut little buds. They would look even more delicious with a golden piercing.

As if reading the thoughts coursing through my mind, my mate pointed at my nether region.

"From the moment I met you, I wondered how many piercings you would have and where they would be located," she said in a soft voice.

I glanced down at my cock that was standing half erect. As soon as she had begun stripping, my shaft stiffened. It didn't bother me that she should have this undeniable proof of my growing arousal. While it could be perceived as offensive, I believed the absence of visible desire on my part when she was fully naked before me for the first time would have been far more problematic.

"I can say without hesitation that every single adult Obosian, male *and* female, has at least a couple of piercings or implants in their private parts," I said with amusement.

"Judging by yours, it's a lot more than a couple," Ciara said, scrunching her face in an unreadable fashion.

I glanced down at my cock, my gaze roaming over the two rows of three round studs on each side of my length, near the base, the barbels at the beginning of the shaft, the one on my head, and the two additional studs right below the glans.

"Indeed. I have ten," I said in a factual manner before studying her features. "Does it bother you?"

To my relief, she shook her head without hesitation.

"Not at all. It's actually kind of hot," she added, looking a bit embarrassed. "Any others?"

"On my tongue," I replied.

She nodded, her face taking on a mischievous expression. "I know. I felt that one."

That made me chuckle, but it also made me want to kiss her deeply again. Chasing that wandering thought right out of my mind, I allowed my gaze to freely—and somewhat greedily—roam over the perfection that was her body.

"A few of them would look extremely hot on you as well," I mused aloud.

To my shock, Ciara immediately stiffened, a frown creasing her brow as she shook her head.

"That's going to be a hard pass for me," she said in a tone that brooked no argument.

Considering her previous comment about finding them hot on me, that response took me aback.

"Why?" I asked carefully.

"While I genuinely appreciate and admire body modification on others—at least when it's well done—I personally do not want any on myself. My pierced lobes for earrings are as far as I go. I don't have anything against it, but I like my physical appearance the way it is," she said in a gentle, almost cautious fashion.

"I understand," I said softly.

She shifted on her feet, looking a little uneasy. "Does that upset you?"

My brow shot up in surprise. "Upset me? Not at all. A little disappointed, maybe. And even that feels like too strong a word. I love the aesthetics of piercings as it is an intrinsic part of my culture, but not an essential one. At the end of the day, it is your body. No one gets to dictate what you do with it. So long as you are happy, that's all that matters."

"But will that make me less attractive to you?" she insisted.

"Ciara, your physical appearance is not your main appeal. The light of your soul is. And yours mesmerizes me. Nothing can ever supersede that. You are beautiful just the way you are. And that will not change, even in sixty years, when we're both all wrinkled, and I have a wine belly."

She burst out laughing. "You mean a beer belly?"

"Yeah, that," I said in an amused tone. "Or whatever humans call that pregnant-looking stomach your males get in their later years."

Still chuckling, my mate stared at my flat stomach with a wistful expression. "My grandfather has a rather impressive one that my granny calls his crystal ball. Whenever he asks her something silly, she starts rubbing it and peers into it as if to find the answer within before responding with something totally ridiculous."

It was my turn to burst out laughing as I tried to visualize the scene. "That will be us in a few years, I guess."

She grinned and shook her head. "Doubtful. I've seen older Obosians. You all remain obnoxiously fit through your twilight years… not that I'm complaining. But let's get you under the water."

I nodded and swiftly twisted my own long hair into a bun so that it wouldn't get wet. I wasn't spending hours trying to let it dry naturally right before bed.

We stepped under the water to wet ourselves. My eyes immediately zeroed in on the way the water trickled down her skin. The most irrational envy surged through me, wishing it was my hands and my tongue gliding over her like that. I wanted to lick each bead that lingered on the dark silk that I ached to explore.

As there was a single bar of soap, we took turns using it, working up a lather before exchanging it. Watching her rub the soap on her body, especially on her breasts and between her thighs had me rock hard in seconds. Although she pretended not to see it, I didn't miss the smug smirk that discreetly quirked the corner of her mouth.

But two could play that game.

Biding my time, I gestured with my chin at her back.

"Want help?" I offered.

"Yes, please," she replied, a strange light burning in her grayish-brown eyes.

She turned around, and my eyes zeroed in on the plump curves of her behind. Tharmok take me! It should be illegal for anything to be so damn enticing. I couldn't decide if I was aching more to grab her cheeks with both hands or drop to my knees and take a bite. Her behind demanded to be bitten.

Reining myself in, I forced myself to look back up as I began to wash her back. Far from distracting me, that only made me even harder. Her skin was so soft, so warm under my touch. Feeling her shiver as my hands glided down her back on each side of her spine had my cock jerk in response. Despite her attempts at remaining stoic, the scent of her arousal wafted to me.

For a split second, I considered growing bolder and slipping my hands around her front to tease her nipples. A part of me believed she wouldn't oppose such an act, maybe even welcome it. But another deemed it more prudent to hold back. It wasn't just the fact that I didn't want her to think me too presumptuous or disrespectful. I needed Ciara to know that she could trust me not to try and seize any opportunity to take advantage of her, especially in a vulnerable setting.

I finished, dropped my hands—with much reluctance at that—and took a step back. My mate immediately turned around to face me, her face unreadable. Her taut nipples, standing to attention, almost seemed to be angrily shouting their dismay at being so utterly ignored and neglected.

Acting nonchalantly, I resumed soaping myself as she stepped under the water to rinse off. Eyes locked with hers, I started washing my cock and my testicles, silently daring her to avert her eyes. The lascivious expression that descended over her features had a bead of precum seep out, thankfully hidden by the soap.

My stomach did a triple somersault when she suddenly stepped away from the water, closing the narrow distance between us to take the soap from me. She was so close, every time she breathed in, the movement of her chest had her nipples brushing against me. For one foolish second, I thought she was going to lean in and kiss me. Instead, she waved the washcloth I had not noticed in her hand.

"Ready for your wings," she said in a singsong voice.

The taunting glimmer in her eyes made it clear she had noticed my disappointment and was reveling in the power she had over me.

"Thank you," I said in a controlled voice while fighting the urge to spank that delicious bottom of hers.

She proceeded to wash my wings in an efficient, but too swift manner to my liking. When she dried them previously, Ciara had taken her sweet time, making the pleasure-torture last to both our enjoyment and dismay. She had clearly wanted to touch my wings with her bare hands, just as I had longed for her to do so.

These games of propriety we play sure are annoying.

And yet, I didn't truly mind them. They built the tension and anticipation. By the time that desire was fulfilled at last, it would make the experience all the more special.

"So how come such a fine specimen of masculinity like you was still single?" Ciara suddenly asked while cleaning the front of my left wing.

I snorted and gave her a sideways glance, more flattered than I would ever admit.

"The obvious answer is that I had not found you yet," I replied teasingly. "But as you can imagine, living on Molvi makes it more challenging to find a partner."

"Right. A prison-planet doesn't exactly sound like an ideal dating-scene," she replied. Although her tone was light and a little playful, I noticed the troubled expression that fleeted over her features.

"It's not," I conceded, "but not for the reasons you think.

Contrary to what most people think, Molvi isn't just one big scary place infested with murderers and psychopaths as well as an army of bloodthirsty, terrifying beasts. All of that is definitely there but contained within each of our Sectors. The rest of the planet is just as beautiful as the wilderness you enjoy here. We do have a capital city with shopping malls, restaurants, entertainment, schools, and various businesses that cater to the day-to-day needs of the people and families who live there."

"Oh, my God! Really?!" Ciara exclaimed.

I couldn't help a smile at the relieved and hopeful tone in her voice.

"Yes, my mate. No Warden would be able to have a family if they couldn't enjoy a normal, safe, and comfortable life there. The problem is that most of the people are already married, or the younger offspring of those couples. Schools on Molvi only go so far. Once the student is ready to move on to more advanced education like a university degree, they usually go back to Vargos, our home world."

"Right. I can see that."

"Obviously, I traveled frequently back home and was invited to many events where my parents tried some matchmaking," I said, unable to withhold an aggravated eye roll that had Ciara chuckling. "My people are also extremely big on ostentatious parties where they flaunt their mansions and wealth on Molvi, which present opportunities to meet a potential partner. But for all its comforts and beauty, life on a prison planet isn't for everyone."

"It has to be very limiting for certain professions," she conceded while circling around me to start washing the back of my wings.

It bothered me that she should do so just then. I wanted to see her face as we broached that sensitive topic. In a couple of weeks —a month at most I hoped—we would be able to get back to our own lives. As much as I wanted to accommodate her, my situation made it to where she would have to be the one to follow. Was that a deal breaker?

"Would that be a problem for you?" I asked softly.

My chest constricted when she didn't answer right away. I glanced over my shoulder to peer at her. To my relief, she didn't look distressed or uncomfortable but appeared to be assessing a few things.

"I don't really care where I live, to be honest," she replied at last. "In recent years, I have shifted more to research, which I can perform almost anywhere so long as there is an advanced enough laboratory. But even that requires occasional travel. Sometimes, we are gone for a few weeks, up to a couple of months."

"We can work that out," I replied swiftly. "Getting you access to a top-notch laboratory would not be a problem. We have a couple of high-end research facilities already on Molvi. As for your traveling, if Kayog and Linsea managed to have such a successful marriage despite each of them having to go to every end of the galaxy, I'm sure we can do it as well."

Her lips stretched into a wistful smile, her face softening with a dreamy expression. "They are so perfect together. I've seen many couples deeply in love even after many years of marriage. But I don't think I've ever been in the presence of two people in such perfect harmony with each other. I'm not the jealous type, but I want what they have so badly."

"We will," I said with conviction. "We are soulmates."

She smiled and finished washing my wings before pushing me under the water to rinse.

"Who is taking care of your Sector right now?" Ciara asked, reaching for a towel.

"My best friend, Kronos. He's the Warden of the Sector right next to mine. My cousin Arthas is also on standby to assist if needed. But I'm feeling guilty about my absence," I admitted sheepishly, while extending a hand to take the towel from her.

To my surprise, my mate ignored my hand and proceeded to dry my chest. Although stunned, I didn't push back.

"Is it a serious problem? Could it undermine your status as Warden of your Sector?" she asked with a sliver of worry.

That touched me more than I could express. I didn't need to be a genius to know she had reservations about settling on Molvi. Someone else might have rejoiced at the thought of my extended absence possibly making me lose my position so that they wouldn't be stuck moving there with me. That her concern should immediately be about me said a lot about her.

"No," I replied in a reassuring tone. "It would take something extremely serious for a Warden to be removed. It is more that I hate being an inconvenience to others. Kronos already has his hands full with his own Quadrants not to mention the fact that his human mate is well advanced in her pregnancy with their first child. I should be there supporting and calming him rather than being a burden."

I barely managed to finish that sentence, my brain getting distracted when Ciara poked her index finger through the plush fabric of the towel to carefully trace around the barbell piercing in my left nipple. The way my mate circled around the areola left no doubt in my mind that she was purposefully teasing me.

She deliberately avoided making eye contact as she finished drying my chest. She brought the towel down to my pelvis. For half a beat, I believed she would pursue the journey down to my cock. I held my breath, bracing for it, only for the wretched female to swipe the towel to the right as she circled to the side. The smug, borderline malicious grin that stretched her lips made me want to put her across my knees and spank her raw.

"Maybe you're not being an actual burden," she said nonchalantly while drying my arm. "If he is so nervous about their first child, you might be doing his wife a huge favor. If he's constantly fussing over her or panicking any time she so much as sneezes, she might be itching to knock him unconscious so that she can get some peace. Keeping him busy might be a blessing."

I snorted and slowly nodded. "Malaya might have yelled at him once or twice about how she was just pregnant and not invalid," I replied with a chuckle.

"See?" Ciara said triumphantly. "But I get it. I also hate when my workload ends up getting dumped on someone else because circumstances make it impossible for me to handle it myself."

An involuntary purr rolled out of my throat when she began drying my back. She likely accidentally rubbed that sensitive spot right at the upper corner near my spine where my wing attached to my back. I wouldn't actually call it erogenous and yet rubbing the muscle right there was always highly pleasurable. It wasn't the type of pleasure that would make you climax, but the type that made you become languid like during a full body massage.

"Oooh! Someone liked that!" Ciara said smugly.

"Someone certainly did," I said, my voice sounding deeper. "That's my weak spot. It's extremely relaxing to have it massaged."

Ciara snorted. "Well, that was subtle…"

"Whatever do you mean?" I asked in an overly innocent voice that didn't fool her in the least.

To my shock—and utter delight—she kneaded that muscle with a bare hand, sending a violent shiver down my spine, followed by another rumbling purr, almost a moan. My mate chuckled, pursuing her ministrations for a few more seconds. I almost whimpered when she stopped.

"Weak spot duly noted. Expect me to shamelessly abuse it to get you to cave in to whatever unreasonable demands I may make in the future," she said with an unrepentant grin.

I laughed. "For that, yes, I would likely give you my soul."

She laughed and resumed drying my wing.

"But what of you, Ciara? Why was such a beautiful, smart,

and successful woman like you still single?" I asked.

"I was engaged to a douchebag, who fooled me for the longest time. After dumping him, I became a lot pickier," she replied dismissively. "I paid closer attention to signs that the person might be a user or a narcissist. For what it's worth, I did meet a few decent men, but something was always missing. Getting into a relationship that was doomed from the start felt pointless. So staying single was simpler."

"As much as I hate that you got hurt, I'm glad that fool showed his true colors before he could claim what was mine. I would have broken the law to get rid of him," I said in a factual manner.

"Amreth!" Ciara exclaimed, her outrage laced with a hefty dose of wonder and amusement.

I glanced at her over my shoulder with an unrepentant expression. "It appears that finding my mate has unlocked my darker side."

"So it seems... And it's rather sexy," she whispered with a smile.

I opened my mouth to reply, but only a shocked gasp escaped me. Eyes locked with mine, she ran the towel over my behind. She lifted my tail, wiping its entire length, her hand closing around the tip before gliding back down, as one would stroke a cock. I swallowed hard as she got back to my right butt cheek. Shifting to the side, Ciara circled back in front of me as she dried my right thigh. I held my breath as she boldly rubbed the towel over my cock. My lips parted, and I sharply inhaled as she wrapped both hands around it to wipe its length. I hated that towel between us, cheating me out of direct contact with her. My mate then took her sweet time wiping my balls, giving them a not-so-subtle squeeze in the process.

My fangs burned with the need to sink into the tender flesh of her neck and bind her to me.

Far from done, Ciara finally broke eye contact as she slowly crouched before me. She carefully dried my legs, each one in turn, her gaze locked on my length. A bolt of fire exploded in the pit of my stomach as she examined it closely. It wasn't my piercings that held her attention, but the chevron-shaped scales that covered the top part of my shaft and the soft spikes that lined its sides. She leaned in so closely, for a split second, I believed she would actually press her mouth to it.

To my dismay, the brat glanced back up at me with a mischievous smile and a provocative glimmer in her eyes.

"Very nice," she said tauntingly as she slowly straightened.

A billion thoughts flashed through my mind, and twice as many words burned my tongue. But something snapped inside me when her hard nipples brushed once more against my chest. Moving at the speed of a striking snake, my right hand grabbed her hair at the nape with a will of its own and drew her face to mine. My tail possessively wrapped around her, flattening her body against mine.

I realized I was kissing her when my mouth brutally pressed against hers in a voracious kiss. The soft rustle of fabric vaguely registered in my brain as the towel fell to the floor as Ciara slipped her arms around my neck. I picked her up, both hands behind her thighs, and she wrapped her legs around my waist. My engorged cock throbbed against her stomach as I deepened the kiss. She sank her fingers through my hair, releasing it from the improvised bun I had tied it into. It cascaded down, and she fisted it on my nape with both hands.

Holding her up with one hand behind her thighs, I caressed her back with the other. Her skin was still a little damp as she had not dried herself after we both rinsed. But I didn't care, and neither did she.

I broke the kiss and locked eyes with my woman. Words weren't necessary. She smiled, her hands tightening their hold in my hair. I smiled back and reclaimed her lips. Chest to chest, I carried her back inside.

CHAPTER 12
AMRETH

Each step towards our room had my blood racing through my veins. A burning desire had a pool of lava swirling in the pit of my stomach. I didn't understand how she could have so easily inflamed me. I meant to give Ciara a prolonged courtship. But right now, all I could think about was how desperately I wanted to lose myself in her, feel every inch of her body wrapped around mine, the sound of her moans in my ears, and the taste of her pleasure on my tongue.

Still supporting her weight with one arm behind her thighs, I blindly opened the bedroom door with my free hand. Ciara eagerly caressing my chest and side was making it even harder to form any rational thought. I wanted… needed more.

I had never entered this room before. As a Warden and Elite Obosian Warrior, my first instinct should be to quickly examine my surroundings to assess any potential threat and tactical details that could be used defensively or offensively should trouble arise. But I only had eyes for the large bed propped in the middle of the back wall.

Still kissing my mate, I made a beeline for it, before carefully laying her down on top of the soft mattress. When I tried to straighten, Ciara tightened her grip around my shoulders, drawing me closer. I chuckled against her lips and gave in. I climbed onto the bed and on top of her. My mate spread her legs so that I could settle between them. Holding my weight with my left forearm resting on the mattress, I broke the kiss and brushed my lips all over her face, and especially on that beautiful crown on her forehead.

Cupping the side of her neck with my right hand, I lifted her chin with my thumb, exposing the palpitating artery that my fangs ached to sink into. But I simply covered her neck with kisses, sucking on the tender flesh in the crook, right before it curved into her shoulder. Ciara's sigh of delight resonated directly in my cock. I kissed a path down her chest, my mouth watering in advance as I closed in on the prize that had taunted me for what felt like an eternity.

I latched on to her hard little nub like a starving male, sucking and licking it in earnest. My mate rewarded me with a voluptuous moan, a shiver coursing through her when I also tweaked and pinched her left nipple with my fingers.

Lifting my head to look at Ciara's beautiful face, I summoned my Lumiak in my index finger and sent a small electric discharge on the underside of her nipple. My mate instantly threw her head back as she cried out. A violent spasm shook her body, and her abdominal muscles contracted a few times. Breathing heavily, she lifted her head to look at me in shock.

I gave her a smug grin, baring my fangs in the process in a way that I wanted a little menacing. Used in the right intensity, at the right place, our Lumiak could sent a blast of pleasure so intense, it flirted with an orgasm, without quite achieving it... Well, unless used directly on the clitoris.

Gaze still locked with hers, I poked out my tongue, slowly stretching it. Her jaw dropped when the tip continued past my chin, down to my jugular notch. Another shiver coursed through her. My grin broadened, and her eyes smoldered when I lowered my head again to lick a trail down her flat stomach towards my even greater prize.

The delectable scent of her musk had my cock throbbing with need. It grew stronger with each second in tandem with her arousal. Finding my woman's petals already slick for me fanned the flames of the brazier burning deep within me. They were the loveliest shade of pink and dark brown with a hint of purple. Although her engorged clitoris was begging for my attention, the need to taste my mate rode me too hard.

I teased her slit with the tip of my tongue, which was pointier than a human's. Ciara gasped, and her left hand closed around my main right horn. That instantly sent a bolt of lust in my groin. I wanted her to grab both my main horns and tug on them. But I could wait. I could only pray she would do that once I was balls deep inside her.

I pushed my tongue in her slit. The tart taste of her essence set my loins ablaze. A hungry growl of approval vibrated in my throat as I pressed my mouth against her sex and sank my tongue even deeper in. A strangled cry escaped Ciara, and her right hand latched onto my other horn. My cock ached and palpitated with the need to claim her, but I focused on my feast.

The sound of her moans in my ears was the sweetest music as I began to fuck her with my tongue. Her inner walls were so warm and soft, imagining how they would feel around my length was driving me insane. I accelerated the movement of my tongue dipping in and out. To enhance her pleasure, I made sure to systematically rub my lingual piercing against the sensitive bundle of nerves of her G-spot.

In no time, Ciara's hips were gyrating, her grip tightening around my horns. It wasn't quite as firmly as I liked, but each involuntary tug still resonated directly in my cock. Only once her legs began shaking around my face did I finally give her clitoris the long overdue attention it deserved.

Without stopping to plunder her tight sheath with my tongue,

I rubbed her little nub with my thumb. I barely brushed against it before my woman went off. She cried out, her body seizing as ecstasy swept her away. Ciara's essence poured on my tongue, and I greedily devoured every drop. My thumb and mouth kept her flying high for a while longer. At last, I relented and lifted my head to peer at her.

My mate looked a little dazed, her lips parted as she breathed heavily. The fast rise and fall of her chest only drew my attention back to her perky breasts. As much as I wanted to bury myself inside her and feel her climax on my cock, I wasn't done playing with her.

I knelt between my woman's thighs and parted her legs wider, leaving her fully bare and exposed to my possessive gaze. Tharmok smite me! She was breathtaking, and mine. All mine. I would have her screaming my name over and over again before the end of the night.

Ciara blinked, startled by a sudden movement at the edge of her vision, before realizing it was my tail joining the party. Her eyes widened as she watched it slither over her stomach, glide over each of her breasts, teasing the hard buds along the way. Her breath hitched when it resumed its journey upward and wrapped around her neck. Resting both palms on the mattress on each side of her, I leaned forward to study her features as I began to tighten my tail, slightly constricting her airways.

I altered my vision to examine her aura for any sign of distress or discomfort. It blasted me with a mesmerizing rainbow of colors that had my mouth instantly water with the need to taste her energy. It took every ounce of my willpower not to give in to the urge to gorge on her emotions.

Although keeping it wrapped around Ciara's neck, I loosened my tail's grip only to extend its tip towards her mouth. Without needing any instruction, my mate immediately parted her lips to welcome it. A low, animalistic growl vibrated through my chest as she began sucking on it in a lascivious way that set my blood ablaze.

Baring my fangs at her, I closed my right hand around my cock, squeezing the base almost painfully to silence its need to erupt. Each motion of her head as she bobbed over my tail resonated straight in my cock. When my woman twirled her tongue around the tip, I could almost feel it on my glans. Fuck, if I let her carry on, Ciara could make me climax just from this. I feared how quickly she would make me fall apart if it was my cock she was lavishing this much attention on.

She gasped, looking almost outraged when I suddenly pulled my tail away. She attempted to argue, but I choked her neck with it, my face stern, making it clear she was to behave. For a split second, I braced for the possibility she might rebel. I didn't want a true submissive as I didn't consider myself a Dom in the traditional sense. However, as much as I liked having control in the bedroom, I didn't oppose the occasional exchange of power if my partner wanted to take the lead.

But right this instant, I wanted to have my way with her, which required her submission. Obviously, I would relent if she clearly opposed it and could only hope she wouldn't.

My heart soared when she suddenly relaxed, yielding to me.

"Good girl," I whispered as I loosened my tail before fully retracting it. "I'm going to feed from you, Ciara."

My tone was almost menacing as I spoke those words. Once more, I wanted her consent. Technically, I could do it without her even being aware of it, and it took nothing away from her. But it would feel too much like a violation, both of her body and her trust.

To my delight, she licked her lips in a way that screamed anticipation and reached for me. I stared at her hands as they caressed my chest, her thumb teasing my right nipple. Her palms were like burning embers on my skin, warming me to the bone. I placed my own hands on her waist, caressing a path towards her breasts as I invoked my Lumiak. She gasped as the electric tendrils set her nerve endings on fire, the agreeable sensation accentuated by blasts of pleasure as I brushed my lightning over her erogenous areas.

Before she could fully adjust to my ministrations, I emitted gradually increasing waves of my *bakaan*. The intensity of my aura acted like a shot of liquid ecstasy directly into her veins. In no time, she was moaning and writhing on the bed from the dueling pleasure of my *bakaan* and Lumiak. Her back arched on the mattress, and she gripped my forearms with bruising force when the tip of my tail found its way between her thighs.

As expected, it was a tighter fit than my tongue, and I shamelessly used it not only to pleasure her, but also to prepare her to receive my greater girth. Tharmok's teeth, she was stunning. Her aura radiated like a kaleidoscope of shimmering lights, bathing her in a mesmerizing halo as she moaned with bliss.

My eyes glowed as I began to feed from her, then nearly rolled to the back of my head as her divine taste blasted through me. Fuck! It was like drinking from the fountain of the gods themselves. I gorged on her emotions, showering her with even more of my *bakaan* to increase her pleasure as my tail relentlessly plowed into her.

Ciara's sharp cry of ecstasy snapped me out of my drunken daze. Her head rolled from side to side as she once more flew high. Even as I stopped myself feeding from her, my fangs ached to bury themselves in her neck, inject her with my essence, and even drink some of her blood. It wasn't something that my people ever really did anymore, but we sometimes indulged in our more primal urges in moments of overwhelming emotions such as this one.

I let my *bakaan* and Lumiak fade, and pulled my tail out of my woman, only to replace it with my fingers. While she continued to fly on the wings of bliss, I kissed and caressed Ciara, with my right hand stretching her to receive me.

Once she came back to reality, I pulled my fingers out, greedily licked her essence off them, then carefully settled on top of my mate. She wrapped her arms around me, the air of wonder in her beautiful grayish-brown eyes—which had almost turned black from passion—turned me into a messy puddle. Obviously, this wasn't love. We still barely knew each other. But it gave me a glimpse of what kind of bond would blossom between us over time.

I couldn't wait.

"My Ciara," I whispered tenderly while brushing aside a damp lock of hair from her forehead. "Do you accept me, my mate?"

"Yes," she whispered back, her voice a little rough from screaming. "I accept you, Amreth."

I smiled, letting the tenderness and passion she awakened in me shine through before I reclaimed her lips. Slipping a hand between us, I aligned my cock with her opening and gently began to push myself in. Despite how wet I'd made her, and how relaxed Ciara was, her body quickly resisted me. I had expected as much, but it didn't make it a lesser blow to my burning impatience to be one with my soulmate.

Invoking the control acquired over years of rigorous training to become a Warden, I forced myself to maintain a slow pace, pushing myself in with careful and shallow thrusts. The whole time, I whispered sweet words of encouragement, kissed and caressed her. My Ciara reciprocated each touch with matching passion.

And then we were one.

Her nails dug into the small of my back as I began to move. Her tight grip on my cock threatened to have me come undone with each stroke. Although meant to procure extra sensations to our female, the spikes lining the sides of my cock were highly erogenous. The way her inner walls squeezed them on their way in and out sent sparks of lightning throughout my nether region and down my legs.

Wrapped in the searing heat of her body, I gradually gave in to the passion she awakened in me. As I picked up the pace, taking her faster, deeper, and harder, my mate lifted her pelvis, meeting me thrust for thrust. An inferno raged within me. I couldn't get enough of her, of the feverish way she caressed and clawed at me, the sweetness of her tongue mingling with mine, and the sound of her pleasure.

But above all, the taste of that pleasure…

I gorged some more on her emotions. My mind screamed for me to stop, but I couldn't. It was too good, too divine. An insane amount of energy coursed through me. My skin felt on the verge of bursting from the overflow of power feeding from her gave me. I wanted to be deep inside her, wrapped around her, and take all of her within me. No beginning, no end, Ciara and me fully intertwined as one.

Before long, I was pounding into her. My wings deployed, aching for me to take flight with my mate and complete our bond. I vaguely feared that my feral instincts would just take over and irrevocably claim her without her consent in my rabid need to make her mine forever. But I was drowning in too powerful a maelstrom of emotions and bliss. So much in fact that I never saw Ciara's climax creeping in.

She suddenly cried out, her blunt nails savagely raking my back as her orgasm slammed into her. Her inner walls clamping down on my cock wrested my own release from me. Throwing my head back, I roared and slammed myself deep inside my woman. My seed erupted with a violence that left me reeling. It shot out into Ciara in powerful spurts of liquid ecstasy. My entire body trembled as I remained buried deep, grinding my pelvis against hers until I was fully spent.

Wrecked, I collapsed on the bed next to her and rolled onto my back, drawing her with me. She breathed heavily, her head resting on my chest. I wrapped my tail and my arms around her slender body covered in a thin sheath of sweat. A shiver coursed through her, and goosebumps spread all over her skin. I closed my wings around her to keep her warm and safe… to keep her close.

"You are mine, Ciara. Now and always," I whispered.

She snuggled more deeply against me and pressed a soft kiss on my chest. "As you are mine," she whispered back.

I smiled.

CHAPTER 13
CIARA

A mreth's wandering hands stirred me from my slumber. Although wonderfully sore, I gladly participated in yet another wild romp with him. My man had not been boasting when claiming that sex with him would be off the charts. Saying he had my girly bits singing arias couldn't even begin to do him justice.

The boldness with which I had initiated all of this between us still blew my mind. I wasn't prudish, but I also wasn't the type to quickly jump in bed with a new date. Sure, Amreth and I had a much stronger connection than that. We were soulmates. That didn't mean we needed to rush anything, though.

My over analytical brain kept trying to rationalize why I had done it, not that I had any regrets. Obviously, having such a fine male, ready and willing to do the nasty with me had been a hard temptation to resist. However, as horny as he made me, my libido didn't control me. It was more than animal attraction between us. I also quickly realized that as much as Amreth qualified as an alpha, he was extremely respectful and protective.

More than once, I perceived his desire to push things a little farther or to be more flirtatious. He systematically reined himself in, making it clear he would let me set a pace that was comfortable for me. I loved how he sought my validation and consent every step of the way. Even when he got more dominant and controlling last night, not once did I feel threatened or coerced. I knew beyond any doubt that a single word would have sufficed to make him back off from pursuing whatever made me feel uneasy.

The way he touched, kissed, and spoke to me made me feel both safe and worshipped. I was falling hard for my incubus.

With much reluctance, we finally rolled out of bed and showered together. As we settled at the table to eat the generous breakfast the Kreelars brought us, Amreth scrunched his face at the food. Considering the substantial amount of meat provided, his reaction made no sense.

"What's wrong?" I asked, confused.

Seeing his pointy elf ears darken and his face take on an air of embarrassment piqued my curiosity even more.

"I'm not hungry," he mumbled.

"What do you mean, you're not hungry? The last few days you've been a bottomless pit!" I exclaimed. "Considering your exertion last night—and this morning I might add—you should be fam…"

My voice trailed off, and my eyes widened with sudden understanding, while his face darkened further. Despite my best effort, I failed to keep myself from bursting out laughing at his mortified expression.

"Did someone give himself indigestion from feeding off his mate a bit too much?" I asked in a taunting tone.

The grumpy face he made was all the answer I needed. I laughed some more, sympathy, amusement, and a hefty dose of smugness swelling within me in equal measure.

"That's your fault for tasting so damn good," he grumbled.

"Sorry… Well, not really. But I doubt there's anything I can give you to soothe your stomach," I said in a mischievous tone.

"It's not my stomach," he said in the same disgruntled fashion. "The energy is stored inside me, and it makes my skin feel on the verge of bursting. Technically, it's comparable to an overfull stomach, but spread throughout your entire body."

"Ouch," I said with sincere sympathy this time. "Is there any way to relieve this?"

He nodded. "I just need to expend some of the energy I stored to make room. Normally, I get rid of excess energy while charging the power crystals of my inmates' various Quadrants. I will just need to go outside and blast some energy."

"Why didn't you do so when we went out to shower?" I asked with genuine curiosity.

"Because I doubt our hosts would have appreciated seeing a swarm of lightning shooting out into the sky over their village," Amreth replied mockingly.

I snorted, picturing the scene. Yeah, the Kreelars would not have been amused at all by this, especially if he was truly blasting a large amount of it. I had seen how impressive the Obosians' electrical discharges could be at lethal levels. It was terrifying.

"I will ask Vala to let me traipse a little distance away from the village to do so."

"Good idea," I replied with a smile.

Moments later, as if in response to his comment, Vala dropped by to inform us that the Kalds of the other tribes agreed to allow us to freely travel throughout their territory, including between their villages with his ship. My mate didn't have to be told twice.

I escorted him outside. He gave me a kiss before flying back to his vessel to get a shuttle that we would use as our own field lab. Before that though, he would go pick up some berries in the forest and make a detour by Bryst to drop them off to Mehreen and Ernst. They could then thoroughly test and analyze them in the deployable lab, which possessed the proper equipment for it.

I burst out laughing again when lightning started to fire off in the distance in the general direction he had taken off towards. It was silly, super cute, and incredibly flattering. Amreth didn't strike me as the type to overindulge in things or to have an addictive personality. That my emotions had been so delicious to him that he couldn't help himself to the point of discomfort was the greatest compliment he could have paid me.

Sighing wistfully, I headed to the office in the village's gathering hall to establish a call with Mehreen and Ernst using the Kreelars' radio communication system. It felt so weird, like I teleported to a dystopian future where society had reverted to the old days where most technology had been wiped off the planet. It felt even stranger without video. Situations like these reminded me how overly comfortable technological advances made us, and how we often took so many conveniences for granted, no longer truly appreciating their benefits until we lost them.

"We made some great progress here," Ernst said proudly. "All of our tests confirmed that it is indeed estrogen killing the females faster. As you know, it interacts with their hippocampus and prefrontal cortex to increase synaptogenesis."

Before he even finished, understanding dawned on me as to what was happening.

"Of course!" I exclaimed. "The disease causes the cerebral mutations which grant them their powers. With estrogen boosting the formation of new synapses, the females' brains are mutating too fast!"

"Exactly, and with those new synapses comes enhanced neurotransmitter activity. Except the prions disrupt the normal function of the neurons, which leads to improper synthesis and damaged synapses. Their bodies get overwhelmed before they have a chance to fight back, and they die," Mehreen said. "We've been running some tests and simulations that show that Gonadotropin-releasing hormone antagonists work on them like with humans and stop their ovaries from releasing estrogen."

I frowned. "That's great, but is it enough?"

"It will significantly increase their chances of survival, especially if we give them the proper GnRH antagonists. Partial stasis might be required to help those whose illness already progressed too much. But if caught early, administering GnRH antagonists to females will bring their odds of beating back the disease to levels comparable to males."

"Great work!" I said with a smile. "Amreth will drop by Bryst in the next couple of hours. He went to get his shuttle, and he'll pick up some berries for you on the way. Please give him some GnRH antagonists so that I can administer it to the females over here who need it."

"Will do," Ernst said, his voice bubbling with excitement. "I've already started doing some research on a way to permanently eradicate strawberries here. But my tests are based on those from Earth. I can't wait to get my hands on the local ones."

"On my end, I'm looking into ways of making the Kreelars immune or at least to significantly dampen the effects. Between both options, we should be able to come up with a viable solution," Mehreen said.

"Perfect. As soon as Amreth returns, we will go directly into the forest to study the soil, surrounding flora, as well as the animals that feed off them. Hopefully, I will get you some useful data."

"Sounds like a plan," Mehreen replied with enthusiasm.

We chatted a bit longer before ending the conversation. While waiting for Amreth, I checked on the patients. To my relief, the treatment we administered was working so far. Obviously, it wasn't a cure, but it stopped the prions from reproducing. Unless we managed to find a cure—which remained doubtful—there would be no miracle healing. All we could do right now was provide an antagonist protocol for those infected to slow the progression of the mutation long enough for their brains to adjust. This extra time would allow them to survive the changes.

I also worked with their healers to train and teach them natural methods using their current technology to test their food in the future, as well as detect infections early on in patients. The idea was not to further upend their society by dumping a whole bunch of advanced technology so that they could reclaim control over their health. They needed to be able to handle it on their own using methods that aligned with their current technological level.

As soon as Amreth arrived, he launched a series of drones to survey the area in search of smaller animals feeding from the berries. In the upcoming days, the Kreelars would organize a hunt to cull the rabid larger creatures that roamed further north. Aku and his tribemates captured a couple of beasts alive for Mehreen and Ernst to run tests on to see how we could also try to save other creatures of those species, should we fail to fully eliminate the presence of the berries on the planet. Hopefully, it would be something akin to a rabies vaccine on Earth.

Amreth finally spotted the perfect location for us to settle the shuttle. It was surrounded by multiple patches of berries and a few Onei lairs. When he first scanned the area, he managed to capture a couple of images of the adorable little creatures.

They possessed the rounder rump of a beaver, but the more slender body and tail length of an otter. They were masters of camouflage, thanks to their green fur that easily blended with moss and grass, the leaf-shaped fan at the tip of their tails, and especially that adorable head with huge eyes, a mousy little nose with a tiny mouth, and a crown shaped like the leaves of a fern. So long as the Onei remained immobile, you would genuinely confuse it for just being part of the underbrush.

According to Vala, they were relatively harmless little mammals, somewhat comparable to bunnies—at least based on how she described them. They mostly fed off of leaves, fruits, and nuts. Under rare occasions, especially when facing food scarcity, they would go for small bugs instead. They were extremely fast, with very strong and sharp teeth that allowed them to break through the shells of the nuts. So while they usually scampered off when frightened, should you catch them, Oneis could inflict some nasty wounds with a bite strong enough to chop off your finger and claws so sharp they would tear you to shreds.

But I had my special weapon in the form of a very sexy-looking Obosian. I took position near a tall bush, with gloves and paddings around my wrists and forearms for protection. The smug brat didn't even use a stealth shield to approach the creature hiding between two thick ropey roots of a tall tree. The wide leaves of the wild plants towering over the berry bushes partially hid the Onei. In truth, if not for the scanner on my armband confirming its presence, I never would have detected it or the berries for that matter.

No wonder the fruits escaped notice for so long, especially since they still hadn't spread far enough south to be in areas where young Kreelars might have played and stumbled upon them.

Amreth began blasting his *bakaan* in a focused fashion towards the location of the creature. He had circled around in the opposite direction from me so that he could herd the Onei towards me should it attempt to flee. Although the area of effect didn't reach my position, I instantly felt hot and bothered at the mere memory of how he wrecked me with it last night.

A string of highly inappropriate thoughts started racing through my mind. I clamped down on them, mentally chastising myself for being such a horn ball. The Onei attempting to flee when it finally noticed Amreth's insanely silent approach snapped me back into focus. The wretched thing was fast. I leapt forward to catch it, but it slipped right through my fingers and kept hightailing it only to suddenly stumble, seeming groggy.

I glanced at Amreth with a hint of outrage and suspicion. He clearly lessened his calming aura, allowing the creature to escape me and only slowed it after I missed. The overly innocent look on his face seemed to confirm it. But before I could speak a word, he gestured in a way that said to hurry before the Onei fled.

I hastened to the little cutie only to see it take off again seconds before I would grab it.

"You son of a gun!" I exclaimed, glaring at Amreth. "Stop it!"

Once again, he took on an overly dramatic expression, but this time displaying the most dishonest air of guilt I had ever seen.

"Apologies, my mate! I got so distracted by your beauty that I forgot what I was doing. Here, let me grab it for you," he said.

"You do that," I replied, scrunching my face at him.

I couldn't decide if I wanted to kick his butt or kiss him. Actually, I wanted to do both. Eyeing him suspiciously, I watched him strut his stuff, his tail slowly swaying from side to side in what I perceived as provoking and mocking. The Onei was still taking the occasional step forward but mostly seemed uncertain as to what it wanted to do, whether to come or go.

Amreth effortlessly picked it up without the slightest sign of resistance. I quickly opened my medical case and retrieved the stylus that also acted as a syringe to draw blood samples. I was just about to reach for sterile cloth to clean the area I would make the puncture in when my mate stopped me.

"Let me get that for you," Amreth offered.

"It's okay. I got it," I replied with a grateful smile that froze seconds later.

"I insist!" Amreth said, before putting the Onei back down on the ground so that he could pick up the round container.

"What the fuck?!" I shouted as the little creature took off and vanished in the underbrush.

"Oops?" Amreth said.

I didn't know what expression was plastered all over my face, but Amreth didn't stay to ask for explanations and just flapped his wings, flying backward to a safe distance from me. He burst out laughing as a string of curse words tumbled out of my mouth. But even as I itched to throw a big rock so that it would smack him right on that smattering of scales between his main horns, I also got the urge to laugh.

I was annoyed to no end to have serious work delayed. And at the same time, I loved seeing this boyish and playful side of him. When he vanished in the forest for a few seconds before returning with the Onei comfortably snuggling in his arms, I watched him close the distance between us with mixed feelings. While I could see the humor in his teasing—and even enjoyed it despite my outburst—I also wondered if he was the type to not know when to quit while he was ahead.

As if he had read the thoughts crossing my mind, he stopped in front of me and locked gazes with mine.

"I promise to behave this time," he said with a serious expression, although I didn't miss the hint of amusement in his voice.

"Good," I said, half-serious and half-playful. "This must be distressing for the Onei."

This time, all teasing vanished from his face as he shook his head.

"He's not distressed. He realized quickly that we would not harm him. I can be a brat at times, but I would never mistreat an animal, least of all for entertainment."

As he spoke those words, he gently scratched the creature behind the long leaf-like scale that appeared to cover its right ear. My heart instantly melted when the Onei stretched its neck and tilted its head to the left to give him better access.

"Wow, he seems to like you," I said softly.

"Who doesn't?" he asked smugly.

I snorted and gave him a playful tap. "Stay still, Mr. Lovable, so that I can draw some samples," I replied in a falsely severe tone.

The creature remained blissfully still in my mate's arms. That calm wasn't fully natural to the extent that I could feel Amreth's *bakaan*, but it was very weak. I suspected that it was now more to keep the animal stoic while I drew the blood and less to prevent it from scurrying off.

"I love pets," I mused aloud. "Growing up, we had a dog, a cat, and an aquarium filled with turtles. I didn't care much for those. They were my father's pets. But I loved the other two. As a traveling doctor, it felt cruel to adopt pets if I couldn't provide them with the proper stability they required. And I didn't want to abandon them for weeks on end. Settling with you on Molvi would fix that."

"And then we'll get you a pet or two… or five," Amreth said with a smile.

I chuckled and gave him an inquisitive look before glancing back at the vials of blood, which I began to label.

"Do you have any pets?" I asked as I placed that first labeled vial in the cooling compartment of the container.

I raised an eyebrow at the almost evil smile that stretched his lips, allowing the tips of his fangs to peek between them.

"I do, but they are of the scary type that no one in their right mind would even consider petting," he said with self-derision.

"Like what? You have a tank of piranhas?"

He laughed and shook his head. "My pets are quite a few meters long, with five heads filled with dagger teeth, and the type of poison that will kill even the most resilient person in a few minutes. They can also fly and stab you with the nasty dart at the tip of their tail."

"Talk about charming," I said with a shudder that only made him laugh more.

"Faernychs aren't friendly. They're bred and raised specifically to guard the forests surrounding our Quadrants. They bond with their Warden which usually keeps them from attacking us personally. But you should never take it for granted. However, their training will definitely prevent them from spraying their acid at us."

"I don't like your pets," I said as I began to scan the Onei, who still appeared content to remain in Amreth's arms.

I couldn't blame it.

"It's okay. They're not really the social type so they won't expect cuddles from you," he added teasingly. "Anyway, they never leave the forest."

I tilted my head to the side and gave him an assessing look.

"So what made you want to become a Warden?"

"It is often expected of the firstborn of a Warden to take on that mantle once they reach adulthood," he said with a shrug.

I peered at him with curiosity. "So you did it out of duty?"

He shook his head. "It is expected but not demanded. After all, the position must be earned. First, you need to possess the Warrior traits, which enables us to summon our Lumiak. Contrary to popular belief, not every Obosian can summon lightning. Or rather, a majority can only summon the type of weak spark sufficient to pleasure a partner during foreplay, but not enough to use in an offensive or defensive fashion."

"Which means some of your people who might have wanted to become a Warden are eliminated by default?" I asked.

He nodded. "It is essential for the role. Even if you could find alternatives to Lumiak when it comes to controlling misbehaving inmates or the wild beasts that roam the surrounding forests, you still need it for the power grid. We generate the electrical energy that powers each Quadrant of our Sectors. Building an electric plant or any other source of energy would not only be costly but inefficient."

I paused running the scanner to stare at him in awe. "So you're literally a walking battery? This thing about expelling that excess energy this morning wasn't just an overly dramatic exaggeration. You meant it?!"

He chuckled and nodded. "If your deployable lab ran low on power due to a long period without enough sun to recharge the batteries, I could max them out for you in less than ten minutes."

I whistled through my teeth as I completed the scan. "I can think of a few people who would love to have you around. Electric bills can be insane on some planets."

"I bet. They would be as well on Molvi otherwise. Truth be told, I wasn't certain I wanted to be a Warden initially."

"Oh? What changed?"

"I wouldn't say anything changed, but more that things clarified themselves for me as I grew older. I always wavered between becoming a Warden or a Judge. You know how humans incentivize their offspring to be lawyers, doctors, or engineers?"

"Yep, absolutely."

"For us, it's a judge, a law enforcer, or taking over whatever the family business is."

"Not a Warden?" I asked, surprised before indicating for him to release the Onei.

The adorable creature, no bigger than your common house cat, peered up at Amreth with an almost offended expression to have thus been discarded. Considering how eager it had previously been to run off, I expected it not to stick around longer than needed. But it didn't flee. After lingering around us a moment longer, it sauntered a few meters from where we stood to go munch on more berries nearby.

"There are no more Sectors left to be assigned," Amreth said as I crouched by the bushes to take some soil samples. "So unless your family owns one, or you marry into a family who does, then your chances of becoming a Warden are pretty much nil."

"Oh, my God! Are there so many prisoners that the entire planet has been used up as Quadrants?!" I asked, stunned.

He smiled and shook his head. "No. Only a third of the planet is currently used for incarcerations. Half is still undisturbed wilderness, and the rest is occupied by the city and residential sectors. There currently is no need for additional space. Should that day come, the competition to secure those new plots will be fierce."

"I'm surprised your people didn't just develop them regardless," I said pensively. "On Earth, any piece of real estate available for development will be exploited to the maximum. Greed is a powerful thing."

"It is," he conceded while handing me another container so that I could place more samples of the surrounding flora. "But that kind of thing tends to lead to corruption and miscarriages of justice. If you have empty facilities, you will want to fill them to avoid running a deficit. In turn, it may drive authorities to arrest people under flimsy excuses and for judges to give longer and harsher sentences than necessary. It will also cause existing Sectors to no longer have enough inmates to make their current operation reasonably sustainable."

"That would be bad for your family?" I asked.

He shook his head. "We're a noble house. Our wealth dates back centuries, with quite a few very successful and lucrative businesses. The raw material we need for some of our factories is gathered in my Sector. But I pay my inmates at market rates for everything they choose to gather. Therefore, financially, it would make no difference for us whether we bought from our prisoners or from some other company."

I smiled. "You have no idea how much I appreciate that you guys fairly compensate the prisoners instead of using them as slave labor. For a long time, that's how humans treated their inmates in privatized prisons."

He returned my smile. "Obosians aren't perfect, but where the penal system is concerned, I genuinely believe that there are many things that we do right. I have enough cousins—not to mention my own brother—who are of the Warrior breed who could have become Warden in my stead. As I was never interested in business management, taking over one of our factories didn't appeal to me."

"I think you would have been a wonderful Judge. Why did you go with the other option?"

He gave me a mischievous look. "I'm a sucker for punishment?"

I snorted and moved to a different patch of plants and trees to gather more samples, while he held the container for me.

"I can see that. But seriously, why?"

"Because I couldn't stay locked inside a courtroom just passing judgment on others," he said, sobering. "I need to be active. I need the outdoors. To become a Warden, we undergo extremely intense training that many actually give up on. Difficulty-wise, it's comparable to your Navy Seals. But to that you have to include aerial combat both with and without weapons. I got hooked despite the hardships of training."

"And that certainly paid off," I said teasingly while giving his body a very meaningful and admirative glance.

He chuckled and bowed his head in a thank you. "However, beyond that, I needed to feel like I was making a difference in people's lives. As a Judge, you condemn them and move on. As a Warden, you can try to help them back on the path of redemption. Each person you helped improve themselves, find their way, and go on to live a righteous and productive life is the greatest victory one could dream of."

My chest warmed for him for the passionate way he spoke of this. It gave me yet another glimpse at the truly good male buried inside his stern and intimidating Obosian exterior.

"Does it happen often that you can redeem your inmates?" I asked in a soft voice.

He pursed his lips, and his shoulders slouched imperceptibly. "Sadly, nowhere near as often as I would like. We have a respectably high success rate with inmates from Q1. But that diminishes almost exponentially the darker the Quadrants. Still, there have been redemptions in Q4 in the past. I endeavor to continue to increase that ratio over time. But what about you? What made you want to become an Interstellar Doctor?"

I smiled and gestured with my head for us to go back to the shuttle to bring in the samples we had gathered.

"Like you, it's a family thing. Both my parents are plastic surgeons. They were extremely happy when I told them that I was following in their footsteps by entering the medical field. But I quickly burst their bubble saying I wouldn't go into plastic surgery. They're still proud of me, but annoyed by many of my choices," I said with a hint of self-derision.

"Like what?" he asked with genuine curiosity.

"Over the years, I received some pretty flattering offers to take on prestigious positions in the medical field. But those roles turn into more of a public relations thing, political and administrative where you just hold conferences, mingle with the stuck up elite, and really lose that hands-on connection with the magic of healing. Like you, I want to make a tangible difference in people's lives. Those fancy roles or my parents' even fancier clinic didn't do it for me."

Amreth opened the door of the shuttle and gestured for me to go in first before following me in.

"Plastic surgery isn't only related to vanity modifications," he countered softly. "For many patients, reconstructive surgery was the only thing that gave them back their lives after a grievous accident or injury, not to mention those born with serious birth defects."

I nodded. "That's absolutely true. Actually, I seriously considered it at first. My parents even offered to add that as a new service in their clinic. But the adventurous bug bit me something fierce. I wanted to go out there and face the type of challenges that I would never encounter in the controlled setting of a local clinic. The worlds and people I have visited and discovered have changed me in ways that I could never put into words. In all the ways that matter, those experiences have made me a better person."

"I understand what you mean," he said pensively. "Working closely with my inmates has also opened my eyes and broadened my horizons. Unless you interact with them directly and over a long period of time, you forget that they're people first, and criminals second. It has forced me to learn about their various cultures and circumstances. As strict as I may be about upholding the law, being a Warden reminded me that people are not born criminals. Society and circumstances are usually to blame. I love that I can try to undo the damage that brought them to that place to begin with."

"Just like I can try to undo the harm caused to my patients whether it came to them intentionally or because of an accident —especially when due to some idiot's carelessness," I said, a sliver of anger seeping into my voice as I thought back on the circumstances that led to the tragedy plaguing the Kreelars. "I just wish I could tell my parents that all is well, and that I will be home sooner than later."

"They already know," Amreth said in a hesitant tone.

Shocked, I nearly dropped the container I was about to place on the counter of the shuttle's hold, which we had turned into a makeshift lab.

"WHAT?!"

He heaved a sigh and appeared to choose his words carefully before answering. "Remember how I mentioned that Maeve helped me track you down here?"

"Yes," I said, the irritation in my voice indicating clearly that I didn't see what that had to do with the question I just asked.

"She requested I send a message as soon as I got visual confirmation of your presence," he explained. "Initially, it would have sufficed for the Peacekeepers—and maybe even the

Enforcers—to come charging in had you been in any kind of danger or displaying distress. So before I got captured, I sent Maeve the recording of the three of you walking out of the lab while I was still scouting."

"Right," I said, tension bleeding out of my back. "That makes sense. But it doesn't confirm that she received it or that she passed it on to my parents. After all, you said yourself that we are in the Dead Zone, and communications with the rest of the galaxy is a gamble at best before the signal travels far enough to be picked up by one of the relays."

"That would have been true if not for the fact that I found Maeve's response when I returned to the ship this morning," he countered.

"What?! Why didn't you tell me that sooner? What does it say?" I asked, feeling somewhat offended.

"It said that they received both my messages."

"*Both* your messages?!" I exclaimed before he could continue, interrupting him.

He nodded. "The first message was the one I told you about. But that first night, when Aku allowed me to go fetch my personal belongings, I sent a second message informing her that we were fine, safe, and that we were voluntarily staying to help cure their people. Without that, they would have sent someone to investigate, and things might have turned ugly. If not the Enforcers themselves, I can guarantee you that my family would have come looking for me."

"Fair," I said, still taken aback by the whole thing.

"When I went to fetch the shuttle this morning, I found yet another message in which Maeve confirmed that all three of your families and the Enforcers have been informed of the situation," Amreth continued. "They won't interfere but remain on standby. In truth, I believe they're either in orbit or not too far from here."

I frowned. "Why? What makes you say that?"

"Her responses are too quick," he replied matter-of-factly.

"Without a relay nearby, it should take on average a couple of days before the signal gets picked up."

"But why didn't you tell me any of this sooner? What's going on? I'm not a fan of secrecy, especially under the current circumstances," I said, staring at him uneasily.

I hated the powerful flashbacks I was getting of my douchebag ex-fiancé. He kept so many things secret so that he could take advantage of me that I now had trust issues.

Amreth ran a nervous hand through his long, silver-white hair, a frown creasing his forehead covered in dark scales.

"I'm stuck in an odd position," he said, sounding frustrated. "I believe they want me to be very discreet."

"Discreet?" I echoed, baffled. "About what?"

"It's hard to explain. It's just various subtle signals woven into the conversation and the messages. I got the distinct impression from the start that I was being somewhat recruited as a free agent for this specific mission so that they could keep plausible deniability if anything went wrong. And I believe there is something much bigger happening for which they need to make sure that no one knows that we're here."

"You think there's some foul play happening?" I asked with a sliver of worry.

Amreth nodded with a grim expression. "Yes, I believe so. I may be overthinking things, but there was a single word out of place at the end of her message. It simply said 'Kalmia' like one would write their name as the signature."

I recoiled. "Kalmia? As in that huge corruption case that resulted in massive casualties?!"

He nodded again. "I can't be certain. But like you, it's the first thing that came to mind."

I shook my head in disagreement. "That doesn't make sense. The berries that are currently killing the Kreelars grew organically over the past decade. The computers' analyses of the spread pattern confirm it. No assassin came here and planted these berries. Animals caused them to be found in all these various places," I argued.

"I don't believe this has anything to do with the berries," Amreth said pensively. "I agree with your rationale as to the fact that the berries spread naturally. But to me, Kalmia doesn't refer to the current situation where an entire species is slowly heading towards extinction over multiple decades. It would rather imply that someone is sending a bunch of assassins to swiftly wipe out the entire Kreelar population."

"But why?!" I exclaimed, refusing to believe anyone would do something so insane, egregious, and immoral.

"So that this story is never exposed," Amreth replied with a conviction that sent a cold chill down my spine. "Aku mentioned that there were powerful individuals who would bring about a terrible outcome for his people if they went public with this from the start instead of kidnapping you."

I nodded. "Right, he said as much to me as well when I challenged him about it. But who could it possibly be?"

"As part of the message I've sent to Maeve, I asked her to dig deeper into the story and the identities of Elias's crew back then. There would be a record of all the members of his team. Maybe looking into each of their backgrounds, we might find a connection."

"If they truly are considering sending assassins, we have to warn the others," I said, my voice tense.

To my surprise, he vehemently shook his head.

"Not the others," he said forcefully. "I agree that we should inform Aku. However, this currently is pure speculation on my part. What if I'm wrong? There's no need to make people panic until we have more solid reasons to believe this is a real threat. Frankly, I hesitated about telling you."

"Why?" I asked, the hurt I felt audible in my voice. "I know we've only just met, but I would trust you with absolutely anything."

"It's not that I don't trust you, my Ciara. I just don't want to freak you out with a bunch of unfounded speculations," Amreth said with a sincerity that eased some of the irrational sense of rejection I felt. "You already have so much on your shoulders that it feels irresponsible to add even more to your plate."

"I appreciate that you're trying to protect me," I said softly. "But honesty is really important to me. I rather have an ugly truth that I can figure out how to navigate than to live in blissful ignorance until reality finally slaps me in the face. I cannot prepare for a blow that I didn't even know was coming my way."

"I apologize, my mate," he said with a guilty expression. "I promise to be more transparent in the future. It just messes with my head that Aku claims I will punish those responsible. I wish he would tell me more than those cryptic one-liners that prompt more questions than answers."

"He can't," I said in a sympathetic tone. "That Seer and Oracle stuff is pretty messy. All the games involving Fate are tricky. If one of them tells you that they cannot go into greater details, you just need to suck it up and accept it."

He frowned and studied my face with undisguised curiosity. "How do you know that?"

"Earth is part of the Galactic Alliance, remember? We hear a lot about Oracles and Seers. If they tell you too much about what they've glimpsed of your future, it can influence your choices the wrong way. They all make a blood oath to always speak the truth but to also never try to dictate the path that one should follow, especially when it comes to Oracles as they see possibilities, not immutable certainties like the Seers. Free will is essential."

"But wouldn't it remain my free will whether to act on it if they told me clearly what would happen?" Amreth argued. "If you tell me that a person will drown at a specific time and place, I can choose to ignore it, go there to try and rescue them, send someone there in my stead, or try to warn that person not to go near the water at that crucial moment."

"Right, but that initial premise would be the kind of thing the Seer or Oracle would tell you," I countered. "The options you listed are the types of paths that an Oracle sees. What she will not tell you is that if you go yourself, you will indeed save that person but drown in the process. She will not mention that if you ignore it, a different person will attempt to rescue the victim and cause a massive disaster that will claim a hundred more lives. She also won't say that sending someone else there will allow them to discover that they were soulmates, or that warning that person not to go into the water at that precise moment will allow them to go to a different place where they will enter into a business deal that will bring prosperity to an entire people severely struggling."

"But why wouldn't they mention those two paths with positive outcomes? Then I could choose which one I believed was more beneficial. I would still exercise my free will," Amreth argued.

I smiled. "Not really. Because at that point, you're merely choosing between the two morally more suitable options. But every path has its own set of domino effects. Your drowning while attempting to rescue her will set in motion the creation of a series of new laws and safety measures around that area that will save countless more lives down the road. So your sacrifice was worth it. The more you mess with any threads of Fate, the more lives end up getting affected whether positively or negatively."

"Which is why the Kreelars' *friends* refused to get involved further. The potential paths they saw had too many negative trickle-down effects," he replied pensively.

I nodded. "Believe me, I hate nothing more than to be told to just wait and see. But I get it. It just warms my heart knowing that some way, somehow, you will bring the sons of bitches who caused all this pain to justice."

"This, I pledge," he said with a fierceness that was sexy as fuck.

I smiled, closed the distance between us, and slipped my arms around his waist. He returned my embrace, his tail wrapping around me as a tender emotion settled on his handsome features.

"Thank you for sharing all of this with me," I said with sincere gratitude. "I'm so happy you're here. You make me feel safe and supported, like everything is possible, and that no matter what hurdle is thrown our way, we shall prevail. Thank you for coming to rescue me."

"Always, my Ciara. Always," Amreth said in a solemn tone.

I smiled and lifted my face to receive his kiss. Yes, this was my soulmate.

CHAPTER 14
AMRETH

Over the following three days, my mate and I settled in a comfortable routine. I loved accompanying her in what I started labeling as our field trips. I assisted in every way possible, although I wished I could do more. Her intelligence, skills, and work ethic never ceased to amaze me. I wouldn't pretend to understand half of the things she was doing, but I was glad to be able to accelerate the process by capturing the animals she needed to test, collecting some of the samples required, and just flying her around wherever she wished.

Above all, I just loved being with her.

I was falling hard for my woman. It was silly how my mind would constantly look for ways to make her smile. Strangely enough, I had this irrational urge to annoy her from time to time. Not so much that she would actually become angry at me, but just enough for her to get that look in her eyes that screamed she wanted to kick my butt. Something about it was sexy as fuck.

Today, we wrapped up our final tests in the region and prepared for our return to Bryst. Ciara did one last round checking up on the patients of the village before we said our goodbyes to Vala.

"Thank you for everything you have done for my tribe," Vala said, her voice deep with gratitude. "I especially want to thank you for what you did for Muti's family. I doubt he ever would have recovered from the loss of his mate. He has loved her since childhood. We had all made our peace with the fact that she would die."

A powerful emotion fleeted over my woman's face as she smiled at the village leader. Pride swelled within me as I gazed upon Ciara.

"She's still fighting and isn't completely out of the woods yet," Ciara warned gently. "But things are looking good now. Although I won't make any promises, so long as the healers continue administering the treatments, I have high hopes that she and the others will make it through."

"Have no fear, Ciara. Your instructions will be dutifully followed. Until you came, we had nothing but darkness on the horizon. Now, the sun rises again. It is with sadness that we see you leave. Just know that you will always have a home with the tribe of Jaln," Vala said.

My mate blinked multiple times to stem the tears pricking her eyes.

"Thank you," she replied with a slightly shaky voice. "But you are not so easily rid of me just yet. We will return to check up on the patients and see how everyone else is faring within a week. In the meantime, do not hesitate to radio call us if anything seems off. Nothing is too insignificant. We cannot take any risks."

"You have my word. Safe journey, Sister."

That last word wrecked my mate. To my shock, both females exchanged a hug. After they released each other, Vala also bade me a warm farewell, but an undeniable bond had formed between her and my Ciara. The village as a whole chanted for us as we climbed back inside the shuttle. I had never experienced something like that before.

"Now I see what you mean by wanting to make a difference in people's lives," I said softly while piloting the shuttle back to Bryst.

She smiled, her face still displaying the strong emotions this sendoff stirred within her.

"They're not always this expressive," she replied with a wistful look. "Some form of clapping, cheering, or offering gifts are somewhat common depending on the situation. Chanting is a lot rarer. Then again, my role rarely lasts until the illness is a thing of the past. Normally, I only stick around long enough to find the cure or treatment. Then I will move on to a different mission, and field nurses or general physicians will stay behind to see the treatment through. So they often are the ones to get celebrated."

I frowned. "That seems a little unfair."

She snorted and shook her head. "Finding the cure is only the tip of the iceberg. Those handling the following days, weeks, and months treating the patients have the hardest work. It isn't easy witnessing so much suffering while trying to give both the sick people and their loved ones hope and the strength to keep fighting. It is heartbreaking every time you have to pull the plug on those who didn't make it. And you keep asking yourself if there was something you could have done better, sooner, or differently that would have saved them."

I pursed my lips and nodded slowly, not having looked at it from that angle. "I see what you mean."

"Everyone in each step of the process is important and essential. So no, I do not begrudge the nurses and physicians receiving most of the accolades in the end. They deserve every bit of it. Knowing that my work contributed to that success is the greatest reward I could hope for. I helped save those lives."

"That you did, my mate," I said with pride.

We landed in Bryst a short while later. Once again, we were greeted warmly, almost like heroes. It was silly, but it struck me that our actions in Jaln reflected positively on them, as if we were a member of their tribe helping one of their neighbors. After all, Aku vouched for us and our intentions.

"More of our people will set off on a pilgrimage in the upcoming week," Aku said as we finished bringing into the deployable lab the last samples Ciara and I had gathered earlier during the day. "We will head out in the morning to clear the main paths to the temple. An increasing number of rabid creatures have been spotted roaming closer to our village and hunting grounds."

"I would be glad to assist you," I immediately offered while setting the container down on the counter. "My drones can help locate all of them, and it will be a lot faster to get to them and dispose of the bodies with my shuttle."

"Thank you. We're grateful for the offer," Aku said warmly.

He didn't need to specify that he had hoped I would. It made sense. On their own, it would take them weeks to scout their extensive forests, with many beasts likely slipping through their nets as they continued to roam around.

"Actually, while you guys are out there, you should mark the locations of the berry bushes and even start uprooting them," Ernst intervened while opening one of the crates we brought in. "I understand the Jaln tribe has already begun exterminating the strawberries in their area."

"We were planning on doing that after the culling," Aku said.

Ciara shook her head. "I think you should get rid of the berries first or at the same time. The type that you have growing here is what we call day-neutral strawberries, which means that they continuously fruit from spring to fall. I had hoped you would have those that bear fruit only once or twice in a season."

"Of course, we don't. That would have been too easy," Aku said, his voice heavy with sarcasm.

"Culling all the rabid beasts will only have a bunch more roaming around so long as the berries are still getting eaten. So until your people have decided what you want to do with these berries and what the best containment method will be going forward, I suggest that you dig them out completely and we can help you adjust the soil's pH to make it more difficult for them to grow again. What we've come up with so far isn't a permanent solution, but it will drastically reduce the probability of more creatures becoming rabid and by extension of making your people sick."

"We can take care of both during the culling tomorrow. The drones can track both the animals and berry patches at the same time. If you dig them out as we go, we can burn them in the shuttle's incinerator," I suggested.

"Excellent idea," Aku said approvingly. "I will round up a few more people to take care of the berries while we hunt."

That night, being back in that first house felt strange. It was almost like being back home. Naturally, I shunned the guest room to share Ciara's bedroom, which also had a bigger bed better suited for my tall frame—not that we slept all that much.

It still shamed me how I repeatedly gorged on her emotions. I couldn't help myself. Over the handful of days spent in Jaln Village, the tribe had started making jokes about my strange habit of casting an insane amount of lightning in the distance every morning. At first, they feared something or someone had infuriated me, prompting me to vent my fury that way. Then their wariness quickly gave way to amusement. When I asked my mate if she had snitched as to the cause of my behavior, she swore her innocence. Judging by her aura, she was speaking the truth.

So how did they guess? Assuming they did...

The thought that they figured it out because of how loud we got was mortifying. Still, it remained a stretch for them to make the connection. Therefore, I convinced myself that they had no idea but were merely entertained by a behavior they deemed quirky.

That morning, Aku and sixteen Kreelars joined me aboard the shuttle. The return would be a little cramped if we planned on flying back with the carcasses of the creatures. In the end, we agreed to burn them on site to avoid bringing back unnecessarily anything that might be harmful to the people.

I released five drones, sending them ahead to scout the neighboring areas of the path the pilgrims would use. In no time, we found the first couple of wild beasts they called a Murthis. Of all the infected creatures, they presented the biggest threat. At least three meters long, and two meters high, the beasts possessed the broad shoulders and sleek body of a predator. Ciara claimed they looked as if a giant lion had a baby with a dinosaur. I had to look up the latter to find out what she meant.

It had a short greenish coat on its underbelly, and green scales along its thick neck, chest, and back. Even bigger scales covered its feline legs and paws, as well as its reptilian tail, which boasted a series of sharp bone spikes along its top side. The head was undeniably reptilian, triangular-shaped, with a wide mouth filled with dagger teeth, and a long, forked tongue. A huge set of horns, also covered in spikes on the upper edge, sprung from the brow and recurved on each side of its face.

Despite its massive size and weight, the Murthis could move at insane speeds. Its jaw was strong enough to cut right through flesh and bone with a single powerful bite. Thankfully, they usually traveled as small packs of around fifteen. Most males only remained with the females and the offspring they sired on them until the cubs were old enough to start hunting alongside their mothers, which normally took about six months. The males would then set off again on their own, although they remained within the territory that they shared with up to ten other males.

Just as I was hoping that we wouldn't have to cull mothers and their cubs, drones picked up a suspiciously large pack, at least two to nearly three times the normal number of beasts. A quick fly over with the drone indicated they were all females with their cubs. They looked nervous, the mothers forming a circle around their offspring.

"The females are joining forces to protect their young from the enraged males," Aku said. "Please tell me none of them are infected."

"The scanners do not show any infection among these females or their cubs," I said with relief.

"Perfect. Let's take care of the sick males then," Aku said.

I landed the shuttle in a small clearing, half a kilometer from the closest rabid beast. As with the first time they captured me, the Kreelars weren't armed to the teeth. You'd think they were simply going off on a leisure stroll in the woods. They all wore those poofy pants with a decorative loincloth on top. Barefoot and bare chested, they had a weapons belt and bracers, with the occasional chest straps.

Where my weapons belt included a blade—not quite a full sword, but longer than a dagger—and a blaster, the Kreelars only had a blowpipe barely thicker than a straw, a dagger, and a small pouch containing the darts they would fire on their targets.

"What?" Aku asked when he caught me eyeing them as we exited the shuttle.

"I was only thinking your weapons are quite minimal to face off against such imposing beasts," I said carefully.

As one, the Kreelars snorted and huffed, looking at me as if I'd said something ludicrous.

"Watch and learn, off-worlder," a female said teasingly.

With the same mind-boggling speed they had displayed when they came after me, the Kreelars took off running in the direction my scanner indicated a couple of rabid males were located. They split into two groups, one climbing on the trees on the left, and the other on the trees on the right. Aku kept running on the ground straight ahead. I activated my stealth shield and took flight, following the leader.

Watching his tribemates swing from tree to tree took my breath away. Now that I was no longer attempting to flee them, I could admire the physical prowess it involved. They easily leapt over six to eight meters to the next tree, catching a branch with one hand, and using their momentum to propel themselves towards the following tree. It reminded me of the hypnotic motion of a pendulum, their bodies swaying from side to side as they caught themselves with the left hand, leapt to the next tree, caught a limb with their right hand, and leapt again in an infinite loop.

The movement of all those Kreelars traveling at comparable speeds and in almost perfect synchronicity made the whole thing resemble some sort of lethal choreography. Acting as bait, Aku dashed forward on the ground towards their target. As soon as the beast noticed him, it charged with a blood-curdling roar. I fought the instinctive urge to swoop down and haul the Kreelar leader out of harm's way.

The bold confidence with which he continued to race towards a feral beast at least four times his mass boggled my mind. Watching him simply whip out his blowpipe felt even more reckless. But his aura indicated no fear, just focus and determination. He suddenly veered towards a tree as the beast closed in on him. At the last minute, Aku leapt at an impossible height over the Murthis. It reared on its back legs to try and eviscerate the Kreelar with its vicious claws but completely missed. Before it could get back down on all fours, at least three or four darts found their marks in its underbelly, fired by the tribemates swarming the trees.

But my eyes were locked on Aku. With phenomenal grace and dexterity, he kicked off the trunk of a nearby tree, caught a branch with his tail, using it to swing himself around back towards the creature, and fired a blow dart at the back of its head. He loosened his tail, using the momentum to land back a short distance from the creature. My jaw dropped as the Murthis staggered under the effect of whatever drug coated the darts. It collapsed just as Aku was running up to it.

Grabbing the thrashing creature by the massive horns framing its head, Aku snapped its neck with one powerful movement. And just like that, it was done. The respect I felt for his people grew a thousandfold. Admiration for their skills was only a tiny part of it. It was the merciful and efficient way they dispatched the animal that truly impressed me. I also loved that, as their leader, he didn't safely sit back at home and let them do the dirty work. He got down into the trenches and took on the most dangerous role.

Despite my stealth shield, Aku lifted his head to look at the exact position I was hovering in, a smug expression on his face. It still messed with my head that they could so clearly see me. I hated how vulnerable it made me feel, which was ironic considering that my people leveraged that very power to track our prisoners.

I nodded in concession before looking for the female who teased me about watching and learning. She was crouching on a thick branch a few meters to my right. She winked at me with a playful grin that had me snorting.

Aku emitted a single high-pitched sound that had all of them moving as one in the direction of the next beast, except for two of the Kreelars who closed in on their kill. They both took a few moments to spray something over the carcass. I presumed it would repel any carrion feeder that might want to take a bite until they could come back and dispose of it. I marked the location on my bracer before catching up to the rest of the tribe. I arrived just in time to see them make quick work of the next target.

Once again, I realized what a deadly army they would be in battle. It wasn't just their speed and efficiency, but also how incredibly silent they were as they literally flew through the trees. Primitive or not, the UPO needed to strike an alliance with the Kreelars and nurture that relationship for the future.

With the next target located a significant distance away, I landed near Aku, the rest of his tribemates also descending from the trees.

"Impressive work," I said as I disabled my stealth shield. "I'm curious though as to why you didn't use your mind disruption ability instead of rushing straight to an enraged beast."

"Specifically because they are enraged," Aku said with a smile. "The mind of a rabid animal is already too confused for our powers to work. Your calming ability could actually slow them down as it makes the target a little groggy."

"I would be happy to do it," I immediately offered. "Although you don't seem to need it."

He grinned at me smugly in a way that had me shaking my head. In that instant, I realized that I would miss him once we left this planet. Under different circumstances, I believed he and I could have grown to be close friends.

"We will remove the berries in this area before we move on to the next beast," Aku said pensively while glancing around us.

"I'll go fetch a hovering platform so that we can bring back the carcasses to the shuttle's incinerator as well as the crates to put the bushes in," I replied.

"Thank you, my friend," Aku said.

Once more, I watched in amazement the efficiency with which each of them worked, their physical strength and stamina easily rivaling some of the fittest Warriors I knew. On more than one occasion, I wondered if they had some sort of a hive mind happening. Nothing specific prompted that assumption. It was just a combination of things in the way they required little communication as they worked collectively towards a common goal.

They formed a line and moved forward as they tore out the berry bushes, stem and roots. A few of their tribemates shadowed them holding the crates in which they dumped the plants while also observing the ground for any signs that anything had been left behind. As they filled them, I grabbed some of the crates, flying them back to the shuttle, and then dumping them into the incinerator.

For now, the Kreelars and my mate's team agreed not to play with the pH of the soil until they better understood how it might affect the surrounding fauna. Although their initial tests indicated that it would be safe to use some aluminum sulfates to lower the pH and make it less suitable for strawberries that thrived on more acidic soils, there was no rush. The current cleansing would give us a long enough reprieve so that more thorough tests could be performed first.

Everyone got back in the shuttle, and we moved to a different sector. They dispatched four more Murthis as well as a handful of less lethal, smaller rabid creatures that still threatened the local fauna.

We moved at a phenomenal pace that hinted we could clear the entire area by the end of the following day. By early afternoon, we flew back to the village for lunch and for the Kreelars to restock on darts. This time, instead of us eating in the meeting room next to the deployable lab in the inner courtyard, our hosts invited us to join them in their gathering hall.

It was common practice for them to eat together, although it wasn't like everyone ate at the same time. While the room could fit the entire tribe, they usually came in smaller groups, like the infants with their parents or caretakers, the farmers and crafters as a separate wave, and then the hunters, although not necessarily in that order. That didn't prevent people from various groups from coming in at a different time or mingling with others. If nothing else, the Kreelars appeared to be very informal, with a strong sense of community.

They didn't have formal currencies. Everything was based on trade, goods for goods or services, whether within the tribe or with their neighbors. That they invited us to share their meal said a lot about how they were now accepting us as friends and not just intruders. Hopefully, it would give us an opportunity to get a deeper look at their society, which they were zealously keeping secret from us.

I couldn't blame them for only showing us the strict minimum necessary for us to accomplish our task here. The less we knew about them, the less they exposed potential vulnerabilities that could be exploited later.

Multiple tables were set in the back corner of the building, with large windows looking out onto the square. A buffet had been laid out on one long table. It was one of my first times seeing their use of electricity with wide trays that kept some of the salads and vegetables cool, and burners that kept the cooked dishes warm.

While the hunters who had accompanied us scattered at various tables, Aku and Enre settled with my mate, her colleagues and me at our own table. We enjoyed the meal while making casual conversation. Most of it was dedicated to our hosts inquiring about our lives off-world. I didn't miss how they skillfully deflected any efforts we made into getting them to open up more about their own people.

Under different circumstances, it might have come across as distrustful if not a little offensive. But he wasn't the leader of his entire species. I strongly suspected that he and the other Kalds had agreed to avoid oversharing as it could potentially impact all of them. As only a handful of them had met any of us, they had no reason to trust us, despite the blossoming friendship we had with Aku.

At least, his questions were harmless. He wasn't trying to pry into anything that might jeopardize our own national security. It was the type of friendly chatter one would have with a new acquaintance regarding our families, hobbies, and what led us to our respective careers.

Just as we were preparing to head out again, my com went off. Intrigued, I glanced at its interface, thinking it was only a notification from my scouting drones having detected more feral beasts. To my shock, it was an actual message.

'You have company.'

"What in Tharmok's name...?!" I whispered to myself.

A set of coordinates and a frequency followed that single sentence. The identity of the sender was unknown. Technically, I shouldn't be receiving this type of direct message here. It was not using basic analog radio frequency, but a digital one which required connectivity.

"What's wrong?" Ciara asked, her face displaying the same curiosity as the others.

I shared the contents of the message with them then redirected one of my drones closest to those coordinates to see what was happening.

"Company?" Aku echoed, his face and voice hardening. "More off-worlder ships came?"

"I'm assuming that's what this means," I said carefully while calling up the holographic display from my bracer to show the camera feed from my drones. "Give me a minute."

At first, it didn't show anything, even when I set the scanner to the widest radius. I recalibrated the device to scan on the frequency provided in the message. Within seconds, it detected a camouflaged vessel a short distance away. My stomach dropped when the zoom in revealed a Nazhral ship.

"Fuck! That can't be good," Ernst said.

"Who are they?" Aku demanded, with a glimmer of suspicion and betrayal in his yellowish-brown eyes. "What are they doing here?"

"Based on the vessel, they belong to a species with a rather bad reputation when it comes to smuggling and piracy," I explained cautiously. "But I have no idea who they are, or why they came here. We're all finding out together. If we were up to no good, I would not be sharing this with you in real time."

Aku appeared embarrassed for implying we might have been double-crossing them. He gave me an apologetic look, and I smiled, indicating I wasn't offended. Under the circumstances, he had every reason to be suspicious of off-worlders.

The drone followed the ship discreetly. Thankfully, I had set all of them to stealth mode to avoid causing any distress to the fauna while surveying the land. As it didn't possess the advanced anti-detection systems of a military-grade drone, I worried that our targets might detect it. However, as the intruders had no specific reason to suspect we were onto them, they blissfully went about their business, apparently not scanning for potential threats.

To our collective shock, their ship headed straight for the Svast Temple. Aku uttered a series of swear words in his language. Enre bared his teeth, the same fury visible on his features. Even though this wasn't my planet or my sacred shrine, I felt personally violated when I watched them land in a large clearing near the pathway that led to the entrance.

"Thank God there are no pilgrims there right now," Ciara mused aloud. "I can't imagine how ugly things might have turned otherwise."

"It seems incredibly convenient," Aku countered, the same anger visible on his face. "Just yesterday, over four hundred of our people were there. Tomorrow, hundreds more will arrive in the morning. How did they know to come today to be undetected?"

That was an excellent question that triggered many more, all of which would likely yield the type of answers I dreaded. But two passengers disembarking from the vessel sent another shock-wave among us. Despite the model of the ship, it wasn't a pair of Nazhrals who came out, but a human and a Raithean.

"What the hell?!" Ciara uttered under her breath.

Although stunned, I immediately directed the drone to capture their images to attempt facial recognition. Unfortunately, as I didn't have network access, I would need to transfer the data to my contact later to try and identify them.

Both intruders walked the short distance up the path to the water by the entrance of the temple. The human remained on the edge while the Raithean went into the water. He waded through the shallow part, occasionally pausing for a few seconds before moving again. And then he dove into the deeper part, completely vanishing from view while his companion observed in silence.

"What are they doing?" Aku asked. "Who are they? And are they a threat?"

Frowning, I shook my head, failing to find a satisfying explanation.

"I'm not sure. They came in a vessel that does not belong to either of their species. But they could have purchased it used in a shipyard for a reasonable price. They don't seem to be doing anything other than the Raithean getting into the water. It is salt water, correct?"

Aku nodded.

"As you can see, Raitheans are an amphibian species. They need to soak in salt water at regular intervals. So it might explain why he is doing this," I said, although my tone made it clear that my own explanation didn't come even remotely close to convincing me.

"Fair enough," Aku said, his voice still dripping with suspicion. "But why our temple? There's plenty of water everywhere else. Some of the areas they flew over on their way to Svast had large, unobstructed shores that would have been a lot more convenient for them to land in. This feels too deliberate."

"Oh God!" Ciara suddenly exclaimed. "This is Kalmia! They're here to kill us all!"

CHAPTER 15
CIARA

A powerful sense of dread washed over me even as I spoke those words. My companions gasped, shock and confusion warring over their features as they looked at me in disbelief.

"What?!" Aku exclaimed. "Kill us all, how? What is that Kalmia?"

I licked my lips nervously as I ran my fingers through my hair, my mind racing as I observed the intruders. Raitheans were frequently referred to as Krakens on Earth. They possessed an upper body similar to humans, with a torso, two arms, and a head, but with thick tentacles instead of hair. And their lower body was made of eight tentacles like an octopus, but only half of them had suction cups.

"Raitheans—the male you see with the human—share similarities with certain creatures from Earth called squids and octopuses. They're recognizable by the tentacles that form the lower half of their bodies instead of legs," I explained. "Generally, they're a peaceful species, but they also possess some extremely lethal abilities."

"Like what?" Aku insisted.

"They can produce pearl-like growths that we call calcareous concretions," I continued. "They're usually shaped like small pebbles or stones. They can be smooth or rough, but usually with Raitheans, they look like red rocks."

Aku stiffened, his face taking on a frightened expression that chilled me to the bone. He wasn't the type to openly show fear.

"There should be no red rocks in the river," he whispered with a look of dread.

"Exactly! I'm not sure why I know that, but—"

"My friend warned us it might happen," Aku replied dismissively, interrupting me. "What exactly do these rocks do? How dangerous are they?"

That comment threw me. I wanted to ask what else his friend mentioned about it, but there would be time later for this.

"Mollusks like squids usually produce pearls or those concretions as a natural defense against irritants, parasites, or wounds. If a foreign object gets lodged inside their bodies, and they can't expel it, they will coat it with some sort of nacre to prevent it from damaging them further. In Raitheans, it's a little different in that they form a coat that is fibrous and not crystallized like nacre."

"All right," Aku said hesitantly, waiting to see where I was going with this.

"Pearls made out of nacre are extremely difficult to destroy whereas the fibrous ones crumble fairly easily under pressure or under extended exposure to something that could dilute them, like water," I explained.

His eyes widened with understanding.

"Normally, the calcareous concretions are not a threat since they usually just contain a wood shard or other similar irritants that embedded themselves inside their bodies. But in a very nasty war involving the Raitheans, we discovered that they could use that ability in a lethal fashion to eliminate massive numbers of people. They possess a natural venom that can inflict a terrible disease comparable to what we call malaria on Earth."

"A lethal disease?" Aku asked.

I hesitated. "It can be if it's not diagnosed and treated quickly. The Raitheans produce very thin darts the size of a needle that they can shoot from the suction cups on their tentacles. They normally fire those from a distance the same way you do with your blowpipes, which is how they infect their targets."

"Fine, but what does that have to do with the red rocks?" Aku asked, sounding a little annoyed and impatient.

I gestured for him to bear with me as I tried to summarize the entire concept even more succinctly.

"The problem is that, during that war, the Raitheans deliberately ate toxic plants which allowed them to secrete a virulent acid that they mixed with their venom before coating their darts with the combination. The same way they wrap a shard or irritant with a fibrous membrane in their bodies, they can wrap their lethal darts with it as well. And they become like time bombs," I said.

"The Raithean is coming out of the water," Amreth suddenly said, interrupting us.

He had swum a considerable distance from where he initially entered. That further worried me. Had he scattered a bunch of stones all over the riverbed?

"Your drone must scan the water for the presence of those rocks," I said, my voice tense.

"I need the parameters for it," Amreth replied. "I can configure this one for now, but I have a second drone incoming. This first one needs to stay with the ship in case they move."

I nodded and swiftly started punching in some parameters, which I hoped would suffice. Otherwise, we would have to wait until they departed for the second drone to arrive and get close enough to the water for the camera to pick up their potential presence.

As he emerged from the water, the Raithean twisted six of his eight tentacles in sets of three, forming a makeshift pair of legs that allowed him to walk in a strange, wobbly bipedal fashion. It was a common practice for their people as they could taste with the suction cups of their tentacles and didn't really care to lick the ground. Granted, they could block the taste receptor, but some crumbs always lingered when they glided on any surface.

To our surprise, as soon as he caught up to the human, both males got back onboard their vessel and took flight. Simultaneously, Amreth's bracer beeped with the drone sending a confirmation that it indeed detected Puricis stones in the water.

"We must go at once and stop them," Aku said even as he jumped to his feet and started marching towards the exit, Enre shadowing him.

"Wait," Amreth said in a commanding tone. "We cannot go after them in the shuttle. If things get heated, their ship will obliterate us. And what of the stones? How long before they poison the water?"

"It will take some time for the fibrous shell to dissolve," I said pensively. "It all depends on how thick he made them. If they knew that the temple would be empty today, but that people would come tomorrow, then he will have made it thick enough to last at least twenty-four hours."

"Which gives us plenty of time to go after them," Aku insisted.

"Yes, but only if my assumptions are correct," I cautioned him. "You can go after them while Mehreen, Ernst, and I go after the stones at the temple. We just need a moment to gather some equipment and hazmat suits."

"If you want to tag along, we need to use the shuttle to fly to the ship," Amreth intervened when Aku opened his mouth to argue against that additional delay. "It wouldn't make sense for us to monopolize both vessels while leaving these stones longer than necessary in your sacred shrine. The drone is currently tracking them. They will not escape. Let's do this right."

Teeth clenched, Aku gave us a stiff nod. "While you prepare,

I will have Sora send a message to Vala and the other Kalds to warn them to steer clear of any water that shares a stream with the temple."

"That's an excellent idea," I said with a grateful smile.

We hurried to the deployable lab and grabbed everything we needed. As we hopped into the shuttle, a million different thoughts fired off in my mind. As soon as we settled down in the passenger seat and Amreth got us airborne, I shared the theories taking root in my head.

"I think I finally got it," I said pensively. "Puricis—the red stone bomb the Raitheans produce—would effectively serve to repeat Kalmia. Anyone who enters in contact with it doesn't just get sick. The acid will also liquify them from within. By the time it has run its course, the person is completely unrecognizable and has turned into a puddle of gore."

"So all the pilgrims would be wiped out?" Aku asked angrily.

"It would be worse than that," I said apologetically. "Puricis is highly contagious, once the symptoms appear. Death is atrocious but comes quickly. The bacteria transfer through mere contact, but especially through the patient's sweat. It lasts for about twenty-four hours. But as soon as the fever breaks, the patient dies within the hour."

"What is this Kalmia you keep mentioning?" Aku asked, looking distraught.

"It was a massacre that took place between two rival cartels," Amreth explained. "One of the cartels poisoned the water source of their enemies' compound. It wiped out everyone. What troubles me is that if the assassins are targeting your temples now, they know that this is the season during which a majority of your people will go into that water. Who would have that kind of information about your customs?"

"No one should," Aku said with helpless frustration. "Even our friends know very little about us. They do not pry the same way we do not pry about them. So clearly, off-worlders are spying on us. Which brings me to your own friends. Who warned you about the assassins?"

"The same friend who told me to come here and rescue my mate," Amreth replied in a factual manner.

"You trust them?" Aku insisted.

"Yes. Without this message, tomorrow or in a couple of days from now, we would be waking up to an irreversible tragedy," Amreth said. "The question is why? Who hates you so much they would attempt to wipe you out when you seemingly just want to go about your lives?"

"The answer is obviously the powerful people our friends told us would come after us with vicious wrath if we went public," Aku replied.

"Tharmok's blood!" Amreth suddenly exclaimed, his eyes widening. "Didn't you say that Elias claimed that the creature at the origin of SS12 decomposed too quickly for them to have anything to show for? That it all but liquified?"

My jaw dropped. "Yes. That's the explanation he gave when people asked about it. This cannot be a coincidence. He used Puricis as a reference to justify everything. But why would he go to such extremes over that initial incident? It doesn't make sense."

"Whatever the reason, they clearly want to wipe out the Kreelars and erase all traces of their existence," Amreth said in a harsh tone, his silver-white eyes gleaming with unyielding determination. "Let's go catch those fiends. They *will* talk."

The five-minute flight to Amreth's ship felt like an eternity. As soon as we landed, Aku rushed out of the shuttle. I understood his impatience. His people had already suffered so much, this new threat would be the final blow.

"You be careful and come back to me in one piece, you hear?" I told Amreth as we stood by the shuttle's ramp.

"I promise, my mate. You also be careful out there. I didn't just find you to already lose you," he replied.

"Not a chance. You're stuck with me," I said with a smile despite the apprehension twisting my insides.

We exchanged a kiss, far too brief, but we couldn't linger any longer. Aku would probably lose his shit anyway, with good reason.

As soon as Amreth exited, I went back to my seat while Mehreen piloted the shuttle out of the hangar to the temple. Barely a minute after our departure, Amreth's ship took off. I clamped down on the dreadful images wanting to worm their way into my mind about all the ways things could go wrong. Reminding myself that Amreth was an elite Warrior and a Warden on Molvi helped alleviate some of my fears.

I really cared about him. The prospect of a life without him was unbearable.

But as we closed in on the temple, I refocused on the task at hand. We quickly donned our hazmat suits. To Enre's dismay, they weren't suitable for him or the other two Kreelars who came with us, in no small part due to their tails.

Further scans of the area thankfully didn't reveal the presence of any other person, cameras, or drones that the would-be assassins might have left behind. It either testified to an excess of confidence or a high degree of carelessness. Whatever the reason, it served us just fine.

As we waded into the water, a wave of anger surged within me. This was such a cowardly and underhanded way of eliminating people who had done absolutely nothing but tried to live their lives in peace. Had we not seen the Raithean get inside the water, the chances of anyone discovering what had happened would have been slim to none.

Due to their relatively small size, detecting the Puricis stones would be nearly impossible if you didn't know of their presence beforehand. And even then, we had to use our scanners as we kept walking right past some of them, which too conveniently blended with the riverbed. We picked up twenty-two pebbles and stored them inside a biohazard container.

"How bad is it?" Enre asked, his voice tense as I sealed the container.

"For the water?" I asked.

He nodded, his back stiff.

I gave him a reassuring smile. "Ernst is taking some water samples for further analysis back at the lab, but all our initial scans show that it is safe. The stones themselves have a pretty thick coating. I'm confident that nothing leaked. We caught everything early enough, and there's no strong current that could have dragged them away. The water is also relatively cold. It slows down the breakdown of the fibrous shell. Had the water been warm, it would have been more problematic. All should be well."

"Thank you," Enre said, his voice thick with emotion. "Our people cannot handle another large-scale tragedy."

His companions nodded, their expressions grim.

"And we're going to do everything in our power to make sure it doesn't happen," I said reassuringly. "Let's go back to the village, test this stuff, and destroy it."

CHAPTER 16
AMRETH

We gave chase to the vessel in stealth mode. Judging by their flight pattern, they seemed to have a very specific destination in mind. I entered a few instructions in my navigation board so that the artificial intelligence would calculate their potential trajectory.

Sitting in the copilot chair, Aku suddenly muttered a string of curse words in his language. I glanced at him inquisitively.

"That map your device is showing is pointing directly to Lenph," Aku said angrily. "It is another temple similar to Svast but located in another territory. We are close to crossing the border."

"Is it illegal?" I asked carefully. "Are there any conflicts between your territories?"

He shook his head. "Kreelars are a peaceful people. We would all be one if the land wasn't so vast and the distances so great. We're all an extended family. But it would be unrealistic for every tribe to attend the same temple. The journey would be too long."

"How many such temples do you have?" I asked Aku.

"Three in total. But those two other territories—Lenph and

Durgh—have not been touched by the sickness. Only the tribes that worship at Svast Temple have been affected. The disease has not traveled beyond our territory."

I nodded grimly. "The berries have not spread beyond your borders, yet. Let's make sure they never do."

I increased our speed to further close the gap with our quarry. I wanted to be able to intercept them before the Raithean could begin to release his poisoned stones in the river. The gods only knew what damage had already been done at Svast Temple.

A glance at the overlay display from the drone's camera feed showed me the area that the enemy ship was flying in, as well as a ghostly outline of the vessel itself. From our current location, we couldn't see through its camouflage.

I tapped a few instructions so that as soon as we were five hundred meters from them, the autopilot would kick in and maintain us at a steady distance from them. The goal was to sneak up on them as soon as they lowered their ramp. Judging by their previous actions at Svast Temple, they were fairly careless and overly confident that no one was onto them.

"What are you doing?" Aku asked when I began typing a message on a different screen.

"Sending images of the two intruders to my friend," I replied. "We have facial recognition technology that might help them find their identities and hopefully locate any accomplices they might have or maybe even who their employer is. We need to find the source before they attempt to strike again."

"Good. They must answer for their crimes," Aku snarled. "We would know—"

An incoming com request interrupted him, startling us both.

"What in Tharmok's name…?!" I whispered.

There shouldn't be such a quick response, let alone a direct com request. There were no relays or satellites nearby. Or at least, in theory…

"What is it?" Aku asked.

"A communication request from my friend. I'm going to accept it," I replied.

He gave me a stiff nod, his tension almost palpable.

A million thoughts fired off in my mind when Maeve's face appeared on my screen as soon as I accepted the communication. She said she would be away on a different mission. And yet here she was, in close enough range to have a live vidcom in an area where that should not be possible.

"Maeve," I said in greeting. "This is Aku, the leader of the tribe hosting us. Aku, this is Maeve, my friend."

"It is a pleasure to meet you, Kald Aku," Maeve replied.

"Likewise," Aku responded in a non-committal fashion, his voice polite but cold.

"I do not mean to be curt or rude, but I cannot maintain this connection too long," Maeve continued. "We're analyzing the data you sent, Amreth. What's your status?"

"We're closing in on them. We intend to confront them as soon as they land. We believe they are headed for another temple," I replied before glancing at the overlay of the drone's camera feed. "In fact, I can see it in the distance. They're almost there. We need to hurry."

"Chase them away from Kestria, but do not give pursuit," Maeve ordered.

"WHAT?! Absolutely not!" Aku hissed. "We're going to catch those murderers, and they will answer to my people."

"They must face justice!" Maeve argued. "The law—"

"To *Dramsta* with your laws! This is Kestria!" Aku shouted, his muscles swelling with anger. "You off-worlders caused the death of countless numbers of my people, and now you dare to dictate how the culprits will be handled?!"

Maeve raised her palms in an appeasing gesture. "We're not trying to dictate anything or to impose our will upon your people. Despite the tragic events that took place, please rest assured that we respect your sovereignty. However, we need irrefutable proof against the people who ordered these crimes and funded this attack so that they can face justice. You cannot kill them."

"Why shouldn't we?" Aku challenged, his anger still audible. "Their remains will be proof enough. Unlike them, we will not use poisons that will liquify their bodies to the point they are unrecognizable."

"She makes a valid point, Aku. Without them alive and forced to testify, it will be harder to prove their guilt," I said in a soothing tone. "The fact that we have their bodies does not mean they came to your home world with evil intentions, or that they even came intentionally. It could be a setup to harm someone we have a conflict with."

"You have your recording devices," Aku countered.

"We do," I conceded. "However, those videos can be doctored, modified to show what we want them to show. Many courts will not grant them a lot of weight when it comes to passing judgment."

"They're landing!" Aku said, his attention shifting to the overlaid display on the screen showing our quarry beginning its descent. "Go faster!"

Unlike Svast Temple, there was no need to walk a narrow path to the river that led to the entrance. A large clearing framed each side of the river, which led to the rocky formation that this temple had been carved into. A few trees, placed at equidistant intervals, adorned the edges of the shore, their long branches almost forming an arch over the river.

"I'm sorry, Maeve. We must go," I said apologetically.

"Please, Amreth! Do not kill them! They're vital to this case!" Maeve pleaded.

"Noted. Goodbye," I replied in a non-committal fashion.

She pinched her lips in resignation and gave me a stiff nod. I terminated the communication and sped towards the temple. I cursed myself inwardly for not having pushed harder earlier.

Despite the long journey we had traveled, I stupidly thought we would have had a bit more time and therefore reined in our speed to reduce the chances of being discovered.

To my surprise, although their ship landed, they didn't lower the ramp right away. In fact, nothing seemed to happen in the five minutes it took for us to catch up at high speed. I slowed the ship down and landed two hundred meters away from them. Still, they remained inside with no sign of coming out.

Another incoming message nearly had me jumping out of my skin. Tharmok's blood! When did I become so nervous? To my surprise, it was an analog signal from Ciara. My initial relief quickly gave way to worry that something might have gone awry.

"Ciara?" I said in lieu of greeting as soon as the communication was established. "Is everything alright?"

"Yes. We took care of everything at the temple," she replied. "If you find more stones, do not touch them. Just send the coordinates, and we will come handle it."

"They are at another temple, right now. But for some reason, they are not coming out of their vessel. Our systems do not indicate that they have detected us, but I'm beginning to wonder," I replied, hating that I could not see her face.

"I'm not surprised," Ciara replied immediately with confidence, taking me aback. "Raitheans need time to create more of those stones. Considering the quantity that we retrieved from the river, and depending on how skilled he is, it should take him about an hour to create a similar amount with a comparable thickness of fibrous shell. That means at least another fifteen to twenty minutes."

Relief flooded through me. "That's excellent news."

"Is Svast Temple safe?" Aku interjected.

"So far, we have every reason to believe that it didn't sustain any damage. The initial tests indicate that the water is safe, but we are going to continue running more in-depth scans," Ciara responded.

"Perfect. We're going to try to prevent them from putting anything in the water. I will message you once things are handled here," I replied.

"Understood. Be safe," Ciara said.

As soon as the communication ended, I turned to look at Aku.

"We can't kill them, my friend," I said in a gentle tone.

His face immediately hardened. I could deal with his anger, but the glimmer of betrayal in his eyes cut me deeply.

"I am *not* letting them escape and then just hope that some off-worlder will catch them and make them answer for their crimes," he snarled. "You above all others, as a Warden of the principal prison of your alliance, should understand that local laws should be enforced when a crime has been committed against the people."

"I do, my friend. Believe me, I do. But these two males are mere grunts in the greater scheme of things," I said in a reasonable tone. "If you choose to torture or kill them, whatever my personal feelings on the matter, I cannot interfere. This is your planet and therefore your rules."

"Exactly. And our rules say they will stand before the Kalds to face our wrath," Aku snapped.

I sighed, my mind racing to find an argument that might sway him. It was an odd predicament to find myself in. As a Warden, and even during my compulsory service as a Peacekeeper as part of my training, I never had to juggle this type of diplomatic conflict. As I'd only ever interacted with member planets of the UPO, we had a set of laws that applied to all, which also took into account their individual planetary laws.

"You have incredible power right now. Dead people don't talk. From them, we can gather enough proof to lead to the masterminds. If they've done this to your people, chances are they have done the same or maybe even worse to others. The powerful people your friend alluded to must be stopped. These two could help us achieve that."

He stared at me for a long time without a word. For a brief instant, I hoped I might have gotten through to him, but his face hardened again.

"They *will* talk," he replied.

I opened my mouth to argue again, but the look in his eyes clearly told me to let it go. Heaving another sigh, I rose to my feet. The suspicion that instantly sparked in his eyes stung again. As much as I understood his anger, I hated how this situation had sufficed to severely undermine the friendship and trust that we had gradually built since our arrival.

"I'm going to place EMP charges on their ship," I said in response to his unspoken question. "They are devices that will release a powerful electric discharge that will destroy their engine and navigation systems," I explained. "Should they attempt to flee, I can remotely activate it and make sure they cannot escape."

Aku immediately relaxed, suspicion giving way to a mix of approval and gratitude. There was no question in my mind that he intended to beat them into a pulp. Frankly, in his stead, I would want to do the same. I only hoped I could talk him down if and when we got to that part.

The main question for me was who and how many ships lurked nearby in orbit. I couldn't tell for sure that Maeve was among them. In fact, I suspected that she had been honest by claiming to be on another mission elsewhere. But the clarity of our vidcom implied that the UPO had likely snuck in a satellite, a relay, or one of those communication ships that acted as a satellite. I was heavily leaning towards the latter option as it would avoid suspicion since such vessels were camouflaged to look inconspicuous if detected.

I only knew of their existence because of my high security

clearance as a Warden, since such vessels had previously been used during raids to apprehend some of the inmates that landed in my Sector.

The UPO couldn't have a small fleet up there. Even if they managed to do so undetected, once they decloaked to catch the assassins—assuming they managed to flee from us—it would create a different issue within the justice system if they raided the Dead Zone without a warrant. One or two vessels were far more likely. But it also meant that the assassins would have an easier time of escaping. The EMPs would make certain they didn't.

I retrieved the EMP devices from the armory as well as a pair of blasters, one of which I extended to Aku. He lifted his nose at it before glancing at me as if I'd done something offensive. Nodding in concession, I put the weapon back in its place and offered him a bracer.

"It has an energy shield that you activate like this," I said, demonstrating it by activating the one on my own bracer.

"That won't be necessary," Aku said.

This time, I glared at him with annoyance. "If things turn ugly with those two males, they will fire their weapons at you. Blaster shots are nasty and will kill you. It's fine if you don't want to use a Blaster as they do require some training, but there's no reason for you not to use a shield. I have no intention of returning to your village without you walking on your own two feet."

"Careful, Obosian. You're starting to sound like you care," he replied in a taunting tone. "But I will be fine. Let's not dally. Based on your mate's estimate, they will come out any minute now."

"At least, use the personal stealth shield feature of the bracer," I insisted with preemptive exasperation, waiting for him to turn me down again.

To my surprise, he pursed his lips before giving me a nod. "The invisibility feature could be useful. I consent to that one."

I gaped at him, my mouth closing with an audible sound when he raised a mocking eyebrow at me. After showing him how to turn it on and off, we quickly discussed our strategy, then exited the ship.

I double checked that his stealth shield was properly activated before we stepped outside of the camouflage radius around our vessel. The look on his face was almost feral. Despite the multiple days spent among his people, Aku had done a great job of keeping us mostly in the dark about them. I didn't know how they chose who would be their Kald, but I suspected that it included not only leadership and diplomacy, but also being the apex alpha. And right now, his face loudly expressed that a savage and ruthless predator lurked within him.

I gestured for him to stand back as I quickly approached the ship. Heart pounding, I snuck up to the back of the vessel, crouching as low as I could to place the EMP charge as close as possible to the engine, but also at an angle that would be difficult to visually notice without having your attention deliberately brought to it.

I was just about to circle to the other side to place the second magnet when the whiny sound of the ramp lowering startled me. My head jerked towards Aku. Through his stealth shield, he appeared to me like a ghostly silhouette. But it hid nothing of the savage expression that descended over his features as he took a defensive stance, ready to lunge forward. I gestured for him not to move just yet. His eyes flicked towards me for a brief second before refocusing on the two males exiting the Nazhral vessel.

Aku removed his blowpipe from his belt while I stealthily approached him. My eyes widened as he extruded a set of vicious claws I didn't realize he possessed. Not even during the hunt against the Murthis had he extended them that much. I knew the Kreelars could extrude their claws a little, which they regularly did to help them more easily climb on trees. But this was something else. It sent a cold shiver down my spine as I realized this could be yet another sign he wouldn't let them live.

"This planet is truly beautiful," the Raithean said as he walked down the ramp in that strange fashion his people did whenever they twisted their tentacles into makeshift legs. "It's quite a shame to poison it and its people. There's no pleasure in killing the innocent ones."

"Who cares?" the man said with a mix of annoyance and contempt. "Don't be a fucking pussy. They're just a bunch of talking monkeys. We don't even have to get our hands dirty to get rid of them. This is the easiest pile of credits I will have made in a long time."

"It's not about the credits," the Raithean grumbled as he stopped walking a few steps after getting off the ramp. "Some things are more important than that."

"Nothing is more important than that, you dumb fuck. Since when have you gotten so damn sentimental?"

He shrugged. "I'm not sentimental. I will not lose any sleep over them. I just take no pleasure fucking over someone who hasn't done me wrong. There's no honor in poisoning people who aren't bothering anyone."

"Dude, spare me the repentant scoundrel act. Just go poop your shit out so that we can get the fuck out of here. There are a few fine bitches on Galathea Space Station that will be bouncing on my cock with all those credits we're making. So get to pooping already!"

"I do not defecate in the water. Creating Puricis takes time, and they must last forty-eight hours before they unravel," the Raithean said with a look of contempt for his companion. "Their people are still traveling here."

"I don't give two shits about any of that. Just get it done!"

"You will care when you do not receive your credits because of a botched job, you stupid human! If the poison releases too early, the flora, fauna, and fish nearby will all be dead by the time their people arrive. They will know something happened. What do you think Marilia will do to us once the Enforcers are alerted?"

My heart leapt upon hearing that name. Was he referring to Marilia Hesper, the CEO of Typhoon Pharma, the biggest intergalactic pharmaceutical conglomerate? That name was too unique to be a coincidence.

The human muttered something inaudible under his breath, the threat apparently convincing him to back off.

"I'm almost done," the Raithean finally said reluctantly. "Give me five more minutes."

"I don't think so!" Aku hissed as he dropped his stealth shield.

I groaned inwardly that he gave us away so soon. The Raithean could have made a few more revelations that would help us round up all the people involved in this mess.

Both assassins gasped as they abruptly pivoted to their right to face us. The human instinctively reached for his blaster while the Raithean raised the two remaining tentacles that he hadn't wrapped into his makeshift legs. Before either of them could fire, Aku shot a dart at the human with his blowpipe. It found its mark into the man's neck. The human's left hand flew to the point of entry even as he tried to fire. The shot went wide, and he stumbled back, the strength of the paralytic on it working at an insane speed on him.

Barely sparing him any attention as he collapsed, his eyes becoming glassy, I darted forward as I activated my energy shield to parry the volley of poisoned darts the Raithean launched towards Aku from the suction cups of his tentacles. They crashed against my shield, making it sparkle. My hands tingled as I invoked my Lumiak and blasted it at the Raithean. He dodged to the left into a roll, before getting back onto his now unfurled tentacles.

This time, he raised four tentacles to shoot a second flurry of darts while slithering in an erratic pattern towards the ramp to make himself harder to target. But I cut him off, flying in his path while blasting more Lumiak at him. Aku was also already on the move. He ran towards the Raithean, jumping at an impossible height to avoid the projectiles.

The Raithean activated his own energy shield, blocking my lightning, but leaving himself open to Aku's dart. He shouted in anger when he felt its sting as it embedded itself in his hip. Realizing he would never make it back onto his ship, and that he couldn't face off against the two of us on his own, he made a dash for the river. He kept his shield raised in front of him while slithering backwards at an astounding speed and firing his own darts at us.

I felt the psionic energy emanating from Aku half a beat before the Raithean faltered. He blinked multiple times and shook his head like someone trying to recover from a brutal slap. I flew towards him, unimpeded, as he was focusing his attacks on my companion, who was still not using a shield. It was a foolish endeavor as the Kreelar was moving much too fast, jumping and leaping out of harm's way at dizzying speed while shooting his blowpipe almost like an automatic weapon.

Many—if not all—of Aku's darts hit their target. And yet, the Raithean didn't instantly go numb or paralyzed like the human had. It struck me then that he was likely coating each dart with his fibrous membrane before the venom could negatively impact him.

But can he truly neutralize them this fast?

That was a question for another time. Despite Aku's psychically disrupting his mind, the Raithean managed to slither all the way to the edge of the shore. I swooped in, hoping to catch him before he got into the water, which would make it extremely difficult to tackle him. To my shock, Aku leapt onto a tree by the shore, right above our prey. He swung around the branch, throwing his tail like a lasso, and latching on to one of the Raithean's tentacles just as he was diving into the water.

Like a gymnast spinning around a horizontal bar, Aku rotated back towards the clearing, yanking the Raithean back with him. He flung him onto the ground with brutal force. Stunned, he attempted to get back onto his tentacles and raise his shield to deflect any attacks from us, but he wasn't fast enough. My Lumiak struck him straight in the chest. His body seized, and he flopped back onto the ground, shaken by spasms. Fighting the urge to zap him once more with even greater intensity, I whipped out my blaster instead and shot him at the highest stun setting. His body jerked once more before going limp.

Aku landed on his feet and ran the short distance to his fallen prey. The murderous look in his eyes sent another chill down my spine.

"He's unconscious for now," I said preemptively while crouching next to the Raithean. "It will last about ten minutes. I'm going to put the control collar on both him and the human. It will keep them from trying to escape or otherwise attempt to attack us. In his case, it will also prevent him from producing his poison darts."

Aku didn't answer. He just stood there, observing me, claws fully extended, and his fingers twitching as if he was fighting the urge to tear the unconscious male to shreds. I removed the collar from my belt and quickly set it around the Raithean's neck before configurating it for his specific species. It would send distinctive neuronal signals inhibiting certain functions.

I moved to the human who was still very much conscious and aware, merely paralyzed. He could still speak and think rationally, but his limbs were too heavy to move. Even his speech was slightly slurred as he began to shower me with insults when I closed the collar around his neck.

"Let's bring them back inside their ship," I said, unnerved by the cold—not to say sadistic—intensity with which Aku was still staring at the unconscious male.

I picked up the human and carried him in my arms back up the ramp. I had mixed feelings about Aku grabbing the Raithean by the wrist of his right arm and dragging him behind him like dead weight. By galactic standards, it would be deemed an abusive and illegal mistreatment of a prisoner. I itched to request that he carry him in a more compassionate fashion but held my tongue. This minor roughness was better than a summary execution.

We took them to the bridge and sat them in the chairs near the science and tactical stations. After shackling them to their seats, I turned to the navigation board and attempted to hail Maeve. To my shock, she once again answered almost immediately. Whatever doubt I still held about them either having a communication vessel or temporary satellite in orbit vanished.

"Are they alive?" she immediately asked.

"For now," Aku replied in a cold voice.

Maeve pinched her lips but didn't argue. "Give me access to their computer. I will show you how."

I followed her simple instructions, and within seconds, the entire navigation board lit up.

"Thank you," Maeve said, her voice tense as she glanced towards my companion who was still towering over the prisoners. She returned her attention to me, her eyes doing all the speaking. "I'm counting on you, Amreth."

I nodded, understanding her unspoken request. It was a tall order, but one I hoped to manage.

"The Raithean mentioned something about a Marilia. I suspect it might be Marilia Hesper. You may want to look into her."

The enigmatic smile she gave me, laced with a hint of triumph in her dark brown eyes hinted that she was already onto her.

"Noted," she replied in a noncommittal fashion. "Maeve out."

Although she ended the communication, I knew the Enforcers' top hacker was currently scrubbing every single piece of data from the ship including their communications logs. Anything that could be gathered wouldn't escape her.

As soon as I joined Aku by the prisoners, he turned his attention to the human, who was conscious and furious. Judging by the general stillness of his body, the paralytic still affected him.

"Who sent you?" Aku demanded, having apparently waited for me to be done before beginning the interrogation.

"I want a lawyer," the human said with arrogance.

"You're on Kestria, you *smarva*! Here, you do not get a lawyer. This is *my* world, and you will follow *my* rules."

"I don't care about your rules, you stupid monkey. I'm not talking without a lawyer," he spat, lifting his chin defiantly.

The fool didn't seem to realize how precarious a situation he was in. He foolishly believed my presence provided him with some kind of protection. On any other world, that would have been true, but not here.

Aku tilted his head to the side, and a menacing grin stretched his lips.

"You know, we recovered the little rocks your friend dropped in the sacred waters of Svast Temple earlier," he said in a sickly-sweet voice. "As we Kreelars believe in treating others as they treat us, I'm feeling rather inclined to give you a bath with them. Our friend Ciara mentioned something about warm water speeding up the experience. Tell me human, what would you prefer? A hot bath or a friendly conversation?"

With each of his words, the human grew a little paler. He had the tanned skin of someone used to working outdoors. He appeared to be in his early to mid-forties, with greasy black hair to his shoulders, a two-day beard, beady blue eyes, and a crooked nose that indicated it had been broken at least once or twice. Tall and lanky, he struck me as the type who promptly tried to resolve issues with a blaster, but who would run from hand-to-hand combat.

"Torture is illegal," he hissed, trying to sound brave despite the fear seeping into his voice as he turned his attention to me. "Tell him!"

"I have nothing to tell him," I replied nonchalantly with a shrug. "You've heard him. This is his planet. Therefore, we observe his rules."

"But you're an Obosian! You are sworn to uphold the laws!" the man exclaimed, his panic steadily growing.

"Exactly. And his people make the local laws. I will abide by them. If the Kreelars authorize torture, there's nothing I can do about it."

"You're bluffing!" he shouted, clinging to denial. "This planet is a member of the UPO. We perform trades with the Sangoths!"

"This planet is *not* a member of the UPO," I corrected. "The Sangoths have a limited agreement with them, but it does not extend to any other species here. This is the Dead Zone. The United Planets Organization has no jurisdiction here, nor do the Enforcers or the Peacekeepers. So, unless you want to see your guts turn into mush, I suggest you start speaking. Because I assure you that Aku will be more than happy to give you a taste of what you had in store for his people."

This time, the seriousness of his situation finally sank in. He licked his lips nervously, his wheels spinning as he attempted to come up with a reply. He glanced at his companion bound next to him only to find him still unconscious. The Raithean would be awakening any minute now, not that he would be of any assistance to him.

"I don't know anything," the human said at last. "I'm just a hired hand. This was one of many contracts. My job was to fly him around so that he could drop his shit in three temples and in the wells if needed."

"Why?" Aku snarled. "Why would you do this to us?"

The human shrugged, his movement barely noticeable due to the lingering paralysis. "It's pretty damn obvious. They told us to exterminate the monkeys and scientists."

A blinding fury swelled within me, not only because of the continued disrespect towards the Kreelars, but also the callousness with which he expressed his intention of murdering an entire species alongside with my mate and her colleagues.

"You would do well to watch your tone, human," I hissed. "You're in no position to talk down to people that are far better than you ever will be. Now answer the blasted question. Why were you sent to kill them?"

"I don't know, and I don't give a shit. They were offering a nice chunk of change, and I just wanted to get paid. Why, and who gets hurt in the process is not my fucking problem," the man replied belligerently.

"You lie!" Aku ground through his teeth.

He was right. A quick glimpse at the man's aura confirmed his deception, and also something else. Treachery came to mind.

What is he up to?

A powerful wave of psionic energy startled me. Not even a second later, the human screamed, and blood started trickling out of his nose. Teeth bared, and a vicious expression on his face, Aku was staring at the man with a hatred that sent a chill down my spine. It took every ounce of my willpower not to intervene. I didn't believe in torture. But then, as an advanced species, I enjoyed many benefits from technology that helped loosen certain reluctant tongues. I wanted to believe that my companion wouldn't push things to a point where I would have no choice but to step in.

As much as I believed in respecting the laws of his people, I could not sit back and watch a murder being committed, no matter how much the victim might have deserved it.

The wave of psionic energy ended just as abruptly as it began. The man's head dropped to his chest, his shrieks fading into pained whimpers as he breathed heavily.

"Speak or I will make you wish you could die," Aku said in a menacing voice. "Your people brought death and suffering to mine with a sickness that nearly wiped us out. And now, you threaten us with extermination. You *will* tell me why."

"I don't know anything! I swear!" the man pleaded.

Aku didn't insist and simply gave him another generous serving of psionic strikes. My stomach roiled, every fiber of my being screaming for me to stop him. This wasn't the way to do it. It troubled me all the more that, although his voice screamed sincerity as far as him not knowing anything, the human's aura continued to say that he was being deceptive about something.

When blood began to trickle from the man's ear, I placed a hand on Aku's shoulder in an appeasing fashion. I didn't say a word. He gave me a sideways glance, our eyes locking for a moment. He clearly wanted to tell me in a less-than-friendly way to back off. To my pleasant surprise—and utter relief—he relented and stopped his attack.

The man wheezed and cried, all his previous arrogant bravado gone.

"He doesn't know anything," the Raithean suddenly said, startling us both.

His head was still bowed, giving us the impression that he remained unconscious. The shorter and narrower tentacles dangling from his head, and which acted as hair, hid his face, reinforcing the illusion he was still passed out. He lifted it, the nictating membrane of his double eyelids blinking as he looked at us with a slightly groggy expression.

"Bruce is just a grunt. He's too stupid for people to confide anything in him beyond the specifics of his tasks," the Raithean said in a tired voice.

"But *you* know what's going on," I retorted.

"I know *some* of what is going on, but not all," he corrected before shifting his attention to Aku. "I don't know anything about the sickness that the scientists are trying to cure. But the continued existence of your people has become too great of a threat now that you have found a way to travel off-world. Our employer cannot risk you exposing them."

"Shut up, Nylar!" Bruce hissed.

"No, *you* shut up, stupid human," Nylar replied, as he gave him a disgusted sideways glance. "We're not getting rescued. But you're too dumb to see it."

"You don't know that!" Bruce countered.

"Look at the monitor," Nylar said, gesturing with his chin at the overlay screen above the navigation board. "The artificial intelligence is currently transferring all our data. They have someone skilled enough to remotely take control of our ship. By now, they've already seen and handled our pre-programmed emergency rescue call. We're screwed. So, we might as well come clean."

"We have indeed taken control of your ship's computer," I confirmed, while narrowing my eyes suspiciously at him. "But why are you suddenly so cooperative?"

"Because either we die here today, have an *accident* on our way back, or meet just as dreadful of fate on Molvi. Any way you cut it, we're fucked. Typhoon Pharma will not want us to speak. So I'd rather do it now for a chance at increased protection from the Enforcers. For sure, they have some of their people out there. There's no way you would have detected us this quickly, or managed to hack our ships in a Dead Zone the way you currently are."

I nodded in concession, my heart soaring upon hearing this

confirmation about Typhoon Pharma's involvement. That his aura also didn't show any deception further thrilled me.

"I knew I shouldn't have messed with such a pretty world, and especially not places of worship," Nylar added with self-derision.

"And yet you did," Aku said harshly. "Why?"

"I had to. It's my job. For the record, I don't know all the secrets, but only that if what happened here gets exposed, it will raise too many questions that will have people look far too closely into Typhoon Pharma," the Raithean replied noncha-lantly. "The problem heavily centers around Noah Montel, the CEO's son from a previous relationship."

"Noah! I know that name," Aku exclaimed. "That was the name of the human that Sora bit."

Nylar snorted. "Obviously. That bastard constantly gets in trouble. Most of my career has been spent burying his shit. After the last big tragedy he caused, I thought he was done for. But Elias Jacobs agreed to take him on his team when no one else would."

"Why did Jacobs do that?" I asked. "And why would no one else take Noah?"

"Credits, of course," Nylar replied in a factual manner. "Jacobs was failing at securing new funding for his research. Noah wants to play field doctor but cannot follow rules and quickly gets bored. In this specific instance, the project wasn't turning out to be lucrative enough."

I frowned, my confusion reflected on Aku's face.

"What do you mean by not lucrative enough?" I asked.

"The research on the Sangoths was always a huge gamble that no one truly believed in. But it was just a facade. Typhoon always suspected that it wouldn't pan out. But it gave them a legal excuse to be on Kestria, despite the Prime Directive. There's a reason why Typhoon tries to get involved in projects on primitive planets. It allows them to always stay ahead of everyone else when it comes to major discoveries. They send people like Noah as scouts to explore forbidden areas of the planet to seek new medicine, plants, or resources to exploit."

"But why attack my people?" Aku challenged. "Surely, your Typhoon doesn't go around exterminating the local population of every planet they try to exploit."

"We don't, but your case was unique in that Noah's action made your people sick," Nylar explained. "There had been many complaints lodged against him over the years for previous infractions and violations of safety and medical protocols. Had Jacobs reported what happened, Noah would have lost his license. Beyond the fact that his mother was always overly protective of him, she couldn't lose the effective agent at exploiting primitive worlds that Noah proved to be."

"I get that. But this all went down more than a decade ago. Our current research indicates that the source of the new disease is caused by an invasive species of berries," I countered. "If that ever came out, Jacobs could argue that there's no proof that his team brought them to Kestria. Various people come to work with the Sangoths under strict permissions. One of them could be responsible."

"Which would have applied if not for SS12," Nylar countered. "That changed everything for both good and bad."

"How so?" Aku asked.

"Without the serum, everyone would have just moved on once your people were cured. But the serum stirred a lot of questions about the source. The work missions with the Sangoths were also a problem. Sooner or later, one of the seasonal workers would eventually discover the Kreelars, which would expose that incident. But the years passed and nothing happened, so we figured all was good. And then the messages began."

"What messages?" I asked.

"Our demands that Elias fix what his team did to us," Aku replied in his stead.

"Except Elias is no longer the weak and nearly broke researcher that he was back then," Nylar said. "SS12 has made him insanely rich and influential. While Typhoon was able to silence him at the time, they no longer have as huge of a hold on him. He started messaging Marilia, Typhoon's CEO, saying they were long overdue to come clean about the incident. Naturally, she did not agree with that. She charged me to make it very clear that he was to remain quiet about the matter and let her handle it."

"Are you saying that Jacobs isn't involved in any of this assassination plot?" I insisted.

He nodded. "Jacobs is an obnoxious ass, but he never wanted to keep any of this secret. Marilia forced him to in order to protect her own interests."

"So what else were you going to do beyond poisoning our temples?" Aku asked.

"Nothing," Nylar responded. "We were going to let my Puricis do its work. In one week's time, we were expected to come back for a second dose if needed."

"But why? We sent out those messages many months ago," Aku insisted. "The attack on your ship was more than two weeks ago. Why come now?"

"Because we received confirmation that you had scientists here treating you. I immediately suspected that it was a trap and told Marilia as much. But she insisted that we come and wipe everyone out."

"What made you think it was a trap?" I asked, baffled.

"Because the Enforcers never leak anything unless they *want* that information out there. And every single time, it's a trap for the idiots and gullible," Nylar said with a dejected expression.

And that much was true. I remembered all too well how they 'encouraged' me to leak similar information about pirate raids involving the Levendoc Corporation after Gaelec completed his sentence on Molvi.

"And yet, you came," Aku challenged.

The Raithean snorted and smiled with resignation. "Like Elias, I didn't have much of a choice. I've been working for Marilia for far too long. Once you get in too deep, there's no turning back until you are set free—which rarely ever happens— or death claims you."

"You are resigned to this death now that you have been captured, but you wouldn't have risked it to avoid wiping out an entire species that, of your own admission, is innocent?" Aku snarled.

To my surprise, Nylar didn't respond right away and took a moment to reflect on his answer.

"Truth be told, you were not people to me… not really. You were merely targets… a task. I don't like hurting anyone who hasn't done me wrong, but that has never stopped me from doing it, if it was my job. Compassion and empathy have no place in my line of work. Just know that it was not personal," he replied in a factual manner.

Far from appeasing him, the Raithean's words further incensed Aku, who bared his teeth at him.

Nylar lifted his chin defiantly. "You wanted the truth, you got it. I never claimed it would be pretty."

"I should kill you," Aku replied, his voice dangerously soft and low. "I should bring you to the people so that they can give both of you a slow and excruciating death. But even that would be too kind."

My heart leapt with hope upon hearing his words, especially when he turned to look at me.

"I hear Molvi is a terrible place to serve on," Aku said.

I smiled. "It certainly is."

"It all depends on which Quadrant you serve in," Nylar said in a nonchalant fashion. "I've already been on Molvi and came out unscathed, as you can see."

"You never served in Dakon's playground," I retorted in an

icy tone. "No one survives their sentences there. And I can assure you, it is exactly where you both will land for your crimes."

The Raithean had the decency to look unnerved upon hearing those words. I doubted he believed he would survive a second sentence on Molvi, but he likely never expected it might take place in the worst Sector on the entire planet. Dakon didn't divide his Sector into Quadrants. All the inmates shared the same space. Therefore, he only accepted the cruelest, most ruthless, and unredeemable criminals. Few people lasted more than a few weeks, some not even a couple of days.

"That sounds like a fitting punishment," Aku said. "May you think of us every day of your stay there."

The beep of an incoming communication had all of us jerking our heads towards the navigation board. Even as I went to accept it, my gut told me what had transpired. Unsurprisingly, Maeve appeared on screen again.

"Let me guess, you've heard everything?" I asked.

She smiled in a non-committal fashion before shifting her gaze towards my companion.

"With your permission, Aku, we can take over from here. I have full control of the ship. As you would likely prefer not to have any additional off-worlders invade your space, I can remotely get this ship off your planet and take these prisoners into our custody to face justice."

He stared at her in silence for a moment before giving me an inquisitive look. That struck me hard, but in the most wondrous way. The amount of trust he was putting in me meant a great deal to me. Once again, my chest constricted at the thought that very soon, we would part ways and likely never meet again. I could have seen us forming as close a friendship as the one I shared with Kronos.

"I trust her with my life and vouch without hesitation that she will see to it that they do not escape justice," I replied firmly.

He nodded then looked back at Maeve. "In that case, they are yours."

"Thank you, Aku. On my honor, I promise that we will bring to justice everyone that was involved in the tragedy that befell your people. Know that your cooperation today will help us save countless other lives as well as avenge even more people wronged by Typhoon," Maeve said fervently. "With your permission, we will contact you in the future to keep you apprised of the developments."

"I would appreciate it," Aku said begrudgingly.

Maeve turned to me, the glimmer of gratitude mixed with an unmistakable spark of triumph almost made me smile. She didn't need to speak for me to know she was congratulating me for a mission accomplished. In that instant, I realized that my initial suspicion that I was being recruited as a free agent had been accurate. The Enforcers hoped all along that things would lead to this outcome. My gut further told me that they always suspected Typhoon Pharma but simply lacked the evidence or enough probable cause to get the necessary warrants for a full-fledged investigation.

"Thank you for your assistance in this matter. Let us know if you require anything to help you resolve the situation for the Kreelars. With this arrest, the UPO is now officially able to get involved and provide any support needed."

"That's very kind," I replied politely, keenly aware of how her words made Aku tense. "We will discuss the matter with the scientists and the Kreelar Kalds so that they can make the decision if they wish for more external assistance."

She smiled again and nodded in concession. This time, I realized that she had not only expected such a response from me, but she had also done it in a teasing way to remind me how she claimed I had better diplomatic skills than I gave myself credit for.

I returned her smile. "Be aware that I placed an EMP detonator near their engine. I can remove it on our way out."

She snorted and shook her head. "Thanks for the heads up, but don't worry about it. We will handle it once we've recovered the vessel."

We exchanged our last farewells.

"Let's go home," I said to Aku when the communication cut off.

The gentle smile he gave me moved me to the core. "Lead the way, Brother."

Ignoring Bruce's pleading voice, we walked out of the ship under the resigned gaze of the Raithean. By the time we settled back inside my vessel, Maeve was already remotely getting the Nazhral ship airborne. It took off seconds before we did.

"Will the other Kalds be angry that you released the assassins?" I asked carefully as we flew back home.

"At first, some will be. But all will align with my decision," Aku said with confidence. "What happened to us cannot be allowed to happen to others. And above all, the leader must answer for the action that they led others to commit. It would be unconscionable to allow those two assassins to take the entire fall, only to be replaced later by others directed by the same foul hand. I want this Marilia and Noah to see their entire world crumble the same way we watched ours slowly die for years."

"And we will make sure they do," I pledged.

"I know you will."

We completed the journey in an amiable atmosphere during which he pointed out a few landmarks of his world, weaving in some of the folklore related to them. As we approached the village, he pointed to a large open area where I could land the ship.

"It's a bit of a walk for you. I could drop you off a little closer over here," I said, pointing at another space sufficiently large to land.

He shook his head. "It's not that much longer to walk. And you can leave your ship there. There is no need for you to leave it elsewhere and fly back."

My brow shot up. "Are you certain?"

He nodded. "Thank you for what you did today. Without your warning, we never would have known, and all of us would have died. Our friends told us you would bring our enemies to justice. But you have exceeded every hope we laid at your feet. Know that all four of you have earned your place among my people."

"You honor us, Aku," I said, my throat tightening as I smiled in gratitude. I still didn't know much about their society and people, but I knew enough to realize this was not simply a polite gesture, but a rare gift.

"Let's go home, Brother."

CHAPTER 17
CIARA

Excited shouts outside had me storming out of the lab. Before the door finished opening, I jerked my head up to scan the sky. As soon as I saw Amreth's ship making its approach, a squeal of excitement escaped me. I ran like a mad woman outside the courtyard, through the village square, and out the gates with everyone looking at me with an amused expression.

Technically, I didn't have the right to exit the inner courtyard without an escort. But something undeniably shifted earlier after our return from the temple. That change had already been taking place gradually in a far more subtle fashion. But today, the tragedy that we helped avert completely flipped everything on its head.

Although I suspected that Kreelars from other villages would continue to eye us with suspicion and wariness, the tribemates of Bryst now fully embraced us.

Amreth landed his ship in a clearing at least three hundred meters away from the village. Although I took pride in keeping fit, I was out of breath by the time I reached the ship, constantly fearing that he would take off again after dropping Aku to go park it on the cliff where he normally kept it.

To my shock—but also pleasant surprise—I found both males walking side by side towards the village. His face lit up when he saw me, and he flapped his wings, flying barely a couple of feet above ground to close the distance between us. I threw myself into his arms, and he caught me. I crushed his lips in somewhat of a brutal kiss in which I poured both my happiness and relief at seeing him back.

Still flying close to the ground, he twirled us around before landing back down. I broke the kiss, buried my face in his neck, and deeply inhaled his scent. A sense of peace and of being at home washed over me. He wrapped his wings around me, holding me close as we quietly remained in each other's embrace.

After a few seconds or countless minutes—I couldn't really tell, nor did I care—Amreth opened his wings and released me. I took a step back and immediately examined him from head to toe looking for any sign of injury.

He chuckled. "I'm fine, my mate. We're both fine."

I continued to pat his chest and arms before stretching my neck to look for Aku, a sliver of guilt twisting my features. I looked over my shoulder to find him standing at a respectful distance to grant us some privacy. He was observing us with an air of almost paternal amusement, which was silly considering I was older than him.

"Are you okay?" I asked him although still leaning against Amreth. "Anyone injured?"

He shook his head as he approached us. "Neither of us are injured, and we were able to stop the assassins before they could contaminate the temple."

"Where are they?" I asked, looking over his shoulder towards the ship as if I could see through its hull all the way into the brig.

"The Enforcers have them," Amreth replied.

"What?! How?" I exclaimed.

"I will explain everything once we get back with the others," Amreth said in an appeasing tone.

My tongue burned with the urge to bombard him with questions. I didn't want to wait, but it also wouldn't make sense to have him go through telling the story twice. Obviously, Mehreen and Ernst, as well as the entire village, would want to know what happened.

We ended up splitting, with Aku rounding up his people inside their gathering hall while the four of us off-worlders went inside the deployable lab. At first, it stung a little that we should not be included, considering our significant contribution in the matter. But Enre and the two other Kreelars who escorted us to Svast Temple already updated everyone about what we did there. This second update would be more about the way their leader handled the assassins and likely actions they would want to take moving forward as a people. In their shoes, I also wouldn't want strangers to eavesdrop, regardless of how friendly our relationship had grown.

As soon as we settled inside the lab's meeting room, Amreth gave us a detailed recounting of the events. We all sat there flabbergasted by all of those revelations, especially regarding Marilia's involvement. And yet, I shouldn't be this shocked. It was no secret that huge corporations often acted in highly questionable fashion when it came to increasing their bottom line or remaining the leader in their field. It was especially true in the pharmaceutical industry. Whoever came up with the first patent stood to make billions of credits. If the discovery permitted treatment across species, then the monetary potential blew up exponentially.

SS12 made Elias Jacobs and Typhoon Pharma obscenely wealthy. And this wealth was about to be siphoned—at least for Typhoon—both as punitive damages and to fund the efforts that would be required to do right by the Kreelars.

With primitive planets under the Prime Directive, it always made things significantly more complicated as you couldn't simply dump a whole lot of credits on them as compensation or share technology. But that was a challenge for people more qualified than me in that field to sort out.

"Wow! Things are about to get seriously ugly for Typhoon," Mehreen mused aloud. "They're such a massive corporation with labs and research teams pretty much everywhere in our sector of the galaxy. Investigating them is going to be an insane undertaking. This could take years!"

Amreth nodded grimly. "It certainly could. But that doesn't mean that consequences aren't going to be felt sooner. The Enforcers will go after the lowest hanging fruits to get a swift conviction and be able to get greater access to everything so that they press further charges from previous crimes later. It just infuriates me that some of them might not be indictable due to statutes of limitation. Still, I got a sense there will be enough of them to make sure they will never taste freedom again."

"They should have come clean rather than attempting to cover for Noah," Ernst said. "I can understand a mother wanting to protect her child, but he was always too much trouble. At the same time, I'm not sure how much it was out of maternal love or simply greed. After all, it couldn't be easy finding someone with the proper medical credentials willing to do that kind of shady work."

"Either way, they're fucked," I said with a shrug. "But what will happen to Elias?"

Amreth pursed his lips as he reflected on the question. "It really depends. Obviously, there will be some repercussions for hiding what happened here. That negligence cheated the Kreelars out of the regular check-ins they would have benefited from over the following years, which would have prevented this tragedy from going on for nearly a decade. It all comes down to how much he was coerced into remaining silent. Based on the

Raithean's statement, Marilia seriously threatened Jacobs. If a crime is committed under duress, he could be exonerated."

"But I thought that didn't apply if it caused the death of another?" Ernst countered.

"The evidence so far doesn't point towards any of Jacobs' actions leading to direct deaths," Amreth said. "He wasn't present or responsible for what Noah did. He promptly treated the Kreelars as soon as he realized they were infected. His crime was not reporting it to the galactic Medical Order. But that was under duress when they had little reason to think the disease would return. And in fact, the cause was a completely different source that he couldn't have suspected and had no idea existed until the Kreelars' friends helped them send him a message."

"And he reported immediately to Typhoon, requesting that they go public," I completed for him. "He just might get away with it, or at least with only a pretty harsh slap on the wrist. Time will tell. Still, the downfall of Typhoon is the best possible punishment. Hopefully, it will send a chilling message to other corporations and conglomerates that use these types of immoral tactics to enrich themselves."

"Hear, hear," Mehreen said.

"But the hour is late," I said at last. "I could use a shower, a good meal, and some rest and relaxation."

"Oh I'm sure you will *rest*," Mehreen said, wiggling her eyebrows.

I glared at her while the other two chuckled.

"Actually, you are indeed going to rest," Amreth said with a mischievous expression. "I believe someone has earned herself a spa day on my ship, which conveniently happens to be parked just a short stroll away."

"Oh hell yeah!!" I exclaimed, prompting my companions to laugh again.

We bid our friends good night, and I didn't balk when Amreth whisked me up in his arms and flew me to the ship. Then again, he remained close enough to the ground that I didn't get queasy with my silly fear of heights.

This was my first time truly getting a proper tour of the ship. Not only was it state-of-the-art, but it also struck me that it was definitely on the higher end of the spectrum as far as luxury went. Although we frequently spoke of what our future would look like once all of this was resolved, we never really discussed petty things such as finances.

I wasn't rich, but I lived very comfortably and sat in the upper half of the middle class. Aside from the generational wealth inherited from my parents, my role as an epidemiologist earned me an enviable income. But it was clear that Amreth belonged to a much higher bracket. After all, he was a Lord.

It always felt funny to think that once we were married, I would officially become Lady Ciara. That made me want to cackle in a very unladylike fashion. Considering how pompous I found most people during events such as the symposium where I got abducted, such a title was somewhat wasted on someone like me. I was just grateful that Amreth didn't seem to be stuffy or a stickler for hierarchy and acknowledgement of his rank. That definitely would have been a problem.

However, I did feast my eyes on the color palette and the decor of the large vessel. I suspected it reflected his own aesthetic at home. For some reason, I had expected a lot of dark colors from varying shades of gray to deep reds, and dark browns. Instead, the interior was mostly white with light beige and the occasional sharp obsidian accents. There was something very Zen and peaceful about it.

"I like this color palette," I said as he led me to the back section of the ship which had four bedrooms, two of them with their own hygiene rooms, and the other two sharing one.

"I'm glad to hear it," Amreth said with a grin. "My home shares a similar color palette. I love how spacious and relaxing it makes the space feel. We have a lot of huge windows, with massive terraces on all three floors of the mansion. I cannot wait for you to see it. Obviously, you will be free to make whatever modifications you wish to make it more appealing for you."

"Judging by what I'm seeing so far, I doubt that will be necessary," I said in all sincerity. "But I definitely cannot wait to see it."

"Well, here's the first glimpse," he said while opening a door on what turned out to be an impressive bedroom.

My jaw dropped at the sight of the massive bed, which occupied at least a third of the space. It looked almost wide enough to allow Amreth to lie on it with his wings spread open. Bedding and pillows in earthy tones added some warmth with a nice splash of color. I barely looked at the comfortable couch in dark wood with plush beige cushions across from a giant vidscreen. To my surprise, there was no breakfast table or work desk in the room. But it was the large abstract paintings adorning the walls that held my attention.

I'd never been the type to be able to drop famous artists' names or invest in outrageously expensive collector art. But I had a genuine appreciation for the work of those who could convey a feeling or stir an emotion with their creation, from a simple drawing to a sculpture or a song. I wouldn't be able to put it into words and didn't think it was necessary either. To me, it was just about embracing whatever emotions it awakened in us. And these pieces resonated with me.

"Yep, I really think I'm going to love your house just the way it is," I said wistfully while admiring the art pieces.

He smiled, kissed my temple, then led me by the hand to an adjoining room.

My eyes nearly popped out of my head when I stepped inside the hygiene room. He had not been kidding by saying he had a literal spa. The room was bigger than most cabins on common cruise ships. The humongous, recessed tub instantly drew my attention. Amreth didn't exaggerate when he boasted about its size. I squealed like a schoolgirl and clapped while he laughed.

I then noticed the even more massive shower that ate up almost an entire wall. On top of the shower heads hanging from the ceiling, a series of body jets lined the wall. Judging by their number and angles, they'd were specifically designed to handle the wide span of an Obosian's wings. No wonder my man had been so miserable without his creature comfort. In the corner, long strips resembling vertical air vents on the wall, and a square one on the ceiling, appeared to act as some sort of dryer.

Across from the shower, a long counter with a double sink sat in front of a mirror that ran up to the ceiling. At the other end of the shower, separated by a privacy wall, a toilet was propped on top of a small platform raising it. Considering the large gap between the toilet and the back wall, I realized the distance and elevation were to accommodate his wings and tail.

"This is an almost perfect replica of the en suite hygiene room in the master bedroom of my home," Amreth said before approaching a swirling pattern on the wall near the entrance with a luminous stone next to it. "And in here, you will find clean towels and other toiletries needed. Just wave your hand in front of the stone."

I gaped as the swirling pattern seemed to turn into a thick liquid, the pattern unraveling to reveal the shelves within.

"Okay, that's super cool," I said, impressed.

He gave me a smug smile. "It is standard for doors on Vargos, and by extension on Molvi. If you ever need to open a door, just wave your palm in front of the stone. To lock it, wave the back of your hand in front of it instead."

"Noted," I said, excited at the thought of all the other wonders I would discover on his world.

"Good. Now take off your clothes, and let's get you wet," Amreth said in a suggestive voice that instantly had my toes curling.

I giggled and complied while he went to fill the tub with water.

"I'll be right back," he said with a mysterious tone, piquing my curiosity.

My gaze lingered on him as he exited the room, admiring his strong back and the way his long tail gently swayed behind him. The memory of the naughty ways he used it had me instantly throbbing in all the right places. Bubbling with anticipation, I finished undressing and neatly folded my clothes on the counter. I approached the tub, which was filling at an impressive speed, and dipped the tip of my toes in to test the temperature. A grin stretched my lips at finding it at the perfect warmth. Walking down the two steps into the tub, I settled in the water with a voluptuous moan.

The soft swish of the door opening behind me reclaimed my attention. My eyes widened upon seeing Amreth followed by a hover tray with two flutes filled with a sparkling beverage that resembled champagne, and two plates laden with sliced exotic fruits in one and luxury gourmet chocolates in the other.

"Oh, my God! Where did you get that?!" I exclaimed, straightening in the tub as he approached and set the tray to hover at the perfect height in front of me.

"I brought them with me with the intention of us enjoying them during our first date after I freed you," Amreth said smugly as he began to strip out of his clothes. "There was actually the equivalent of strawberries dipped in chocolate as part of the menu. But under the circumstances, I figured we'd seen enough of those for a while and left them out."

I snorted, both amused and touched by his thoughtfulness. "Damn, you're so sweet!"

"Normally, I would take umbrage at being described as such, but this time, I'll allow it," he said teasingly. "I didn't exactly free you, but we have cause to celebrate."

"We do," I concurred while feasting my eyes on my man. "In more ways than one."

To my surprise, he didn't join me in the tub but sat sideways on the raised edge, his feet remaining on the floor. Amreth reached for the two flutes, handing me one. I took it, my heart fluttering as he locked eyes with me with a depth of affection that messed me up.

"To you, my Ciara, the greatest blessing the Gods could have ever bestowed upon me. I always wondered what my soulmate would be like. I hoped she would be kind, smart, funny, affectionate, and of course law-abiding," he added with a teasing wink, making me chuckle.

He sobered and gently caressed my cheek with his knuckles.

"But you exceeded all of that. You're bold, courageous, compassionate, and selfless. Day after day, I watch you working yourself to the bone to save these people with empathy and respect. Not once have you even contemplated how succeeding in this endeavor could bring you praise and acclaim. You only care about their welfare. And it shines through. You cannot begin to understand how proud I am to claim you as mine."

My throat tightened, and stupid tears tried to prick my eyes to join the party. I didn't think I was doing anything special other than what was necessary and right. But his response was moving me to the core.

"I love that you aren't afraid to speak your mind, to stand firm by your beliefs, and to go after what you want. And above all, I love how happy I feel simply being by your side. The mere thought of seeing your face and of hearing your voice makes me smile. I'm falling in love with you, Ciara. I cannot wait for us to start our life together."

"And I cannot wait to start our life together either. You, too, have exceeded my wildest dreams. Every quality you listed about me, I could throw right back at you. My biggest fear had been that you might be too rigid. But you're extremely humble, open-minded, and willing to see things from someone else's perspective. You're protective without being controlling, principled but not self-righteous, disciplined and yet playful, and above all, you're the best cuddler in the world. Those winged-hugs are just next level," I added teasingly.

He snorted and shook his head at me.

"I love that you didn't think twice about coming to rescue me. I love that you swiftly adapted to the new situation and didn't hesitate to do the right thing, even to the detriment of your own career on Molvi. You're just as selfless as you claim me to be. And everyone here sees it. I'm even more proud of you than you are of me."

"I doubt that's possible," he said, trying to sound playfully grumpy to hide how much my words moved him.

"Believe me, it is. You possess so much power that you could easily abuse, and yet you always look for the peaceful option that will avoid bloodshed. You make me feel safe, respected, and valued. I'm falling in love with you, tail, wings, horns, and all."

"Piercings, too?" he asked.

I burst out laughing, while he chuckled affectionately.

"Yes, piercings too. Especially those ones," I added, casting a meaningful glance at his crotch.

"Good! Because by the time we return home, I suspect the Conclave will bestow more algarium to me as a reward for my contribution in solving this crisis. Start thinking where you'll want me to add those piercings."

My jaw dropped, while he chuckled smugly.

The Conclave was the highest legal authority on Vargos, the Obosian homeworld. Algarium was the rare metal they used for their piercing, all of which had to be earned through remarkable deeds or achievements. I needed to inquire about what earned him all the ones that currently adorned his body.

"Until then, to us," Amreth said, not waiting for my response.

"To us," I repeated as we clinked our glasses.

We drank. It turned out to be something more like a fruity rosé, although it could very well be an Obosian version of champagne, not that I particularly cared. I'd never been big on alcohol. But this was delicious.

To my surprise, Amreth didn't partake in the goodies on the two plates, but moved behind me, crouching at the edge of the bath, to give me a proper shoulder massage. A loud purr tumbled out of my throat.

"Eat, my mate, and enjoy being taken care of," Amreth said.

"You're not eating?" I asked, reaching for one of the chocolates.

"Nope. I'm leaving space for the mouth-watering feast I intend to indulge in a little later," he replied in a suggestive tone that made no mystery as to his underlying meaning.

A pleasant flame sparked in the pit of my stomach as I gave myself over to the massage and enjoyed a few more of the treats. He used his *bakaan* at a very low level to make me even more relaxed. With a vocal command, he activated the sound system which began playing some soothing Obosian music.

I finished my drink, munched on a few more fruits and chocolates, then cast the tray aside as Amreth released my shoulders to circle around the bath. My heart leapt when he got into the massive tub, which still had plenty of room for at least one other adult to comfortably join us. However, Amreth sat across from me at the other end instead of snuggling with me. Only then did I realize that he was about to give me a foot and leg massage. Another loud purr tumbled out of my throat. I leaned back against the tub, the back of my head resting on the elevated edge while getting pampered by my man.

His touch was magical. It took me a moment to realize that small tingling was due to him using minute amounts of his Lumiak while massaging me. I briefly wondered if it wasn't a risky endeavor as water was a huge conductor for electricity. But at forty-six years of age, I trusted that he would know by now what was safe and what not to do with his powers.

By the time he was done, I was totally languid, my entire body feeling like it was floating on a cloud. Amreth got out of the tub then activated the bubble jets. The warm water immediately began to roil all around me, giving me yet another full body massage that had me turning into a puddle.

My mate chuckled smugly as he leaned forward to kiss me. I returned his kiss, wishing he would snuggle with me in the tub. But he straightened and headed to the shower. Feeling a little bereft, I groggily watched him begin to wash himself. It was indeed quite the spectacle seeing all those body jets blasting water at him and especially at his wings.

He looked like a pagan god as he spread them wide. My mouth watered as I watched him raise his arms to start washing his hair. It exposed every inch of his scrumptious body to my greedy eyes. The ambient light reflected just the right way on his piercings, further drawing my attention to them. I swallowed hard, remembering how they felt on my tongue, as well as the small scales and soft spikes along his length.

He turned around to face the body jets as they blasted the front of his wings. My gaze glided over the strong muscles of his back as they rolled beneath his grayish-brown skin. It followed the path down his spine which curved into his long tail. Although somewhat thick at the base, it didn't hide the deliciously round globes of his behind. My fingers itched with the urge to grab them with both hands. Then again, I also wanted to give each cheek a solid bite.

He lifted his face to the raining water from the shower heads. After a moment, he stopped the water, then turned around to face me again. Eyes closed, he rested his palms against the glass doors, head slightly bowed. Only then did I hear a very subtle whistling sound, which I assumed to emanate from the dryer. Seconds later, I indeed noticed the movement of his long, silver-white hair indicating that wind was blowing through it.

I realized I had stepped out of the tub when I started walking towards the shower. Amreth's eyes snapped open half a beat before I reached the shower. His silver-white irises, which had almost been completely swallowed by the black sclera surrounding them, suddenly expanded to their normal size as he locked gazes with me. He straightened and dropped his palms from the glass doors. I pulled them open and stepped inside, the lukewarm draft of the dryer rolling over me in a gentle caress.

Without a word, I closed the distance with my mate and placed my palms on his chest. I lifted my face to receive his kiss, which he generously gave. Our tongues mingled, sending a bolt of desire coursing through me. It was narrower than a human's, with a slightly rougher texture that enhanced every sensation, especially in naughty places. Even the piercing in the middle of his tongue added to the experience.

He cupped my nape with his right hand, the left one gliding down my back in a gentle caress before settling on my behind. I immediately broke the kiss, not allowing him to take control of the moment. He was naturally dominant in the bedroom. While I usually had no problem yielding on that front, right this instant, I wanted to sate my hunger for him under my own terms.

He didn't try to restrain me when I started peppering kisses alongside his jaw and down the curve of his neck. I loved the soft texture of his skin, which felt slightly leathery in comparison to a human's. The chevron shaped scales on his shoulders tickled my palms as the edges scraped against it while I caressed him.

My mouth ventured further down to his left nipple. I had grown quite addicted to sucking on the little barbell piercing he had there. Seeing what enjoyment I derived from it always made me feel guilty about not having piercings of my own for him to play with. I still didn't think I would ever get any, but I was less adamantly opposed to it now that I had grown familiar with his.

The fact that he never brought it up again or even remotely tried to pressure me to get some played a large part in it. I loved that he truly respected my bodily autonomy and liked me just the way I was.

The deep rumble of his approving moan resonated directly in my clit. There was no greater turn on than the man you loved being so incredibly sensitive and responsive to your touch. Amreth never seemed to get enough of me, just like I constantly craved him. I licked and laved his nipple for a while longer, sucking on the little bud while pinching the other one with my left hand.

I resumed my journey downward, pausing to grant a bit of attention to the other piercing in his navel. Feeling his abdominal muscles contract beneath my palms further fanned the flame growing in my belly. I rubbed my hands all over them, before tracing each chiseled groove with my tongue.

Amreth took a hissing breath when my right hand caressed a path down between his thighs to boldly wrap around his length. Fuck me! I would never tire of the otherworldly feel of his cock in my hand. His *xinnix*—the small spikes lining the sides of his shaft—the two sets of scales on the upper side of his length, and the numerous piercings scattered along the length and at the head provided a multitude of sensations that had me throbbing with anticipation. Anything it did to my palm as I began to stroke him would be multiplied a thousandfold inside me.

I crouched before him, feasting my eyes on the perfection that he was. Leaning forward, I immediately started teasing the slit of his head with my tongue before drawing circles around the glans. My other hand fondled and squeezed his testicles, reveling in their unusually smooth texture. Amreth's fingers slipped through my hair, gripping it loosely enough not to restrain my movements, a strangled sound emanating from him when I licked his entire length a few times before taking him into my mouth.

Saying he was massive couldn't even begin to give him justice. Oddly enough, I was the one feeling cheated that I couldn't take a lot more of him inside my mouth. I truly wished I could properly deepthroat him. But I compensated by stroking him in counterpoint to the movement of my mouth. The deep, growling sound of his moans in my ears had me soaking wet in seconds. My breasts felt heavy, and my nipples ached with the need for attention.

Despite his phenomenal self-control, Amreth began to gently rock in reaction to my ministrations. The first time he did, I feared he would destroy my tonsils once passion overtook him. Thankfully, even when pleasure rode him hard, he never forgot to keep me safe. For a completely irrational reason, it spurred me to want to make him lose it even more, like in some masochistic need to push his limits.

I loved his taste, slightly spicy like sweet ginger. Unfortunately, he too often deprived me of the pleasure of fully savoring him. It was an odd craving to have developed specifically for him considering I had never been too crazy about swallowing. And yet, I loved everything with him and could never get enough. Amreth just had an issue with climaxing first. He obsessed about making sure I got off at least a couple of times before he could enjoy his own release.

As if he'd read the thoughts crossing my mind, Amreth began to gently tug on my hair to pull me away from him. By the way his abdominal muscles were spasmodically contracting and that his legs were slightly shaking, he was on the verge of toppling over. Refusing to be cheated out of my prize, I tightened my grip around the base of his cock and accelerated the movement of my head bobbing in front of him. When he attempted to tug a bit more forcefully, I resorted to the shameful tactic I discovered would make him come undone in seconds.

I grazed my teeth against the sensitive spikes of his *xinnix*. To him, they were like external G-spots. Right on cue, his body seized, and his hand fisted painfully in my hair as he cried out. Although I had deliberately provoked this, I nearly choked on the first powerful spurt that shot into my mouth. I swallowed, preparing for more, but the wretched male yanked himself back, holding my hair too tightly to allow me to try and hang on.

He hissed and closed his hand around the base of his cock, right below mine still trying to stroke him. Amreth squeezed it tightly, stemming the flow of his seed. I licked my lips in a lascivious way, a mischievous glimmer in my eyes mixed with a sliver of disapproval for not fully letting me have my way with him.

But even as he continued to slightly shake from the throes of bliss, he stared at me with an almost feral expression that clearly expressed I had been a bad girl, and he was going to punish me for it. The throbbing between my thighs went into overdrive as I braced for his retaliation.

And it came swiftly.

"You like to play dirty?" he said in a growl. "Two can play that game."

An insanely powerful wave of his *bakaan* slammed into me. I cried out, my back arching as a violent orgasm swept me away. Two strong arms scooped me up right before I would collapse onto the tiled floor.

Clinging to his shoulders, my body shaking, I tried to regain my bearings as fire ran through my veins, and my clit throbbed almost painfully. Amreth's chest against mine vibrated with a smug chuckle. He kissed the white spot on my forehead—my crown as he called it—then brushed his lips along my temple down to my right ear.

"How about a different game?" he whispered in an almost malicious tone.

Still too dazed, I tried to ask what he meant. But he caressed my behind, his hand slipping between my thighs and curving around to reach my clit. The only sound that came out of me was another shout of ecstasy as he zapped my engorged little nub with a lightning bolt of Lumiak. My eyes rolled to the back of my head as I was once more swept away.

Wave upon wave of bliss crashed over me as Amreth kept me flying high with a mix of his *bakaan* and strategic uses of his lightning in erogenous areas between two caresses. It took me far too long to realize that his tail had joined the fray, dipping in and out of me in a frenzy, while my mate covered my face and neck with passionate kisses.

A third orgasm claimed me, this time building gradually instead of the savage way Amreth had triggered the previous two. I was clinging on to him for dear life, wanting more and yet fearing I would shatter into a million pieces. My brain could barely process the sweet words he spoke to me, my mind too addled by overwhelming pleasure. The endless strings of moans tumbling out of me and my blood roaring in my ears made it even harder to hear what he was saying.

And yet, when he pulled his tail out of me to replace it with his thick shaft, his words pierced through the lustful fog clouding my thoughts.

"One more time, my love. On my cock… Together…"

As with every time we coupled, he filled me to the brim, his non-negligible girth stretching me to what felt like my limits. And yet, I couldn't get enough. Each thrust wrested one strangled moan out of me after another. Between the spikes of his *xinnix* and the piercings lining his shaft, my inner walls were subjected to an indescribable sensual assault that had me singing arias. The barbell piercing on his head, and the scales on the upper side of his shaft systematically rubbed against my G-spot with deadly accuracy, both going in and out, driving me insane with pleasure.

The world around me ceased to exist, my entire universe narrowing down to the feel of him, in and around me. An inferno was consuming me from within, each nerve ending set ablaze by a whirlwind of sensations.

Amreth started pumping into me harder and faster, his breathing becoming labored and coming out in short, loud bursts in my ear as he drew closer to the edge. Before long, he was pounding into me, gripping my behind with both hands, his partially extruded claws digging into my cheeks. His cock was wrecking me as my ultimate climax came rushing towards me with the unbridled fury of a tsunami.

My spine seized, and a blinding light exploded before my eyes as I once more fell apart. My inner walls clamped down on Amreth's cock, intensifying the feel of his spikes, scales, and piercings inside me. He joined his voice to mine, his hands on my bum tightening their grip almost painfully. It surprised me that his claws didn't break my skin.

His seed shot out inside me, bathing my battered insides with a searing flow as he continued to rock in and out of me. He crushed my lips with a voracious kiss, swallowing my moans of ecstasy. He broke it, and I buried my face in his neck, shattered and boneless. I vaguely felt him half stumble back, then lean against the wall, likely trying to regain his own bearings. How he managed to hold on to me defied logic. I was just grateful for it.

Raining water showering down on us snapped me out of my daze. I felt too steamrolled to move, but I didn't have to. With a tenderness and infinite care that messed me up, Amreth washed us both, and kept me cradled in his arms, kissing me and whispering words of love as the dryer blew warm air on us.

He then carried me back to his room, laying me down carefully on the large mattress before joining me. Amreth drew me on top of him, his tail and arms wrapped around me, and his massive wings blanketing us.

I fell asleep in the arms of my mate, feeling safe, loved… home.

CHAPTER 18
CIARA

In the week that followed the capture of the two assassins, many diplomatic discussions dominated most of our interactions with the Kreelars. Now that the cat was out of the bag, the UPO and the Enforcers formally made the offer that Maeve mentioned to Aku and Amreth. They wanted to provide personnel and technological resources to help find either a cure or a treatment and eradicate the strawberries invasion.

Where previously I would have automatically encouraged a primitive species in their situation to accept that assistance, the short amount of time spent here among them truly helped me better understand their reluctance. These people suffered from genuine trauma from their interactions with off-worlders. The genocidal attempt only multiplied their distress a thousandfold.

Furthermore, I wasn't naïve enough to believe the offer was purely altruistic. Yes, the UPO and the Enforcers wanted to do right by the Kreelars, but they also sought to ingratiate themselves with them, laying down the foundation for future alliances.

Although my colleagues, Amreth, and I fully earned their

trust, the Kreelars weren't as keen to extend the same to others. At the same time, even with the deployable lab and Amreth dealing with most of the scouting, there were too few of us for the extent of the work to be done. Having a complete team, especially for analyses, running simulations, and preparing the treatments would significantly accelerate our progress. More importantly, access to top-of-the-line technology that was missing in the deployable lab and connectivity to the infinite database of the Galactic Medical Board would make a huge difference.

Although the Kalds initially refused to allow any additional off-worlders to land on their planet, they consented to the permanent placement of a relay satellite in orbit to finally give us the connectivity we required. They also agreed to a team remaining in orbit aboard a scientific vessel to pick up a lot of the slack from us.

By the end of the following week, we developed a serum that coated the prions with a substance that prevented their absorption. It wasn't an antidote but a treatment for those who were already infected. We still strongly encouraged vaccination, but felt confident that this medication would work.

The biggest debate for them as a people was to decide what they wanted to do about the strawberries. The new powers that these mutations introduced were now a permanent part of their people. Our research actually indicated that this mutation was always intended to occur down the road as part of their species' natural evolution. The prions only triggered it much sooner than they were ready for.

The question was whether to eradicate the trigger and allow their people to try and get back to their normal timeline to the extent it was possible, or to now take control of that evolution and activate the mutation on their own terms. The reality was that, even if they managed to get rid of every strawberry out there, that psionic ability already existed among their people now. Some children would be born with it, and others might suddenly develop it, while it remained dormant among others. It would create a different class of people in their population that could cause a rift or power imbalance that could derail their entire future.

If they embraced it, they could grow the berries themselves in a controlled environment and deliberately administer it in small quantities to their people before puberty. Combined with the medicine we devised, they could ensure a safe mutation for all.

Whatever their choice, it still required the eradication of the berries in the wild. And that reopened the discussions about allowing off-worlders onto their planet. We'd already been here for a month. With the main crisis now averted and all the people infected stabilized and safely mutating, we could no longer justify holding Amreth here, away from his duties.

In truth, he technically could have left in the couple of days following the arrest of the assassins. But we needed him to play chauffeur with his shuttle. Had Amreth left his shuttle and gone back home with his ship, Mehreen, Ernst, and I would have been too busy with scientific work to do all the taxiing. Anyway, he didn't want to leave me behind, which secretly made me happy.

In the end, in great part thanks to my mate, the Kalds eventually agreed to allow five small teams vetted by Amreth to come eliminate all the strawberries, as well as track down, treat, or put down any infected animal. Each team consented to be supervised by a couple of Kreelars assigned to them. As it would take many weeks to complete the task, accommodations were provided for them in the inner courtyards of the village they were paired with.

After even more debates, the Kreelars decided that individuals—not their tribe or the Kalds—would choose whether to trigger their mutation. We set up a special greenhouse in each of the three temples where their Adhias—who served as their spiritual leaders—would supervise the growth and administration of the berries. As of the age of ten, had the mutation not occurred on its own, a Kreelar could decide whether to consume the berries, which would be given to them by an Adhia.

I spent my last week on Kestria going over additional training on the Kreelars creating their own detection tests, treating infected patients with supervised cases of people deliberately consuming the berries. Mehreen and Ernst agreed to remain until everything was done, which would likely take at least another three months.

However, I volunteered to take part in the follow-up check-ups which would take place every six months for the first two years, and then once a year for the next three, with a final visit in the tenth year. With the relay satellite, they now had a direct method of contacting us for help should anything go awry in between check-ups. Naturally, Amreth would escort me on those visits. It was less to protect me than to hang out with his new buddy. If I didn't like Aku and Vala so much, I'd almost be jealous.

The day of our departure wrecked me. I always felt a little emotional when leaving a mission, but this one took it to another level. Vala, the healers, and Adhias I worked with came to see us off. Seeing Muti and his two children blew me away.

The entire village gathered in the square. To my shock, they formed a perfect circle around Amreth and me in multiple concentric rings. Every person held the hand of their neighbor and intertwined their tail with the one from the person in front of them, in the smaller ring. As the inner rings counted less people, one person out of two would have their tail intertwined with two people. Vala, Aku, Enre, and two Adhias surrounded Amreth and me as we stood face-to-face.

I held both of my mate's hands. While his tail was intertwined with Aku's, Enre and one of the Adhias wrapped their own tail around each of Amreth's calves, while Vala and the other Adhia did the same with me. Every single person in the village was fully connected, hands and tail, forming an unbroken circle.

As one, the Kreelars began to sing a haunting melody that had chain goosebumps erupting all over my skin. From time to time, the Adhias would speak words in their language while the people continued to sing. I didn't know what they were saying, nor did I need to. Aku mentioned they wanted to cast the blessing of a traveler on us. But at a visceral level, I believed it went far deeper than this, that they were making us official members of their tribe.

Amreth had described a somewhat similar scene at the temple when he first flew over there to scan for infected animals. That they would involve us in a ritual that clearly was sacred to them moved me to my very core.

When the singing ended, people dropped their hands and tails but remained in a mostly loose single circle around us. Muti and his offspring approached us. My throat tightened as he handed a beautifully embroidered folded fabric, which turned out to be a blanket with various symbols, including the emblem of the Jaln tribe.

"My beloved and I made this for you. She wanted to be here, but she is still recovering," Muti said with a voice strained with emotion. "I weaved the blanket, and my Ranae embroidered it with the symbols of life, love, and happiness, because that's what you gave back to us. Every time you wrap it around you, know that it is our arms and our hearts hugging you."

"Thank you, to both of you," I said, my throat almost too constricted to speak. "Helping you is a great blessing in and of itself. I will cherish this gift."

He placed his palm on his chest and bowed his head. To my

surprise, each of his children in turn grabbed my right hand and pressed their foreheads to its back. Simultaneously, they wrapped their tails around my calf. It was brief, and they immediately released me before taking a step back and beaming at me with their adorable little faces.

I returned their smiles, my heart filling to bursting. The family retreated when Vala and Aku moved forward. They each held one of those ornate bead necklaces their people wore, although they weren't just beads. They resembled sculpted stones with crystals or precious gems trapped inside. I wouldn't compare them to geodes as their exteriors rivaled the most polished pebble, and the interior crystal or gem was much too clear, smooth, and iridescent.

The necklaces also seemed far more elaborate and luxurious than the ones the tribemates commonly adorned themselves with on the daily.

"This is an *ondishae*," Vala said, holding the necklace before me, while Aku did the same with his before Amreth. "It is both an important identity symbol and community bond. Every Kreelar receives one the day they are weaned from their mother or wet nurses, around the ages of seven or eight. In the years that follow, as they form close relationships with others and carve their place among the tribe, so will their *ondishae* grow."

"Grow?" I echoed with curiosity.

"It has two parts. The *ondi*," Aku explained, removing the central part of the necklace, which turned out to be a single chain with a string of seven larger gems. "And the *shae*," he added, showing the other, much larger part, which had four chains, each one adorned with countless small, sculpted stone-gems. "The first stone of the *ondi* represents the tribe you belong to or were born in, while the others indicate the other tribes that claim you as kin or friend."

I pressed a palm to my chest as his meaning sank deep. Seven gems... Seven tribes claimed us.

"The *shae* are tokens of friendship from people whose loyalty, respect, or love you have earned by some great deeds," Vala continued. "They're not given lightly, as the entire family unit must be in agreement before it can be bestowed, which represents on average between four to eight people who must all concur it is warranted. Your *shaes* each count one hundred and twenty-seven stones."

"We have no words," Amreth said, his voice filled with the emotions I felt.

"No words are needed," Aku said in a slightly teasing tone. "One is not expected to wear their *ondishae* daily. As it is heavier, the *shae* is usually displayed in our homes in a place of honor. But it is common to wear the *ondi* as a necklace, wrapped around our bracers, or integrated into our belts."

He raised his forearm in an ostentatious fashion. Only then did I notice that he indeed had his *ondi* nicely secured to his bracer. I previously simply thought he had adorned it with embedded gems.

"This is a present from all the Kalds and their tribes for what you have done for us. You are Kreelars, if not by blood, at least in heart. You will always be welcome here," Vala said in a solemn voice.

I mumbled a thank you as she clasped the necklace around my neck. Although not uncomfortable or painful, it was undeniably heavy, which explained why no one would wear it daily—assuming they received this many tokens. It struck me then that it acted like a charm bracelet, but where good deeds potentially earned you a new one.

To my surprise, Aku placed the *shae* around Amreth's neck, but bound the *ondi* around his wrist. Vala drawing me into her embrace reclaimed my attention. She hugged me in an almost maternal fashion, even though she struck me as potentially being a couple of years younger than me. I returned the gesture with the same affection.

She released me, kissed my forehead, then took a step back. "May the divine lights always shine on you the same way you cast away the darkness that suffocated us. Until we meet again, Sister, may your days with your mate be filled with all the happiness you deserve, and more."

"Until we meet again, may all darkness always stay at bay, and may you and your people receive every blessing," I said.

Just as we were readying to leave, Aku pulled out a blowpipe from his weapons belt along with a pouch. Once more, I was stunned by my lack of observation skills. The same way I'd missed his *ondi* on his bracer, I hadn't noticed that he was equipped with a second blowpipe and extra dart pouch. He extended both to Amreth, who took them with a raised eyebrow, his air inquisitive.

"You may not call yourself a skilled hunter until you can defeat your prey using nothing more than your blowpipe and your natural physical attributes, excluding psionic powers," Aku said tauntingly.

Amreth snorted as he accepted the gift from him. "Is that a dare?"

"It is," Aku confirmed with an almost malicious grin. "When next you visit, we shall see how you fare against a Murthis."

"Challenge accepted," Amreth said with a smugness laced with a hint of arrogance. "Make sure to invite plenty of other tribes to join the feast that night. I will bring back enough meat with that little blowpipe to feed at least five of them."

We all burst out laughing while I shook my head affectionately at Amreth. Both males sobered, then Aku placed his hand on my mate's shoulder.

"Safe journey, Brother. Until next we meet, may the sun and the stars always light the path you travel," Aku said.

After a few more goodbyes, and friendly hugs with Mehreen and Ernst, we were off to a new adventure—the biggest and most important one for me—my new life with my soulmate.

As soon as we left the planet, my first order of business was to call my parents. Seeing both of them cry, especially my ever-stoic dad did quite a number on me. Like Amreth previously mentioned, they knew I was fine. But there was still a huge difference between being told something and then seeing it with your own eyes. They weren't too thrilled to hear I wasn't coming home but going straight to Molvi. As impressed as they were with my mate, like most people, they had a dreadful image of the prison planet. In their minds, it was a scorched world, festering with demonic creatures, putrid waters, and the air filled with sulfuric toxic fumes.

It wasn't until Amreth sent them images of his home and of the surrounding landscape that they finally relented a bit. They still pouted about me not coming back to Earth. It actually made me feel guilty. In their shoes, I would likely also want to hold my baby to reassure myself that they were indeed fine. At the same time, I'd been on countless missions and stayed away from Earth for two or three years in a row, only talking to my parents once a week through vidcom. But the promise of us flying them over to either Molvi or Vargos for our wedding in a couple of months further mollified them.

The two-day journey to Molvi ended up being like a mini honeymoon with Amreth going out of his way to pamper me in every way possible. Obviously, we made sure to get creative with every room and surface of the ship. That didn't stop me from squeezing in a few minutes to check in with Mehreen and Ernst.

The UPO and the Enforcers remained disturbingly quiet. It shouldn't surprise me considering this type of major case would require some huge investigation and for them to take very careful steps. You didn't want the culprit to get off on some technicality because you botched things by rushing too much. I didn't doubt Marilia knew by now that something had gone wrong with her assassins. She would likely try to eliminate as much incriminating evidence as possible, although I suspected she did so over the years in the eventuality of such a turn of events.

I wanted to see her face justice for all the pain and suffering she either provoked, enabled, or perpetuated. But above all, I wanted Aku and the Kreelars to be vindicated. He placed a tremendous amount of trust in us. The brunt of his experience with off-worlders had been beyond negative. If the UPO and the Enforcers failed to deliver on the justice they promised, the damage to the blossoming relationship we were building with them would be irreparable. I just hoped some news or consequences would come soon.

Our arrival on Molvi took my breath away. Despite the beautiful pictures Amreth shared with my parents and him telling me about the beauty of the prison planet, I hadn't been able to shake the lingering fear that it would be a dreadful and depressing place. But my mate had not been boasting when he compared Molvi's landscape to the wild and untamed beauty of the Kreelars' homeword.

Amreth's house—*our* home—nearly had my eyes popping out of my head. Again, he'd shown me images, but reality exceeded anything I ever could have imagined. Its sheer size left me speechless. Apparently, as was the case with the mansion—not to say castle—of every Hell Lord, his house was carved directly inside the top of the mountain. It had three stories with expansive terraces on each level, wide enough to accommodate at least two hundred people. An Olympic-size pool took up most of the lower-level terrace. A natural waterfall poured into it. An inner courtyard allowed for more floor to ceiling windows on the inner parts of the house, keeping it from feeling claustrophobic.

Like with his ship, the house was mostly white with some light-beige and dark-brown or black accents. Multiple plants and fragrant flowers gave it the splash of color needed to make it warm instead of clinical. Even more stunning gardens and flora carpeted the ground at the bottom of the steep cliff below the terraces.

"This is gorgeous," I said, leaning against the railing of the main terrace as I gazed on the garden below and the luxuriant forest that spread endlessly beyond. "This looks like a perfect setting for a picnic."

To my surprise, Amreth barked with laughter as he looked at me as if I'm lost my mind.

"A picnic for the plants, yes. Definitely not for us," he said, amused. "Every single plant down there, including the grass, *will* kill you. Some will take their sweet time doing it, keeping you alive in the worst agony as they slowly devour you, others will kill you instantly, their spores basically making your veins and capillaries bursts like frozen water in a pipe, and then you have those who will either suffocate you before they eat you, or spit the most virulent acid in existence at you so that you get lique-fied—including your bones—and they'll absorb the nutrients through their roots."

"What the fuck?!" I exclaimed, horrified. "Why would you keep shit like this around?"

"Because it is part of the defense and deterrent systems to prevent prisoners from escaping," Amreth replied in a factual manner. "For the record, the prisoners are informed in advance of all the lethal defenses set around their Quadrants and throughout the Sector. If they decide to take their chances regardless, it's on them."

A shudder coursed through me as I examined the colorful, almost peaceful-looking garden below.

"Why make it so damn pretty and inviting if those freaky things are about to go apeshit on you? Why not make it gnarly vines with thorns the size of daggers, giant mushrooms with the types of neon colors that scream 'I'm-about-to-fuck-you-up-beyond-recognition' instead?"

Amreth laughed again and gave me an indulgent smile.

"Because I have to look at these plants every day when I relax on my terraces. I would much prefer a pretty view to a gnarly one."

I pursed my lips, still distraught by it all. "Fair enough, I guess. But now the question is how many times have you 'enjoyed' the spectacle of one of your inmates getting slaughtered by flowers?"

He chuckled some more, seemingly amused by my dramatic expression. "Peace, my love. It has never happened. This is the last defense… well, minus the cliff, which is impossible to climb. Nobody has ever survived attempting to cross the forest. There are plenty of nasty things roaming in there, including a river with even nastier critters. Do not fear, my mate. This house is safe, and you will not be subjected to the less savory things that occasionally happen in the Quadrants."

"Right," I said, sounding far from convinced.

He smiled. "Don't be so distraught, my Ciara. You will not find these lethal plants in the rest of Molvi. They're bioengineered specifically for our Quadrants and strictly contained within them. But come, it's time for you to meet our Nundars. They've prepared a proper feast for us and are impatient to meet you."

My pulse immediately picked up, and tension stiffened my spine. As curious as I was to meet the elusive familiars that Amreth spoke so fondly of, I couldn't help but worry that they might not respond well to me. They carefully chose whose house they would join as they were extremely sensitive to people's emotions. What if they disliked mine? What if my aura was so unbearable to them that they'd considered leaving Amreth rather than being subjected to my mere presence?

Cut it out, woman! You're Amreth's soulmate. They are bound to love you!

That slightly appeased me, but sensing my nervousness, my mate soothed me further with his *bakaan*. I gave him a sheepish smile of gratitude.

"Do not fret. They already love you. I can sense their excitement. Normally, they just hide and wait a few days to formally introduce themselves to give the partner time to adjust to their new home. But they cannot wait to meet you. Your aura beckoned to them from the moment you stepped out of the ship."

My stomach fluttering, I let Amreth lead me by the hand inside the house. The humongous floor-to-ceiling glass patio doors parted before us to reveal a large, formal living area. Once again, it had a very Zen feel to it but luxurious enough I wondered if a professional interior decorator had achieved such a marvel.

However, it was the two dozen strange beings who greeted us inside who retained all my attention. They were bipedal with a very long, striped neck topped by a head shaped like a cone. Their faces weren't quite flat but had a bump of a nose almost shaped like a snout above a pair of very thin lips. A long, fur-like mustache, a paler beige color than their skin, framed their wide mouths. Their feet resembled star-shaped hooves, and a thick tail trailed far behind them. They wore long, embroidered tunics that reminded me of Medieval outfits.

They peered at me with big, curious eyes brimming with kindness.

"Welcome home, Master. Greetings, Mistress," a voice said in my head as all the Nundars pressed their right hands to their chests.

Only then did I realize that they only had two extremely long fingers in each hand, tipped with two-pronged claws. But I remained focused on their words.

Although I knew I had *heard* that greeting, it had not been actual words or a real voice, like when a telepath communicated mentally with us. It had been more like a transfer of thoughts that I simply understood. Amreth mentioned in passing that they had a form of hive mind. They didn't use individual names, and you should always address them as a unit. I didn't know which one of them had spoken on behalf of the others.

A part of me felt like I should be somewhat freaked out by these strange beings. And yet, I instinctively found myself smiling and feeling at ease. That they were spiritual people shone brightly. There radiated an aura of peace and kindness that you just wanted to wrap yourself in.

"Thank you," Amreth said affectionately. "Ciara, meet my Nundars."

"It is a pleasure to meet you," I said warmly.

"Nundars prepared a feast. Earth recipes shared by Lady Malaya's Nundars. We serve when you're ready."

That messed with me. I had yet to meet Malaya, the wife of Lord Kronos, Amreth's best friend. But that our Nundars would go through the trouble of learning human recipes to make me feel welcome moved me to the core.

Amreth puffed out his chest, pride and gratitude oozing out of him in response to his Nundars.

"Thank you, my friends. That's very thoughtful. We'll eat once I finish giving my mate the tour of her new home," Amreth said.

As one, they bowed their heads before scattering. To my surprise, a handful walked past us and exited the house through the large patio doors while the others headed in the opposite direction, deeper in. It then dawned on me that the first group was likely going to retrieve our personal belongings from the ship.

"They're amazing!" I whispered, my voice filled with awe.

"They are, and they think the same of you. I can't wait for us to be bonded so that you can see their auras like I do. They shimmered with even more beautiful colors for you than they ever do for me. My feelings are hurt," he said with a pouty expression.

I burst out laughing. "Don't be jealous of my irresistible

charm! But hey, take heart. Hang around me long enough, and it might rub off you! Then you'll be as lovely as I am!"

He snorted. "If that's what it takes, expect plenty of rubbing in the foreseeable future," he said, his voice filled with promises.

I laughed and let him give me a tour of the mansion I would now call home.

EPILOGUE
CIARA

The next month on Molvi turned out to be quite the whirlwind. Between strengthening my relationship with Amreth, familiarizing myself with my new homeworld, and sorting my career, time just flew by. But my neighbor and new BFF Malaya was a huge blessing. Having gone through that entire relocation process, she had all the tricks and tips to make everything as painless as possible.

Saying she was an angel couldn't begin to do her justice. Malaya was funny, witty, and always eager to help. I actually had to chastise her about resting with her huge belly as she drew nearer to delivering her first child. Seeing her going through that pregnancy also alleviated many of my concerns about future babies with Amreth. Women often complained about how their fetus kicked their bladder and kidneys around like they'd stolen their lunch money, but Obosian babies were natural protectors.

From my understanding, they could feel any discomfort they caused their mothers and would instantly police themselves not to negatively affect her. Sure, they were overly massive, but not to a debilitating extent.

As Malaya was the official Reporter of the Conclave and of

the Enforcers, she got to write the earth-shattering scoop about the mass arrests of Marilia Hesper, her son Noah Montel, and countless other associates. The downfall of Typhoon Pharma sent shockwaves throughout the industry. The pharmaceutical giant was put under guardianship while justice followed its course. Naturally, Amreth and I gave Malaya an extensive interview going in-depth about the hardships and devastation the Kreelars endured.

Elias Jacobs's reputation got slapped hard as he was swept up in the legal tsunami. However, he had been preparing for that day for years. Within hours of the first indictments going public, his army of lawyers were already filing motions to dismiss with an impressive amount of supporting documentation and detailed precedents justifying why he should be exonerated from all responsibility due to the coercion and duress Marilia subjected him to for years. And then the statute of limitation also kicked in.

The weasel had been clever enough to have written communications where he expressed his need to go public, which systematically got shot down with less-than-subtle threats. I doubted real moral anguish prompted those requests. He was just cleverly covering his ass.

In the end, he got off with a stern reprimand and substantial fine—which was really nothing considering the wealth SS12 earned him. Although a part of me wished he'd face some more severe consequences, I couldn't really argue against the outcome. After all, none of this tragedy could be pinned on him specifically. He never encouraged or condoned Noah's sexcapades which triggered the initial encounter. Noah smuggled the strawberries without his knowledge or consent. And he had no reasonable motive to justify a search of his team's belongings or for tracking their movements.

This could have happened to any other research team leader with a scumbag teammate.

The entire process would take at least a couple of years

before all indictments and trials were completed. But at least, Marilia, her son, and closest acolytes were guaranteed a trip to Molvi. It surprised me that Amreth hoped they wouldn't end up in Dakon's Quadrant. I would have expected him to wish the worst fate on them. But they would die too quickly there. In a Sector like his or Kronos's, they would suffer for years before they died.

Did it make me a monster that I also wished extended pain for them?

All that mattered was that Aku and the Kreelars were more than satisfied with the outcome, especially after confirmation that the investigation revealed more wrongdoings to other primitive species. In fact, the UPO set up the most insane lab on Molvi. They effectively recruited me to perform advanced research in various fields pertaining to primitive species. Most of them concerned the very planets negatively affected by Typhoon Pharma's mercenary actions. Thankfully, none of the ones discovered so far had suffered something as tragic as the Kreelars. However, one of the most disgusting cases we discovered involved their beauty products division. They had been tampering with the food of wild reptiles in order to modify their skin and scales. Once the creatures finished molting, the pharmaceutical employees would swoop in and gather the skin to be used in absurdly expensive rejuvenating creams.

The tampering negatively affected those animals, causing their shedding to be extremely painful and reducing their life expectancy. It also made those reptiles improper for consumption by the primitive species that used to hunt them and for whom they were a major dietary source.

As much as I hated that such things ever occurred, I was on cloud nine as those had always been the types of projects I aspired to work on. Furthermore, it made Amreth beyond happy knowing that I had a fulfilling career right here on Molvi. Even though he tried to be laid back whenever we discussed our future together, I could see deep in his eyes the fear that he would fail to make Molvi a good enough place for me to settle in permanently.

As he predicted, the Conclave bestowed three hundred grams of algarium to him for his contribution to saving the Kreelars. In reality, he should have only received half with the other gifted to me. But as we weren't officially married just yet, they couldn't give me any as those were reserved for Obosians—which applied by extension to their spouses and offspring. It still touched me that they would include my share in his so that he could give it to me once our wedding took place in a few months.

The wretched thing just kept being postponed with everything else that was happening, not to mention the fact that both his parents and mine were going crazy wanting to have the biggest and baddest wedding combining human and Obosian rituals. Amreth and I would have been fine with eloping. But we were happy to let our parents have fun with this madness, so long as they shouldered the burden, which they eagerly did.

Tonight, two weeks after being honored by the Conclave, I returned home and settled my personal shuttle on the landing pad at the edge of the main terrace. I made my way down the ramp only to find Amreth waiting for me by the entrance with a mysterious expression. That he was still wearing his breastplate set all my senses on high alert. At this hour, unless some incident called him back to one of his Quadrants, my mate liked strutting about bare chested, the same way human women whipped our bra out the minute we returned home from work or errands.

"What's going on?" I asked before stretching my neck to look over his shoulder to see if we had an impromptu guest.

I couldn't think of who it could be as he would normally have warned me in advance, even if it was just Kronos and Malaya. Anyway, he was comfortable enough with both of them not to wear a top or breastplate in their presence. In more ways than one, they were like siblings to us.

"I have a surprise for you," he said with that same unreadable expression.

"A good one I hope?" I said, my curiosity piqued but also laced with a hint of worry.

"I want to believe it will be," he replied, his gaze locked with mine.

I closed the distance between us. That he instantly drew me into his embrace, his expression softening with a tenderness bordering on adoration instantly lifted some of my tension. He leaned down and gave me a passionate kiss that had my toes curling and my knees feeling wobbly. Barely five months had gone by since we first met following his rescue attempt, but it had sufficed for me to fall madly in love with my incubus. I always expected the initial passion that burned so fiercely between us our first couple of times together would eventually settle into something tender and comfortable with time. But it only seemed to keep growing, like a million lifetimes would never suffice to sate the hunger and fever consuming us.

He released me, took my hand, and lured me to the large table by the pool. Only then did I notice two tall glasses, a bottle of sparkling wine set to chill, and a medium-sized box between them.

"What's that?" I asked, intrigued. "What are we celebrating?"

"I finally decided how to use the algarium, but I need your consent to proceed," he said, a hint of nervousness seeping into his voice.

"*My* consent?" I echoed, taken aback. "Like you said so well yourself, your body is yours to do with as you please. You do not need my permission to pierce whatever part of your body you wish. And you're educated enough on the topic not to make a choice that could be detrimental to your health or welfare in the long run."

"You are correct," he said carefully. "But this time it also involves *your* body."

I stiffened, and my face immediately closed off as a cold shiver coursed through me. Not even five minutes prior, I had been thinking just how madly in love I was with this male. Could he possibly have so little respect for my boundaries that he would try to guilt trip me into getting piercings after I clearly expressed this was a no go for me? Did he think that by having them already made, I wouldn't have the heart to refuse him?

"It's not what you think," he added quickly upon seeing my physical reaction. "You stated that you unequivocally would not get piercings, and I respect that. What I have in mind will not require any body modification from you."

"Ooookay," I said carefully, tension bleeding out of my shoulders as I glanced at the box. "Then what is it?"

Amreth reached a hand towards the table. To my utter annoyance, instead of taking the box to reveal its contents, he picked up the bottle then took his sweet time opening it and then filling the glasses. I glared at him, but he continued to grin smugly with a dare in his eyes.

Challenge accepted!

Two could play games. While he was halfway through filling the second glass, I swiftly attempted to snatch the box. Just as my fingertips were brushing the surface, Amreth's tail wrapped around my wrist and yanked my hand away.

"Hey!" I exclaimed in outrage.

"You naughty girl!" he grumbled. "No touching allowed."

"You said it was a gift for me," I argued before reaching for it again with my free hand.

The wretch released my wrist, and wrapped his tail around me at lightning speed, flattening my arms against my sides, and binding me like a freaking sausage.

"What the…?"

He chuckled and stared at me with an insufferably smug expression while his eyes sparked with mischief.

"An item only becomes a gift after it has been given," Amreth said in a slightly chastising tone. "This box was not given to you. In fact, what it contains is *not* for you."

Shocked, I stopped fighting against his tail binding me and gaped at him in surprise and confusion.

"It's not?" I asked, kicking myself inwardly for repeating the obvious.

He shook his head with a taunting expression. "Nope. This one is your gift *to me*, should you accept mine first."

This time, I just stared at him speechless, my mind drawing a blank as to what the heck was going on. To my surprise, instead of growing even more smug and mischievous, Amreth suddenly looked a little nervous, almost shy as he unwound his tail restraining me.

"In the months since we've met, I've fallen madly in love with you, my Ciara," he said in an almost solemn tone. "As Kayog deemed us soulmates, it has from the beginning been a foregone conclusion that you and I would marry. Our parents certainly are going all out on that front."

The sliver of derision with which he spoke that last sentence made me snort and then nod in agreement. But I felt even more confused as to where he was going with this. If not for his initial sentence reiterating his love for me, I would be on the verge of hyperventilating at the prospect he was preparing to dump me.

"It feels like none of this was ever handled the normal and proper way. Everything was kind of done backwards. But I want to do this right. You *deserve* to have this done right," he said, making my heart flutter.

My breath rushed out of me when Amreth took a step back before getting down on one knee. Eyes bulging, I watched him fish a small box out of his pocket and then hold it before me.

Tears started pricking my eyes when he opened the lid to reveal the most stunning engagement ring. It looked like they had weaved algarium into the types of twists I occasionally did in my hair. In the center, the twists created a delicate receptacle which held a beautiful Kreelar stone, matching the color of my eyes, and engraved with the symbol for eternity.

"I want us to be one, now and always, in body and soul, because we chose and love each other. I want you to bond with me, and for these rings to be the physical representation of the commitment we make to each other, in accordance with your culture, while also embracing mine. Will you have me, Ciara?"

Cue the dam bursting.

Tears drenched my cheeks as I cried and laughed while blubbering my consent. My hand shook as he placed the ring on my finger. The oddest mix of amusement at my silly reaction and joy at my acceptance played on my mate's gorgeous features. When he finally gave me the box from the table so that I could put the other ring on his finger, I nearly dropped it too many times to count from emotion, making him burst out laughing.

Eventually, I succeeded then threw myself into his arms. It was silly for me to have such a reaction to what technically was a mere formality, but this truly made it perfect. The thoughtfulness with which he came up with a way for me to partake in an important aspect of his culture while respecting my boundaries meant the world to me. That he would do it in such a way, making it clear that he didn't take me for granted just because everyone saw us as a foregone conclusion made me feel loved and valued.

He claimed my lips in a possessive kiss that instantly set my blood ablaze. I reached for the clasps of his breastplate, eager to have an unfettered access to the perfection that he was. To my surprise, Amreth caught my wrists, stopping me. He broke the kiss and locked eyes with me as I stared at him in confusion.

"I want to bond with you. Do you consent?" he asked, his eyes flicking between mine.

My heart leapt. I licked my lips nervously, excitement and a sliver of fear making my stomach flutter. Obosians could only bond once in their lives, linking their soul for eternity to their chosen partner. Even the death of their spouse would not allow the survivor to form a new bond with someone else. They truly married for life. So for him to ask me to bond with him was not a commitment made lightly. He truly meant for us to be together for as long as we drew breath.

The bond itself didn't scare me. I was more than all in. But they normally did this while flying. My wimpy self would more than likely ruin the moment peeing myself or flat out puking in fear because of the height. Based on the description Malaya had given me of her bonding flight with Kronos, it put to shame even the wildest, most neck-breaking rollercoasters out there. Although she skimmed over the details, it involved quite a bit of naughty play. The bond also caused quite a bit of pain for humans while it slightly modified us not only to enhance our immune system, but also to grant us the ability to see souls, although not to the same extent as a pureblood Obosian.

But it would take a lot more than that to keep me from bonding with the love of my life. My fear of heights be damned. I wouldn't let it ruin the best thing that had ever happened to me.

"Yes, Amreth, I consent. I want to spend the rest of my life with you," I said in a slightly shaky voice.

"My love," he whispered, reclaiming my lips with a fervor that wrecked me.

He lifted me up, and I instinctively wrapped my legs around his waist, focusing on the feel of him around me and clamping down on the first hints of fear trying to take root in my heart. To my shock, Amreth didn't take flight with a single powerful flap of his wings as was his wont. Instead, he casually started walking towards the house without breaking the kiss. When the giant doors parted open with a soft swish, I pulled back to look at him inquisitively.

He smiled tenderly. "Flying is not required. Your comfort and welfare are all that matters. Wingless Obosians can bond too while remaining land bound."

My chest constricted with love for my mate and guilt for depriving him of the full experience of bonding.

"You're so wonderful to me. I'm sorry for cheating you out—"

"You're not cheating me out of anything," he interrupted sternly as he made his way to our bedroom. "I can fly any time, any day. The bond isn't about zipping through the sky, it's about two souls coming together. I couldn't care less where or how we do it. I just want my soul to be one with yours."

"You're so damn perfect. I don't know what I did to deserve you," I whispered, my voice filled with emotion.

He snorted. "You won't say that the next time I pester you just for the fun of it."

I chuckled, nodding as he carried me inside our room. He could be an insufferable pest, making me both want to strangle and kiss him. But all such thoughts flew right out of my mind when he set me back down in front of our bed. How was it possible for anyone to make me feel so loved with a single look?

We didn't speak, our hands doing all the talking as we mutually rid ourselves of our clothes between gentle kisses and caresses. In this instant, there was none of the usual unbridled lust that normally fired us. It was pure love and infinite tenderness. He carefully picked me up and lay me down on the bed before joining me. For the next eternity, he worshiped every centimeter of my body, his hands and tongue on me bringing me slowly to a gentle climax, unlike the earth-shattering ones he often gave me, and which left me a complete wreck. This one had me flying high, shrouded in a cloud of bliss and complete well-being.

I understood that he was preparing me for the bite that would seal our bond. Before I fully came back down, he settled on top of me and carefully began pushing himself inside. I would never tire of the feel of his massive cock stretching me and filling me to the brim. His scales, *xinnix,* and piercings against my inner walls and my G-spot quickly had me cresting again. He kissed me, our tongues mingling while he gradually accelerated the movement of his hips.

He broke the kiss and lifted his head to look at me. One glance at the expression on his face turned my voluptuous moan into a strangled gasp. His silver white irises had shrunken so much they all but vanished in the black sea of his sclera. His bared fangs appeared longer, sharper, their tips glistening with a drop of what I suspected to be his bonding essence. But it was the feral way he stared at me, like a savage beast about to devour its prey that had my stomach do a couple of backflips.

Before I could do or say anything, Amreth moved at the dizzying speed of a striking snake and buried his fangs in my neck. An intense burning sensation exploded at the puncture point. I opened my mouth to cry out in pain, but a shout of ecstasy came out instead as he immediately blasted me with a powerful wave of his *bakaan,* wresting an instant, powerful orgasm from me.

Simultaneously, something appeared to break inside him, and he unleashed his passion on me. His fangs still filling my veins with his essence, my mate fucked me hard, each stroke of his massive cock sending blistering bolt of fire coursing throughout my entire body as one insane wave of pleasure after another crashed into me, fueled by both his body wrecking me and his aura whipping my blood into a frenzy. This endless whirlwind of bliss drowned out the burning sensation of his acid-like essence eating me from within.

My brain knew that this pain should have me writhing in agony. And yet it was endless moans of ecstasy that tumbled out of me as I sank my nails into my mate's powerful back. Pleasure almost too much to bear steadily built within me as I lifted my pelvis to meet him thrust for thrust as he pounded into me. At the same time I finally realized that he had pulled his fangs out of me, I also noted that the overwhelming sensations sweeping me away didn't exclusively belong to me.

I was now also feeling Amreth's pleasure as if it was my own.

A violent orgasm slammed into me. Half a beat later, he threw his head back, roaring his own release, filling me with the searing heat of his seed. A blinding light exploded before my eyes, and the echoes of Amreth's climax resonated inside me with such brutal force that I feared my mind would fracture. It created an endless loop of his pleasure feeding mine and mine feeding his, until there was no beginning or end between us, just an infinite crescendo of ecstasy.

We were one body, one soul.

He collapsed on top of me, his body shaking with the same spasm of bliss as mine did. To my surprise, he rolled onto his side, facing me, instead of onto his back before pulling me on top of him as he normally did. Feeling bereft and cheated of the cocooning warmth of his embrace, I groggily opened my eyes to stare at him, only to realize the same bright light still blinded me.

I blinked a few times, confused as to what was off. Then the light began to shimmer in the most stunning iridescent pattern in a circular fashion as Amreth's face began to emerge from the luminous glow. My jaw dropped in sudden understanding as the blinding glare receded to form a mesmerizing halo around my mate's head.

"Oh God! I see it," I whispered, transfixed.

Amreth smiled at me with infinite tenderness and joy.

"Yes, my mate. You can now see my soul in a way no other living being ever can or ever will. I love you. My light, all that I am, all that I ever will be is yours, Ciara."

"As I am yours. You are my heart, my love, the other half of my soul, now and always."

He finally rolled onto his back, drawing me into his embrace and closing his wings around us. Safe and sheltered in the arms of my beloved, hearts and souls intertwined, I was home.

THE END

SAGUL

ONEI

MURTHIS

FAERNYCH

NUNDAR

KRONOS & MALAYA

An Alien For Christmas

OTHER
True As Steel
Alien Awakening
Heart of Stone

ABOUT REGINE

USA Today bestselling author Regine Abel is a fantasy, paranormal and sci-fi junkie. Anything with a bit of magic, a touch of the unusual, and a lot of romance will have her jumping for joy. She loves creating hot alien warriors and no-nonsense, kick-ass heroines that evolve in fantastic new worlds while embarking on action-packed adventures filled with mystery and the twists you never saw coming.

Before devoting herself as a full-time writer, Regine had surrendered to her other passions: music and video games! After a decade working as a Sound Engineer in movie dubbing and live concerts, Regine became a professional Game Designer and Creative Director, a career that has led her from her home in Canada to the US and various countries in Europe and Asia.

Facebook

https://www.facebook.com/regine.abel.author/

Website

https://regineabel.com

Regine's Rebels Reader Group

https://www.facebook.com/groups/ReginesRebels/

Newsletter

http://smarturl.it/RA_Newsletter

Goodreads

http://smarturl.it/RA_Goodreads

Bookbub

https://www.bookbub.com/profile/regine-abel

Amazon

http://smarturl.it/AuthorAMS